# Caught in a Waking Nightmare

Tony moved warily back towards the car, then turned, realizing Lili had made no move to follow him.

She was standing where he had left her. She had pulled the black lace shawl tighter around her, and her head was angled forward, so all he saw was a cascade of glossy black hair.

"Lili . . ."

Her head snapped up. The face wasn't Lili's.

The face was barely human. It was too long and narrow, with piercing red eyes and fanglike teeth. The mouth was drawn back into a snarl. The creature threw back the shawl to reveal her nakedness. Tony saw she had the breasts of a woman, but they were covered with pale green scales that extended down to hooves like those of an ox. The shawl itself, fluttering in the pewter-gray light, became the huge dark wings of a nightbird. Her hands were now crooked claws tipped with razor-sharp talons. The horror screeched at him, making a sound no human throat could have made . . .

For Roland Nelson, for friendship and support while traveling
through the dark & light.

An Armadillo Press Book

THE DREAMING

A Berkley Book published by arrangement with
The Armadillo Press

PRINTING HISTORY
Berkley edition/February 1989

ISBN: 0-425-11433-3

A BERKLEY BOOK® TM 757,375
Berkley Books are published by The Berkley Publishing Group,
200 Madison Avenue, New York, NY 10016.
The name ''BERKLEY'' and the ''B'' logo
are trademarks belonging to Berkley Publishing Corporation.

PRINTED IN THE UNITED STATES OF AMERICA

10  9  8  7  6  5  4  3  2  1

# THE
# DREAMING

by Robert D. San Souci

BERKLEY BOOKS, NEW YORK

# Prologue

## When the Sleeper Wakes

STIGESVILLE IS A dying piece of the American dream—the husk of what was once a thriving steel city in Crane County, Pennsylvania. Situated on the Wonamey River, near the point where the south-flowing waters suddenly swing west to join the Allegheny, Stigesville is north of Pittsburgh, the nearest major metropolitan area.

The city proper straggles along the eastern shore of the river. Across the October-gray water, the Skeffington Steel mills—which once provided most of the town's wealth, and work for so many townspeople that Stigesville was jokingly called a "company town"—now struggle along with one quarter of the former floor crew. Since the end of summer, there has been talk of reduced orders for its steel, and further cutbacks.

After World War II residents gradually began moving to housing developments such as Green Ridge and Forestview, on the outskirts of the city. Most of the businesses have gravitated from the town center to the Long House, a mall adjacent to the suburbs and the east-west highway that bypasses Stigesville miles to the south.

The area around Skeffington Square, once the city's commercial and cultural heart, has been abandoned to squatters, drifters, punkers, and fringe businesses—enterprises such as the Shenzhen Kung Fu School, several heavily barred pawn-shops, adult video-rental stores, Betty Anne's Boutique and Wig Emporium, and small ethnic grocery stores where Vietnamese, Armenian, and East European foodstuffs offer an alternative to the more familiar items stocked at the neighborhood Day-'n'-Nite and OneStop minimarts.

Two or three of these marginal shops are often sandwiched into hastily subdivided structures that once housed concerns such as Walton's Department Store ("Where Fifth Avenue Meets Cabot Street") and La Grande Maison Restaurant. But such here-today, gone-tomorrow businesses are less a sign of any real economic vitality than an indication of further decay.

If the failed steel mills and haphazardly thrown-open shops along Cabot and Hudson Streets are two constant reminders of just how far Stigesville has slid, the third, and by far the most dramatic, is the Hotel Bethel. Once the city's social center, its grand ballroom hosted, in 1905, a meeting of some of the most influential steel magnates in the country to celebrate the formation of the short-lived United Steelmakers Association. The event featured the appearance of some of the most influential officials of what was then the world's biggest business. J. P. Morgan, Charles Schwab, Judge Elbert Gary, and William Skeffington—not only was the latter born and bred in Stigesville but also he managed to put it on the map—were among the seventy-three luminaries gathered at the vast, round table under the Bethel's crystal chandeliers. A hand-tinted photograph of the event was still displayed in the ballroom, long after the Association had fallen victim to infighting and indifference.

The hotel, a four-story brick building, on then fashionable Cabot Street, has been abandoned for nearly fifty years, following a fire that gutted the west wing in 1937. The windows are boarded over, though a few, on the second and third floors, reveal occasional glass panes still intact above the weather-beaten wood strips.

What were once gardens frequented by wealthy guests have become thickets of dusty brambles, nettles, and withered wild roses. The pool has cracked, and only an oily black residue of rainwater and leaf matter remains at the deep end. The squash courts that once hosted the "bright young things" of another age now host field mice and an occasional stalking cat.

Curiously, vandals have left the silent hulk of the building undisturbed. The spear-tipped, rusting iron fence and the chained and padlocked gates through which elegant carriages, and later limousines, once passed have always presented a barrier that few have attempted to cross.

In summer, the hotel's crumbling facade wavers behind veils of shimmering heat; in winter, the distortion is like looking through a polished sheet of ice. But no one ever sees the place without a sense of some rippling effect in the air, some need to pass a hand over the eyes as if to clear one's vision. There is something unreal and dreamlike about the building, with its empty grounds, sealed windows, and sloping green roof, broken by gambrel windows that reveal what once were storage areas for the luggage of long-term guests, or cramped living quarters for the hotel staff.

Fallen sea-green roof tiles, crisscrossed with silver snail trails, litter the weed-choked paths around the building's perimeter, where smartly dressed couples once strolled. The hotel is a derelict—as dead and out-of-date as would be the shell of the *Titanic* suddenly transported from the icy Atlantic deep to the center of Stigesville.

Inside the hotel, on this day in late October, a young girl struggles toward consciousness. Amid the dust and rot, her fingers clutch convulsively at a coverlet of frayed silk. Her grasp shreds the brittle material. Her dark hair is splayed out on a pillow cover yellowed by time.

Her eyelids flicker but don't open. She whimpers and moves her head slightly to the right, then back again. The dream that torments her is not yet ready to relinquish its hold on her. She is drawn down into deeper consciousness again, but the suffocating layers of sleep are beginning to lose their hold—like a mummy's wrappings being peeled away. For the first time in half a century she can sense light as a gentle pressure on her eyelids; deep in the blue-black sea in which she floats and dreams, she is aware of the susurration of her own breathing, soft waves hitting an unseen shore. The sound whispers to her of a nearly forgotten world she left long ago. It hints her time of dreaming might come to an end.

That she might escape the nightmare that has held her for so long.

Outside, the world is declining into cold, darkness, and decay. In the silent, musty, dust-clogged room, the girl sleeps on. The ocean of her dreams has become a landscape of shadowy, deserted streets lined with empty houses, all built of dusty bricks and jammed so tightly together that they form a continuous wall. The sky overhead is a starless expanse of watery gray mist, backlit by an unseen moon. Her dream-self is running down the dead streets, at once tantalizingly familiar and terrifyingly strange. She can still hear breath-waves somewhere beyond the maze of interlocking streets; frustrated, she turns a corner, only to find still another row of silent houses facing a mirror image. Not as much as a scrap of paper moves in the street.

She hurries on, determined to get beyond the limits of the dead city. Around her, the housefronts flicker and melt and change at the edge of her vision, though when she looks directly at them, they appear solid enough. Once or twice she pauses to pound on a door or tap on a window, but there is no response. She might as well be knocking at a mausoleum.

And then, ahead of her, she sees the huge, dark building she remembers as a place of danger and horror. She touches her fingers to her lips and makes a soft, frightened sound—

(Asleep in the dusty room, the sleeper moans. The sound causes a questing mouse to freeze suddenly, ears alert, nose anxiously testing the air for the smell of danger. The creature senses her fear and suddenly bolts through a hole in the crumbling hand-patted plaster.)

—and turns to run, but the houses behind her have shouldered together; the street she had just followed is gone, like a miraculously healed gash. The unbroken wall of brick houses curves away to the right and left, forming a ring around the vast, four-story building on a gently sloping hill of grass that looks like black velvet in the gray twilight.

The foot of the rise is protected by an ancient iron fence, entwined with blood-red roses and serpents whose green-black skins gleam wetly, whose eyes are fire-bright rubies.

Narrow tongues dart in and out; fangs drip thick venom the color and consistency of coagulating blood.

Horrified, the girl draws back. But there is no place to retreat. The smooth wall behind her—no longer showing a trace of doors or windows—has moved nearer. Even as she watches, the rust-red embrace of the wall tightens, the walls reshaping themselves instantaneously into a corridor that terminates in the massive carved doors of the building, beyond the section of passage blocked by the fence of serpents and roses.

The surface behind her is moving her forward, urging her toward the deadly fence and the doors beyond it. She is almost to the fence; her proximity sets the snakes writhing and hissing. They coil back, ready to strike.

Then the fence is gone. She is in a tiny, square room. Red walls meet red floor and ceiling seamlessly. The huge, dark doors are temptingly ajar. They open inward. Soft, flickering red light seeps through the doors, inviting her inside as though a fireplace, warmth, and cozy companionship lay within.

But she knows what is waiting for her. . . .

"I won't go in," she says aloud.

Now the room is shrinking all around her; in an instant it is no larger than a closet. A coffin. Instinctively she touches her throat, but what she had hoped to find at her neck is gone.

The sides of her prison are pressing against her arms; her knees are forced up toward her chest; her head is being pushed forward and down simultaneously. And the walls have grown blisteringly hot. The heat is unbearable.

Still, she tries to endure, to resist. She is drowning in red-hot pain. Above her, a rectangle of shimmering, silver-white moonlight filtering through seawater promises coolness and an end to her suffering.

She will not give in; she groans and twists, trying to force back the red-hot agony that embraces her eagerly.

(In her twilight room, the sleeper cries out and desperately pushes aside the coverlet; tears of pain and frustration squeeze out from under her still shut eyelids.)

But the suffering is more than she can stand; her will to resist dissolves in a final searing moment of pain. She screams and clutches for the cool, wet light overhead—

—and steps into a shadowy room draped in black curtains as fabric woven of spider silk. At the far end of the room a tall female figure stands, swathed in veils of the same silken material. The room is suffused with light, though the girl can see nothing but billows of soft black everywhere. In the uncertain light the figure sometimes seems less than a head taller than her; sometimes it looms to twice her height.

"Come closer, child." The figure's voice is a dry rasp, muffled by the gauze drawn across its face. It makes the girl think of a burn victim talking through thick bandages.

The girl takes a step, then stops. The veiling seems to grow finer and coarser from moment to moment, as though it were smoke from an erratic fire. Sometimes she can almost see the hidden features. She has the impression of black, unblinking eyes that glitter as hard and metallic as a spider's . . . full, sensual lips that gleam redly, moistly . . . a flash of white teeth frighteningly sharp and long.

"Don't resist me, child." The voice is seductive, yet it repulses her. It makes her skin crawl, as though thousands of insects were crawling over her face and neck, hands, and bare feet—wherever her dream-flesh isn't covered by the silky white garment in which she is clothed.

(Still fast asleep in the dusty hotel room, she instinctively moves a hand, brushing aside invisible tormentors. The dreamer is soaked in sweat.)

She backs away.

A beautifully shaped hand, the long, graceful fingers tipped with crimson, beckons her. But she shakes her head.

The hand gestures impatiently. The girl sees her father's body appear on the softly rippling floor between the figure and herself. His right arm is still in the sleeve of his brown, Sunday-best coat, which is bunched under him. His left hand is frozen in position, reaching for his throat. Dried black blood clots his throat and crusts the shredded front of his best shirt. The monogrammed letters on his breast pocket, which the girl's mother had sewn, are also flecked with blood.

The girl screams and tries to look away, but she is powerless to turn her head, or even close her eyes.

"Worse will happen to you if you continue to defy me," threatens the shrouded figure. "And it will go worse for this one too." The hand moves slightly.

The man on the floor begins to scream; his eyes are filled with terror and pain; he can see nothing else. The girl is not allowed to call to him; she can't even press her hands to her ears.

The hand moves again. Now it is an old woman's hand, withered and veined. The joints are swollen and stiff; the skin is bruised and covered with age spots.

The girl's mother, her neck savaged, her dress and coat streaked with blood, shrieks and jerks like a broken doll on the floor, her head lolling from side to side like a blossom on a broken stalk.

"No," the girl manages to whisper. "None of this is real. I won't let it be real."

The hand—skeletal, stripped of all flesh, tipped with yellow, cracked nails as sharp as talons—gestures a final time.

A third small figure blends its screams with the others'.

"*Mickey!*" the girl howls, recognizing something resembling her brother. He is the worst of all. Unable even to faint, she sees that the creature who drained blood from her parents has taken . . .

*More* from the little body.

It's . . . *incomplete*, she realizes, refusing to let her mind take in the full horror of what has been done to the boy.

Impossibly the hysterical child's wailing continues.

"Send him—them—away, *please*," she begs, unable to bear a minute more of their torment, which is growing more real with each passing moment.

"When you agree to return to that other place and bring me what I need."

The screams are deafening her. She can feel—*taste*—the terror radiating from the twitching, impossibly alive bodies. She tries to blink away the hot, wet tears pouring down her cheeks.

"Let them go," she says weakly.

"And—?"

"Yes! Yes, damn you! Yes, yes, *yes!* To whatever you want."

The room is suddenly quiet. There are only the two of

them—the girl in white and the black-shrouded figure—in the chamber, facing each other.

"Then here is your final warning," the figure rasps. It moves closer to the girl. Now it is as tall as she. The veiling dissolves. She is looking at death. *Her own death*. She sees her familiar face hideously caricatured in the desiccated features of a freshly disinterred corpse. The white garment she is wearing is mimicked in the stained and filthy grave cloths wound carelessly around the body. Worms are gathered in the folds; a black beetle, like a traveling beauty mark, crawls across a parchment cheek toward the eye sockets, in which the girl sees her own tormented eyes dimly reflected as though in circles of smoked glass.

Withered arms reach out to her.

Helplessly the girl extends her own arms, and the two embrace in a grotesque parody of affection.

She was wrapped in cold, darkness, and suffocating fear. She was flooded with understanding of what the other wanted from her.

Dead lips rasped into her left ear, "Go back. Wake up. Become who you once were. Become—"

"Lili," the girl whispered in the dusty hotel room, crossing in an instant the razor-thin infinity between dreaming and waking.

Amid the grime and rot, her eyelids flickered, then she blinked herself awake.

Momentarily disoriented, she continued to blink into the gloom. Bits of her dream, like fragments of a shattered mirror, spun around her. She glimpsed insect eyes behind a veil; screaming mouths flecked with blood and saliva; a skeletal hand reaching for her. Some images whirled away harmlessly; some lacerated her, leaving a residue of pain. Buried deep in her brain, one icy splinter remained, reminding her of what she had promised to do, and what would happen to her if she failed to obey.

She touched her throat and felt the thin chain she had failed to find in her dream. She traced the curve of the silver pendant where it lay just below the hollow of her throat: the pendant was a tiny drop of warmth, comfort, and hope.

Her fingers grew suddenly numb, and Lili held her breath in horror as, clumsily, her own hand, under some other control, pawed at the bauble, then yanked it free of the chain. Her arm jerked painfully as the fingers spasmed open and the silver bauble was tossed to the floor with a soft *ping*.

She sank back into the yellowing bedclothes, and lay for a moment breathing heavily.

*It's a warning,* she told herself.

Painfully, sensation returned to her arm and hand.

Above her dust-shrouded bed, the horizontal rays of the setting sun hit a pane of exposed glass above the cornice breaking the light into a spectrum. A radiance of blood-red, orange, yellow, green, blue, indigo, and violet, crisscrossed with fine black lines cast by spiderwebs, splashed the wall across from her.

Dust sifted from the cracked plaster overhead and rose from the crumbling mattress as she sat up. Dust motes spiraled in the thick sunlight near the ceiling, pinpoints of brightness and color. But she felt smothered with dread.

Sitting on the edge of the bed, Lili touched her face, stared at her long-fingered, pale hands, tested the hardwood floor with her bare feet, feeling its cool smoothness, the fuzzy layer of dust on it, each speck of grit under her soles. Each sensation and texture underlined that she was awake again, *alive again.*

A fly buzzed near the boarded-up window. She heard the insect hit the glass with a *tunk!* Its buzzing became more frantic. *Tunk! Tunk!* It hit the glass repeatedly.

Feeling as though she were moving through syrup, Lili climbed unsteadily to her feet. She thought only of helping the insect go free, of letting just a tiny particle of life escape the oppressive atmosphere of the hotel. But the window was nailed shut from the outside. A number of the panes were cracked. For several minutes she just stared helplessly. Her thoughts, in painful slowness, strung themselves together into ideas—as though her thinking processes were a string of marcasite beads.

Then things began to fall into place. *I could push out one of the panes of glass,* she thought, *and let the fly escape.* But at that instant there was a final *tunk!* and the insect dropped onto the shadowed window ledge. Half fearfully, half wonderingly, she touched the tiny blue-black corpse with a fingernail.

Then she drew her hand back suddenly, as though the

insect's death might contaminate her. In her mind she glimpsed a death's-head from which her own eyes stared out at her. She had escaped from her nightmare but not from the terror that had followed her back to the waking world. Reminders of death were all around her—most tellingly in the moldering ruin in which she moved like a tiny creature trapped in the belly of a dead beast. And death was *inside her*, too, she thought, like a poisonous worm in a flower.

She had been returned to life, but the hands of death reached out of her dream to fasten icy fingers around her heart and brain. She stared at her own pale hands, and for a terrifying moment saw them wither and rot before her eyes, becoming death's own hands. The vision was gone in an instant, but she continued to stare at her open hands in horrified wonder.

She shuddered and crossed quickly to the door. It was hard to turn the key, from which a metal fleur-de-lis stamped with HOTEL BETHEL dangled, in the lock; the aged wood, swollen with damp, protested with a groan and a sound like splintering wood when she tugged it open. The noise startled her as it ripped through the cloying silence of the hotel.

The yellowing wallpaper in the corridor outside was water-stained and mildewed. To Lili the walls looked diseased; she walked down the center of the passage to avoid touching them. All of the doors along the wide passageway were shut tight. Walking down the carpeted hall, her bare feet making the faintest whisper on the thick, crumbling pile, Lili sensed that, behind each panel identified with tarnished metal numerals, someone slept, as she had done. She imagined these dreamers, locked away one to a room, like insects—bees, perhaps—in the cells of a monstrous hive.

Were they haunting the same dream-city she had just escaped? she wondered. Were they, even now, running down illusory streets to confront the horror at its center? For their sakes she wished them a sleep as dreamless as death.

Twice she paused to test doors she passed, but they were locked. Inside the second room she was sure she heard someone murmuring, then protesting more loudly. She pressed her ear to the panel, wondering if someone else—it was a man's voice, she was sure—was being released from his dreams, as she had been. Or was he merely stirring in his sleep, troubled by some nightmarish image?

Even as she listened, the frightened babbling subsided into murmurs again. Then the room inside was silent. She touched the knob again, then pulled her hand away. The brass oval burned her skin with cold. She was sure she could hear a new sound inside: the rustling of silken material, like curtains in a wind or a robe brushing the carpet. Lili thought of the tall, veiled woman who had, with a gesture of her hand, shown her horrors enough to haunt many lifetimes.

There were more faint cries inside the room.

A second voice spoke in a rasping whisper; the words were indecipherable.

Lili's nightmare came back to her with devastating clarity. She fled the nearness of that unseen other, running down the hall, though she knew in her heart no real escape was possible.

She paused at the junction where the hallway veered toward the right, running past more closed doors to the head of the grand staircase, where the waist-high balustrade threw an intricate pattern of shadow in the gloom. Beyond the gaping head of the stairs, the corridor ran on until it was lost in shadow. No stray sunbeam eased the waiting darkness there. Though one memory told Lili the wing contained only an L-shaped corridor, the mirror image of the one in which she paused, other memories warned that the shadowed hallway at times became an avenue from the familiar world to terror. She had followed the interlocking hallways into the heart of a nightmare so powerful that even waking could not loosen its hold on her.

Someone, concealed in the darkness opposite, was laughing at her. The rasping sound was distressingly like a death rattle. Even as she watched, a darker shadow detached itself from the gloom. The frighteningly familiar figure—wrapped in black veils, so tall that the top of its head almost brushed the hall ceiling—continued to laugh mirthlessly.

Suddenly dizzy, Lili swayed and reached out her right hand to steady herself. She felt as helpless as a small child in the face of the chilling power she could feel radiate from the specter. She saw herself as an insect hammering self-destructively against a thick pane of glass. Rebellion, just the slightest disobedience, would leave her lifeless, lost in the gathering dusk.

The laughter ceased. But Lili could feel the hard, lifeless eyes boring into her from the shadows. Feeling so weak that she had to lean heavily on the stair railing, she descended the stairs to the main floor. In her wake, chill silence coiled down the massive staircase from the shadows above, to fill the entryway below.

On the ground floor, in what was the lobby, the afterglow of sunset filtered in blades through narrow cracks where the outside doors sagged in their frames and imperfectly boarded windows from which most of the glass was gone. Chill air came through with the light, causing Lili to shiver even more.

The tall, shadowy figure lingered at the head of the main staircase. *Watching her.*

She pulled open one of the tall doors; its splintered casings, which had once held thick, beveled-glass panels, now framed a patchwork of thick boards. Some of the heavy nails holding these in place had been driven all the way through the wood: the tips of the nails jutted from the dried, fissured oak.

These doors opened with far less noise than the bedroom door on the second floor. The cold air cut through her thin shift and made her bare feet ache, but she stepped out onto the broad porch in spite of her discomfort. The chill and the last light of day—such a contrast to the gloomy hotel interior—cleared her head.

When her eyes had adjusted to the twilight, she gazed at the waking world hungrily—like a traveler glimpsing home after being away for a lifetime.

The sun was gone behind the western hills, but the sky was still bright with the afterglow. She could make out a single star, where the gold shaded into blue. It was so beautiful, she felt she could stare forever, never moving. But the terms of her return could not be denied; the beauty she could almost taste turned bitter. It was gathering dark, not the fading sunlight, that claimed her.

Lengthening shadows from the rusty iron fence crept toward her, like a row of threatening spears. They stretched along the cracked and weed-choked drive, almost to the edge of the broad steps leading up to the porch on which she stood.

A car went by in the street. It was strange-looking, almost like something she remembered from a *Flash Gordon* or *Buck Rogers* comic strip. The dark-haired young man who was driving slowed the car to stare openly at her. Through the rolled-down car window she could see the pale oval of his face above his bulky blue jacket.

This glimpse of the first human face she had seen since awakening filled her with undefined sadness and longing. But her own emotions were suddenly drowned in a palpable wave of hunger and fear that boiled out of the darkness behind her. For a few moments she experienced what seemed to be the flood tide of another's frustration and desperate need, so intense that it threatened to burst her brain.

Then the car and its driver passed out of sight down Cabot Street. The welter of bewildering sensations ebbed back into the shadows of the hotel. She felt as weak as a nearly drowned person hauled out of the waves at the last possible moment.

Night swallowed the hotel grounds. A second car, headlights blazing, shot around a corner with a squeal of rubber. It paused near the padlocked front gates and gunned its engine. Lili clasped her hands over her ears. The driver rolled down his window long enough for someone to throw a can in the direction of the hotel. Lili heard loud laughter that was cut off abruptly once the window was rolled up again. The driver revved the engine again, peeled rubber, then roared off down Cabot Street.

Lili slipped back into the waiting dark of the Hotel Bethel, closing the door firmly behind her.

The presence still lingered in the shadows at the head of the grand staircase. Lili could feel the raw hunger and a curious hesitancy that clung to the gaunt, veiled form. Then the figure melted into the shadows and vanished.

Lili stood where she was, staring at the place where the creature had been hovering only a moment before.

She was awake, she thought despairingly, but her nightmare was going to go on forever.

# One

THE ENGINE WOULDN'T start. Tony Kovacs turned the ignition key several times and pumped his foot on the gas pedal. What he got was a sound like tin cans run through a blender. "Shit!" he said. "This is great, *just great!*"

Angrily he slammed the flat of his hand against the steering wheel. "If anything is going to go wrong, it's going to go wrong today, right?" He snarled at the dashboard through clenched teeth. So far he'd been hassled by his teacher, Mr. Murduch, over his math grades; had been told by Janet Dillon that she was canceling their date Saturday because she was driving into New Jersey to spend the weekend with a girlfriend of hers who lived in Lincoln Park; and had just walked out in the middle of an argument with his father over some point so trivial that Tony had forgotten what it was in the shouting match that stemmed from it.

He tried the engine again. Another half dozen cans were Osterized. "Why me?" he bellowed loudly at the roof of the car. The overhead light, its bulb exposed since the dome-light cover had disappeared months before, gave no answer. The dome overhead had vanished on one of the occasions Vic had borrowed the car. Tony's uncle, a Vietnam vet, was "not accountable" (that was the phrase Tony's mother used) for such lost or missing items—or for much of anything, Tony thought bitterly. His uncle was not even responsible for himself, since his nephew had to "go fetch" (Tony's phrase) most evenings and bring the man home from his usual hang-out in Skeffington Square.

Which task was going to be goddamn hard without a car. Tony dreaded the thought of busing it downtown and escorting Vic back on the coach. He'd done it before, often resulting in Vic hassling the driver over his unwillingness to give a "vet's discount" on Vic's say-so. Worse, everyone on the bus had kept staring at the two of them as though estimating just how wacko they *both* were, the space-cadet uncle and his teenage keeper.

"Please start, please just friggin' *turn over*," Tony whispered, giving the dashboard an encouraging pat on its faded and split padding. Hardly daring to breathe, he switched on the ignition one more time.

And sighed when the engine caught. Disaster averted again. He gave the engine a few minutes to warm up, and used the side of his hand to help the minimally effective defrosters clear the windshield of fog. The radio in his mother's car had long since given up the ghost, serving up nothing more than bursts of static. He'd given up trying to get his brother-in-law, Jerry Blount, who worked part-time at Ferro's Garage, to help him tune up the car and fix its worst problems.

At the very least, Jerry could fix the radio. The lack of it was a very real problem for Tony; without it, he had to endure Vic's moody silences or, worse, his ramblings about 'Nam and what had happened during the war while they returned home every evening from the Square.

His uncle's babblings were getting farther and farther out, Tony thought as he pulled away from the curb. For the most part, Vic would talk about ambushes and what had happened to some of his buddies who hadn't been lucky enough to survive their tour of duty. He always claimed that his problem "readjusting" to life in the States was the result of being exposed to a mind-altering experimental gas that was being field-tested against the Vietcong. Whenever there was a report in the newspaper or on TV about the defoliant Agent Orange, which had ruined the health of so many vets, it would trigger Vic's accusations that he and his buddies had been exposed to what he called "Agent Mindfuck."

Tony thought his uncle was using this to explain the fact that he was no longer able to cope with life. He was certain

that Vic had had a nervous breakdown right after he was
discharged, but that his uncle couldn't admit to himself that
his mind had let him down—not his government. Tony's
mother, Maria, had been convinced by her younger brother
that the unlikely "agent" existed. At one time she had threatened to try to seek out other victims nationwide and start a
movement to uncover what she insisted on calling a "conspiracy of silence."

Tony had advised against it, arguing (to no avail) that there
had never been even a whisper of such a thing in the news
media. Yet it could have been as big a story as Agent
Orange—too big to keep a lid on it for so many years.

Tony's father had put his foot down in terms of any attempt
to get even local attention from veterans' organizations or
concerned citizens' groups. And Daniel Kovacs had a hefty
foot: Maria Kovacs had backed off a cause on her brother's
behalf. But her husband, and the rest of the family, remained
neutral on the question of what had caused Vic's initial
breakdown. Only Tony continued to challenge the "unknown-
agent" theory, and he was honest enough to admit to himself
that such arguments were a way of blowing off steam. The
real frustration came from his unwilling role as Vic's keeper.

He couldn't wait for high school to be over, then he'd leave
Stigesville—it was only a dead end—and go somewhere, to
work, to school, anywhere to get away from this. He'd even
toyed with the idea of enlisting, but seeing what had happened to Vic kept pushing that option back into the hopper.

And Vic was getting worse. Tony had tried to point this out
to his mother and sister, but they both suggested he was
making a lot out of nothing. The thing was, they didn't hear
Vic moaning and tossing in nightmare-riddled sleep. Tony
sure as hell did. He was forced to share a room with his
uncle, since his sister Elene, her husband Jerry, and their
daughter Leslie had moved in—"temporarily, only until Jerry
gets back on his feet financially" was how his mother explained it—and ousted him from his room. Losing his own
space had been the final insult. "Come June, come graduation," he said aloud, "I'm outa here!"

He swung the battered old Chrysler station wagon sharply
onto Cabot Street, narrowly missing a pair of young men,
heavily bundled against the cold in down jackets and knit
caps, wandering along the crosswalk. One of them made a

graphic gesture and yelled something Tony couldn't make out through the closed car window. The boy didn't have the energy to return the gesture, so he ignored it.

He had been on the borderline of complete exhaustion for nearly a week now, and he knew this was causing a lot of problems at school. And at home, since he was on a short fuse about everything.

Vic had managed to wake him up three, four, five times a night for days, raving on about wartime horrors and worse. Sometimes he would subside into mutterings, then sink back into a quiet sleep. More often Tony would have to get up, pad across the attic bedroom to where his uncle, drenched from night sweats and thrashing from one side of the bed to the other, would be wrestling with the covers as though they were alive, or clawing the air under the sloping roof as if it were filled with spiderwebs or vines.

On these occasions Tony often would find himself unconsciously making his hands into fists, angry at being denied the sleep his body was screaming for.

Yet at the same time, seeing his uncle in such obvious distress made him feel, in spite of his anger, sorry for Vic.

Tony would shake the man awake as gently as he could, to avoid startling him, which had, more than once, resulted in a scream that had roused the whole sleeping household. Once Vic was conscious, Tony would just keep patting his shoulder and make reassuring sounds, until it sank in that the man was safe and had escaped whatever terrors had been stalking him in his dreams. Then, if the boy was lucky, Vic would drop back off and give him a few hours of desperately needed sleep before the next round of nightmares began.

Sometimes, however, Vic would tell Tony what he had dreamed; the process of talking it out seemed to dull the fear, so that he could eventually nod off. On these occasions Tony would be treated to horrifying descriptions of legs being blown off, or, worse, being *found;* a Marine writhing in agony, having just impaled his foot on a pongee stick liberally smeared with excrement; a lieutenant who had collected Vietcong ears and wore them on a length of nylon fishing line around his neck, found one morning at his guard post gutted like a fish, his trophy necklace missing, along with his own ears, nose, fingers, toes, and genitals.

But even the horrific edge of those accounts had been

dulled for Tony by hearing them repeated again and again. During the week past, however, something new had been added: Vic had been plagued by nightmares of demons, werewolves, monsters of all sorts. These would get woven into the Vietnam settings and stories in bizarre ways.

One of the grossest, to Tony's way of thinking, had recurred for seven nights running.

"We're entering a village that's just been pounded by friendly fire," Vic said, his face soaked with sweat. "I can see my buddies fanned out on both sides of me as we move in. It's early morning, and we're trudging through ground fog up to our asses. There's a lot of smoke from burning huts in the air; it stinks of burned meat. All around us are bodies—all women's and children's bodies—in the tall grass.

"I nearly stumble over one. It's—it *was*—a young girl. Her face is beautiful, eyes closed, lips open just enough to show perfect white teeth. Her black hair is still partly held in place by a mother-of-pearl comb, but it's long and mostly tangled up in the wet grass.

"But, you see, you see," Vic would rasp, reaching up to grab Tony's wrists, pulling the boy's face closer to his own, "the rest of her was blown away. There's just her face and neck and then the stomach sac still attached to the gullet and her intestines twisted around it like so many bloody ropes.

"I can feel my breakfast coming up," whispered Vic, "when her eyes pop open. She begins to laugh at me. Then the screams, and snaps her teeth like an animal. *Then the head, with all these guts hanging down in strings, flies into the air and comes for my throat.*

"My rifle is gone. I yell for my buddies, but they're gone too. There's nothing to do but run for it. So I'm running across fields, only now it's jungle and it's night. Behind me, I heard this thing screaming and screaming." (At this point Tony would have to pry the encircling fingers free of his wrist, because they were cutting off his circulation.) "When I look back, I can see her white teeth gleaming in the moonlight, and her entrails, slick with blood, shining like fireflies in the dark.

"I run faster, but it does no good. Suddenly I feel her head slam into my back, feel the teeth biting through my shirt, and I'm screaming myself hoarse until you wake me up."

Even worse, for Vic, were the secret things that lurked in the shadowy corners of his dreams. These never showed themselves; they played cat-and-mouse with the helpless dreamer—pursuing him but never quite catching him, taunting him with the illusion that he could escape when, in his dream-state, he knew he could never really get away. "When they're through playing games with me," he whispered to Tony, as if afraid they were, *even now,* listening in the shadows of the attic room, "when they're ready, they'll grab me, and I'll never be able to get out. I won't wake up ever again."

These dreams convinced Tony that his uncle was losing his last toehold on reality. References to these nightmares—missed by everyone but Tony—began to crop up in Vic's infrequent conversations with other family members. When Tony suggested getting his uncle a shrink, or even signing him in to a veteran's hospital somewhere, his mother bristled and told him to pay more attention to his studies and "let the adults make some of the decisions around here."

Tony was driving past the deserted Hotel Bethel. It loomed, dark and forlorn, in the gathering dusk. Boarded-up windows, weed-filled grounds, and the rusting iron fence made it look, to Tony, like the setting for a grade-D horror film. As a kid he had dared others to find a way over that fence and into the ruin—and had been dared by his friends to do the same thing. But none of them had ever done it. Something held them back; something kept even the boldest from scaling that fence.

Stories circulated about a boy who had tried to scramble over one night and impaled himself, only to be discovered by his parents the next morning, the sharp tip of one iron spike pushed all the way through the muscles of his left arm, the point of a second spike thrust through his lower jaw, piercing the roof of his mouth, the spike having entered the brain. On the anniversary of his death (rumored to have happened on Halloween in 1941), the tops of two fence palings supposedly dripped blood. For a long time clusters of kids on their way to school played the gruesome game of looking for the bloody uprights. Traces of peculiarly red rust on adjoining palings were cited as proof of the event, even though the location of the palings in question seemed to vary from year to year around the perimeter of the fence.

There was also the persistent story of people who had disappeared near the hotel shortly before the fire that had signaled the end of the Hotel Bethel as a viable commercial venture in 1936. But the lack of grotesque details gave the second story much less currency among Stigesville's children.

Whatever the reason—fear generated by the old stories, a lack of real bravado among several generations of youngsters, or something else—the hotel grounds remained off-limits and unviolated for half a century.

That particular evening, the hotel struck Tony as merely sad—a pathetic holdover from a bygone era in a city fast following the building into ruin. He shook his head, remembering how, when he was eight, he had ridden his bicycle with several of his closest friends to search the fence for traces of post-Halloween blood. He recalled how the hulking building had awed him then; he had not dared to touch the fence or the padlocked gates while he searched with the others for fresh blood. There had been several false alarms, but no one had found any gore before they had to leave for school or risk detention.

Suddenly Tony stepped on the brakes. Running on automatic, he pulled the Chrysler over to the curb to avoid blocking traffic. Leaving the engine idling, he rolled down the window to be sure he was seeing what he thought he was seeing.

A young girl, dressed in what looked like a white robe, was standing on the deeply shadowed porch of the Bethel. He couldn't make out more than her figure and the suggestion of a pale, oval face. She looked ghostly, afraid.

Once he was past his initial astonishment, Tony pegged her for one of the drifters who often took up residence in the abandoned buildings downtown. Most of them tended to wander away with the onset of cold weather, but a few hardy souls would stick it out into the heart of winter. From time to time the newspapers would report that the police had found a body in this or that shell of a building. Most of them were unidentified; though once, in Tony's freshman year at Stigesville High, a classmate of his had run away. Her body had been found weeks after her disappearance, in the basement of what once had been a dry-cleaning establishment, a block from the hotel.

The papers had made much of the fact that foul play was suspected, but the story died away unresolved, though the girl's parents had made a valiant effort to keep the case active. They had even brought in a psychic detective who had worked with police in New Jersey and Vermont, but the woman had, according to a small item Tony had stumbled across, buried on the next to last page of the *Stigesville Herald*, left suddenly, returning the fee the victim's parents had paid and insisting that she wanted nothing more to do with the case.

It probably had been only a matter of time until squatters laid claim to the palatial ruin of the hotel. Once the police got wind of the invasion, Tony was sure they'd clean out whoever had decided to settle there. The tall, slender, white-clad figure was probably just another runaway from some hick town nearby; or, more likely, someone heading to California or New York who had gotten down on her luck. He wondered if she was a loner, or part of some tribe that had staked out the building as its turf.

She had retreated farther back into the shadows. There, she struck him as the perfect guest for the deserted hotel.

Her dress was nothing more than a slash of whiteness in the dusk. . . .

Then she was gone, swallowed by the pooling dark under the portico.

Tony popped the car into first. It had grown late, and much darker, in the few moments he had been staring at the figure. Shivering, he rolled the car window back up. Most of the heat from the frail heater had escaped. His teeth were chattering. He wondered how Vic and his friends could stay out-of-doors for such long stretches when the weather had grown so severe.

But even Vic had his limits. If it got too cold, he would wander off with the last of his buddies, and Tony would have to comb the pathetic bars and eateries in the area until he found Vic sitting with a beer or an untouched sandwich and a cup of cold coffee in front of him. Vic went through the motions of socialization, but outside of talking about 'Nam, he seemed to have no way to connect with the world outside himself. He might order a drink or food by rote, but he forgot to drink or eat most of the time.

At home, at the dining-room table, Vic always sat beside Tony's mother. Without making an issue of it she would see that he ate what was set in front of him—and saw to it that her brother had the second best of everything. Her husband was served first; he had the best. She was diplomatic enough to keep her husband happy, and unthreatened by the attention she gave her younger brother.

Sometimes, though, when Daniel Kovacs had had too many beers before dinner (something that was happening with increasing regularity), he would bait his brother-in-law, commenting on Vic's scruffy "buddies," his lack of personal grooming, and his meager contributions to the family's upkeep, now that Daniel and Jerry Blount had been laid off by the steel mills.

At times like this Tony's mother would work overtime to deflect her husband's barbs. Tony thought her efforts were a waste of time: his uncle had a mind-shield that nothing seemed able to penetrate. At such times Vic seemed to retreat even further into himself, and nothing Daniel Kovacs said would get a rise out of him.

But these skirmishes always set the stage for full-fledged rows between Tony's mother and father. When Vic had wandered off to his room, and the others, sensing a major storm brewing, had discreetly withdrawn, Tony could hear, even in the living room, with his headphones on and David Lee Roth blasting in his ears, the drawer- and door-slamming and the shouting that generally went on for more than an hour until a truce was declared.

Vic was still in the park when Tony parked the car. Unwilling to shut the engine off if he could help it, he rolled down the window again and shouted, "Yo, Vic! Your ride's here." Then he waved to his uncle, who was one of a half a dozen guys dressed in olive-drab or camouflage-pattern army-surplus coats huddled on the broad concrete steps at the park's entrance. Vic glanced up, shrugged, and returned his attention to a heated debate between two men sitting hear him.

Tony waved again, and was ignored.

Muttering to himself, he turned off the engine (with a silent plea to the god of starter solenoids that it would start up again) and climbed out of the car. Instinctively he looked both ways, though there was no traffic on Cabot at the moment. Not surprising, since there was no place worth going *to* in Stigesville, he thought sourly; the only place to go was *anywhere else*.

When he reached the opposite sidewalk, Tony glanced farther up the hill to where the upright slab, with it bronze medallion of William Skeffington, gleamed like a huge tombstone in the fading light of evening. On one of the four stone benches that surrounded the memorial on all four sides, two teenage punks sat Indian-style in heavy powwow. Now and then they paused to eye the vets and displaced mill workers below. Tony had the impression that their confab had something to do with the elder men. He knew there was no love lost between the younger kids in their outrageous punk plumage, and the exclusively male, mostly military gray-or-green contingent at the park's entrance.

Both groups claimed the park as their turf. Over the past year there had been several blowups. One punk had threatened an old-timer with a knife; two of the vets had later beaten him up and broken his wrist. The police chief had managed to cool things out, but the potential for violence was always just a spark away from the explosion point.

Today the tension seemed more explicit than usual. For days now, Tony had sensed the whole town was on edge in some unclear, though clearly *felt*, way. *Bullshit*, he thought with a sigh, *it's just Vic keeping me up with his goddamn nightmares. It's not the town, it's me.*

"Yo, Vic," he called, trying for a buddy-buddy tone of voice that he didn't feel. Vic looked up and blinked several times, finally saying "Tony" in a flat voice that gave the boy no clue as to what was going on in his uncle's mind. Sometimes Vic would just come along without an argument; sometimes he would angrily explain to Tony that he still had important matters to settle with his buddies; usually he just ignored the boy, until Tony took him by the arm and steered him to the parked car.

"Pat's gone," said Vic a moment later. The comment came from left field. It took Tony a minute to shift gears and respond, "Where'd he go?" He was trying to remember who Pat was. He glanced over the suddenly silent men, whose attention was shifting from Vic to himself. Then he realized one of the regular faces was missing: the emaciated redhead with the scraggly red beard who had been at Nham Diep the same time Vic had been there. Pat McKenna. Pat was the guy Vic always claimed had saved his life.

"He didn't *go* anywhere," snapped Vic, "but he's sure as hell *gone*." For the first time in ages Tony saw something other than indifference in his uncle's eyes. Now there was something troubled in those dark eyes, set so deep in their sockets. The look reminded the boy of the way the man stared wildly all around him when he first came to after his worst nightmares.

"His room over at the Delaware House"—a run-down hotel where several of the men lived, surviving on welfare or military pensions—"is paid up through the end of the month," said Sag Miller. "When I didn't see him for two days, I had the manager open up his room. He's gone, but all his stuff's there, except the pants and jacket and shoes I saw him wearing on Wednesday."

"Did you try the hospital?" asked Tony.

"*And* the police," Sag said, sounding disgusted. "No one knows anything, and they don't give a crap. He's just another leftover they'd just as soon not think about."

"He'll turn up," said Tony automatically, not wanting to get drawn into the conversation. He suspected that McKenna, who could sock away incredible amounts of Irish whiskey, was sleeping off a bender somewhere. Maybe he'd died of exposure in some back alley, or broken his neck stumbling down a flight of stairs. *It's not my problem*, Tony reminded himself. Aloud he said, "Vic, we've got to get going, or we're going to be late for dinner."

"I saw him in a dream," said Vic, making no effort to stir, "the night I woke you up."

*Pick a night, any night*, thought Tony. *You've managed to keep me awake the better part of a week*. "I don't remember" was all he said to his uncle. Then, "Look, we've got to go, or Mom's going to be real pissed off."

He reached for his uncle's shoulder, but Vic twisted away. "Wait, now, just *hold on*," he said. "There's something important I've got to get straight."

*You've had more years than I can count to sort things out already*, Tony reflected. *I'm not looking for any breakthrough in the next few minutes*. But he waited, knowing that Vic was in a mulish mood and unlikely to be budged until his current train of thought got derailed.

"I saw him in my dream," Vic continued doggedly. "We were back in 'Nam, walking the perimeter of the camp together, when the ground collapsed under us. I thought we'd fallen into a Vietcong tunnel, but we just kept going down, down, until we landed on the floor of a cave that must have been as big as Carlsbad Caverns."

This description was new to Tony. But it all seemed part and parcel of Vic's usual run of dreams, so he had to make an effort to appear interested.

"Pat was hurt in the fall, but I wasn't," Vic continued. "I tried to help him up, but I couldn't touch him without making him scream about how much he was hurting. Way up, so small it looked like a star, was the hole we'd fallen through. I didn't dare yell, because Charlie might hear. I sat and tried to talk Pat through some of his pain, but he just kept screaming about how he was all smashed up inside. I tried to keep my hand over his mouth, but he chewed my palm half off.

"Then, suddenly, he stopped yelling. I risked lighting a match to look at him. He was dead, long dead. His skin had dried tight as parchment over his bones. I let the match go out, but a circle of light stayed around Pat. I tried to back away from the body, but I was paralyzed.

"Then an ugly old woman—not Vietnamese, but no white woman, either—hobbled into the circle of light around Pat's body. There was a smell of rotten meat that clung to her. . . . She was wearing some kind of black robe that was stained and filthy.

"I tried even harder to move, but it was no use. I couldn't even turn my head away, or close my eyes. Suddenly she squatted down beside the body and began to gnaw on his fingers. I'd have welcomed Charlie, even, to get away from that monster. Suddenly she let go of the corpse's hand. With her nails—they were as long as a tiger's claws—she scooped out his eyeballs. They were dried into two black marbles. She—she ate one, smacking her lips like she'd just had a real treat. Then she held one out to *me* . . . pushing it toward my mouth, as if she were going to force it down my throat.

"I didn't dare open my mouth to scream because of what she was going to do. Somehow I knew that my only chance was to wake up. *Wake up wake up WAKE UP!* I told myself. She just kept smiling and nodding and shoving the—

"But I woke up," Vic concluded, "before she could make

me swallow. And I'm sure, *sure,* that my dream means something. Because Pat is gone, and he died in that dream.''

He looked around at his buddies, but their faces were noncommittal blanks. They'd seen enough of the war and what it had done to others, thought Tony, and they've probably fought their own demons too. They didn't have to believe a word of what Vic was saying to experience the truth underneath.

Their reticence took the fire out of Vic. The fear in his eyes subsided. The familiar look of indifference returned.

"Plenty of strange things going on," offered Sag Miller, fishing a cigarette out of the pocket of his army-issue parka. "I don't like to think of Pat getting caught in the middle of it. The poor bastard's suffered enough."

"He's sure as hell not alone," said someone behind Tony. The boy didn't bother to turn around. He quickly reached for Vic's arm, pulling the man to his feet. This time his uncle didn't resist, standing up and brushing off the seat of his pants. "See you, guys," he said. A few grunted at him—the kind of sound that served equally as a greeting, a good-bye, or for punctuating their endless conversations about what had gone wrong in 'Nam and with the world they had come home to.

Tony was never comfortable around these men. Sometimes, with their haunted eyes and their pale skin, they reminded him of creatures out of *Night of the Living Dead.*

Their progress back to the car was interrupted when Vic went into a coughing jag. He bent forward, his arms wrapped around his midriff, coughing his guts out. Tony reached out to steady him, but Vic waved him away impatiently. These spells were coming more and more often—more severe each time. Tony's mother talked about "chronic bronchitis," but the boy was beginning to wonder if there wasn't something more serious involved. Vic was a heavy smoker, ever since he had returned from Vietnam. And Tony knew more than tobacco was involved. He had seen his uncle sharing a joint with his buddies on more than one occasion.

If mind-altering chemicals weren't the cause of his uncle's distress, they certainly had aggravated the problem. One look at the zombies Vic hung out with made Tony want to go places, not wind up facing a mental and emotional dead end like his uncle.

And there was no denying that the guy was a mess, Tony thought, shaking his head. Too clearly he imagined the chest-wrenching pain and the fear of suffocation that went with these extreme spasms. For all his impatience with the situation, it made him uncomfortable to have to stand by and not be able to help someone who was in such a bad state.

But Vic eventually straightened up, taking one or two reassuringly deep breaths. The coughing had given his normally pale skin an unhealthy ruddiness.

"We've got to get home," Tony said when things seemed back on an even keel.

"Fuck off," Vic said with a snarl. He shuffled off toward the car. Tony trailed after him, several steps behind. Vic paused, his fingers around the handle on the driver's door. *Jesus,* thought Tony, *here we go again.*

"Gimme the keys," Vic said. "I'm driving."

Reluctantly Tony handed the keys over. His uncle slid behind the wheel of the car, adjusting the seat to accommodate his longer legs. Tony hoped he wasn't too far gone tonight; he didn't *seem* too badly off, but he knew just how misleading such an impression could be where Vic was concerned. But Vic always seemed able to handle the car, even when he was halfway to the Twilight Zone. He walked around and put his hand on the passenger-door handle, waiting for Vic to unlock it.

Vic revved the engine. Tony could feel his fingers sticking to the cold metal. Then the handle was wrenched from his grip as Vic pulled away from the curb. He drove half a block, hung a U-turn that nearly nailed the other two cars whose drivers both leaned on their horns, then started back down Cabot Street toward home.

"Hey!" Tony shouted, running at the Chrysler, yelling at Vic as the car roared past him. "What the hell do you think you're doing?"

But his uncle ignored him. The station wagon receded down the street, its taillights shrinking to twin red stars in the dusk. Then the car wheeled around a corner and was gone.

"Fuck!" Tony muttered, still staring after the Chrysler, vaguely hoping to see it reappear.

It didn't. Vic might be working out some anger that had focused on his nephew. He might just as easily, Tony knew, have forgotten him from one moment to the next. Like one of the numerous gloves or mufflers Vic left on a bus or a bench somewhere. *Nice to count about as much as mittens,* he thought, pulling his own pair out of a pocket of his down jacket. He had stuffed his knit hat in the other pocket on his way out of the house, so he wasn't too badly off.

Still, he was stranded. His options were phoning home, which meant his father or brother-in-law would have to tear themselves away from the six-o'clock news and the sports roundup to pick him up. And his father certainly—both, in all likelihood—were pretty well sloshed by now, since they'd been well into a six-pack before he left. Whichever one came, he could count on a boozy argument—and the outside chance they'd crack his father's car up in the process.

*Screw it!* thought Tony. He'd take the bus back. But after waiting impatiently, pacing back and forth behind the bench, waiting for the coach, he decided to begin walking home. If a bus came, he'd run for it; meanwhile he'd be warmer if he kept moving.

Jamming his hands in his jacket pockets, he set out east along Cabot Street.

# Two

TONY WALKED ALONG at double time, constantly looking back over his shoulder for the headlights and the illuminated destination sign of the bus. Half the street lamps on Cabot were burned out or shot out, leaving dark pools of shadow through which he moved as quickly as possible. For all that the streets were apparently deserted, he wasn't fool enough to assume that there weren't plenty of "leftovers" around who would be only too happy to separate him from his wallet—and maybe beat him up for the sheer hell of it. The *Herald* editorials had been addressing "the downtown crime problem" lately, urging police action.

These thoughts made him twice as watchful. But, like everything else in town, the Stigesville Municipal Transit (SMT, officially; "Smut" to Tony's classmates) was breaking down. He used to keep their powder-blue schedules for the downtown runs in his wallet, but he realized ages ago that the printed times had nothing to do with when a bus might actually appear. It was a standing joke the buses were "leased out" to drivers who drove only if and when the "spirit" moved them.

He paused by an illuminated phone booth but put off calling home for a few more minutes. The trade-off still didn't seem worth it. Tony's only companion was his own reflection as he hurried by the darkened shop windows.

Looking at his slender, pale image, the boy knew he'd be an easy mark for any serious mugger.

Fortunately the aching cold, aggravated by sudden blasts of wind, seemed to have driven potential trouble off the streets.

He stepped off the curb, straining his eyes to look as far back along Cabot Street as he could. No trace of a bus. Apparently the cold had driven the coaches off the street too.

Tony passed an Armenian grocery with dusty jars of olives and tins of chick peas stacked in the window; a butcher shop with white enamel trays still clotted with drying blood and a sign advertising the daily special, which had been taped to the inside of the glass but was now drooping into a pool of pinkish juice; Devore's School of Cosmetology; the comic-book and recycled record store.

Although the record store was closed, several punks lounged in front of its door, as if there were no place else for them to go. They passed around a single cigarette in a kind of ritual. Their raggedly chopped hair shone red, white-blond, jet-black, green in the sulfurous light of a street lamp. One gangly guy had twisted his hair into spikes that gleamed with glue.

Tony slowed as he noticed that several of them had wrapped their wrists and ankles with chains. Heavy leather jackets, vests, pants, skirts, and boots were the uniform. Tony debated crossing the street to avoid them, then decided it was stupid. While Tony wasn't about to force an issue, he wasn't a coward, either. He knew how to throw a good punch: Daniel Kovacs had taught his son the rudiments of self-defense as soon as he was old enough to make a fist.

Tony pushed on by, straightening up to his full height. One young girl, who looked like an old fourteen, stared intently at Tony as he hurried past near the curb. Without obviously returning her glance, he felt the pressure of her gaze. He picked up on the stark white makeup and the black smudges painted under her eyes. It was like being watched by a corpse. The whole knot of them was strictly from *Return of the Living Dead,* with a heavy-metal rock score provided by the boom box perched on the shop's single step. He felt the back of his neck prickle at the thought of his own vulnerability.

But they let him pass unchallenged. At the corner, soft, muted music seeped from behind the door of a social club. Its windows were painted black; a single yellow bulb generated a cone of light in front of the entrance. Beside the door—a pitted sheet of metal with a circle of dark-tinted glass at head height—leaned a black man in a shiny, steel-blue polyester suit. The man seemed oblivious to the cold. He had a bottle wrapped in a brown paper bag clutched in one hand. He eyed Tony suspiciously, then said, "Out kinda late, aren't you, my man?"

Tony's hands, still buried in his jacket pockets, clenched into fists. But the man just spat indifferently into the gutter and pushed through the door into the club.

It wouldn't take much, Tony realized, gradually letting his fingers relax, to imagine a single wrong turn taking you into the Twilight Zone. The town, the people, seemed more unreal the closer you looked. *Invasion of the Body Snatchers?* Maybe. Except no self-respecting pod would want to grow into one of the creeps hanging out in front of Comix and Recordz. Of course, Stigesville was such a *burg,* it made a weird kind of sense to think of it attracting aliens who were weird even for *aliens.* Then, impatient with the cold and the empty streets, he suddenly broke into a jog. *Might as well get in a little training for track, so the evening isn't a total waste.*

But, of course, it had been shot down when Vic took off with the car. He was going to be good and late for dinner, and his father was sure to bitch about letting Vic drive. Any way you sliced it, it was going to be a shitty evening. He debated going by Janet Dillon's house, then remembered she had cut classes early to leave for New Jersey.

"Oh, a Friday night in this old town is a Friday night in hell," he chanted over and over as he jogged homeward. Every half a block or so, he'd swerve out into the street to watch for the long overdue bus. Not a sign of it. A few cars passed him. Once, he tried to flag down a car he thought belonged to a classmate; but the middle-aged woman driver only glared at him, as if he were a certified pervert, and accelerated. "Thanks, thanks, thanks, and the same to youuuuu." He varied his jogging chant for several choruses, then went back to his "Friday night" mantra.

He was getting pretty warm inside his jacket and sweater. He slowed his pace, not wanting to overheat himself. A little more than a trot, he climbed the gentle slope of Dreamers Hill. The Dreamers Hill neighborhood had once been the most fashionable part of the city. It was now in decline, like

the rest of Stigesville, but it hung on to some remnants of its
upscale past. The gabled rooftop of the Bethel Hotel loomed
above the less fanciful outlines of Georgian brick town houses,
and the low, flat roof of a Louis Sullivan bank papered with
demolition notices.

Tony knew that this was where new projects were supposed
to go—part of an attempt to revitalize the downtown area—if
state funding ever came through. Meanwhile this section was
even more deserted than elsewhere, except for the odd squatter.

And rats. Tony could hear them scurrying to safety at his
approach. He purposely made as much noise as he could: He
hated rats. His uncle had recently killed one in the basement
of the family house. More animated than Tony could remember seeing him, Vic had thrown his whole energy into getting
rid of the rodent. When the rat had eluded traps and ignored
poisoned bait, Vic had traced out the creature's escape route
through the basement.

When shrieks from Tony's mother and sister, Elene, as
they fled up the stairs from the family room where they had
been watching TV alerted the rest of the household to the fact
that the rat was momentarily holed up behind the stereo, Vic
went into action. Tony was drafted as backup.

Vic carefully positioned a wooden box around the corner of
the passageway that led from the family room to the basement
storage area and the garage beyond. When Vic gave the
signal, he and Tony carefully began pulling the stereo away
from the wall. Daniel Kovacs and Jerry Blount sat on the
steps drinking beer, watching like rooters on the fifty-yard
line, offering encouragement but no help. The women refused
to come downstairs. Given a choice, Tony would have pre-
ferred being anywhere else. *Willard* and *Ben* were Creature
Features he had never been able to sit through. And the
ending of *1984*, required reading in his junior year, had
creeped him out totally.

Following Vic's instructions, he kept inching the stereo
farther away from the paneling, until the dislodged rat had
broken and run. Tony had given a shout and backed away,
but Vic had grabbed the ''outdoor'' broom used for sweeping
the sidewalk and lunged after the animal.

While the frantic rat, momentarily thwarted and confused
at finding its escape route blocked, clawed at the wooden

box, Vic slammed it with the flat of the broom. Then, laughing, he clubbed the stunned animal to death.

"Got the sucker," Vic said finally, gasping for breath after his exertion. "Got him."

Then he leaned the broom against the wall and left with Tony's father and brother-in-law. Tony was left with the job of scraping rat meat into a shoe box and dumping it into the garbage can. Two splotches of blood had soaked into the porous concrete, and he wasn't satisfied until a paste of cleanser and water removed every trace, except for two pale ovals where the bleaching agent had bleached the color out of the floor. Even now, when he saw those spots, he shuddered.

The once elegant town houses that commanded an imperial view of the Wonamey River were mainly empty shells cracked open by vandals and the weather. Graffiti covered any smooth surface. Anything of value—lead pipes, ornamental tiles, fancy wooden trim, stained glass—had been carted away long ago.

BULLDOGS STOMP WOLVERINES was scrawled in faded red paint on a boarded-up doorway, a reference to the old rivalry between what had been the town's two high schools before dwindling enrollment compressed the two student bodies into one. Now the Bulldogs were as gone as Eastridge High—further evidence of just how far Stigesville had slid.

Tony's mother often said that before he was born, the city was different, full of life. But as far as Tony was concerned, things had always been at zero. He and his family were trapped in a dead-end town, but he didn't intend to stay trapped. He didn't know what he was going to do with himself, but he knew he was going to do it somewhere else.

Only the Hotel Bethel—set off by itself in the center of the ravaged Dreamers Hill section—brooded, aloof and somehow clinging to a bit of its old dignity, behind its rusting iron fences and its bramble-filled gardens.

There was talk that the place had been for sale for years, though no one was certain what real-estate agents were handling it. Tony's mother swore that she had seen several red-and-yellow COMMERCIAL PROPERTY FOR SALE signs affixed to the main gates some years back, but her husband disputed that. The fact that there was no interest in the property was hardly surprising in a city that barely seemed able to support a few motels as its periphery and a handful of downtown "residential hotels" catering mostly to the elderly, those on welfare, and a changing cast of transient characters.

Much less comprehensible was the way it had come through the years unscathed by youngsters bent on exploration or out-and-out vandalism. It was almost as if there were a *Star Wars*-type of force field around the place that let stray cats and dogs and pigeons through, but never any humans.

Now, as Tony reached the corner where the north and east segments of metal fence met, he thought again of the girl he had seen standing on the porch. As long as he could remember, he had never seen anyone inside the railings. He wondered how she had gotten in. Had she climbed the fence, or had she, more likely, found a gap in the apparently secure barrier? If it wasn't so cold and dark, Tony would have been tempted to circle the perimeter to see if an obvious bent railing or broken lock would give her secret away.

As it was, he merely slowed to a walk, staring at the Bethel's blind, boarded-up windows. On a night like tonight, with the moon just rising over the point of the Dreamers Hill Congregational Church—itself a holdover from the town's flourishing past but one that still held regular services for a dwindling number of parishoners—it was easy to imagine the old hotel haunted by ghosts, or hiding some even more sinister secret.

*Sinister secret. I'm beginning to think like the Hardy Boys mysteries I read in the third grade,* Tony thought, kidding himself. *Pretty soon I'll be seeing ghosts.* But, nearer the main gates, he stopped suddenly, startled at hearing a rustle in the branches of a tree just inside the fence.

A moment later an owl launched itself from one of the uppermost limbs, gliding with deadly accuracy on broad, dark wings toward something it had spotted in the tall grass. With a sudden snatch of its claws, it had the tiny, struggling creature (a field mouse, Tony guessed) locked in its talons as it curved back toward the tree.

Watching the silent, dark shape, the boy thought of Vic's nightmare of the flying head and its dangling intestines. The owl, settling back on its perch, began tearing its meal into gobbets, gulping the morsels greedily.

Tony was about to continue on his way when, just beyond the palings, he spotted a single, ragged white rose. It was impossible that the flower could have survived the cold, but there it was. He stretched his fingers between the iron railings until the tips were just touching the unlikely petals. He had the idea of picking it and taking it home to his mother or to his niece, Leslie, his sister's only child.

His mother would appreciate it as a pretty flower, nothing more; he was sure Leslie, a curiously precocious child with "some of the Gypsy in her"—as her grandmother, Tony's mother, would often say—would appreciate the late-blooming rose for the small miracle it was. The six-year-old child had a seriousness and an almost mystical turn of mind that amused and sometimes worried the women of the household; these qualities irritated and seemed vaguely to threaten her father, Jerry, and grandfather, Daniel. They were always a little curt, even sharp, with the girl—especially if she was in one of her dreamy states, chattering on about angels in the garden or hearing the trees whisper "green words" to one another.

He managed to wedge his jacketed shoulder a bit farther into the space between the railings; now his fingers were just . . . almost . . . *yes!* . . . encircling the hard green stem where the downward-pointing thorns had left it unprotected.

"Please don't," someone said.

"Huh?" Tony said, startled. He would have jerked his arm back out through the fence, but the shoulder of his jacket was caught on some sharp barb of metal. He stopped tugging when he heard his jacket rip.

It was the girl he had seen earlier in the day. She was standing only a few feet from him. He couldn't imagine how he hadn't seen her approaching. With the exception of scattered trees, most of the ground covering was little more than waist-high.

Still, it was so dark that he could hardly see her face, framed in a tumble of long straight black hair. The white shift she was wearing gleamed in the light of the rising, nearly full moon. He suspected she was about his age.

"Let me help," she said, moving closer. Her voice was whisper-soft, but it had a clarity that made up for what it lacked in volume. Now he could see that her eyes, staring at him from under bangs cut straight across her forehead, were large, slightly almond-shaped. They gave her a faintly Oriental look. The irises were jade-green, and the pupils appeared unnaturally large, but Tony remembered enough from biology class to know that was an effect of the eye adjusting to the night.

Her nose was gracefully sculpted, though a hair's breadth more generous than suited a truly classic look. And her lips were a bit less full than perfection demanded. Or maybe the tight set of her lips, the line of them as level as the cut of the bangs above, made her mouth seem thin. There was no happiness or real distress in her face, just a vague suggestion of sadness begun by her mouth and completed by her eyes.

Her neck was long and slender. The vee neck of her dress revealed a tarnished silver chain at her throat; the necklace supported a single twisted loop. Clearly there had been a pendant of some sort that, Tony thought, from the distortion of the loop, might have been yanked away by someone in anger.

"I'm caught," said Tony unnecessarily. She was making him feel klutzy and ditsy and antsy all at once.

"Sit still a minute," she said as he tried to loosen the snag. He remained firmly caught. Then she was working away at his jacket as a smell of flowers filled the night air: a summer day in the tropics and plants were blooming all around. Her perfume, he guessed; he had never smelled a fragrance quite like it. He savored it as her long, slender fingers worked his jacket free of the fence. It made him feel sexual in a general way. He was only feeling slightly aroused: the strangeness of their meeting, his growing discomfort in the cold, the counterbalance of some deeper, undefined hesitancy. But he was aware of her in a heightened way that could very easily turn to real hunger.

The loose sleeve of her shift brushed the side of his head. Out of the corner of his right eye, he was aware of the pale skin of her arm. It was an almost unhealthy white, but it had the sheen and richness of fine marble. The skin was cool, smooth, firm when her arm momentarily touched his ear.

"There," she said, straightening up suddenly, "you're a free man."

Cautiously Tony withdrew his arm. A few blue nylon threads clung to the fence.

"Thanks," he said. For a couple of moments they stood there awkwardly, staring at each other. Tony found himself wondering why she wasn't shivering with the cold; her silky garment looked as though it were meant to be worn inside only. Below the hem, which was trailing on the ground, he saw the tips of white leather slippers that looked like ballerina footwear. It was all very weird, but he was intrigued.

"I'm glad you didn't pick the rose," she said at last. "It should be left where it is."

Neither her eyes nor her voice suggested she was a space cadet or on drugs; there was nothing about her that reminded him of the losers who drifted into Stigesville, hung around downtown for a while, then moved on. Of course, he had been around Vic and his buddies enough to know that someone who seemed perfectly sane could go loony tunes from one breath to the next. He stayed alert.

"I'm sorry," he said, feeling as though he were a child just scolded by his mother. "I didn't mean—" He stumbled to a stop, not sure what he did or didn't mean. Something about her confused him, made it hard to keep any single thread of thought from becoming entangled. He knew he was behaving like an idiot. And now there was a trace of amusement in her eyes; her lips altered into what might, just might, be the ghost of a smile. He grew more self-conscious at the thought that she might be laughing at him.

"So, uh, what's your name?" he asked suddenly, trying to get things back on track.

"Lili," she said in her throaty near whisper. "Lili Sarossy. It's a Hungarian name."

"That's wild," said Tony. "We're Hungarian, too—I mean, my family. Kovacs. I'm Tony—Anthony Ferenc. The middle name is for my grandfather—Kovacs. Say, how do I get in there? It's ridiculous trying to talk through these bars like we're in a prison visiting room."

She didn't answer. Instead she took a step back toward the hotel, raising her hand slightly, as though he had said something threatening. "You"—she shook her head—"you shouldn't come in here. It's dangerous."

"Sure, if I try to climb the fence or something. But I'll just get in the way you did. Or did you climb over yourself?"

"I . . . climbed? No, no. But the way I came in is locked now. All the gates are locked," she said, as if that decided the matter.

"Well, unlock one of them. There has to be a way for you

to get out." A thought struck him. "Or does someone else have the key?" He wasn't sure he wanted to hear the answer.

She seemed distracted, as if she were listening to a voice only she could hear. *Loony Tunes time?* Tony asked himself. Finally she said, "Yes, there's someone else here." Her voice was dull now, like someone delivering a memorized speech, her attention focused entirely on reciting every word in its proper order.

"A man?"

"Yes. A man. Several men." Tony was far more disappointed than he should have felt after such a brief meeting. "Women too," she said. She looked at him as if waiting for a cue so she'd know what her next line was.

"Those guys in there . . . One of them your old man?"

She looked puzzled. "Some are old," she said with a shrug, "and some are quite young. None of them means anything special to me."

"No boyfriend?" he asked. His hopes weren't down for the count, after all.

"Oh, no. They're just . . . *sleeping there,*" she offered with another shrug. Her mind was clearly light-years away from their conversation, but the words were exactly what Tony wanted to hear.

"Just using it as a crash pad, huh?"

That drew a blank.

"A place to stay for a few nights."

"No"—she shook her head—"longer than that."

*Long enough to get to know you better?* he wondered. Out loud he said, "Don't they like visitors?"

"No," she said emphatically. She seemed to have resolved some debate in her mind. He sensed she was back in full touch with their situation. "You don't want to come in here." She took another small step away from him. "It would be foolish. You wouldn't be safe."

"Wait!" he cried, "please! Don't go." If there was a danger to him, then he sensed it as a danger to her also. If the Bethel was a nest of psychos, she shouldn't stay.

"I have to go inside," she said, turning away from him. But she lingered, as if unable to take another step.

Moonlight streaked her glossy black hair. Everything about her seemed designed to snare him. He was enchanted by her hair, her fragrance lingering in the chilly air, the pale bit of right shoulder revealed where the loose top of her shift had pulled to one side. These were like so many fishhooks catching at him, drawing him to the girl by the threads of desire. Was she really telling him to go? Or was she playing him like a fish on a line to tease him, tangle him more completely in her nets, put him utterly at her mercy?

It didn't matter, he realized. He was already captivated. Any game playing on her part would be redundant. "I have to see you again," he said simply. He hoped she was hearing the very real longing in his voice.

Without turning, she started to shake her head, then stopped herself as suddenly as if she had been paralyzed in place. She made a tiny, desperate sound, like a small animal in pain or frightened by the scent of something dangerous approaching.

"What is it, Lili? What's the matter?" Tony leaned up against the railings, clutching at them with his hands. Beneath his skin, the metal was vibrating. His hands tingled, as if a low charge had electrified the fence around the hotel. He heard a humming in his head, growing louder as his ears pressed against the rusty pickets. *"What's happening?"*

But she remained frozen in position, unable to answer.

Now Tony could hear the sound of a door being wrenched open. He could make out the scream and *poppling* of tormented wood. It had to be the entrance doors to the hotel, but the sound would have done justice to a giant's front door and the portals of hell.

The beams of the moon overhead seemed to dissipate before they reached the hotel grounds. The Bethel was a vast, shadowed hulk. Inky darkness filled the grounds between the front of the building and the fence.

Tony could hear someone or some*thing* striding toward Lili and himself. If it was a man, he was a big mother, Tony told himself. He remembered Lili's repeated warnings and tried to break free of the fence, but his hands felt locked in place.

Then he heard a *whuffling* and realized some large animal was charging at them. Since Lili went with the territory, she would be safe. But, at the very least, he stood to have his captive fingers chewed like so many strips of beef jerky. "Oh, please! God! No!" he muttered.

Then the lights of the SMT bus lit the scene briefly. Instantly he heard Lili shout, "Go back!" He did not know whether her cry was directed at him or at the creature bounding across the hotel grounds. In the same moment she raised her right hand; her thumb, index finger, and middle finger were splayed out, the other two fingers were folded in toward her palm.

He had a fragmentary glimpse of something white and moist, like the insect grubs he sometimes turned up when digging in his mother's garden. Then whatever power held him stuck to the fence pickets died. Because he had been so frantically trying to pull free, the sudden release sent him staggering backward. He was almost to the curb before he regained his balance.

The girl had vanished into the shadows. There was no sound, no trace of the animal.

He debated his best course of action for a second, then turned and sprinted for the bus that was nearly a block away, intercepting the bus at the next stop.

On board, catching his breath, he tried to sort out everything that had happened. In the end he decided that the darkness, an overactive imagination, and simple panic had combined to confuse him.

He tried to tell himself he was well out of the situation— that the whole scene was loonyville, and Lili was probably Queen of the Wackos.

Whatever the truth behind everything that had happened, Tony was sure of only one thing: He had to see her again.

# Three

SIX-YEAR-OLD Leslie opened the front door before Tony had a chance. His niece was wearing brown corduroy overalls and a red-and-white-striped T-shirt, both liberally daubed with dry paint, the result of her insistence on helping her father repaint the tiny sewing room that had been converted to her bedroom. She was swinging a clear plastic bag that held the pieces of her lotto game.

"You smell like flowers," she said. "Grandpa and Grandma are mad at you 'cause you're so late. We already had dinner. Meat loaf. My mother made it. It's crumbly."

"Thanks for the news update," said Tony, making light of what was probably the prelude to a major row. "I think you mean *crummy*."

"No, I mean, it falls apart when you stick your fork in it." She considered a moment. "But it's crummy too. Will you play lotto with Mom and Grandma and me?"

"Maybe later. If things don't get too crazy around here. I want to fix a sandwich or something. I'm starved."

"They're waiting for me. I better go," Leslie said, running down the hall toward the stairs leading to the family room. He could hear the portable TV going in the living room, and assumed his father and brother-in-law were watching *Magnum, P.I.* reruns. He wondered if Vic was in with them, or if his uncle had already retreated to the attic for the night, to lay

41

with his arms folded under his head, staring up at the pictures of Grand Canyon and the southwestern deserts he had thumbtacked to the slanted ceiling over the bed.

Tony hadn't noticed his mother's station wagon when he came in, but the Armbrusters across the street were having one of their big parties, so parking was at a premium. He assumed Vic had parked farther down the street, or maybe around the corner.

Crossing the dining room, he saw that the table had been cleared, but no one had bothered to shake the cloth free of crumbs. Several gravy spots and a large damp area where something had been spilled and hastily blotted up marked his father's place at the head of the table. All in all, family dinners were something he could easily live without.

The old dishwasher was making its usual hissing and gurgling sounds. He yanked open the refrigerator door and removed a plate with a plastic-wrapped brick of meat loaf, some lettuce, mayonnaise, ketchup, and a half gallon of milk. Four slices of pumpernickel from the bread box rounded things out. He set down the meat loaf, unwrapped it, and began sawing at it with a serrated knife.

Leslie had been right about its being *crumbly*. The grainy loaf disintegrated under the knife blade. He wound up with a lot of mini-slices and chunks. He slathered ketchup on two slices of bread, arranged the odds and ends of meat loaf with his fingers, threw on some lettuce for good measure, spread the tops of the two sandwiches with mayonnaise, and set it all in a baking dish taken from the dish drainer. Filling a mug with milk, he carried his meal to the kitchen table, savoring the peace and quiet.

Two bites into his sandwich, however, his father came into the kitchen. He was carrying an empty Stroh's beer bottle. "Where the hell did you come from?" Daniel Kovacs demanded. "And why weren't you home earlier? Your sister fixed a real nice dinner for us. You could have given her the courtesy of eating some of it."

"I got stuck downtown," he said, shrugging. "And I'm eating her meat loaf now." He hadn't intended that last remark to sound so argumentative, but as soon as the words were spoken, he recognized they could be interpreted as "mouthing off," depending on his father's mood.

But the older man had other things on his mind. "Where's Vic?" he asked.

Tony felt his stomach knot up. The mouthful of sandwich tasted like cardboard. "I thought he was upstairs," he said cautiously.

"Didn't he come home with you?" Daniel Kovacs asked, suddenly suspicious

"He didn't wait for me," said Tony, setting his sandwich back in the casserole dish. He didn't look up at his father. He waited hopefully for the sound of the refrigerator door opening. That would signal that his father had returned his attention to a replacement beer and away from Vic's comings and goings. He heard an encouraging click; a moment later he heard his father rattling another Stroh's free. *Now, back to the living room,* Tony prayed.

No such luck. "You left food out on the sink," said his father.

"I might want more."

"The milk will sour."

"Not in five minutes," Tony replied. *Be cool, stay cool.*

"Why didn't you drive around until you found your uncle? There aren't *that* many places he goes."

Tony tried to shrug that one off.

"Or did you let Vic have the car?" Daniel Kovacs said, with the superiority of a police detective having just trapped a key suspect in a lie.

This time Tony swiveled to face his father. "I didn't *let* him take the car. He *took* the car and left me to walk home."

"How'd he get the keys?" Daniel Kovacs placed his hands, one still holding the unopened beer, on his hips, striking a pose straight out of a photograph from his days as a Marine drill sergeant. The hard line of his mouth and eyes offset the softness of his beer belly and the homeliness of his worn-out terry-cloth slippers.

Tony gave up. "I *gave* them to him. I was going to ride shotgun. Only he locked me out and took off. I thought he'd be home an hour before me." The fluorescent light fixture overhead was reflected as a lozenge of light on his father's head, which was bald except for a gray-white fringe badly in need of trimming. *It's like a hole in his head,* thought Tony, *letting any light in there leak out—because sure as hell, none is getting in.*

"God almighty!" his father shouted, "you haven't got the brains you were born with! Letting Vic drive off in your mother's car! And if he's not home now, then where the hell *is* he?"

"Ask Vic!" Tony snapped, slamming his fist on the Formica tabletop with a satisfying *whump!* "*He's* the one with the car, not me!" He was tempted to throw the sandwich platter across the room but thought better of it. It would only make things worse—and he (or his mother) would wind up cleaning it up.

"I sure as hell *will* ask Vic when he gets back. But you know damn well—" He stopped suddenly, glancing at the swinging door leading back into the dining room. He listened; then, satisfied no one was overhearing but still cautious, he lowered his voice and hissed, "We know that one's not responsible for what he does. That goddamn war. I still don't know what the hell *that* was all about—just that I'm the one who's got to deal with a brother-in-law who's got a screw loose."

"Yeah, well, what about me?" Tony demanded. "I seem to be the major responsible party as far as Uncle Vic's concerned."

"Ah, *you!*" his father said disgustedly, "I get so tired of hearing how you've had to do without. I'll tell you what's 'doing without': It's my father coming over here from Hungary and getting started in the coal mines. It's my parents working to raise their kids through the Depression. And it's the work I was doing for Skeffington Steel, until the bastards laid me off because of all that Japanese and Korean import steel."

"I know all that, Pa," said Tony wearily.

"You don't know anything, Mr. Too Smart for His Own Good. You don't even know enough to keep the keys out of the hands of a stark raving lun—" His last word became an abrupt throat clearing. His father's already red face had gone an even brighter tomato shade as he looked past Tony toward the dining-room door.

Turning, Tony discovered his mother and Leslie, standing just inside the kitchen. After an embarrassing minute Maria Kovacs said, in her most matter-of-fact tone of voice, "We just came up for some cans of 7-Up." To her granddaughter she said, "Leslie, go get the soda."

The youngster obediently headed for the refrigerator, while

her grandfather stood aside. Tony could see from the way her eyes were darting from one adult to the other that Leslie wasn't missing a thing.

When she had three cans of soda and had shut the refrigerator door with elaborate gentleness, she tried to linger. Clearly she didn't want to miss anything. But Maria Kovacs quickly said, "Take those down to your mother. I'll be there in a minute."

"I can wait. She's not that thirsty."

"You were the one who was so thirsty," said her grandmother.

"Well, I'm not thirstiest anymore."

*"Leslie."*

"Yes, Grandma," said the girl, walking slowly across the kitchen in the hopes of hearing something before she was out the door. But everyone waited in silence until they heard her footsteps thumping in audible frustration down the short flight of stairs to the family room.

"I *wish* you'd be more careful!" said Maria angrily to her husband. "You *know* little pitchers have big ears—but that one has a pair of satellite dishes on the side of her head. She doesn't miss a thing. And kids that age *repeat* what they hear."

"I know, I know," said Daniel placatingly, "but our genius here gave Vic the keys to your car and waved him off into the sunset, in spite of all our warnings."

This effectively turned the spotlight on Tony. His mother, momentarily distracted from his father's gaff, turned on the boy with a mix of worry and anger. "Oh, Tony, you *didn't let Vic have the car, did you?"*

"Ma, he took the keys away from me. Well, he didn't exactly *take* them away, but we were supposed to be coming home together. I was going to ride beside him in the front seat." He didn't like the way he was beginning to sound like a whining child trying to avoid a spanking. He concluded simply, "When I went to get in the car, he drove off. There was nothing I could do. You know how he gets. It was let him drive or have a real bad scene downtown."

"Where did he go?" his mother wanted to know.

"Anywhere his mood and half a tank of gas will take him, for chrissake. *How do I know?"*

"Don't talk like that to your mother," Daniel Kovacs warned.

"Will you both stop acting like cats and dogs and *try to help me decide what we're going to do?*"

"Sorry, Ma," said Tony. He looked longingly at the sandwich that was growing soggier and less appetizing with each passing moment. But then, his appetite was pretty well gone, too, he realized.

His father shrugged, suggesting he was getting a bum rap and that his wife's anger was misdirected.

"I think someone should go and look for him. Someone should take your car, Dan, and drive around until they find him. We know there are only a few places he goes to over and over. It shouldn't be too hard. And someone else should go along, so that one of you could drive my car back. I don't want Vic on the road at this time of night. *Certainly not if he's been drinking at one of those bars he hangs out in.*"

"This was Tony's doing," his father said, waving in his direction with the bottom of his Stroh's bottle. "Tony should be the one to *undo* it."

"I don't care *who* goes," Maria said angrily, "as long as someone goes. And someone else goes along to drive back."

"Jerry can go," said Daniel, heading for the kitchen door. "He knows how to work the transmission of your car better than I do."

Too worn out to challenge his father's non-logic, Tony shoved the sandwich plate away from him and picked up the mug of milk. He was totally aware of his mother staring at him, but he couldn't gauge whether or not her anger was subsiding, now that action was being taken and he had been volunteered.

"I don't know what I'm going to do," she said finally. "Vic seems to be getting worse, not better." The angry edge was gone from her voice; there was only a mix of worry and weariness. She sounded as worn-down as Tony felt. Vic was getting to them both with his nonstop problems.

Tony set the empty milk mug down on the table and licked his upper lip before continuing. Trying to sound as reasonable as possible, he said, "Mom, Vic needs *help*. He needs a shrink really bad. Maybe he needs to go to a hospital for a while."

His mother shook her head. "He's threatened to kill himself if anyone tries to lock him up," she said. "I can't take the responsibility. I'd never be able to live with myself."

*"Mom,"* he said, *"None* of *us* can live with *him* anymore. Do you know what a *strain* he's putting on this family?"

"He's my brother," she said, some anger returning, *"I* know what that means, no matter what the *rest* of you think."

She had fallen back to the classic he's-my-brother position that effectively blew any further arguments out of the water. It was a given, an absolute, an incontrovertible fact that could not be gotten around. The blood link between sister and brother could withstand any logic from any source. Tony had tried attacking this point countless ways; in the end he had merely beaten his head against the it's-a-family-matter barrier that allowed for no suggestion of outside help.

When he would remind his mother that Vic had gone to shrinks years before, she'd simply say, "You can *see* how much good they did him."

It was cure Vic or kill them all, Tony thought. That was his mother's program. She might get worn down enough to admit she wasn't getting very far with it, but she always managed to rally enough to rebuff any suggestion that the answer might lay outside what the family could do for Vic.

"Jeez! Nice goin', bro," said Jerry Blount, slamming in through the swinging door. "Letting Vic go off joyriding and to hell with *my* evening and the things *I* gotta do!"

*Like what?* Tony wanted to ask. Like not missing reruns of *Cannon?* But there was already enough tension; he kept his mouth shut.

"I'm very worried," said Maria.

"All right," Jerry said with a sigh. "C'mon, bro," he said, waving Tony to follow, "I'll get out Dad's car, and we'll go find our wandering boy. But this time you damn well hang on to the keys, hear?"

Tony gave a last look at his sandwiches to confirm what he already suspected. The scene in the kitchen had killed his appetite.

Once Jerry had backed the car out of the garage and they were headed back downtown, Tony's brother-in-law began giving him a hard time about Vic. Tony tuned him out as best he could, staring out the window at the depressing streets rolling by.

When they passed the Hotel Bethel, Tony felt a thrill of
fear and an even stronger hope that he'd see Lili again. But
the place looked as abandoned and dark as ever. Not a
glimmer of light anywhere hinted that a group of squatters
had holed up inside. He imagined they were very careful to
black out any rooms where they might use flashlights or
candles. Under the best of circumstances, they would be
busted by the police for trespassing. If they were dope dealers, as he suspected, given the girl's fear and her insistence
that he stay away, they'd be ten times as careful not to let
anything odd draw attention to the Bethel.

"Tell me where's the best place to start looking," Jerry
said.

"Go to Skeffington Park. No harm in starting with the
most obvious. After that, I'll direct you."

But there was no trace of the Chrysler station wagon near
the square. After that, they hit several bars (Jerry had to go
into those to ask after Vic), then some coffee shops and the
lobby of the Delaware House. Tony had to check these out
while Jerry kept the family Ford idling at the curb.

Most of Vic's buddies had nothing to offer. One old guy at
the Delaware—not a vet, just someone who attached himself
to Vic's group during the warmer weather—said he'd seen
Vic heading west along Mather Road. "I tried to get him to
stop and give me a ride, but he didn't seem to see me,"
Tony's informant said.

"Why would he go that way?" asked Jerry when Tony
passed along this latest bit of information. "There's nothing
but a few houses and some run-down barns out there."

"The old cemetery's out there. One of the bus lines goes
out to Four Corners. It's a half-mile walk from there. He's
done it six or seven times. He's told me. A couple of times he
asked me to drive him out there. One Saturday, I did."

"And?"

"Nothing. We wandered around a little—they've got some
really old tombstones out there, going back almost to Colonial
times. Vic sat in the shade of a tree for about an hour. I read
old grave markers until I got bored. Then we came back."

"Why did he want to go there?"

"He said being there let him get back in touch with some
of his buddies who had died in 'Nam."

"They're buried there, huh?" asked Jerry, turning off Cabot and driving along Penn.

"No, I don't think anyone he knows is buried there. But he said being around so many dead people made it easy for him to get in touch with his friends. He said he knew they were trying to get in touch with him from time to time, but it was like trying to hear a weak radio signal. He could hear much better in the cemetery."

"Jeez," said Jerry as he swung the Ford onto Mather Road West, "I didn't know he thought he was talking to the friggin' dead. Guy's a walking *basket case.*"

"So what else is new?" Tony commented.

"Your folks should do something about him. He's really in bad shape."

"Mom won't listen, you know that. I've brought it up a hundred times, and she's shot me down every single time. 'He's my brother.' End of discussion."

"Yeah," said Jerry. "Shit."

They drove some distance in silence. Single houses, or two or three in a cluster, dotted the road. Most of the windows they passed were dark. Once they passed a well-maintained fence, painted white, that screened a neat little farm from the road. Twin yellow lamps illuminated the open gate with a buttery light. Through the gateposts Tony had a glimpse of a farmhouse, all its downstairs windows aglow. It was like a cheery little oasis in the cold and dark.

Wherever the houses weren't, the forest was. Thick woods of pine, spruce, and maple—ravaged by the approach of winter—massed on either side of the road. Once a deer, startled by the headlights, bounded across the road and disappeared in the brush.

When they reached Four Corners, not much more than a small shopping center consisting of a OneStop Supermarket, Pizza Mia, Laundromat, self-service gas station, and Raiko's Nursery, Tony pointed at the side road leading to the old cemetery.

It was almost eleven o'clock. A lousy Friday night had come to a dead end in Tony's book. He hoped to God that Vic was here. At this point he just wanted to crawl into bed, pull the covers over his head, and sleep without so much as dreaming.

\*    \*    \*

The old cemetery had once been attached to the meeting hall of a curious religious sect called the Dreamers. Lured by the promise of religious freedom, they had come to Pennsylvania before the time of the French and Indian Wars, establishing a small community in 1746. Refugees from persecution in some small Eastern European nation, they kept their own customs, language, and counsel. They raised most of what they needed themselves, traded on necessity with the friendly Indian tribes near them, and kept their dealings with other Colonials to a minimum.

They were a suspicious lot, quick to turn strangers away from the gates of their town (the name of which appears variously in Pennsylvania annals as Stigesville, Strigesville, and Stryxtown). Four Corners is built on what was once the town center. The Dreamers kept their meeting hall somewhat apart and located their cemetery beside it.

Of their religious beliefs and practices, little information has survived. For a time they were lumped together with sects such as the Shakers and Quakers, but any similarities between the Dreamers and such better-known religious bodies was superficial. Members of this sect were guided by dreams that came to individuals when they slept in certain "blessed places." The Dreamers appear to have been a surviving pagan sect that had, in many ways, closer affinities to Native American religions than to the Judeo-Christian tradition.

Contemporary accounts, in which it is hard to separate fact from hearsay, rumor, and wild speculation, suggests that the main religious observance was a twice-yearly sequence of dances held at summer and winter solstice for the express purpose of "inviting the spirit who lives in our dreams to partake of the life of the people and give us power." This spirit was envisioned as a "sister," who danced invisibly, along with her snake-dancing worshipers, providing gifts of prophecy, healing, and power over their enemies (of whom the Dreamers had increasing numbers).

The spot selected for these gatherings was the place of "profoundest dreaming," which they called High Holy Hill. It was located a distance from the town and church, on a neighboring hill that at one time had been a place of "powerful medicine" to a vanished tribe of Indians and was shunned by the Iroquois and Huron peoples who came after them.

Much later this became the Dreamers Hill section of modern Stigesville.

The taint of "devil worshipers" clung to the Dreamers while they flourished. Their Christian neighbors shunned the town and even avoided the roads running near it. Many Indians were also troubled by their strange white neighbors and secretly called them the Serpent People (perhaps in reference to their twice-yearly dances), linking them with mythological beings who once threatened the people, until they were defeated by a benevolent thunder spirit.

The Dreamers—men, women, and children—were massacred in the autumn of 1763. The town and community hall were burned to the ground. This was the period of the uprising of the Six Nations, led by Pontiac, when turmoil and bitterness turned previously friendly Indians against whites and set enraged frontiersmen to slaughtering peaceful Indians. It was officially reported that the Dreamers' community had been obliterated by the Indians in reprisal for their defeat at the hands of the British Colonel Henry Bouquet and his force of five hundred men the summer before at Bushy Run, near Fort Pitt.

However, a number of rumors circulated that the Dreamers had been exterminated by their white neighbors, who used the circumstances of the Indian uprising to mask the crime and rid themselves of the "devil worshipers" in their midst. There was talk of the entire town being "possessed by wickedness," which "provoked all the inhabitants—men, women, and children—to frenzies of blood drinking and cannibalism." While no proof of this has come to light, the story persists to this day.

In time a new group of settlers established themselves on the site of the destroyed town, kept the name Stigesville, and turned the place into a moderately prosperous town, until the birth of the steel industry and the town's coal-rich setting brought boom times in the late nineteenth and early twentieth centuries.

A Methodist church was built on the site of the old Dreamers' meeting hall, the cemetery was consecrated in a properly Christian fashion, and the Dreamers became little more than a curious bit of Pennsylvania lore.

"Slow down," said Tony. "That's the church over there."

"Yeah, I remember," said Jerry, reducing speed. The well-kept redbrick church, its white, needle-sharp steeple gleaming in the moonlight, crowned a grassy knoll. The tiny rectory adjoining the church was dark. Some fifty yards beyond, the waist-high fieldstone fence surrounding the cemetery came into view.

"There!" Tony cried, pointing. "I see the car."

The station wagon, parked haphazardly, its rear end jutting dangerously into the narrow road, was only a few feet from the iron gates to the churchyard.

It was empty. Jerry parked right behind it and shut off the engine.

"Where is he?"

"Inside the cemetery," Tony answered.

"Shit! He'll freeze his buns off! He's probably frozen to death already."

"It's not that cold," said Tony, climbing out of the car. "Besides, he had his heavy jacket on." He slammed the door, cutting off Jerry's comment.

His brother-in-law subsided into fierce muttering. "Son of a bitch didn't even close the car door" was all Tony could make out as Jerry walked over to the Chrysler and shut the driver's door properly.

The gates stood wide open onto the expanse of stone monuments, interspersed with trees and shrubs.

"You go to the right, I'll go to the left," Tony suggested. "Circle around inside the fence, and we'll meet at the back."

"Why not just give a couple of good yells?" Jerry wondered.

"Because we'd probably wake up the pastor. We're trespassing, and I don't want any more hassles. You can call, but keep it *soft,* okay?"

"Yeah, sure," Jerry responded impatiently.

They started out, pausing to call Vic's name every few paces. After a short while Tony couldn't hear his brother-in-law any longer.

Around him, the cemetery seemed much vaster in the dark than it ever had by daylight. The cold night air pressed in heavily on him, swallowing his calls almost as soon as they'd left his lips.

He found himself treading carefully, to avoid stepping on graves wherever possible, trying not to think of the generations of dead underfoot. It didn't work. Trying *not* to think of something was always the surest way to keep the thought front and center in his consciousness. Now all the horror films that detailed in explicit, gory detail what happened to idiots who went traipsing around cemeteries at midnight began replaying in his mind.

There was no sign of Vic: just an endless expanse of moonlit graves and shadows in all shapes and sizes. And a substratum of dead underneath, sleeping the sleep of the dead, dreaming dreams of heaven or hell. Maybe disturbed at having someone walking around above them. Waking up—

*Knock it off!* he warned himself. *Things are bad enough without letting my imagination run wild.* He called Vic's name, louder than he should have, eager to find his uncle and get out.

In answer he heard a short, sharp cry. It sounded as though someone had just hurt himself.

"Vic?" he called into he night. "Jerry?"

A whimpering sound, like a child crying, came from somewhere off to his right. He called again, but there was only the sound of distress—fainter now, as if the person crying were moving away from him or growing weaker.

Tony left the little gravel path, headed toward the sound, ignoring the fact that his way led directly across several graves. He was in an old part of the cemetery now; many of the marble tombstones had been scoured almost clean of carving by wind, rain, and winter cold. All of the monuments were tilted out of true. As though something huge had passed—

*Cool it, Kovacs,* he ordered, *before you freak yourself out.*

A moment later he stumbled over Vic, who was sitting with his back to a tombstone. The cracked marble slab, rounded at the top, supported the carved figures of kneeling, weeping angels facing each other. Their hands were pressed to their faces to stanch their tears; the tips of their upraised wings nearly touched. Tony grabbed the monument to steady himself, and to keep from sprawling across his uncle's feet.

The moon was behind the tombstone, so Vic was sitting in the shadow. His legs were outstretched; he had drawn the hood of his jacket over his head so Tony could see nothing of his face. His hands were buried in his coat sleeves, mandarin-style. He was so still that only the whimpering from the shawdowy area of his face gave proof he wasn't a corpse propped up against the gravestone.

"Are you hurt?" Tony asked hastily, his eyes adjusting to the darkness, enabling him to make out the man's figure more clearly.

Vic just kept on whimpering.

Tony hunkered down beside him, shaking him by the shoulder.

"Vic, what's the matter?"

There was a sudden surprised intake of breath, as though the other man suddenly realized he wasn't alone. Then he pushed weakly at Tony's hands, trying to shove the young man away. "Don't hurt me anymore," he pleaded in the voice of someone pushed to the limits of endurance.

"Pull yourself together, man," said Tony, restraining Vic's weakly flailing hand. "No one's going to hurt you."

Vic's head swung back and forth, denying what he was hearing. "They're out there. Not my buddies. They were waiting for me."

Another bummer Vietnam memory, Tony decided. Or maybe he fell asleep and had a nightmare. Aloud he said, "C'mon, Vic. We'll get you home and you'll be fine."

"No! Don't move! They've got us surrounded. We're dead meat."

"Snap out of it!" Tony insisted. He had the urge to slap the man across the face; but he was more afraid that would be just as likely to start a fistfight as stop Vic's panic—given the man's short fuse. *"Charlie isn't out there. This isn't 'Nam."*

"Not then, *now!*" Vic began struggling weakly against Tony's grip. "Not Charlie, *her*. And the others." His efforts to break free ceased; he collapsed like a rag doll against the tombstone. "They're waking up *now!*" His voice was little more than a whisper. "They need me to help. They want me to be one of them. I won't, I can't, *don't let them make me.*"

Now Tony had his bearings. He was sure Vic was flashing on being captured and tortured by the Vietcong, before he'd been rescued. He took hold of Vic's shoulders and shook the man gently. "You're all right, soldier. The Marines have landed. You're a free man."

Suddenly Vic began to laugh, as though Tony had just made the greatest joke in the world. "But she's inside my head," he explained, in between bursts of hysterical laughter that creeped Tony out. "They *all* want to get inside my head. And how can I get away then?'' His hard laughter was making him gasp for breath; Tony was afraid he would go into a coughing spasm. He shook the man harder; Vic's head bobbed forward, then back suddenly, hitting the gravestone with a loud *thunk*.

Tony was frightened, but the blow sobered Vic. He cursed softly and rubbed the back of his head. ''Shit! You trying to kill me?''

''I'm trying to get you pulled together enough to get the hell out of here,'' Tony snapped back.

''It doesn't matter,'' said Vic dully, his anger dying away as quickly as it flared. ''She's in my head. I'm just dead meat. Might as well leave me here.''

''Who the hell is 'she'?'' Tony demanded. *And where the hell is Jerry? The turkey must have heard us by now.*

''Ask her yourself; there she is,'' said Vic, pointing past Tony's shoulder before turning his face to the freezing marble and beginning to whimper again.

Tony turned. For a minute there was nothing but moonlight and shadows thrown by the monuments and the trees. Then he saw *something* near one of the crazily leaning tombstones he had passed only minutes before.

At first it was only a thickening of the air. Then it seemed more substantial, like dark smoke in the chill air. It kept changing, curling in on itself, spiraling outward and upward, growing denser, then more transparent. It was as uncertain as a poor television signal, as fluid and shifting as ink in a glass of water. One moment it appeared like an old woman wrapped in blue-black rags; then it was a younger woman in pale blue veils.

Suddenly it was a girl in white, moving toward them.

''Lili?'' breathed Tony, knowing that was impossible. But she was there.

''Make her go away,'' begged Vic like a frightened child. ''Please, *make her go away!''*

''Lili!'' Tony called. ''Come help us.''

But it wasn't Lili on the path. It was a phantom hag swathed in black. Her face was covered with boils and blisters; her thin lips were drawn back in a snarl revealing black gums studded with yellowing teeth. Her fingers were tipped with nails that looked more like talons to Tony. As she drew closer, she reached for them both.

A wind swirled around her, shredding her gauzy black

garments. Tony felt the night grow appreciably colder, but no wind of the real world stirred the shrubs near the tombstone.

The apparition, stripped naked by the unnatural wind, cupped its withered dugs in its bony fingers. Then the creature threw back its head and laughed and screamed: Tony wasn't certain which, nor was the boy certain whether he had heard the sound with his ears or only in his mind.

A second howl split the night and threatened to split Tony's head in two. He pressed his hands to the side of his head, but the sound sliced through his brain like a cleaver. He was aware of Vic bellowing something incomprehensible, but he didn't dare remove his hands from his ears.

Now he could see that the hag's belly was swollen like she was eight or nine months pregnant. She arched backward in a nearly impossible curve; the mountain of her swollen belly gleamed whitely in the glow of the moon, which was just beginning to set. Suddenly the flesh began to split in two, then burst open. Out poured scorpions, worms, snakes, cockroaches, beetles, spiders, centipedes, maggots, and innumerable other creatures. A living wave of squirming and crawling things swept toward Tony and Vic as they cowered against the nearest gravestone.

"*Jerry!*" Tony yelled, trying to haul Vic away from the advancing flood of slithery things. The man clung to the side of the monument and wouldn't be budged.

"Hey, guy! I thought you were the one who wanted to keep things quiet," said Jerry. "I heard you all the way across the place. And the minister heard you, too: I saw a couple of lights go on in the house beside the church."

The hag with the burst belly, the horde of insects and reptiles she had given birth to, had vanished. Tony heard himself breathing heavily; he heard Vic muttering to himself, still huddled protectively against the grave marker.

"Did you see anything?" Tony asked Jerry. "Didn't you hear anything?"

"Only you, bellowing like a stuck pig. Oh, great! I see Vic's doing fine too. What the hell happened?"

"I saw—" Tony looked across the empty expanse of graves on all sides. "I thought—" He stopped. What could he say that would convince anyone—himself, for openers—that he'd done anything but freak out? Vic had spooked him into seeing what couldn't possibly be there. Given his present level of stress and lack of sleep, why shouldn't he see things?

"Listen," Jerry said quickly, "I don't know what was going on, but we've got to get Vic out. I'll bet you even money that whoever's in that house over there"—he jerked a thumb toward the church rectory—"has already called the police. Let's haul ass."

Jerry was right. The first thing they needed to do was avoid a confrontation with the police in the middle of the night, when they were clearly trespassing.

Tony took Vic's right arm, Jerry his left. Together they hauled the man to his feet. They hustled him toward the gate. He didn't put up any argument, but he just kept saying over and over, "She's still there, you know. She was dead. I killed her. Later, when we were going back, we found the body, swollen, crawling with maggots, and—"

"Just what we need," Jerry hissed. "His friggin' *war memories*."

They were supporting Vic now. He had gone limp but not unconscious; he continued to babble on about what had happened to him in Vietnam. And about a dead woman who had followed him home, halfway around the globe.

Tony and Jerry shoved Vic into the front seat of the Chrysler. "Where does he keep the keys?" Jerry wanted to know as he deftly began searching each of Vic's pockets.

"Forget that now! I've got a spare set. Let's split and meet back at the house."

"Fine with me. I got better things to do than get busted."

Jerry went back to his car and started the engine. He popped it into gear, hung a U-turn, and was headed back toward Four Corners.

Thanks for waiting to make sure this rattletrap starts, thought Tony bitterly. He turned the key in the ignition for several false starts. On the seat beside him, Vic slid down until the back of his head was resting on the back of the seat. Tony was wondering if they should run for it when the engine caught.

He swung around sharply, his teeth rattling as the car's tires jounced over several rocks on the shoulder. Then he was following Jerry back to Four Corners and home. When he reached Mather Road East, he breathed a bit easier.

"I think, if you saw her, too, you're in trouble," said Vic.

He was resting the side of his head on the back of the seat, staring at Tony. In the dim light of the car interior, the whites of his eyes seemed to glow unnaturally bright as he watched Tony.

His nephew was about to make a comment when he heard the distant sound of an approaching police siren. Carefully he slowed to five miles below the speed limit. He was glad he was driving the Chrysler; the station wagon didn't seem like the sort of getaway vehicle to attract police attention.

A short distance along the main road, he passed a police car headed in the opposite direction, its lights and sirens going full-tilt. When it had disappeared behind a stand of pine marking a curve in the road, Tony dared to exhale slowly.

"How are you—?" he started to ask Vic. But the man was fast asleep on the seat beside him.

*That's where I want to be,* thought Tony. *Sound asleep, so I can wake up tomorrow and write this whole day and night off as a bad dream.*

What else could it be?

# Four

BUT WHEN TONY was finally able to crash that night, the sleep he got was anything but restful. Instead he was plagued by nightmares in which he ran through a subterranean labyrinth of tunnels with damp earthen walls and chambers filled with horrors: clutching hands reaching up from the dirt floor; bat-winged creatures that screeched and snapped at him and had clusters of human entrails gripped in their claws; and a row of distended bodies, blackened skin drum-taut and beginning to split open to give birth to obscenities.

Sometimes he would catch a glimpse of Lili far down a corridor, or just turning a corner and being lost to view. He would call her name and hurry after her, but each corridor brought him face-to-face with some new fright: a blind creature, an ape covered with greenish-white hair, an old woman sitting by a bonfire cutting the flesh away from her bones with a paring knife and tossing each gobbet onto the fire that brightened from yellow to blood-red with each feeding.

When he finally fled back to consciousness, he lay for a long time listening to Vic's light snoring. The man had slept all the way home in the car. Tony barely had been able to rouse Vic enough to get him upstairs and into bed, before he was out cold again.

Tony had been afraid that there would be more arguments that night, but his father was too exhausted to do more than

shake his head, make sure the front door was locked, and
mutter that he hoped his son would "make sure this sort of
Mickey Mouse routine doesn't happen again." For his part,
Tony deferred any comments until the next morning. Sleep
had seemed the only idea worth pursuing; now, lying awake
in the darkened attic room, sleep had become a lousy idea,
since it promised only terrifying nightmares.

Instead he tried to piece together a coherent picture of what
had happened to him that day. The easiest answer—that he'd
been imagining things—was not very satisfying. It raised the
question of whether he was beginning to lose his grip on
reality. Just like Vic. And it worried him that what he thought
he saw and felt earlier at the Hotel Bethel had impacted so
strongly on his senses that he could still feel a tingling in his
palms and recall the exact pitch of the humming he had
heard. Worse yet, his experience at the cemetery had been so
terribly real that just recalling it sent residual panic through
him. Why was the image of Lili at the heart of both terrifying
events?

And what was he to make of the fact that Vic apparently
saw pretty much the same thing as they huddled in the
shadow of the tombstone? Had he just been getting a hit off
Vic's ramblings? he wondered. But, replaying the incident in
his mind, he was sure he had seen the apparition of the hag
*before* Vic had begun talking about the corpse of the old
woman in Vietnam.

There was, of course, the very weird possibility that Vic
had been able to project an idea into his mind. Tony was
familiar enough with science fiction to know that a lot of
people believed in telepathy—or at least believed it *possible*.
Had his mind picked up what Vic imagined? Was it some
thing like a case of "mass hypnosis," like when a whole
group of people thought they saw a UFO?

The idea that Vic (or anyone, for that matter) could tamper
with his mind made Tony very uncomfortable. Yet, as unpleasant as that possibility was, it made a kind of sense. He knew
that his grandmother Eva (his father's mother) had said many
times that he and Vic had "the Gypsy" in them. She claimed
that "special gifts" were a kind of blood heritage that had
been handed down to certain members of the family from a time
hundreds of years before, when their Magyar ancestors lived
in Hungary and had intermarried with Gypsies living there.

Tony's father and brother-in-law considered such talk the prattling of a senile old woman. His mother and sister kept open minds on the subject and would sometimes recall incidents where one or the other had dreamed an event before it happened, or knew the phone was going to ring before it did. But Tony had never believed much in "special gifts" —especially not any that he might have inherited.

After this evening and night, however, he wasn't so sure. . . .

Most of all, his thoughts turned again and again to Lili. His mind conjured up her face, her voice, the way she looked in the moonlight for the few minutes they had talked. It frightened him to think that she was hanging out with dangerous people. He tried to tell himself that she had fallen in with such a group by accident, but he was too much of a realist to deny that she might just as easily be there because she was a user, a pusher, or worse.

He knew next to nothing about her. She was a complete mystery to him; and he made up his mind, whatever else happened, to find some answers. He'd never met anyone quite like her; the way she intruded into his thoughts when awake—*and* his dreams while sleeping—was unlike anything he had experienced before.

Vic slept on. He hardly shifted in the bed at all—a dramatic change from all the previous nights of tossing and turning and shouting himself (and Tony) awake.

It was ironic that with the gift of a night of peace and quiet, Tony couldn't get to sleep. His mind kept spinning around events and possibilities without providing clear answers to why things might have happened the way they had.

At length he gave up. Pulling on jeans and a shirt, he tiptoed quietly out of the bedroom and closed the door softly behind him. He'd put on the headphones and try to find a late-night "creature feature" or, failing that, listen to music in the family room.

The household slept all around him. On the second floor, he heard his father's loud snoring, while someone—his sister, maybe—was murmuring too softly for him to understand what she was saying. He only hoped, for her sake, that she was having sweet dreams—and that none of his nightmares had spilled over into her sleep, the way he half suspected Vic's insane imaginings had slopped over into his own mind.

Maybe in the morning he'd go to the library and get out some books on mind power and dreams and things like that. He also knew that Janet Dillon had read all the Shirley MacLaine books on reincarnation and spirits; Monday, he could ask her—

Thinking about Janet made him think about Lili. How would she fit into the pattern of his life?

"Huh!" He laughed into the darkness of the downstairs hall, thinking what a joke it was to refer to his life as having any "pattern." He was going nowhere, and he was just about there. He thought of the fairy tale about the steadfast tin soldier who was set adrift by street boys in a paper boat along a rain-swollen gutter. What lay ahead? Rats and sinking and fish and finally being burned up in a fire.

He flicked on the light in the family room, staring at the fireplace that hadn't been lit in years, pending repairs on the chimney that would probably never get made. Jerry had rigged up a plywood cover that kept out the worst drafts.

Tony thought of the tin soldier's boat growing waterlogged in a canal, disintegrating, the water closing over his head—

He'd have to make some real decisions soon. The appointment with the school counselor he'd been putting off couldn't be put off any longer. At present the Army (despite his anxieties stemming from what had happened to Vic) seemed the only real avenue to schooling and some success in the world. He doubted his grades—good this year, but only because he'd finally gotten his act together enough to graduate after three years of not really caring, of assuming he'd go with the flow and not worry about things—could get him any kind of scholarship. He knew he was bright enough when he put his mind to it. Since there would be no money from the already strapped family resources, his only other option might be a work-study program somewhere.

He put a mental check mark next to his mental note to set up an appointment for counseling.

Maybe, just maybe, there'd be a way to get the boat to dry land before it fell apart completely.

He settled into a corner of the couch and, feeling cold, flipped on the little electric heater with his stockinged toe. The quartz heater quickly turned a cheerful cherry-red, encasing his feet and legs in warmth. One of his mother's sweaters was draped across the back of the couch, and he pulled it over his shoulders, because his T-shirt gave little protection from the perpetual damp chill in the family room.

The heat felt good; it relaxed him. The faint smell of his mother's cologne clung to her sweater. He had a flash of himself as a small child sitting on her lap while she read fairy tales to him. His favorite had been the one about the little mermaid who was transformed into a human girl by the sea witch who lived in a house built of the white bones of shipwrecked men and who let ugly, fat water snakes crawl all over her. Though the little mermaid got herself a soul, the fact that she had never gotten her prince, and had to die into the bargain, had always made him sad.

The steadfast tin soldier had been his second favorite story. But that had ended sadly, with the soldier burned to a heart-shaped lump of tin and the pretty paper princess he had loved caught in the fire so that nothing was left of her but a single spangle burned as black as a lump of coal.

Funny how well he remembered those stories, even though he hadn't thought of them in years. Maybe the unreal events of that night were bringing them to mind. And maybe some of it had to do with Lili (here she comes again!), who had had a strange, almost magical effect on him. Talking to her through the fence, he might as well have been talking to someone in an undersea kingdom. Seeing her on the porch was like the tin soldier seeing the little maiden standing at the open door of her beautiful paper castle.

The pleasant warmth was making him drowsy. He had no interest in turning on the stereo or flipping through late-night TV shows. The tensions of the day were slipping away.

Curious that fairy tales with such sad endings had been his favorites. Maybe, even as a kid, he'd begun to realize that "happily ever afters" weren't in the cards. As long as he could remember, his parents had had arguments, sometimes over money, sometimes over all sorts of things. Vic had gone bravely off to war but had come back to no hero's welcome, and problems that seemed likely to last the rest of his life. And his sister's marriage to someone who reminded Tony uncomfortably of a younger version of his father seemed to say that they were all caught on a treadmill with no hope of breaking free.

But Tony was determined to break the no-win cycle. It had never seemed so clear to him before that night that the power to do it lay squarely with him. He could do it, or he could blow it and wind up another loser hanging out in Skeffington Square, waiting futilely for the steel mills across the Wonamey to go back to full production.

His eyes were closed now. He thought of the tin soldier sailing on to his fate.

*"Onward! Onward! Soldier!"* he murmured, remembering one of the lines he had memorized and would repeat when his mother reached the appropriate part of the story and nodded to him. But what had been the other line?

*Scritch. Scritch.*

Tony popped his eyes open at the sound, blinking in the light after being half asleep. Had he imagined the noise?

*Scritch.*

It was coming from the fireplace. Something was scratching on the other side of the plywood insert. He felt a chill, thinking of the rat he and Vic had gotten rid of years before. He remembered the bleach spots on the basement floor.

*Scritch. Scritch.* He listened attentively. It might be a bird that had gotten trapped in the chimney. But he knew that was impossible; there was a baffle at the top, through which no bird could get. Squirrel?

He wasn't about to remove the wood and find out by himself. Still with his mother's sweater around his shoulders, he padded across the cold linoleum. There was a fragment of sound (*Scr—*), then silence; he had the vision of a critter—he tried to think *squirrel*, but it kept coming out *rat*—aware of him and waiting to see what *he* was going to do.

"Scram!" he said, thumping the board softly, hoping to startle the creature back up the chimney or out whatever way it had arrived.

Whatever was on the other side suddenly began scrabbling with real frenzy, causing Tony to jump back. That rat knows it's got a real wimp out here, he told himself. He remembered a detail of the tin-soldier story that he'd forgotten earlier: the part about the black goblin that suddenly popped out of the snuffbox like a horrible jack-in-the-box. He had a sudden vision of the fireplace filled with a mass of goblin that was teasing him, luring him close, before it would burst the flimsy plywood barrier and—

To break that train of thought he leaned over and knocked several times on the wood, much louder. So loud, in fact, he wondered if he'd wake somebody up. But, truth be told, he could use a little moral support right now. He debated just shutting off the light and going back upstairs to bed, but that seemed the most cowardly thing to do.

*Wimp!* he told himself. It annoyed him to think of being routed by a field mouse (this image seemed less threatening than a rat or squirrel).

Sitting on his heels at arm's length from the plywood sheet, he listened. No more scratching sounds came from the other side. He figured whatever was there was listening and trying to decide what to do next.

"What are you doing?" asked a sleepy voice from behind him. It startled him so that he sprang to his feet as he whirled around with a grunt.

Leslie was standing at the bottom of the stairway. She was fussing with the belt of her blue bathrobe. Her pink, pajama-clad legs ended in green frog slippers. The right frog's head was cross-eyed; the left was a Cyclops, since one of the goggle eyes had long since fallen off.

It wasn't exactly the cavalry, but it was company.

"There's something alive in the chimney," Tony explained. "I'm trying to scare it off."

"What is it?" Leslie crossed the room, satisfied with the bow she had tied to keep her robe fastened. She peered at the fireplace, her hands tucked into her bathrobe pockets. "Will it bite?"

"I don't know what it is, and I don't want to get close enough to find out if it bites," said Tony. "I just want to get rid of it."

"I don't hear anything," the child said, stepping closer.

"Hey, not too close. It could be a rat."

"Ugh!" Leslie made a face and took two giant steps backward from the hearth.

"Of course, it could be Santa Claus," Tony teased.

She just shot him a look that let him know what she thought of that. "There isn't any Santa Claus. And, besides, it's too early for him to be stuck in our chimney."

"Maybe he's been in there since last Christmas."

"Did you hear anyone say anything?"

"No, just scratching."

"Well, someone like Santa would yell for help. So it's some poor stuck animal or something." She considered a moment. "We should let it out and put it in the yard."

"No way, Jose! If it wants out, it can go the way it came. Remember, it could be a rat."

"You're probably just saying that to scare me."

"Then I'm scaring myself too."

"I guess we could wait and see if it goes away by itself. We could watch TV."

"What are you doing up, anyway?"

"I had a nightmare. It didn't start out so bad. I was a princess in a castle. But then something big and red and full of teeth came to the castle window and was trying to get in. But I woke up, only there was still something trying to get in at my bedroom window, so I put on the light. Then it went away. But I didn't want to sleep anymore, so I came downstairs to watch TV. That's when I heard you hitting the fireplace."

"I guess everybody's having nightmares tonight," said Tony, keeping his eye on the plywood panel. "I sure don't hear anything back there anymore. Maybe I was having a kind of nightmare."

Leslie went to the quartz heater and held her hands out to it, warming them. "Can you have a nightmare when you're not sleeping, Tony?"

"I think it can happen, if you're tired enough."

"I don't like that idea very much. When you're asleep and you wake up, you know a monster can't get you. But if it could come when you're awake, then you couldn't run away and it could get you, couldn't it?"

"Yeah," he said uncomfortably, "I guess it could. Look, it's all quiet on the western front. Why don't we watch TV a little bit, then we can both go back to bed."

"But put the sound on real low so we can hear if the thing in there still wants to get out," said Leslie.

*Killers from Space* was what they decided on . . . a fifties science-fiction piece of crap with aliens with pop eyes that looked like the eyes on Leslie's frogs. They wheeled the TV stand close to the couch and kept the sound to a murmur. From time to time Tony nervously glanced at the boarded-up fireplace, but he heard nothing and saw less.

The heater kept them nice and warm. Leslie nodded off pretty quickly. But Tony felt more awake than ever. His eyes were burning from lack of sleep and his frequent rubbing of them. But his mind continued replaying the day's events, remixing them with tin soldiers and paper princesses and goblins and an old witch whose body writhed with snakes.

*Scritch. Scratch. Scratch. Scratch.*

Tony was fully awake in an instant. He stared at the fireplace. The sounds were louder now. They suggested something much larger than a rat was back there. He thought of the dog that had come running across the Hotel Bethel's grounds while he was pinned to the fence.

*Scratch. ScratchScratchScratch.*

That sucker is *big!* thought Tony. Time to rouse the troops.

He reached for Leslie, but she was gone. "What?" Had she gone upstairs? No, now he could see her, crouched down in the recliner chair in the farthest corner of the room, the corner between the stereo cabinet and the wall. Funny, he didn't remember her getting up from the couch.

The TV, which was between him and the girl, was still going, but the screen was a mass of static now.

*ScratchScratchScratchScratchScratch!*

"Leslie, c'mon, we're going upstairs. I'm going to need your father's help. Or Vic's."

"I can't," she whined. "I'm afraid, Uncle Tony."

He held his hand out to her, but she shrank even farther back into the old leather chair. It all seemed very out of character, but there was no time—

*Scritchscratchscritchscratch*

—to worry about that now. He ran to her and tried to scoop the child into his arms; but she squirmed free, wildly beating the air in a burst of pure panic. It was like trying to get a hold on an ocotpus wearing boxing gloves.

"Leslie, honey, please, *please don't!*"

Wood splintered. Whatever was in the chimney was coming through. Tony grabbed his niece and turned to confront the creature, protectively tightening his hold on the child.

The plywood screen exploded outward. Fragments and splinters shot across the room with such force, they imbedded themselves in the Naugahyde couch and in the sheetrock wall behind it.

A coil of tentacle the thickness of a tree stump snaked across the room, cutting Tony and Leslie off from the stairwell. Black water, stinking as though it had gushed up from a sewer, began to flood the room. The tentacle twisted and arched, probing each corner, touching each object. *Searching,* Tony realized, *for us.* It would only be matter of moments before the questing thing found them, and then . . .

The dark water was soaking his pant cuffs. The stench was turning his stomach. Leslie's hands wound around his neck so tightly, she threatened to cut off his wind. Making as little noise as possible, he climbed up onto the leather seat of the chair. The probing tentacle was investigating the stack of records on the far side of the stereo cabinet.

*Where is everyone?* Tony wondered. *They must have heard the room being torn apart down here!*

The tentacle was no longer interested in the records. It was making soft patting sounds along the side of the turntable in the stereo cabinet, accompanied by a chorus of greedy, sucking sounds.

Time was running out: Tony's only options were to try to fight off the creature or make a break for it. But the thing had looped out from the fireplace in such a way that it had effectively drawn a noose around them. The back of the television set, only a few feet away, was giving off sparks. The dampness in the waterlogged room clearly didn't agree with the old portable on its ancient roll-around stand.

The tentacle was moving past the stereo now, touching the single box speaker that was the last object between Tony, Leslie, and the nightmare of black flesh. One way or another, Tony had to *do something* fast. More sparks shot from the back of the TV set and from the outlet in the wall to which it was connected as the TV extension cord looped down, almost touching the pooling water.

Trusting to equal parts of his junior-year chemistry lab and reruns of the original *Thing* on Creature Features, Tony went into action. He pried Leslie's arms from around his neck, though she began to scream that he was going to die if he let go of her. But he shoved her, more roughly than he intended, as far back into the chair as he could. Then, balancing on the edge of the recliner, he stretched toward the TV stand.

As the chair rocked dangerously underneath him, Tony felt his fingers encircle the frame tubing of the stand. With a jerk he managed to pull over the stand and the television it supported.

The TV hit the water with an angry flare and an electrical hissing. The overhead light flickered and dimmed, then came back on.

The agonized tentacle writhed and twisted itself into agonized corkscrews as the water became an electrical death. It was absurd that no one had been awakened by anything that was going on, but at the moment Tony's main worry was that the flailing tentacle not knock Leslie or himself into the water.

"Die, you mother!" he snapped, holding on to both sides of the chair. His back was to the mass of flesh, but he could hear it lashing at the water, as if that were the cause of its pain. He was protecting Leslie with his body; she seemed to have fainted, but he could feel her breath against his cheek.

The overhead light dimmed again, brightened, then went out for good. Shivering from terror and soaked to the skin with ice-cold water, Tony tried to keep his teeth from chattering as he listened and tried to guess what was going on in the dark behind him.

The thrashing grew weaker; the screaming subsided into moans and whimpers and finally faded into sudden silence.

Not daring to move—hardly daring to breathe—the boy listened for any hint of movement or faint splash of water.

Nothing. Was the creature dead, stunned, or merely playing possum? Presumably the water carried a deadly charge. Their situation was better, but, he realized, all things were relative. They were still a long way from being out of the woods— trapped by the very device that appeared to have rescued them a moment before.

The fact that Leslie was still out made things a fraction easier; at least he didn't have to contend with her hysteria. Degree by degree, he shifted around on the generous seat of the recliner, until he was sitting alongside his niece, the two of them wedged tightly between the rounded armrests.

He was looking ahead into absolute darkness, except for a faint rectangular patch that defined the stairwell to the main floor. The only sound was the mingled breathing of the two of them in the chair.

For a span of time that seemed infinite, he sat with his arm protectively around the thin shoulders of the still limp child. When he could stand it no longer, he fished a quarter out of his jeans pocket and tossed it as far as he could. He heard it nick the far wall, then drop into the water with a soft plop. He waited to see if the noise roused anything, but nothing stirred. He tossed a second quarter on a shorter trajectory; heard it plop and sink without causing any kind of reaction.

The third coin, a nickel this time, hit something mushy and solid. He tossed two pennies in what he judged to be a little to the right and left of his original target point. Both of them hit with the same mushy sound.

Beside him, Leslie stirred, then said, "No!" very sharply. She began to twist under his arm; he had to use both hands to keep her in place.

*"Sit still!"* he ordered. "If you move, we're both dead!"

She froze. Then, in a sad, frightened little voice, she asked, "Can't I wake up yet?"

"In a minute, sweetheart," he said, trying to sound as reassuring as he could. He could hear so much nervousness in his voice, he doubted she was the least bit comforted. "For now we both have to sit tight and ride this out."

He could tell from her sniffling that she had begun to cry. He relaxed his hold on her just enough to let her wipe her eyes, but he was alert to any sudden, panicky movements on her part.

And then, crazily, the room began to fill with soft-blue-green light. At first Tony wondered if it was some bizarre side effect of the mix of electricity and water; but the luminescence seemed to be seeping out of the walls and ceiling, as well as rising from the floor.

Around them, the walls dissolved. Still in the recliner, they were floating on an unnatural blue ocean. The waves were really the gentlest of ripples. The chair rocked only slightly from side to side. The sky overhead was pink and curiously flat-looking, full of unmoving clouds that looked as though they'd been painted on.

"Oh," said Leslie, "there's my castle!"

Where there had been only smooth, electric-blue water before, there was now a tiny island ringed with glossy-stemmed palm trees that blossomed into uniform bunches of harsh, artificial green leaves. In the exact center of the island was a castle that seemed to be made out of paper, with scraps of paper doily for curtains at the window.

Someone was standing at the doorway of the castle. Tony

couldn't see her clearly, but she was wearing a white gauzy dress, a dainty blue ribbon draped over her shoulders, like a scarf. At her throat was a silver ornament of some kind that sparkled in the light of the sun. As Tony watched, the figure stretched out her arms to them in a kind of welcome, as the chair floated gently onto the island.

"This is insane," Tony said.

"Oh, Uncle Tony, don't spoil it. That's my castle, where I'll be a princess. Except . . ." Leslie paused, as though remembering something unpleasant. But the thought escaped her. She began to wave to the white-and-blue figure at the castle door.

"Don't touch the water," cautioned Tony.

"Why?"

"Because——" But he had forgotten what made him say that. "Because you'll get wet," he ended lamely.

Then the chair drifted almost to the edge of the island, where an unseen wave, stronger than any they had felt, lifted the recliner and deposited it gently on the shore.

"May I climb down now?" asked Leslie.

"Yeah, sure."

She ran the short distance across the mounded brown paper (and it *was* brown paper, Tony discovered, when he bent down and brushed his palm along it) to the young woman who was waiting to gather her in.

*"Onward! Onward! Soldier!"* Tony urged himself on with a chuckle, not sure why he had thought of that line but pleased with the sense of it. There was a second line that came right after it. He paused, trying to remember the next part, though Leslie and the woman in the white and blue were waving impatiently to him. *"Onward! Onward! Soldier!"* he said again, and the second line came easily enough: *"For death thou canst not shun."*

He began running for the castle, suddenly afraid. But the brown-paper island underfoot had gotten wet and soggy. His feet sank into a surface the consistency of wet papier-mâché.

He fought his way toward the castle, where Leslie was shouting, "Hurry, Uncle Tony! Please, hurry!"

But the ground was the consistency of glue now, and he could barely tug one foot free before the other was swallowed up. Now he could see dark water stains soaking the castle walls. The odd-looking palm trees tilted crazily, as their bases sank into the softening brown mass.

The castle was crumbling too. Leslie kept calling to him, but he knew he was never going to make it. Blue water was spilling over the curving shore of the island. All the palm trees were down. The castle was falling in on itself. He forced himself closer to the gate.

Leslie had vanished. Only the white-and-blue figure remained, standing on a crumbling piece of porch. He was close enough to see it was Lili.

"Help me!" he called, reaching out to the young woman.

But he saw that she was nothing more than a cardboard shape dressed in paper clothes, with a blue paper ribbon around her neck.

Lili crumbled into the blue water that rose over the porch and suddenly swept the castle away.

Tony was swimming now. The last of the island had dissolved. The palm trees had sunk.

There was no trace of anything but electric-blue water and flat pink sky with painted clouds.

"Help!" he shouted.

Then, drawn by some impulse, he looked down into the depths below him. Far down, but rising hungrily toward him, was a vast shape around which coiled black, snaking tentacles. Cruel red eyes locked on his own, and a gaping maw lined with three rows of teeth opened beneath him.

He stopped calling for help and began to scream his lungs out.

"Uncle Tony, wake up, you're having a bad dream," said Leslie, shaking him. "You're gonna wake up Grandpa, and we'll both be in trouble."

*Killers from Space* was just going into its closing credits on the television screen. The family room was just as he'd left it; the plywood screen fit snugly over the fireplace.

Leslie snapped the TV set off. "I think I'm ready to go to sleep now," she said. "I think maybe you'd better go up to your own bed too," she added.

When he paused to snap off the light in the family room, he turned suddenly, afraid that something was rushing out of the dark at him.

But there was nothing. Still shaken, he followed Leslie up the stairs.

# Five

AFTER THE NONSTOP weirdness of Friday night and Saturday morning, Tony fell asleep and stayed asleep until nearly noon. When he made his way downstairs, his father, who was buttoning his jacket preparatory to heading off somewhere (probably downtown to drink beer and watch the football game at Delahanty's Bar) said, "Well, Sleeping Beauty has arisen."

Tony ignored the crack, thinking only of coffee. As he pushed his way into the kitchen he heard the front door slam behind Daniel Kovacs. *Good riddance,* he thought sourly.

There was still a cupful of lukewarm brew in the Mr. Coffee on the sideboard. He could hear his mother and Jerry talking out in the backyard.

He rummaged two slightly stale bear claws out of the bread box and wolfed them down. Still hungry, he was in the middle of pouring out a bowl of Wheat Chex when Jerry and his mother walked into the kitchen.

"Just the man we wanted to see," said Jerry. "I'm going to work on Mom's car. I'll need you as support squad."

"Great," said Tony through a mouthful of cereal and milk.

"Look, young man," his mother said, "you use that car more than anybody else, so you just plan to help."

"All right already!" he said. "Can't you let a guy finish his breakfast first?"

73

"Looks more like lunch to me," said Jerry, glancing at the clock and raising his eyebrows Groucho Marx style.

"Hah. Hah. Hah." Tony poured out more Chex.

"Isn't Vic up yet?" asked his mother.

Tony shook his head. "He's still out like a light. You might want to look in on him. His breathing sounds a little off, like he might be coming down with a cold or something."

"I'll just bet it's the bronchitis, what with all his running around last night." She stuffed her mittens in the pockets of her quilted coat and hurried out of the room.

"I'm ready to start whenever you're ready to give me a hand," said Jerry.

"In a minute, okay?"

"Fine. Gives me a chance for a beer break." Jerry pulled a can of Stroh's from the fridge and sat down across the kitchen table from his brother-in-law. He popped the top, took a swallow, and smiled at Tony.

"Where's Leslie this morning?" Tony wondered aloud.

"She went with Elene. Rummage sale at her school. I told them they could look all they wanted, but they damn well better not bring back any junk."

"Jerry, have I ever told you that you sound more like my father every day?"

"Plenty of times. Have I told you you sound more like a pain in the ass every minute?"

"Plenty of times."

"Then let's call a truce," said Jerry, punctuating his remark with a long pull on his beer. After a loud belch he said, "We'll be working most of the day. I want to give the car a solid going-over. Hope that's not going to screw up your day too badly."

"I haven't got anything better to do. And I'm tired of wondering if the car's going to start every time I turn the key." He picked up his bowl and coffee mug and set them in the sink. He rinsed the dishes, staring for a long time at the water puddling in the drain. Drying his hands on the dish towel, he asked, "Did Leslie say anything to you about a nightmare last night?"

"She said *you* had one and she had to wake you up. Come to think of it, she said *she* had had one too. But she couldn't remember hers. Speaking of which, I don't think you should be encouraging her to stay up and watch that crap you're always watching."

"I think she only wanted company until she felt sleepy again."

"Yeah, well, next time just send her back to bed. Tell her you'll get me up if she doesn't do what you tell her. That should put the fear of God into her. She knows what a bear I am when I have to get up in the middle of the night." Jerry eyed Tony closely for a minute. "Is there something else you want to talk about? You look like you got a lot of worries on your mind."

"No thanks," said Tony. "Let's get to the car before Dad gets back and decides to supervise us."

"Good thinking," said Jerry, crunching his empty Stroh's can with a loud crunch. He tried to lob it into the garbage pail in the opposite corner of the kitchen, but it fell short.

"Nice shot," said Tony as Jerry sheepishly picked up the crumpled can and deposited it in the pail.

"Get ducked," Jerry responded good-naturedly, heading for the back door.

"I'll get my jacket and be right out," Tony called as his brother-in-law pulled the door shut behind him.

As was always the case with a "Jerry project," Tony played gofer, chasing after missing wrenches, nuts, bolts, wire, and frequent beers for the head mechanic. When there was something heavy to be lifted or a lot of elbow grease to be applied, he always wound up with the lion's share of the work.

Also in keeping with Jerry's approach, they tried to do everything on the car at once: repairing the generator brushings, checking the timing, changing the oil. Somehow Jerry managed to come through wearing a minimum of oil; Tony ended up looking like he had just serviced every car in the Indy 500.

Shortly before five, Jerry announced, "I have to take the car and pick up Elene and Leslie. You can clean up the last of this."

The "last of this" meant cleaning the driveway, which had several large oil stains from the afternoon's work. Tony was tempted to go off and leave it, but he knew that would be the first thing his father spotted. And since Daniel Kovacs was sure to come home with more than a few beers under his belt, it would mean a major row.

He was finishing off the driveway just as Jerry returned with Tony's sister and niece.

"Runs like a dream," said Jerry. "You did a good job on the driveway."

"It's my speciality," said Tony. "When the driveway shines, *I* shine."

"Kid should write ads for TV," said Jerry to Elene, who was struggling to pull two sacks of groceries out of the back of the station wagon.

"Uncle Tony, look what I got at the rummage sale," cried Leslie. She held out an odd-shaped board with numbers and letters all over it.

"That's a nice tray," he said offhandedly, putting away the last of the tools they had used on the car.

"It's *not* a tray," said Leslie, clearly offended. "It's a Ouija."

"Like what you use to wash windows?" Tony teased.

"No, Uncle Tony, you mean a squeegee. But this is a Ouija. It talks to ghosts."

He looked closer at the thing, recognizing it now as a favorite prop used in the best of the worst haunted-house films.

"Here, hold it," ordered Leslie. "Then I can show you the rest."

When he was holding the board, she reached in her pocket and pulled out a heart-shaped bit of wood on three small legs. It looked a little like a trivet. "This," Leslie said, "is a planket. It points to a letter, and then you can see what the ghost wants to say."

"Planket" didn't sound right to Tony, but he couldn't think of the right word. He turned the triangular bit of wood over and over in his right hand, holding on to the board itself with his left hand.

Elene called to Leslie to come inside.

"I've got to go now," she said, taking back her treasures, "but my mom says we can do it after dinner tonight."

"I'm not going to be here," said Tony, "but you can show me how to work it later on."

"Okay, bye!" called Leslie, running after her mother.

\* \* \*

"Where are you going?" Daniel Kovacs asked when Tony got up from the table before dessert and asked if he could borrow the Chrysler.

"Out," he said, with a shrug.

"I'd like a little more information than that, mister."

"Dad, I'm seventeen. I deserve a little privacy."

"Fine, fine," his father said. "Only you can damn well *walk* to your 'privacy.' " He had arrived home in a foul mood, and things hadn't improved over dinner. Tony's mother was distracted because Vic was running a fever, and she worried that he might be entering the early stages of bronchitis. This brought up the previous night's escapade, the blame for which Daniel Kovacs placed squarely in Tony's lap. Tony had barely been able to get through dinner. He had already decided to walk or bus it, if he couldn't get the station wagon. It galled him that the combination of outright cost plus insurance premiums, in a town where there was only the scuzziest work for the lowest possible pay, had made it impossible for him to get wheels of his own.

"It's my car," his mother said wearily. "I promised it to him this afternoon. Let him take it, Dan."

"Jeez! It's a friggin' conspiracy," her husband muttered. But he made no objection. Tony felt a little of his anger subside.

Once he was away from the house, however, he realized he had no clear idea of what he wanted to do. But some deeper part of him had a game plan; without consciously meaning to do so, he found he was driving toward Dreamers Hill and the Hotel Bethel. The image of Lili Sarossy drifted through his mind again and again as he neared the old hotel.

Some obscure prompting had him park the Chrysler three quarters of a block away. His jacket collar up around his throat, his knit cap pulled down over his ears, he walked down the opposite side of Cabot Street, feeling like a burglar casing a house.

An orange-and-blue SMT bus lumbered into view, then rolled away down the street. *Where were you when I needed you?* Tony wondered. Then he considered: If the buses hadn't been running off-schedule the night before, he never would have met Lili. *Chalk one up for Smut's rotten service,* he amended.

The night was dark; the sky was heavy with rain clouds, though Tony could sometimes glimpse the moon through cracks in the cloud cover. He pushed his hands deeper into his jeans pockets.

Behind its rusting fences, the old building looked more forlorn than ever. Not a glint or glimmer of light betrayed a sign of life. The grounds were a tangle of shadows and, when the moon broke through the clouds, odd patches of moonlight.

Once he thought he saw a pale, oval face at a third-story window, where no boards hid a pane of still intact glass. But it vanished when he watched it more closely. He decided it was only a reflection of the erratic moon, or headlights from a passing car.

Tony crossed the street and headed west, following the hotel's fence. Once or twice he was tempted to put out his hand and let his fingers slap the railings. But vivid memories of panic, his fingers locked to the metal, the sound of a giant unseen dog in the bushes made him snatch his hands back before he actually touched the hotel fence.

At the gates he stared for a long time at the tightly closed double doors, shadowed by the porch roof. But no one was standing there tonight. With a sigh he continued up the street to the corner of Paxton, where he turned south, still walking the perimeter of the fence. He had some vague idea that he might discover how Lili and her companions got in and out of the hotel. But the side gate on Paxton Street was still sealed fast. Experimentally Tony rattled the gate, but the huge, old-fashioned lock held firm.

Of course he could bring a hacksaw or borrow Jerry's welding torch. But he knew that even the increasingly lacka-daisical Stigesville PD would nail him if he tried anything so foolish. And there was something repellent about trying to cut or burn his way inside the hotel. He eyed the upthrust pickets and had a sudden, gut-wrenching vision of himself impaled on the spikes, his legs thrashing wildly, his mouth and lungs filling with blood.

He shook his head to clear his mind. He even touched his chest absently, as if to assure himself no metal spikes had ripped open the flesh there. No, he decided, he would have to find the secret way through the fence on his own, or wait to be invited in by Lili.

He was almost to Hudson Street, which ran parallel to Cabot, behind the hotel. Inside the fence, matted clumps of shriveled rosebushes and browning geraniums thrust a few brittle leaves and twigs between the palings.

Suddenly he paused. He heard something scuttling in the underbrush. Instinctively he stood away from the fence, continuing his walk at arm's length around the hotel block.

Whatever it was, it had to be small—a mouse, or maybe a kitten, or (he hated to think it!) a rat.

It was odd how he was drawn to the hotel—well, to Lili—only to find himself confronted by something that made his skin crawl, made him want to get away fast. No one needed an elaborate system of fences and locks and man-eating watchdogs to keep him out, he thought, teasing himself. Just let a lazy old rat waddle through the leaves and he'd never try to force his way in.

He took a step forward, his invisible buddy inching forward. He decided to continue on past the back gates, where the stretch of cracked, but still reasonably intact, driveway would reveal the creature if it persisted in following him.

At the Hudson Street entrance he paused, straining his eyes for any trace of movement on the momentarily moonlit drive. When nothing broke from one line of shrubs bordering the fissured concrete to the bushes on the opposite side, Tony decided the mystery critter had abandoned the game.

A few paces farther along, however, he heard the rustling again. He broke into a run for the southeastern corner of the hotel, at the intersection of Hudson and Stanwix. But when he stopped to listen, he heard a telltale crackling of dried leaves as the thing caught up with him. What had seemed mostly puzzling, and even amusing now, began to bother him. *What's there?* he wondered, and, more worrisome, *Why is it following me?*

Prowling around the deserted hotel was becoming less interesting by the moment; even if he suddenly discovered a way inside, he wasn't at all sure he'd try it anymore. He had no desire to set foot on the turf of whatever was following him.

He was just rounding the massive brick pier, where the south and east fences joined, when he saw movement far down the street. A dark figure materialized outside the Stanwix Street entrance to the hotel grounds.

Tony forgot about the Bethel's bothersome watch-rat; he was so excited by the possibility that he had found a secret way into the place. He still wasn't about to go inside in the dark, but he could do some exploring while it was still light.

The figure, muffled in an overcoat and hat of some kind, stretched out an arm toward the gate. With only the inadequate light from a street lamp illuminating the scene, Tony couldn't decide whether the man (or woman) was locking the gate, or merely rattling it to make sure it was secure.

Satisfied, the figure glanced up and down the street. Tony ducked back behind the masonry pier, feeling like one of the Hardy Boys. He wanted to giggle. Then, seeing the figure walk briskly up Stanwix toward Cabot, Tony followed, hugging the shadows. The rustling persisted, but he managed to ignore it.

He paused briefly to rattle the street gate himself but found it locked as tightly as all the others. Somehow they must have found keys inside, or had them made—whoever *they* were, these people with whom Lili was mixed up. It didn't matter at the moment: Tony had already made up his mind to follow the retreating figure. Maybe it would tip him off to what was going on in the hotel. Although, what he'd do about it was up for grabs. He didn't particularly want to be found shot to death in some back alley. But the lure of playing detective, and the mystery surrounding Lili, tempted him to follow a little farther.

The figure reached the corner and turned west on Cabot, walking rapidly downtown. Tony waited as long as he could before following. His rodent companion was still dogging his own footsteps. There was something so silly about following someone while being followed himself (by a goddamn *rat!*) that he had to suppress the urge to giggle again.

He was also struck by the absurdity of spending a perfectly good Saturday evening playing cops and robbers. Was it further proof that he was going off the deep end? he wondered. *All I need to do is find out I'm following Uncle Fester,* he thought, *and that the Addams Family is vacationing at the hotel. And Lili is their long-lost cousin. Then you can book me into a padded cell for my vacation,* he told himself.

*I sure as hell won't be able to tell Janet any of this,* he decided. *She wouldn't understand. And she especially wouldn't understand about Lili.*

The figure ahead crossed to the far side of Cabot, continuing in the same direction. When he was sure he wouldn't be noticed, Tony did the same.

The guy turned down a side street. After a reasonable interval, Tony did the same.

This new street was much darker than Cabot. The streetlights had failed (or been broken) in greater numbers here. There were far more empty or boarded-over windows; fewer neon signs or night-lights to signal still struggling businesses. The cars parked at the curb seemed older and more banged up; several had fluorescent orange stickers affixed to their windshields, warning that the car would be declared abandoned and towed unless their owners made other arrangements. This thoroughfare—named Minsi Lane, according to a street sign that had been knocked askew by a careless driver—seemed to Tony to express real desolation at the heart of the city.

The object of his attention was walking a bit more slowly. Tony, clinging to the shadows—and there were plenty of them along Minsi Lane—could see the person glancing frequently from side to side, as though searching for something. Whatever was going on, Tony felt he was going to find out very soon.

Then the figure in the overcoat and slouch-brimmed hat disappeared. One minute he was about a block's length ahead of his pursuer; the next, Tony was eyeballing a deserted stretch of sidewalk.

After a moment's puzzlement he realized the figure had stepped into a doorway or down an alley. Had he reached his destination? Tony wondered. There was the disturbing possibility that he had discovered he was being followed and had ducked aside to see what Tony would do. The idea of the tables being turned, of himself becoming the hunted, chilled the boy. *Back off*, an inner voice warned. *Get your ass in gear and split!*

But the feeling of having some answer within his grasp overrode all objections. He waited an extra long time to see if the man would reappear. Then, feeling the hairs on the back of his neck prickling at the thought of just how dangerous a situation he could be getting himself into, Tony headed up the block. He hugged each shopfront, sidling quickly across any well-lit patches, alert for any sounds ahead. The street seemed so quiet, he imagined he would be able to hear the sound of a gun's safety being released, or a trigger being drawn back while someone drew a bead on him. . . .

In spite of the biting cold, he could feel sweat gathering in his armpits. His mouth was so dry, he was having a hard time swallowing. His mental warning system was bleeping *Don't-don'tdon'tdon'tdon't* with the persistence of a phone receiver left off its cradle.

He passed two deep-set doorways. One was screened by an accordion grate; the other was empty, except for a litter of wind-deposited papers. It stank of stale urine. Someone had left an empty Thunderbird bottle standing on the stoop.

*Nice neighborhood,* Tony thought, making a conscious effort to calm himself down.

Beyond a grimy expanse of barred display windows containing only dust and dead flies, the boy discovered an alleyway entrance. It had to be where the guy had gone, he reasoned. There wasn't a sign of life anywhere up or down the street.

He took several deep breaths to calm himself, then cursed the way his heart continued to pound inside his chest. He had a hunch the answers lay somewhere along the shadowed passage ahead; he also knew that the danger level would shoot into the full-tilt boogie red zohc the moment he set foot in the alley.

Trusting to his hearing and prepared to hit the street sprinting like he'd never sprinted in any track meet, Tony entered the narrow space between facing blank gray walls. Every few steps he paused, listening, ready to sprint for his life.

The passage was clogged with damp, rotting papers and several disintegrating brown boxes filled with mildewed rags. *Just another Saturday night in the city,* Tony thought, swallowing yet another threatening giggle. There was a lingering smell of urine, not as strong as before but persistent enough so that he had to hold his hand in front of his nose.

The alley turned sharply to the right. A nine-foot wooden fence separated him from the back of a movie theater. Several metal doors, set flush in the wall beside him, offered no hiding place. Unless his quarry had slipped through one of these, the guy was still somewhere ahead.

Tony quietly tried each door, finding each sealed fast. He pushed on.

Abruptly the alley opened into a large, roughly square area formed by the meeting of the side and rear walls of half a dozen buildings. Most were blank, though a few had dark and securely barred windows overlooking the area. A row of rusty garbage cans, most of them turned on their sides, debris scattered across the cement, lined the wall opposite where Tony stood, still in the passageway.

From somewhere on his right, out of his line of sight, came a soft rustling sound and an even softer moan. Tony stood for a moment, frozen in place, while he debated splitting immediately, or taking one quick look around the corner and *then* splitting.

Curiosity got the best of him. Steadying himself by placing his hands flat against the unpleasantly damp and chalky wall nearest him, the boy moved his head into position a fraction of an inch at a time. After what seemed an eternity, he edged past the corner of the building so he could see where the sounds were coming from.

At first he could only see a darker blot of darkness in the pool of shadow filling the courtyard. Then, as his eyes adjusted, he made out the trench-coated figure, apparently kneeling, facing away from him. The guy was moving slightly; it looked like he was searching through a pile of old rags in the corner. Was this some drop-off point for dope? Tony wondered. If so, was the guy on a pickup or delivery run?

He heard the moaning again; it seemed to come from the guy. If this was a pickup, Tony reasoned, maybe he was suffering withdrawal symptoms. And if the guy was in bad shape, he wasn't nearly the threat he might have been.

Then a second thought struck Tony. Someone like that might really freak out. Hadn't he read somewhere that psychos had superhuman strength?

Something white flopped over onto the cement near the edge of the trench coat, which was pooled around the guy's knees. A wad of paper? But the shape seemed—

Tony strained his eye to see, then felt his gorge rise suddenly.

*A hand. It's a fucking human hand and arm.* Now he could see the fingers clenching and unclenching weakly. Too scared for the moment to move, he realized the bundle of rags the man was kneeling over was *a person*. The guy's victim was the one doing the moaning, not him. *But what's he doing to the poor bastard? Robbing him?*

*Get out of here!* His brain ordered his feet. But the lines of communication were momentarily downed by shock.

In that instant the kneeling figure spun around, aware that he'd been discovered. Tony heard an angry sound—somewhere between a snarl and a hiss—that was unlike anything he'd heard from a human throat before. He saw two eyes flare—bright and startled and alien—as a cat's or deer's eyes caught by a flashlight or headlight beam. He had the impression of thick black hair and eyebrows, a long face the color of moonlight on snow, and sharp teeth and lips flecked with diamonds and rubies, which his mind instantly translated into saliva and blood.

Then he was racing back down the alley, the message having reached his feet.

Behind him, he heard the snarling again—louder, the walls of the court and passageway acting as a kind of echo chamber.

He had almost reached the street when he felt his back stiffen, his shoulder blades strain together, his whole body tighten up to present as small a target for the bullets he sensed would be pumped after him at any instant by his pursuer.

"Hey! Help me! Please! Anyone! *He's got a gun!*" Tony shouted at the top of his lungs. He was running down the middle of Minsi Lane, hell-bent for Cabot, hoping someone somewhere would call the police.

He glanced over his shoulder.

The guy was gaining fast. Too fast. No one except a top athlete could have overtaken Tony in a sprint, but his pursuer was sure as hell going to do it.

He managed an extra burst of speed as terror flooded his system with adrenaline. Why hadn't the guy shot? he wondered. Then he remembered he hadn't seen any gun in the guy's hands. Just a glimpse of long fingers tipped with stained nails.

But the eyes, the sounds the guy was making . . . *He's a psycho*, Tony thought. *People like that can rip an elephant apart with their bare hands*. He knew he'd heard that someplace. And just his glimpse of the guy told him it had to be true.

A sedan turned down Minsi. As Tony ran toward it, trying

to flag it down, the driver swerved into the oncoming lane, narrowly avoiding running Tony over. The sedan roared past Tony's pursuer and was gone. The drama in the middle of the deserted street interested the driver not at all.

Tony, without breaking stride, risked a glance behind him . . .

And groaned.

The guy was almost on top of him, gaining on him almost effortlessly—like a man in peak shape. If he was into dope, Tony realized, it sure hadn't affected his performance.

The guy plowed into him, knocking the wind out of him, tumbling them both across the street into the gutter. Tony tried to yell for help but found his face pushed into a black mix of mud, oil, and rot. He tried to heave himself out of the muck, but his assailant was riding him, forcing his head down into the suffocating mess.

*I'm going to die oh God I don't want to die don't let me die I'm going to die.* Tony's brain was a jumble of frantic, helpless messages. The weight of the man was crushing him; the guy's hands were on the back of his head, pushing him deeper into the ooze. Tony couldn't find purchase anywhere to try to flip his body over and unseat his attacker. His own hands kept slipping in the mud; the lack of oxygen was making him desperate; he was losing his coordination. He had a horrible vision of himself flopping around in the muck like a fish without the sense to know it's been reeled in to its death and hasn't brains enough to die.

*I don't want to die,* his mind kept insisting, urging him to struggle on, even though he was blacking out.

Then, abruptly, the weight was gone from his back; the hands were gone from the back of his head.

Sobbing, Tony lifted his head out of the goo, raising himself shakily to his hands and knees. He shook his head from side to side to free it from the worst of the gunk. He spat repeatedly, but he could feel grit all over his teeth, could taste nothing but oil and rot.

Hands hooked under his armpits. Someone firmly hauled him to his feet. Wiping off his face with the back of his hand, Tony saw the old man in a maroon down jacket who was trying to help him up. He was carrying a cane, tucked under his arm like a riding crop. A thatch of white hair and rimless spectacles gave the old man a teacherish look. A patch of scar tissue, running from his left cheek down below his coat collar, suggested he had been terribly burned at one time. Tony guessed him to be sixty or seventy, at least; but he was as strong as an athlete many years his junior.

In a sudden panic, Tony searched the street for any sign of his attacker. The man had disappeared.

"I—he—"

"It's all right," his rescuer said. "When he saw me, he ran. You're safe now."

Tony was shaking. Dimly he heard the sound of a police siren on Cabot, turning onto Minsi Lane.

"Someone must have seen what was happening out here in the street," said the old man. "They must have called the police. Come with me; I don't think the police can help very much." He took the boy's arm and urged him back down the street.

"Nnn-no." Tony gasped, breaking free of the old man's grip. "Suck-sucker's a kill-killer. Po-police need to arres-arrest him."

"I'm afraid they'll be more trouble than anything else," said the man, walking quickly away from Tony. His iron-tipped cane made sharp clicking sounds on the sidewalk. "Need a wit-witness," Tony called after him.

But the man turned the corner and was gone an instant before the police car, lights and sirens going full-tilt boogie, pinned Tony in its headlights. A voice ordered him to "Freeze!" and Tony, relieved to see the two officers climbing out of the sedan, was only too happy to obey any order they flung at him. Without being told to, he raised his hands and said, "Boy, am I glad to see you guys."

# Six

THE NIGHTMARE OF his near murder was over, but a strangeness clung to everything that followed.

When the police had pieced together a coherent story from his frantic attempt to tell everything at once, the officer had hustled him into the backseat of the car. They made him stay put while with drawn guns they checked out the alleyway and courtyard. They were gone four or five minutes before the younger policeman, a sandy-haired jock Tony was sure had been a senior during his freshman year at Stigesville High, returned and motioned the boy out of the car. He escorted Tony to the cul-de-sac at the end of the alley.

Just retracing his steps, Tony felt his palms growing sweaty and the hairs on his neck beginning to stand up. Every crumpled cardboard box or soggy rag, highlighted by the glare of the alley lights on top of the police car, was a vividly remembered obstacle to his panicked flight.

Some illumination from the strong floodlights made it around the right-angle turn in the passage, but none of it reached as far as the blind court. The officer's partner was standing in the middle of the enclosure, shining his flashlight around, randomly picking out a closed door, a grate-covered window, an overturned garbage can. "No one here now," he reported needlessly. "Show us where you saw the guy and the victim."

"In the corner there." Tony's voice seemed to boom out in

the echo chamber formed by the surrounding walls. He glanced nervously around, as though the sound of his voice might bring back his would-be killer.

The beam of light swept back and forth over the spot, revealing nothing but a mat of waterlogged newspapers and filth. After a minute the second officer, taller and rangier than his partner, snapped off the light. Turning to Tony, he said, "I don't know what you saw or what you *thought* you saw, but there's nothing there. We've checked all through that mess." The boy could hear the distaste in the man's voice.

"Let's get back to the patrol car, Mike," the jock suggested. "We can fill out our reports at the emergency room."

"Hey, I'm okay," Tony insisted.

"We play it by the book," said Mike.

Out on the street, a few people hung around, curious to see what the police were investigating. *Where were you when I was getting the shit beat out of me?* Tony wondered.

Most of the onlookers melted away as soon as the officers stepped out of the alley. A few hung around long enough to assure the police that no one had seen anything relevant, though several wanted to point out what a scandal it was that no one could walk the city streets, day or night, without risking a mugging, or worse. No one knew anything about the old guy with a cane and a burn-scarred neck when Tony described him as the first person on the scene. The officers gave curt, noncommittal responses and quickly wrapped up the interview.

"I really don't need a doctor," Tony tried again as the patrol car pulled away from the curb.

Officer Mike sighed. Then he picked up the radio microphone and began updating police headquarters while his partner drove toward Skeffington Memorial Hospital.

Tony had given them a substantially edited version of his misadventures. He had just been taking a long walk to "blow off steam" and had turned down Minsi Lane without really thinking about where he was going. He had been passing the alley when he heard a moan. "I thought, you know, some wino or someone might have, you know, hurt himself." Hearing the officer matter-of-factly report his Good Samaritan actions, Tony, sitting behind the wire screen between the driver's seat and the backseat of the police car, felt his face go red. It sounded even phonier on replay.

Listening to the drone of the reporting officer, and the terse radio responses, Tony was reminded just how deadly his game had become. He had only to touch his scraped cheek and smell the oil-and-rot stink that clung to his jeans and jacket and filled the cab to realize how close to biting it he had come. But he couldn't bring himself to tell the police about the hotel, yet; not until he had had a chance to warn Lili away from the place. Once she was out of there, he was going to phone the hot line and turn in the dealers—including the psycho who had tried to kill him—anonymously.

From time to time the reporting officer asked him for a clarification of some point. Tony tried to keep his answers consistent. Apparently no glaring errors turned up, since officer Mike seemed satisfied.

"Probably one of your transients," the jock suggested. "I'd bet it was some strung-out pot head. You probably heard him moaning back there; they can get pretty wild when they're on something."

"There was another guy back there. I saw his hand. And the guy had *blood* around his mouth and on his teeth."

"Probably chewing on his tongue. I saw a guy who chewed half his tongue off and swallowed it. Drugs," he added. Then he shook his head and returned his full attention to driving.

In the emergency room of Skeffington Memorial, a bored-sounding, stubble-faced intern checked Tony over, cleaned his few minor scrapes and cuts, and pronounced him fit. Tony had to fill out several forms guaranteeing payment for the services; because he was a minor, the hospital had to call his parents to get additional information and authorization from them.

Tony could hear his father shouting halfway across the nearly empty waiting room. The nurse, trying to calm Daniel Kovacs down enough to get the answers she needed, finally rolled her eyes, then gave in and held the receiver out to Tony.

He grabbed the phone in the middle of one of his father's angry commentaries on life, doctors, crime, and his son's lack of common sense—audible to everyone within earshot.

When he finally was able to get his father to listen, Tony quickly assured him that he was fine, that the doctors and police had everything under control.

Daniel Kovacs insisted on talking with the police. Wearily Officer Mike confirmed everything Tony had said. There would be a report and follow-up in the next few days.

Then Tony had to repeat everything to his mother, who sounded hysterical. "I just don't believe this. First Vic, then you—"

"What happened to Vic?" asked Tony, jolted by her unexpected comment.

"He's wandered off. While we were watching the Saturday Night Movie. Jerry and Elene are out looking for him now. He can't have gone very far, can he? He's been running a fever all day."

"No, Mom," said Tony. "He'll be fine." Mechanically he gave her a list of Vic's hangouts. She wrote them down to pass along to her daughter and son-in-law when they phoned in. With a few more assurances he was able to turn the phone over to the nurse, who finally got the information she needed to fill out the forms on the clipboard in front of her.

The nurse handed him the phone again.

"Do you want us to come down to the hospital?" his mother asked. "Jerry has your father's car, but we can borrow the Thompsons', I'm sure."

"No, no, I'll be fine. They, uh, just want to keep me here a little while longer. For, um, observation, I think." The nurse gave him a funny look and shook her head. "Just to be sure there's, you know, no concussion or anything." She shrugged her shoulders and turned her attention to more pressing matters. "The car—oh, yeah, the police are bringing it over here right now. They'll leave it in the parking lot." He was relieved to see that the two police officers were seated on adjoining orange plastic chairs in the farthest corner of the waiting room, deep in a debate over some item on the police report form Officer Mike had nearly completed. "In fact, I think it's out there now. Look, I gotta go," he added hastily, seeing the officers rise and head toward him, the point of contention evidently resolved. "Um, somebody needs to use the phone. See you later. Yes, *I'm fine.* I love you too. Good-bye."

He surrendered the phone to the nurse as Officer Mike handed him a form.

"Read this over; if there's anything wrong, let us know.

It's an interim report. We'll probably have to get a fuller report later. If it looks okay, sign there.''

Tony hastily glanced over the mix of facts, half truths, and outright lies. He scribbled his signature, feeling like he had just sold his soul to the devil.

"We'll take you back to your car now," the blond officer said.

"Great," Tony replied, hoping his guilty conscience wasn't showing.

Fifteen minutes later they dropped him off on Cabot Street beside the Chrysler. They waited while he climbed in and started up the engine. Dutifully he made a show of switching on the headlights and adjusting the rearview mirror. When he saw that they were going to wait until he was under way, he pulled out, waving to them.

He drove to the corner of Paxton and turned left. In his rearview mirror he saw the patrol car cross the intersection and continue on down Cabot.

He turned left again onto Hudson, slowed, and brought the car to a stop across from the back entrance to the Bethel. How, exactly, he was going to proceed from this point wasn't clear to him. He had no reason to assume he could find his way into the hotel any better than before. As a precaution, he opened the rear door of the car and took a tire iron out of the wheel well. He hefted it several times, feeling better with the solid metal bar in hand. His need for a weapon reminded him just how dangerous the Bethel might be.

But he felt an obligation to try to warn Lili about the psycho and the fact that he was going to blow the whistle on the others who were hiding out in the Bethel.

The strangeness of the past two days hit him all of a sudden. Weirdest of all was his desire to protect Lili, though he had only seen her twice and had exchanged no more than a few words with her. He sensed he was acting out of proportion to their brief encounter. He also recognized that he had no clear reason for his belief that she was innocent of whatever was *really* going on inside the abandoned hotel. Still, to betray Lili to the police would be to betray himself. A glimpse of her, just hearing her voice, had established some deep, undeniable link between them. It puzzled him, pleased him, frightened him that he seemed to have no real choice in the matter of Lili. His emotions were calling the shots, and he stumbled blindly along the course set for him.

He returned to the Stanwix Street entrance, where the evening's nightmare had begun. The street was as empty as the hotel grounds on the other side of the fence.

Tony hunkered down to take a closer look at the lock. The keyhole had been scraped free of rust, as though it were used regularly. Eyeing the bolt, he saw it was used frequently. Ready to snatch his finger away at any instant, he touched one of the iron palings with his finger; he felt nothing but gritty rust. Emboldened, he let his finger trace out the curve of the scrollwork that extended waist-high on the gates. No electrical pulse; no hum.

He shook the gates on the off chance something might give. It didn't. He watched the darkened facade and blind windows for a few moments. When it was evident no one had been disturbed by his efforts, he threw his shoulder against the ironwork. The gates refused to budge.

There seemed to be no way in but to climb over the fence. He considered the gatepost or the corner pier, deciding that the latter, with its random pattern of dog-teeth bricks, offered the easiest and safest way up and over.

He returned to the corner of Stanwix and Hudson. When he was sure no pedestrians or cars were approaching on either street, he hooked the tire iron in his belt and began climbing, using the outthrust brick ends as toe- and handholds.

Only a short way into his ascent he was assailed by waves of vertigo so severe, he had to freeze in position, until his heart rate slowed down and the dizziness subsided. *Shit! You'd think I was scaling friggin'* Everest! he thought. He had never had any problem with heights before; suddenly he felt the electric tingle of fear in his wrists and ankles. He was convinced that if he stopped moving, he would remain stuck in place—unable to climb higher, not daring to climb down.

He risked a glance back over his shoulder. The sidewalk seemed hundreds of feet below him—as if he were clinging to a mountainside or looking down from the Empire State Building, not scaling a masonry pier less than fifteen feet high. *Don't freeze, asshole!* he warned himself. *Keep moving.* It was the same advice he remembered getting as a kid from his father before he went cross-country skiing with some friends while he was still in grade school. "If you get lost in the snow, keep moving. If you don't, you'll fall asleep, freeze, and die."

He kept going, though the plane of the fence post seemed to be tilting forward. He had the horrible sensation of climbing *out* as well as up. If the patterned brick surface tilted any farther, he thought nervously, he was going to find himself climbing parallel to the sidewalk. He would come crashing down onto the cement, break every bone in his body and bleed to death, as bone splinters ripped through his skin, stabbed into his brain, and ruptured his eyeballs—

*Stop that!* Some inner alarm was trying to short-circuit the too vivid images that were already making his palms slippery and making it harder for him to risk moving the toe of one tennie from the lip of one brick up to the next. He fought back the temptation to look down again. Instead he looked *up*. The two-tiered cement capstone was only a hand's breadth away. He concentrated on the dusty gray line of capstone, rejecting the images of tilting surfaces, his body twisting frantically as he fell—images that grew more intense the closer he got to his goal.

But he persevered. His fingers closed on the lip of the capstone. Dangling from it, he inched his way around the corner of the pier until his knees were level with the topmost rail that supported the row of ornamental spikes. Gingerly he maneuvered his body until his right foot was resting on the rail, taking some of the burden off his overtaxed arms. Just as carefully, he brought his left foot up. As he relied on the capstone ledge to balance himself, he was acutely aware of the rusty, wicked-looking spear point between his feet, aimed sharply upward at his groin. He remembered hearing about people in medieval times who were executed by being impaled on sharpened spikes driven up between their legs, so they couldn't pull themselves free but could only sink farther onto the deadly skewer—

He cut that line of thought off very fast. It was more of the same negative thinking that was proving the hardest barrier to overcome. And he was too close to his goal to give up now.

He leaned his body toward the inside corner of the pier, letting his feet rest on the rail as long as possible, keeping as much weight off his arms as possible. When his hands had a firm purchase on the capstone, he swung his body free of the

fence. His legs were now dangling some twelve feet above
the leaf litter and weeds of what had been one of the Bethel's
elegant gardens half a century before. He angled his feet
closer to the pier facing and scraped his toes up and down
until he found bits of the ornamental brickwork that gave him
purchase. Easing one hand down, he found a solid handhold
before he let go of the capstone lip. Then, swiftly, he re-
versed his climbing procedure, descending to the ground in a
few minutes.

The moment he dropped to the spongy soil near the base of
the pier, he whipped out the tire iron, ready to take on all
comers. But the rising wind was the only thing moving in the
overgrown garden.

Now that he was on solid ground again, scaling the wall
seemed remarkably easy. Surely, Tony thought, lots of others
must have made the same climb. Yet no one in his memory
had ever heard of someone doing what he had done.

Maybe the place creeps people out, so they don't *want* to
try to get in, he speculated. After all, just thinking about what
*might* have happened to him had almost scared him off. More
than that, it had almost made him *fall*. Once he found Lili, he
would get her to run away as fast as possible. He was
counting on her having a key to the gate. He didn't relish the
idea of climbing back over the fence, and he doubted the girl,
who had seemed so pale and thin, had ever had the strength to
try such a thing. The only real problem he could foresee was
her not having a key in her possession. There was also the
chance that she would simply *refuse* to run away; what he
would do then, he hadn't the foggiest. Be cool, think positive,
he thought, giving himself a pep talk.

Still keeping the tire iron at the ready, he began moving
around toward the back of the hotel, figuring a rear entrance
would give him a chance to scope things out. He didn't want
to blunder in on the psycho or his buddies, or worse. He
knew the suckers played for keeps, and he had no desire to
become dead meat.

He stopped suddenly. Someone was moving in the shadows
ahead, wandering in and out of a curved row of graceful
white columns supporting a flat cement roof. He vaguely
remembered seeing the structure, like part of a Greek temple,
gleaming in the moonlight when he had parked the car earlier.
Reaching into his memory, he recalled someone pointing it

out to him years before as a pavilion that shaded one end of what had been the hotel's Olympic-size pool.

Using several sprawling shrubs to screen himself from view, Tony circled closer to the figure. The person, a woman, was wearing a dark robe or shawl of some kind. He thought it might be Lili, but he was still too far away, and the dense clouds scudding across the sky made the moonlight uncertain. He wanted to be sure it was her before he revealed himself.

She paused, head tilted to one side, as though she were listening to a voice inaudible to him. Then she stepped out from under the roof to stand on the topmost of the broad, flat steps that led down to pool level. She was looking directly across the oval shadow of the pool toward where he was crouching behind a brown-leaved clump of hydrangea.

The moon came from behind a cloud and lit the scene long enough for him to know for certain that it was her.

Jamming the tire iron into his belt, he stood up. If she was surprised to see him, she didn't show it. Instead she moved gracefully down the steps and began to walk slowly toward him. To Tony it seemed she was moving like someone in a trance. Maybe she was sleepwalking. He ran to her, skirting the edge of the pool. He could see that the gold-speckled blue tiles on the bottom were covered with matted leaves and dirt. The cement walls of the pool were cracked, and many of the tiles had fallen off, to join the litter below.

The deep end of the pool was a stagnant pond covered with decaying leaves. Occasionally the light breeze disturbed the covering enough to show oily black water reflecting the moonlight, looking uncomfortably like the wet, black flesh of something hidden in the damp and rot.

"Lili!" he called not too loudly, not wanting to spoil his good fortune at finding her outside and alone.

She stopped and stared at him—blinking as though she had only just discovered him. "Tony," she said in a disconcertingly matter-of-fact tone. He had the curious impression that she had been expecting him all along. But that was impossible. "How did you get in?" she asked, again in a flat tone of voice that hinted she had no real interest in his answer but was merely saying the expected thing.

Now that he was close to her, he could see that her eyes had a vagueness that suggested her thoughts were light-years away from their meeting. "Are you all right?" he asked. He reached for her hands, which grasped the long, silky tassels fringing a black, Spanish-looking shawl. He stopped short of touching her. He felt he couldn't touch her unless she invited him to.

"I'm fine," she said. Holding the shawl closed with her left hand, she suddenly reached forward and grabbed his right hand in her own. Suddenly animated, she whispered, "Oh, you shouldn't be here! You can't stay! Please go!"

Her fingers were cool and just a little moist, circling his own. "You've got to come with me," he said. "You can't stay here. Those guys who live here are *trouble!* The police—"

She released his fingers, stepping back suddenly. She shook her head as if what he were saying had overloaded her with too many ideas at once. "Why would the police want to come here?" she asked finally.

"Because of the dealing that's going on."

"What are you talking about? I don't understand what you're trying to say."

"*Drug dealing!* What the guys who live here are into, if my hunch is right."

The flatness had returned to her voice. "Tony, there are *no* other people here."

"But I've *seen* one of them. He tried to kill me."

Her interest flared suddenly, "Oh, Tony, no!" Then it subsided just as abruptly as she said, "You're mistaken. I'm alone here. I've always been alone here."

"Don't try to protect them!" Tony pleaded. "They're not worth it. If the guy I met is any sample, they're all psychos."

"Come with me," she said suddenly, towing him along by the hand. "I'll show you how empty this place is."

"But last time I saw you, *you told me there were people here who wouldn't like me coming over the fence.*"

She paused halfway to the back of the hotel. "If I said anything like that, I only meant I didn't want you to hurt yourself getting inside. But I don't remember my exact words."

Seeing how earnestly she looked at him, he began to wonder just how accurate his memory of the event was. Then he said, "There was a dog. They sicked a dog on me."

"Dog?" Lili thought about it for a minute, then said off-handedly, "Oh, it must have run away. I haven't seen it since that night. Come *on!* You'll see that I'm telling the truth."

No longer sure of anything, Tony let himself be led up a

short flight of steps into an empty passageway carpeted in a rug that was more mildew than pile. It made unpleasant squishing sounds underfoot. What light there was came from open double doors on the left. Passing these, he looked into a room where the spindly remains of ornamental trees rose like broken umbrellas from huge planters. Set among the dead trees were wrought-iron tables and chairs, to which a little white paint still clung, though they were, for the most part, crusted with rust. The walls and part of the roof of the room were made of plate glass, though the former had been boarded over, and much of the roof had broken away or was obscured by leaves and branches. Still, it let in enough moonlight to reach the hallway where Tony and Lili stood.

"It was the solarium once," Lili said. "It was beautiful all those years ago."

"You make it sound like you saw it the way it was," Tony said.

"I still do," she said, urging him along the passageway.

Now they were crossing a vast dining room. A cobweb-shrouded chandelier hung from the shadows overhead, like a monstrous cocoon. Scattered about were tables of all sizes, from round ones suitable for a single diner or an intimate twosome, to a vast oval near one end of the room that could have seated three dozen people. Rotting linen still clung to a few of them. Four tarnished silver spoons and a dusty soup tureen were the only items on a vast, marble-topped sideboard running half the length of one wall.

"This would make a perfect setting for a Dracula movie."

She either didn't hear him, or didn't feel like responding.

There were sepia-toned pictures, so water-stained and dark-ened that it was hard to guess their subjects, lining the walls of the dining room near the exit doors. After several attempts at deciphering some, Tony gave up and followed Lili, who had gone ahead into the huge lobby.

She stood in the center of the immense area, near the foot of the stairs, turning like a ballerina, whispering, "Empty, empty, you can see that it's empty," over and over again.

Except for her soft chanting, there wasn't a sound to be heard in the place. The rooms they had crossed were silent; the shadowy gallery at the head of the grand staircase was as still as a tomb. Precious little light seeped in between the boards over the windows, or followed them through the dining-room doors. Lili continued to spin like some ghostly dancer. Nothing else moved. There wasn't draft enough to move a puff of dust.

Yet Tony felt increasingly uneasy. He was suddenly daunted by the weight of years, memories, shadows and . . .*something else*, something that he couldn't give a name to. It was a feeling: like being watched by someone invisible.

Tony crossed to Lili and grabbed her hand, putting an abrupt stop to her whirling. She gasped in surprise, but the look (insofar as he could make it out in the oppressive gloom) she gave him was dreamy, distant, unfocused. "I want you to come upstairs with me," she said. "I'll show you my room. And if you don't believe we're alone, I'll open as many other rooms as you want, until you *do* believe me."

She started up the stairs. He began to follow her, but he suddenly felt an overwhelming sense of terror flooding down from the darkness above.

"I . . . I can't," he said helplessly. The nameless, shapeless dread did what all his previous vivid fancies had been unable to do: stop him dead in his tracks.

"Tony, what's wrong?" she called down to him from ten steps up.

"I don't want to go up there," he said with a shrug.

"Well, it's not fair that you're not going to let me prove to you that I'm alone," she said, sounding as if it didn't matter in the least. Suddenly she ran down the stairs two at a time, saying, "Then we'll have tea in the kitchen." She laughed, airily dismissing his inability to set foot on the stairs as no reason to spoil their visit.

Happier with each step away from the grand staircase, Tony walked quickly after Lili, following her back into the silent dining room and out through swinging doors, which had once been padded in leather. The leather had burst, letting tufts and coils of dirty white material free. Grime-filmed circular glass windows were inset in each door—too filthy to give a glimpse of what lay behind them.

The shadowy kitchen beyond was filled with huge institutional stoves, rows of sinks, floor-to-ceiling cupboards, and what Tony guessed were the doors to walk-in freezers. An occasional dusty soup ladle or egg whisk hung from huge black iron overhead racks, like the spokes of wagon wheels.

Lili led him to a small table set below a pair of boarded-over windows. To Tony's relief she pulled out two candles, which she set in mismatched holders—one shaped like a crystal rose, one merely a polished glass hemisphere. The candles, when Lili lit them, created a cheerful circle of light; light that glinted off the chain of silver links she wore around her neck. But Tony remained uncomfortably aware of the darkness that pressed in on the circle of light, and the shadows that danced when the candle flames flickered. He couldn't imagine how Lili could stay here alone, night after night, without becoming totally spooked.

From another drawer she pulled out a small can of sterno, a packet of loose tea leaves, a quart container of water, and a small pot. She set to work, brewing the tea on the counter. She directed Tony to teacups that had been carefully set in a nearby cupboard. These, which had been stored with the cup upended into the saucer, were relatively dust-free. He assumed she used these regularly. He slipped off his jacket and hung it on the back of his spindly wooden chair.

"Where did you get the supplies?" he asked, making conversation.

"Around."

When he was sitting down again, waiting for her to fill the cups, he asked, "Where did you come from before you wound up here?"

"I was born here. Then I went away for a while. Now I'm back."

"It's a pretty dead place. Why would you want to come back?"

"Just to see it again, I guess," she said, not really sounding interested.

"Will you stay for a while?"

"Of course," she said, as if that were the most obvious thing in the world.

"Do your parents live around here?"

"They're dead." For the first time he heard dismay in her voice.

"Sorry. Do you have any brothers or sisters?"

"I had a brother. Michael. Mickey. He's dead too." Now there was a bitter edge in her voice. *Nice going,* he thought, berating himself. *Any more polite conversation and you'll have her in tears.* He shut up and fiddled with the candle holders, turning first the rose, then the spheroid, around and around.

She delivered steaming cups of tea to the table. The smell of it wasn't bad, but it wasn't particularly appetizing, either. It tasted funny to Tony—stale, like one of the home remedies his grandmother would brew to help Vic through a bout of bronchitis.

The second swallow was more agreeable. By the third, he felt it really wasn't bad at all. He was enjoying this small-scale mad tea party in the ruin of the old hotel. Just sitting across from Lili, watching the candlelight bring a soft glow to her skin and a new liveliness to her eyes, seemed an extraordinarily wonderful way to spend a night.

He was vaguely aware that he should be heading home, should have headed home a long time before. But Lili refilled the cups, and he was suddenly so tired, so very tired, that he couldn't imagine walking back to the car, let alone driving home.

Lili was talking to him, but her words seemed to be dissolving in the candlelit air between them. She was beautiful, and he was in love, and he was also so tired that he had to put his head down on the table for just a minute. . . .

He fell asleep with his forehead resting on his right forearm, his left arm stretched out across the table.

He was awake enough at one point to realize Lili had cupped the fingers of his outstretched hand in her own.

(He was sitting in a sunlit parlor, with white curtains at the window and a white cat curled on the sill. Across from him, an old man with a thatch of white hair was sleeping in an old-fashioned wing chair. He wanted the old fellow to wake up, because Tony knew the man had something important to tell him. But the man slept on, and it was dark outside the window, and the growling, dark shape crouched on the sill wasn't a cat any longer.

Then the room was gone.)

Tony woke up long enough to flash on the fact that the candles had burned halfway down, and Lili was bent over his arm, kissing the crook of it gently.

(An old man with rimless glasses and leaning on a cane was walking toward him down a street lined with globes that seemed to *suck* the light into themselves, so it was getting harder and harder for Tony to see him, the closer he came.

The man was trying to say something, but for all his straining to hear, the boy couldn't catch a single word.)

Suddenly he sat bolt upright. The candles had burned down almost to the holder. His left arm had fallen asleep and was filled with pins and needles when he tried to move it. *How late is it?* he wondered.

He looked around for Lili and found her standing some distance away, staring at him with a curious expression. He had the impression that she had just come back into the kitchen from another room. "What time is it?" he asked, rubbing his eyes.

"Nearly dawn. There are no clocks working here."

"I've got to get home." He pulled on his jacket, treating his left arm gingerly because it was still aching. "Will you be all right here?" he asked. "There was a guy hanging around the gate on Stanwix Street earlier. He tried to kill me."

"You don't have to worry. I'm sure he won't come back. And I always lock the room I stay in. I think of this as my home, you know. I feel very good about it."

"You can't stay here very long," said Tony. "You're already trespassing. Someone's bound to see you coming or going one of these days."

"Then," she said, "I'll have to worry about that one of these days, I guess."

"When will I see you again?"

"Come again in three days. I'll meet you at the Stanwix Gate whenever you come over."

"I'll come by early enough so I can take you to dinner."

"No, I prefer to stay here—just for the time being. I can't explain; it's—well, if you want to see me, we'll have to stay here for now."

He wanted to see her very much. Whatever ground rules she wanted to set up, he'd abide by. The whole thing was so off-the-wall that he was finding a perverse logic in it all. "Why not tomorrow?" he pressed.

But she just shook her head. Then she said, "Come on, and I'll let you out the gate."

Moving like someone in a dream, he followed Lili through the first graying light of dawn. Feeling reckless, he tried to kiss her, and she let him. Her lips felt as cool and damp as her hand, but the warmth he was feeling more than made up for it.

When he had slipped through the gate, he heard her lock it firmly behind him. The simplicity of his exit seemed downright funny to him after scaling the walls and risking monsters (of all sizes) in the bushes and—what? a black goblin crouched at the head of the stairs?—in keeping with the best fairy tales and starring him as "Indiana" Kovacs. But it all had the headlong pace and somehow *logical* wackiness of a dream. He felt high, like he'd just stepped off a ride that was one part roller coaster and one part haunted house.

And he was feeling, for all his bone-weariness, more alive than he'd felt in months.

Crazy-wonderful end to a crazy-horrible adventure, he thought. *I think I'm in love,* he told himself as he walked back to the station wagon. *Correction: I know I'm in love.*

Looking at the car's roof and windshield, crusted with ice and gleaming dully in the dawn light, he added, *I also know the shit is going to hit the fan when I wander in this late. Correction: this early.*

But in Tony's estimation, what had happened so far that night made whatever was going to happen worth it.

# Seven

WHEN HE LET himself into the house, Tony discovered his mother asleep in a corner of the couch. She had dozed off still sitting up, probably waiting for him to come in.

Or Vic. He had forgotten that Vic had vanished earlier. Had his uncle returned in the hours before dawn? Tony wondered. He'd find out as soon as he went upstairs.

He tiptoed in to readjust the quilt around his mother and gave her a kiss. In many ways he felt sorriest of all for her for everything that seemed to be going wrong in the house. There were a lot of times when he wondered, after listening to one of his father's beery tirades or verbal snipings, why she didn't just go away. Elene had her family and wanted her own house as soon as she and Jerry could get some money put aside; Tony was planning to leave as soon as he graduated. He hated to think of her going on, day in and day out, with only her husband's nagging and abusive ways, and Vic growing more loopy every day. But he knew she never would. She had been shocked when he suggested she could leave Daniel and take up a life on her own. She had grown angry *with him* for suggesting it.

It was her decision, but he didn't like it. It made him feel guilty about the escape route he had blocked out for himself. It made him fell small and selfish.

But what alternative was there? he asked himself. Stay and

live out the rest of his days picking up piecework, living at home, becoming a kind of unpaid servant and companion, the way Poor Ida, his spinster grandaunt, took care of her older sister, Tony's grandmother?

Or stay, maybe find a better-paying job, marry someone like Janet Dillon, and settle into a backs-always-to-the-wall situation like Jerry and Elene? That choice, which had once even seemed a workable compromise, no longer had the least attraction.

Not since he'd met Lili. Not since he'd crossed some peculiar border land where the deadly, dull shape of his life had suddenly become filled with unexpected adventures and colors. Even the dangers that had so dramatically disrupted the *thud* of one routine minute following another were welcome. Though, he thought, touching the scrape on his cheek and flexing his still sore left arm, *a little of that chili goes a long way*.

He brushed his lips against his mother's forehead and continued on upstairs.

Vic was asleep in his bed. His lower lip was cut and swollen; it looked like he'd been punched in the mouth. *Rough night in Jericho for both of us, pardner,* thought Tony, shucking his jacket and jeans. Somehow the events of the night before were making him feel more at ease with himself and his world. He really felt sorry for Vic.

His entry into the room, as quiet as it had been, disturbed Vic on some subconscious level. Still asleep, the man was making vague brushing motions over his face, as though chasing away a swarm of gnats.

He murmured something and shifted about in the bed. Then he repeated it louder, taking more agitated swipes at the dream-insects. "Nham Diep"—Tony could make out the words now. Vic was repeating them over and over in his sleep.

Tony immediately recognized the site of the bloodiest fighting Vic had seen during his stint in Vietnam. Mosquito Ridge was what the Americans called the place. Years ago Tony had looked up the place in a book in the Stigesville High library. He had found the red dot in a South Vietnamese province called Da Trang, not far from the Cambodian border.

Vic would often refer to it, but never at great length. It was the tragic heart of his whole miserable hitch in 'Nam. Tony had pieced together enough fragments of information to know that half Vic's company had bought it in an abortive attempt to take the position, studded with high-caliber machine-gun nests, back from the Vietcong. What had started out as a routine operation for the Americans and their ARVN allies had turned into a bloodbath and a rout. In trying to escape, Vic had run smack into a band of enemy guerrillas and begun a nightmarish three weeks of torture and near madness in the network of tunnels that honeycombed Mosquito Ridge.

It was only when Vic's buddy, Pat McKenna, had managed to drum up support for a commando attack on the ridge that he had been rescued and returned to Saigon for hospitalization. The physical marks of torture and privation had healed completely; the inner scarring had left him an emotional cripple. He had never gone back to the front; he had gone home on a medical discharge. As it happened, he was one of the last to leave before the Tet Offensive, which marked the beginning of the end for American hopes in South Vietnam.

"Nham Diep," Vic muttered again. He sounded like his nose was stuffed up.

Tony leaned over him and restrained the man's restless hands. "Easy, big guy, you're home now. That was a long time ago."

"The dark," Vic said, letting his arms go limp. "She's there in the dark." He coughed sharply a couple of times.

"No, she's not," Tony said, patting Vic's shoulder in an attempt to soothe the frightened child Vic had become. "There's no one there. You're having a nightmare, that's all." He touched his uncle's forehead and found it was warm. The guy had some bug, that was clear.

Vic's eyes were open, but he hadn't left his dreamscape. Thickly he said, "She wants to swallow me, like she did before. Eat me alive and keep me in the dark with her, forever." Then he smiled a crafty smile. "But I'm making plans. My buddies and me, we aren't going to let them get us this time."

"No one wants to get you. Go back to sleep." *And let me get a little sleep while you're at it*, Tony pleaded silently.

"She's got a big surprise coming," said Vic with a smile. Then he frowned suddenly. Sounding like a petulant child, he

said, "Go away. Don't make me talk. I'm too tired to talk."
In a moment he was asleep again. He turned onto his side,
breathing more easily.

Over a late Sunday breakfast Daniel Kovacs informed his
son that Tony was going to have to pay "any medical or other
expenses" that resulted from the assault the night before, if
these weren't covered by the family's limited insurance. Tony
wondered just how big a bite that would put in his meager
savings account—his "getaway" money. This news and not
enough sleep were fast eroding the good feelings he had gotten
from being with Lili.

He didn't have the energy to argue with his father, who
clearly didn't want to discuss the matter at all. Daniel Kovacs
kept his face buried in the Sunday edition of the *Stigesville
Herald* and only spoke when he wanted more coffee or
hotcakes.

Vic was still asleep upstairs. Everyone else seemed sub-
dued, preoccupied. Even Leslie, normally a blast of energy in
the morning, seemed moody.

"Did Vic come home on his own?" Tony asked Jerry. "Or
did you have to round him up?"

Jerry, forking a last morsel of bacon up to his mouth, said,
"He was in that hotel lobby we went by the other night—"

"The Delaware House?"

"Yeah. Anyhow, he was talking with some of those"—Jerry
shrugged and made a face—"he hangs out with. They were
bullshitting about guns and battles and crap. I got the impression they were replaying some war stories. As soon as they
saw me, they clammed up, like they were afraid I'd hear
something I shouldn't. Who the fu— Who *cares* about that
stuff? It's ancient history. I just wanted to get Vic home. I
guess they were all ready to knock it off, because the party
broke up real fast. Elene and I got Vic into the car without
any argument." He ate the bit of bacon.

"What happened to his mouth? Looks like somebody slugged
him."

"Nobody would say. Who knows what sort of scrapes he
gets into when there's nobody around to keep an eye on
him?"

Tony could tell from the angle of his father's head and the
fact that the man hadn't turned a page of the paper in a long

time that Daniel Kovacs was listening to what Jerry was saying. And the question of his responsibilities around Vic was a sore subject between father and son.

Tony decided to change the subject. He asked Leslie, "What's the matter with you? Get out of the wrong side of bed this morning?" Daniel Kovacs turned a page of the sports section.

"No," she said, looking up from a plate of hardly touched pancakes, "I got out of the same side I always get out of. But I kept waking up all night because I was afraid."

"Of what?" Tony wondered.

"Sometimes there's someone who wants to hurt me in my dreams. But then I wake up, and I know I'm not dreaming anymore, but I know she's just outside my window or right outside my door."

"What does 'she' look like?"

"I don't know. If I open my door or the curtains, she'd get me."

"But if you can't see her," Tony asked reasonably, "how do you know she's there?"

"She just is," his niece answered. Her tone of voice suggested that all the reasonableness in the world wasn't going to change her belief.

"Maybe you just dreamed you were awake," Tony suggested.

The idea intrigued Leslie, then she shook her head. "It doesn't matter. I'm afraid of her in my dream, and I'm afraid of her when I'm awake. So it doesn't matter."

"What does she look like in your dreams?"

"I don't remember."

"I think," said Jerry, pouring himself a fresh cup of coffee, "it might be better if we just didn't talk about this anymore. Less said, the sooner she'll forget." To his daughter he said, "If you're not going to eat any more, why not take that plate out to the kitchen and help your Mom and Grandma with the dishes."

Leslie dutifully carried her plate through the swinging door into the kitchen.

Jerry gave his full attention to his coffee. His father-in-law never looked up from the sports section. Tony, taking his own cup of coffee and the national news section of the paper, retreated gratefully to the living room couch.

*   *   *

By one o'clock, the gray overcast had turned into a rain-storm. With much grumbling, Daniel Kovacs pulled on a rain slicker and went out to gather his mother and aunt from their apartment on the other side of Stigesville, to bring them home for the weekly family dinner. Daniel always did this one bit of chauffeuring. For all he complained about it, he never asked anyone else to go for Grandmother Eva Kovacs and Poor Ida Palko.

Characteristically the two elderly women wore identical coats and floral-patterned scarves (purchased at the same sale on one of their infrequent forays to the shopping mall outside of town, escorted by Daniel Kovacs); similar dark skirts, white blouses, and sweaters (Eva's was dark green, Ida's navy blue); interchangeable orthopedic shoes. Their gray hair was drawn back in matching buns; their eyes—watery blue, equally birdlike—darted everywhere, missing nothing.

Tony pecked each old lady lightly on the cheek, tasting face powder and smelling lilac water. Grandmother claimed the most comfortable armchair in the living room; Poor Ida perched nervously on the edge of the couch, as near her sister as possible.

Tea was brought to them. The cookies Elene had baked provided the first major topic of conversation. Tony knew the rules of the game required spending at least fifteen minutes with the old girls before splitting, but after five minutes he thought he was going to go out of his mind with boredom. He had the mind-numbing sensation that Eva and Ida were, between them, going to reconstruct the recipe for every cookie and pastry they had baked since leaving Hungary.

The other adults listened politely, smiles frozen in place, eyes beginning to glaze over. No one noticed when Leslie got up and left the room. Tony decided to take a cue from his niece's escape and slip away himself. He planned to walk over and have a few beers with his friend, Ted, who never seemed to have any problem scoring a six-pack.

He had considered going over to the Hotel Bethel earlier, but the rain, and the fact that his mother needed the car to do some last-minute shopping for dinner, discouraged him. Besides, Lili had made it clear she wanted to be alone, and some inner voice told him he could really screw things up by going against her wishes. Even if they made no sense to him.

Before he got up from the dining room chair he had placed near the hall entrance so he could make an easy getaway, Leslie came running back into the room. "We can play Ouija!" she announced excitedly.

Aunt Ida, who had been explaining for the umpteenth time how chocolate-cream *rigo jansci* came to be named after a famous Hungarian Gypsy, lost her train of thought and fluttered her hands in embarrassed distress.

Tony's Grandmother took charge of the situation. "What are those?" she asked, pointing to the objects Leslie was carrying.

The child brought her treasures close to her great-grandmother. "It's a Ouija board and a planket. To talk to ghosts, and they can talk back to us."

Eva gave a disapproving *tsk!* and shook her head. She looked past Leslie at her son. Daniel Kovacs shifted uncomfortably in the second-most comfortable chair. "It's a devil's toy," said his mother darkly. "Children shouldn't play with such things."

"Oh, really, Nona," began Elene, "I don't think—"

"I know what I know," said the old woman. "When I was a little girl in the old country, there was cousin of mine who lived in Gajcsana who was visited by *liderc,* a . . . a . . ." She groped for the English translation.

"Like a vampire," said Ida.

"Precisely. The creature came down from the sky like a star, blazing with flame. Then it took on the form of a handsome young man and tried to get my cousin Sophie to run away with him. But her father, my uncle, discovered that the young man wasn't human, so he locked up the house and refused to let the creature see his daughter. When the *liderc* saw that he couldn't have his way with the girl, he turned back into a star, like a roaring fire. Then the ball of flame floated into the sky, covering the house and barn with sparks and setting the thatches on fire, so that the man and his neighbors only just saved the buildings.

"Sophie always said she didn't know why the creature had come to her. But once, in secret, she told me she had bought a love charm from an old Gypsy woman. She brought the wickedness on herself by tampering with such deviltry," Eva concluded. "And the child here shouldn't be playing with such things."

The old woman looked at each of the family members in turn. "There is Gypsy blood in all of us. Sometimes it gives us 'special gifts' that are a blessing. But it also brings with it very great dangers."

Tony could see Leslie alternately staring wide-eyed at her great-grandmother, and then at the Ouija board in her hands.

"There are spirits—good and bad—who are attracted to those who have the 'gift.' And there are the ghosts of the dead who hover around some people of Gypsy descent because the blood-magic draws them like starving beggars to the feast of life. Sometimes these ghosts can inhabit the body of the newly dead or the weak-minded. Then they go in search of the blood to—"

Jerry cleared his throat. "Uh, Nona, that's an interesting story, but . . ." He gestured with his head toward Leslie. Eva Kovacs blinked a moment, as though not sure what he meant, then she smiled grimly and nodded. "That's enough of such talk," she said. "I only wanted to remind all of you that some things are best not treated as a joke."

"But I got it at a *rummage sale*," said Leslie. "It only cost twenty-five cents." With a sigh Leslie took her board and planchette out of the room.

"Next time, spend the twenty-five cents to light a candle in church," Eva called after her. "Ida! Tell us about the poppyseed strudel you made last week."

As the conversation returned to more homely topics than ghosts and vampires, Tony made his exit. No one seemed to notice.

He had just reached the second floor on his way to the attic room to get his coat and hat when Leslie called to him softly and beckoned him to her room at the end of the hall.

"I'm *not* going to throw my Ouija out just 'cause *she* doesn't like it," Leslie said when she had closed the bedroom door behind them. "Anyhow, it's broken."

"What do you mean?"

"When I tried to talk to a ghost, with Mommy and Grandma, it wouldn't do anything except give me silly answers that I know was Mommy making them up. She said she didn't, but she did."

"How do you know it wasn't a ghost giving you answers. I'll bet ghosts can be silly if they want to."

"Maybe. But I could see Mom pushing it. So none of the answers were real."

"Well," said Tony, starting for the door, "hang on to it, don't show it to Nona again, and maybe it will work next time."

"Couldn't we try it now?"

"Leslie, I've got to go out—"

"Please, Uncle Tony. *Please.*"

"Oh, all right. But only for a few minutes."

"Good. I've got it all ready on the bed."

"You sure know your way around me, don't you." Tony laughed.

"Well, you're the only one who'll do junk like this with me," said Leslie, sitting near the head of her bed and gesturing to Tony to sit at its foot. She had set the board directly in the center of the circus-pattern bedspread.

"Put your finger on the little planket like this, next to mine."

"Don't worry. I've seen enough of this in the movies to have a pretty fair idea how it works."

"Okay, then ask it a question."

"I can't think of anything off the top of my head. Why don't you start?" Tony suggested.

"Okay. Are there any ghosts in my room?" Leslie intoned solemnly.

After a minute the heart-shaped wooden platform shifted slightly on its wheels to point to YES.

"Did you make it do that?" asked Leslie suspiciously.

"Swear to God, I didn't."

"You ask the next question," she said, satisfied he wasn't cheating.

"How many ghosts are here?" Tony asked, trying to keep from grinning.

The tip of the heart pointed to the numeral 1.

"What's your name?" asked Leslie.

Pointing to each letter in turn, the planchette spelled out R-O-S-E.

"Rose! Her name is Rose!" said Leslie, bouncing up and down on the bed in excitement.

"Easy, you'll bounce the board onto the floor. My turn. Where do you come from, Rose?"

H-E-A-V-E—

"I hope she's not going to be sick!" Tony laughed. Leslie ignored his outburst.

—N.

"Heaven. She lives in heaven. I don't think you should make fun of a real live ghost, Uncle Tony."

He was going to point out the humor in what she had just said, but thought better of it.

Outside the house, the rain was pouring down. Leslie hadn't bothered to turn on the lamp in her room, so what gray light there was came through the corner windows, filtered through the sheets of water running down the glass. It gave Tony the impression that the bedroom was under water. He was growing bored with the game and beginning to feel claustrophobic in the tiny room.

"It's your turn," said Leslie impatiently.

"Oh, um, are there any other kids in heaven?"

"That's a silly question," Leslie commented, "There are lots and lots."

"Let's wait till we get it from the horse's . . . planket." Tony smiled.

"What horse?"

"Never mind; here's the answer."

YES.

"I already knew that." Leslie sniffed. But the mention of a horse seemed to inspire her next question. "Do you have pets in heaven?"

He was trying to decide how many more such questions he would have to provide answers for when the planchette suddenly moved under his fingertip, independent of any guiding pressure from him.

D-A-N-G-E-R.

"Danger? That's not a right answer. Uncle Tony, is it you doing that? Or Rose?"

"It's not me," said Tony. Something in his voice convinced Leslie he wasn't playing games. Not anymore.

L-I-L-I—

*Lili?* he wondered. Maybe he was manipulating the wheeled platform unconsciously.

—T-H. The planchette stopped.

"Lilith?" Leslie sounded out the sum of the letters. "That doesn't mean anything."

"Maybe it's only part of a sentence. Lili th . . . Lili *the* . . . Lili *thinks*. Something like that."

"Who's Lili?"

"Someone I know."

"How does Rose know her?"

"Don't ask me. This is getting too weird for me."

"It's going again," Leslie said needlessly. He could feel the planchette moving under their fingers again. It moved more purposefully now, the tip darting rapidly from letter to letter.

E-M-P-U-S-A.

*Empusa?* That was garble. He tried running the letters together, but that only gave him *Lili the mpusa*.

"More, Uncle Tony."

S-L-E-E-P-I-N-G-N-O-W.

"Sleeping now," Leslie translated.

D-R-E-A-M-I-N-G.

"She's dreaming. Who's dreaming? Lili or Rose?"

W-A-K-I-N-G-S-O-O-N.

"Which one of them will wake up soon? Rose, this isn't any fun anymore," Leslie complained. "I don't understand, do you, Uncle Tony?"

"Not a bit of it," he said.

Another word. D-A-N-G-E-R again.

The planchette stopped moving.

"Rose?" Leslie called out hopefully. "Can we talk about heaven some more?"

The planchette remained stubbornly unmoving. Tony, feeling very funny, found he hadn't the least desire to continue the game.

Annoyed, Leslie picked up the Ouija board and planchette and stuck them in her toy box, from which she took out her lotto set. "Want to play?" she asked.

"Not right now, pumpkin. I've got to go see Ted. Maybe after dinner. But you could take it downstairs and see if Great-grandma or Ida will play."

"I'm mad at Great-grandma. She doesn't like my Ouija."

"Well, you can always stay up here and sulk," Tony teased.

"Well, anyway," said Leslie, following him out of the bedroom, "she's never said lotto came from the devil."

"True enough," agreed Tony, running upstairs to his room.

Vic was still asleep as he got his jacket. Before he left, he grabbed one of his school notebooks and wrote down the message from the Ouija board. *Danger. Lili the mpusa. Sleeping now. Dreaming. Waking soon. Danger.*

It was all pretty straightforward, except for the business about Lili. Maybe it was like one of those word games on the comics page of the *Herald.* Maybe the letters just needed to be rearranged to make sense. Or maybe you had to substitute other letters. Like in a cryptogram. Only, those were usually a lot longer than five letters. *Mpusa.*

Before he put on his jacket, he took another look at the bruise inside his arm. It had grown to the size of a fist. He still didn't remember hitting it when he was struggling with his attacker, but he sure must have. The skin was broken at the center, where the discoloration was most pronounced. Well, he decided, considering what *could* have happened, this was pretty tame.

He shoved the sheet of paper he'd written on into the top drawer of his desk, having no desire to fool with it any longer. Ted and his six-pack were waiting. The steady downpour outside, and the guarantee of a good soaking while he ran to Ted's house, wasn't any deterrent to Tony. He had to get away. The walls are closing in on Captain Midnight, he thought as he ran down the stairs with a wave to everyone in the living room and a promise to be home in time for dinner.

# Eight

MONDAY MORNING, TONY was so tired, he could hardly drag himself to school. He kept falling asleep in English class, though he usually found it interesting.

Time and again, he touched the spot under his long-sleeved shirt, where the flesh was bruised and puffy. Why that particular injury should bother him more than any other was something he couldn't puzzle out. But he wasn't worried about it. The doctor had given him a clean bill of health. And he had had a tetanus shot two months before, when he cut himself helping Jerry work on a neighbor's car.

He had an appointment with Mr. Hargis, one of the school counselors, but the man turned out to be a pain in the butt, as far as Tony was concerned. He kept harping on about Tony's lousy grades so far that semester. Tony wasn't about to bring up the family situation, so he just gave noncommittal yeahs and nos as Hargis ragged on.

When he was finally able to bump the counselor's needle out of the you're-letting-us-all-down-but-yourself-most-of-all and there-might-not-be-a-berth-for-you-on-the-track-team-next-spring-if-your-grades-don't-improve grooves, Tony found the man was a less than great resource as far as career options. His ideas of what job opportunities lay beyond Stigesville were limited to the thuddingly unimaginative ("You might check out the opportunities over in Pittsburgh; I know some people in personnel at the Jones and Laughlin Steel Corporation'') or the wildly fanciful (''You seem to have a real talent for writing; you might try getting a job at a quality magazine like *The New Yorker* or head to Hollywood and try your hand at screenwriting'').

He only seemed to have solid information on ways to earn money for schooling by enlisting in the Army. Though he tended to sound at times like an Army recruiter, he was pretty clear on the amount of monies Tony would have to draw on after two-year or four-year hitches.

Tony left Hargis's office with a copy of a booklet titled ''The New GI Bill & the New Army College Fund'' but not a whole lot clearer on his options.

Janet Dillon met him by the banks of lockers, between math and study hall. It was only when she laughingly asked, ''Have you been trying to avoid me, or what?'' that he realized he *had* been ducking her. He had found his thoughts revolving around Lili; Janet would only complicate things.

She had set her books in her open locker and was leaning against the door, watching him. Her long, honey-blond hair half hid her right eye. Her soft, frosty-pink lipstick glistened appealingly in the raw overhead light. Her hands were tucked into the pockets of her tan, mid-calf-length skirt. She was wearing a snug-fitting, silky white blouse with a turtleneck collar. Her hip-length sweater, black with deep red piping at the cuffs and hem, was new to him; he guessed she had picked it up over the weekend. She wore immaculate white crew socks and dark brown loafers.

Somehow, on Janet, the easy lines and loose, baggy clothes only reminded Tony what a great body she had. And he knew that her seemingly casual pose was calculated to show that off to the best advantage. He knew her expression—appealing and demanding at the same time—well enough to know that he wasn't going to be let off the hook easily.

''Well?'' she said.

''I had . . . you know . . . an appointment with Hargis this morning.''

''About grades or careers?'' she asked, not letting him off the twin skewers of her eyes.

''I wanted careers. He talked grades. Hargis is a bozo.''

''*Anyone* could have told you that.'' She leaned forward to brush something invisible off her knee. ''So, uh, are you going to avoid me tonight?'' She tossed her head back, then ran her right hand through her hair, pulling it back into shape, not disturbing the blond lock that remained artfully positioned over her right eye.

He paused a beat too long. She said, "Did you forget we're going out with Ted and Sandi tonight?"

"No, I— Look, I've been having a lot of hassles, and—"

The deafening sound of the bell signaling last period before lunch drowned out his explanation.

"I've gotta run," Janet said, grabbing her books out of the locker, slamming it shut, and spinning the combination lock. "See you later!"

"Yeah," said Tony to the rapidly emptying hall. "See you around." He had forgotten the date; he'd have to hit his mother or sister up for a loan. *Bummer*. With all the vigor of a condemned man walking his last mile, he trudged along to study hall.

At lunch, Tony took his brown bag to the bleachers overlooking the track field. The cold kept all but a few hardy souls indoors. But he wanted the space to think some things through.

As he munched his dry bologna-and-cheese sandwich (no one had remembered to buy mayonnaise over the weekend) and sipped lukewarm coffee purchased from the cafeteria vending machine, he tried to sort out his feelings about Janet, about the two of them, and, most important, what was going on between himself and Lili.

Images of the girl kept dancing at the edge of his consciousness: Lili walking in the moonlight, sitting across from him in the glow of candles, standing between him and something unseen in the dark.

*Obsessed*. That was the word that kept coming to mind. *I'm obsessed with her*, he thought over and over, until the words became meaningless. It couldn't be healthy, getting so hung up on someone he hardly knew. That much seemed clear. And yet, just thinking about her made him feel more alive, *more adult*, than he'd ever felt before. That much was also clear.

But it wasn't a romance to soft instrumental music, or maybe Lionel Ritchie singing in the background. It was loony tunes all the way. She was living in the old hotel, he had nearly gotten himself killed hanging around her, and there was something else in the shadows of that empty building that frightened him more than the scariest movie he'd seen as a kid.

There was something unreal about it all. He was sitting, freezing his butt on a bleacher bench, chewing stale bread, and washing it down with nearly cold coffee that tasted like cardboard—you couldn't get more real than that. And yet he was impatient to see a girl who looked and acted totally out of tune with the world of cold coffee and bologna, who lived in an Edgar Allan Poe haunted palace, and who made him feel and act like Prince Valiant. Cold coffee by daylight; weird tea with Lili at midnight. How did it all add up?

He was so busy thinking that he didn't notice the lone, black-clad figure approaching the bleachers. The spiked hair, the black leather collar studded with brass rivets, the ankle-length black coat flared at the waist, and the Frye boots—it was SoHo. A punk who was also a senior, though he seemed to spend more time in detention or on suspension than he did in class. At the moment he was the center of a minor tempest over his right to dress as he chose, versus the school dress code, which was loose but had *some* limits. None of SoHo's classmates knew what his parents did, but it was clear that they had money. SoHo never wanted for money; he drove a van that was painted black and had rows of skulls painted along the side like nightmare racing stripes, a huge skull painted across the rear of the van that incorporated the rear windows as eyes.

SoHo had also turned up one day in September, accompanied by a lawyer, shortly after a confrontation between the principal and SoHo over what the boy could or could *not* wear to school. The lawyer had spent more than an hour in the principal's office, while SoHo went to his next class. The rumor that buzzed around the cafeteria that afternoon was that the lawyer had threatened to sue the principal and the school district for violation of SoHo's civil rights and for discrimination.

The talk was, there was a lot of legal maneuvering going on behind the scenes. The fact was, SoHo dressed as he damn well pleased.

It was clear to Tony that SoHo was heading toward him. Since SoHo was someone Tony made it a point to steer clear of, he was not looking forward to the unexpected meeting at all.

"Yo, Kovacs!" SoHo called up to him, leaning his elbows on the bottom railing of the bleachers. "C'mere a minute." He summoned Tony down with a two-handed, palms-up, all-the-fingers-crooked gesture that made Tony think of every cheap hood in every cops-and-robbers film he'd ever seen. *But then,* he decided, *I've always gotten a 'cheap hood' hit off of SoHo as long as I've known him.*

Tony wasn't about to buy any of that snap-to-it crap. He held up the remains of his sandwich and yelled back, "I'm eating my lunch, and I like where I'm sitting. You want to talk, *you* come up *here.*" He patted the bleacher bench beside him for emphasis.

SoHo shrugged and headed for the steps at the nearest end of the grandstand. A moment later he climbed up toward Tony, sitting near the top row of bleachers.

"So, uh, what's up?" asked Tony.

SoHo stood two rows below him; their eyes were almost level. "You got an uncle who hangs out down at the park," SoHo started right out. "I see him there a lot. He seems to be head honcho of that bunch of creeps."

You're a great one to be calling Vic a creep, thought Tony. But the only response he gave was a wary, "So . . . ?"

"So, some of your uncle's buddies hurt some of my buddies."

"That's ancient history," said Tony. "Why bring it up now? Besides, the way I hear it, it wasn't Vic's friends who started it. Though they sure *finished* it," he added with a smirk.

"Battles and wars, Kovacs, *battles and wars.* That was a battle; the war isn't over yet."

"Give it a rest, SoHo. Don't be a sore loser. Those guys don't give a shit about you, as long as you and your friends don't mess with them."

"Well, someone's been messing with *my* buddies," said SoHo, jamming his hands in his pockets and rocking back and forth on the bench. "Two of them—Trick and Razz—have fuckin' *vanished.* Like, into thin air."

"Why tell me about it? The police—"

"Gimme a break, Kovacs. One, the police don't give a shit about my buddies. They'd fuckin' *love* it if we *all* split. Two, just before Trick and Razz were taken out—"

"Aren't you jumping to some pretty heavy conclusions?" Tony challenged.

SoHo ignored the interruption. "Just before that, they mixed it up with your uncle and some of his fuck-brained Green Berets on Saturday."

Tony thought of Vic's swollen jaw. His uncle had sullenly refused to offer any explanation for how he'd gotten it. The pieces fit, though he wasn't about to admit that to the boy standing in front of him. SoHo's coat was flapping in the wind; he looked like an oversize black bird.

"How do you know? Were you there?" Tony asked.

"I was around."

"Yeah, I can guess. If there was a fight, you were safe on the sidelines, egging it on. A perfect little general." He knew he was pushing it, but the guy was an asshole.

"Don't fuck with me, Kovacs," SoHo warned. He kept his voice low, but the threat there was not an empty one. Tony had the mental picture of a sidewinder coiling in on itself, rattles quivering, ready to strike. The guy isn't too tightly wrapped upstairs, Tony cautioned himself.

"Just tell me what you want," said Tony, "then let me finish my lunch."

"I want you to warn commander uncle and his Green Berets to lay off my buddies. And I want Trick and Razz back. Or there's going to be some ass kicked."

"Better make sure your own ass is kick-proof," snapped Tony. Then he tried a last shot at reasonableness. "Couldn't your buddies have gotten bored and gone off to Pittsburgh or New York or somewhere?"

"They didn't come home Sunday night. The chicks who live with 'em haven't seen them since that morning."

"My uncle didn't have anything to do with that," said Tony, sounding more certain than he felt. "Besides, the same thing happened to one of *his* buddies not long before. The guy just walked out of his apartment and never came back."

"Score one for our side," said SoHo nastily. "You just let those creeps know that a lot worse will happen to them."

"You threatening my uncle?" Tony demanded angrily. He stood up and glared down at SoHo.

SoHo shifted on the bench slightly but stood his ground. "I'm giving everybody a friendly warning, that's all."

"Go fuck yourself," said Tony. He had enough on his mind without this spike-headed lunatic adding to it. He started to gather up his books and the remains of his sandwich.

With a growl SoHo launched himself at Tony, catching the boy off-guard, throwing him back against the bleacher bench. Tony's books went flying; the wind was momentarily knocked out of him. Then SoHo was on top of him. Pummeling each other, the boys sank into the concrete walk-through between the raised wooden benches.

When he could breathe again, Tony laid into SoHo with a ferocity that surprised even himself. The other boy's attack had tapped into some reservoir of anger and frustration in Tony. In fighting back he was lashing out at a lot of things. He realized he'd been holding in a lot of shit that he was finally letting go of.

SoHo quickly realized that he'd misjudged things. He suddenly broke free and scuttled back along the concrete strip. To Tony the other boy looked like some kind of big black insect. He started after SoHo—

—then froze, when SoHo whipped a switchblade out of his coat pocket, flipped it open, and held it defensively in front of his chest. "C'mon, Kovacs," SoHo challenged. "Come for me, chickenshit."

"Easy, man," said Tony, climbing slowly to his feet and backing away, palms up.

"C'mon, Kovacs," SoHo repeated.

"Easy. Truce." He could hear the distant bell signaling the end of lunch period. He could also see Mr. Dunn, the football and track coach, and Mr. Norris, the assistant coach, strolling in the general direction of the bleachers, clearly deep in conversation. Tony gestured toward the men. "We've got company. Witnesses. I don't want trouble. And you don't need trouble."

Still breathing heavily, SoHo shot a glance at the two coaches, who had just discovered the boys in the bleachers. Mr. Dunn was shouting something about getting back to class.

SoHo hesitated an instant. Then the switchblade vanished into his coat pocket.

"You say anything about my blade and you're dead meat," he warned. "And you give my message to those friends of yours." He leapt down one, then two rows of benches, and turned back to Tony. *"Battles and wars,"* he said. Then he was going for good, the sound of his Frye boots marking each step he took.

*Great*, thought Tony. *Everyone's gone bonkers. I wonder if I'm going to* live *until the end of the week.*

"Kovacs! Haul it!" yelled Coach Dunn.

Tony hauled it.

The only bright spot of the day for Tony was meeting with the yearbook staff after last period. His class's graduation exercises in June would be the centennial commencement of Stigesville High. In honor of the hundredth continuous year of the school's existence, the senior class planned to issue a yearbook that would include a look back at the history of Stigesville High and the city of Stigesville itself. Tony had volunteered to write several of the historical articles; for all that the town was a dead end at present, he knew it had an interesting history. And he liked the idea of writing articles that he *knew* were going to be printed in a souvenir yearbook that people would keep and look at year after year. He felt it gave him a chance to do something important while giving him a sliver of immortality.

At the yearbook staff meeting, Ms. Fischer, the moderator, suggested Tony begin his research at the newspaper morgue of the *Stigesville Herald*. If he was free that afternoon, she suggested, he could stop by, get to know the place, and meet her friend who managed the newspaper archives.

Curious to see this "morgue," Tony agreed. Ms. Fischer gave him a lift to the newspaper offices and introduced him to her friend, Harry Poundstone, a dusty, dried-up man of indeterminate age with an even drier sense of humor. "You bring an Exacto knife in here," Poundstone warned, "and you'll find your balls under *B*, your prick under *P*, and your ass out in the street."

But the old guy was thorough enough in walking Tony through the archive resources. The boy realized most of the history of Stigesville resided in the yellowing newsprint and microfiche spools in the basement of the *Herald*. He flashed on a moment in the future when the long abandoned city, its buildings fallen into ruin, would be discovered by future archaeologists who would uncover the treasure trove of the *Herald* archives and piece together the whole history of the place. Maybe they'd even find a copy of the centennial yearbook with some of his features among the wreckage of Stigesville. . . .

"Your mind just wandering?" asked Harry Poundstone. "Or were you shooting up while I was lecturing you on the master file?"

"Gimme a break," said Tony with a smile, having gauged the guy.

"So," said the archivist, "where do you want to begin?"

"I don't know. . . ." At first he wasn't sure he wanted to spend any more time in the place. Then a sudden thought struck him. "Yes, I do. What can you show me on the Bethel Hotel?"

"The hotel?" asked Poundstone, rubbing his chin. "Why would you be interested in that?"

"We're doing a series of things on the, um, famous buildings in the city," he ad-libbed. "For the yearbook."

"I think I could guess that since you're on the yearbook staff and researching articles for the yearbook, the yearbook might enter into this somehow."

Tony grinned, putting the best face on what was obviously a put-down from the archivist.

Poundstone said, "There hasn't been anything much to say about the hotel in almost fifty years. There it stands, and it's likely to remain standing for who knows how long. I've heard it's been up for sale since Year One. And I hear the city routinely makes adjustments on the tax rolls because it's so much useless property, though it was declared a Pennsylvania historic site somewhere along the way. But the Historical Commission has never gotten around to restoring it; and they've sure never directed many tourists in our direction, if downtown business is any indication."

"What about when it still was run as a hotel?" asked Tony, recognizing that Harry Poundstone was dangerously close to a lecture on Stigesville's current economic crisis. It was just the sort of ragging that his father got into and wouldn't let go; so he moved to short-circuit it real fast. He had no intention of spending the rest of the afternoon listening to Poundstone's political and economic theories.

"There was a bad fire in 1936," the old man reflected. "It gutted one of the wings of the hotel. After that, the owners just sort of . . . *lost heart,* I guess I'd say, for want of a better phrase. They closed the place down and moved to the south of France somewhere. Tried to open a hotel in one of those Riviera towns. Bad luck for them—the war came along pretty quick. No one ever knew what became of them."

"How did the fire start?"

"Arson. That was pretty clear. But who or why . . ." Poundstone shrugged. "That's another matter."

"Could I see some of the papers from 1937, and a couple of years before that?" asked Tony.

"Yes, but they're all on microfiche. Do you remember what I showed you about working the viewer?"

"Sure," Tony said.

Poundstone went to a bank of metal files behind his desk. In a moment he returned with half a dozen microfiche spools. "I've brought you 1937, 1936, and 1935. Each spool covers six months, January to June and July to December."

Though curiosity made it tempting to start with the most recent spool, Tony decided to look through them in proper sequence. Working through the 1935 microfiche spools, he quickly screened past items on the collision of the passenger liner *Mohawk* and a Norwegian freighter *Talisman* off the New Jersey coast, with a loss of thirty-five lives; terrible dust storms hitting the Midwest, destroying crops and causing farm families to abandon their homes; the Social Security Act becoming law—plus a welter of local items about weddings, births, deaths, and so on.

Zip, as far as Tony was concerned.

In 1936, he discovered, heavy rains and melting snow caused the water to rise as high as fourteen feet in the streets of Johnstown and caused 171 deaths throughout the Northeast; Franklin D. Roosevelt was elected for a second term; *and a series of disappearances hit Stigesville*.

In the course of three months, from August through October of that year, seven people disappeared from the city, including four members of the Sarossy family.

*Sarossy*.

Tony read the article carefully. According to the published report, neighbors who hadn't seen the family for several days, summoned police to a house on the outskirts of town. Inside the modest frame house, the authorities found things apparently in order, with only spoiled milk and fish that had turned to indicate something was wrong. The car, described by neighbors as an older Studebaker, was also gone.

Clothes and shoes in the closets, together with luggage still stored under the bed in the master bedroom, indicated the family hadn't left on any long trip. Nor had they mentioned so much as an overnight stay anywhere.

The family was well thought of by their neighbors, though some found the parents' accents (still very heavy, though the elder Sarossys had lived in the United States nearly nineteen years) and some of the old-world customs they clung to off-putting. Laszlo Sarossy had worked in the bookkeeping office of the Skeffington Steel Mills. Agnes Sarossy had worked part-time in a local bakery.

They had two children, a boy, Michael, who was five.

(*Michael. Mickey.* Lili had said that was her brother's name.)

*Their daughter was named Lili.* Lili had been sixteen at the time of her disappearance.

Skimming through other *Herald* articles, Tony found little useful additional information. They were members of the local Hungarian Reformed Church, had kept very much to themselves, and had expressed no worries for their own safety as far as anyone could recall. It was as if they had simply walked out one day, locking the door behind them, deciding never to return.

The similarity of names was startling. Tony wondered what the family connection was, though it was obvious that Lili had been named after the girl who had vanished.

The mystery was never solved. The father's Studebaker was located in the parking lot of the Hotel Bethel. A few guests reported seeing a family matching the description in the lobby of the hotel one Sunday afternoon. ("Clearly," the person interviewed said, "they were not *our* sort, if you know what I mean, so naturally I couldn't *help* but *notice*. I thought, perhaps they'd come to visit some of the staff and had used the incorrect entrance. . . .")

But the police wound up pursuing will-o'-the-wisps. No solid leads came to light. Eventually references to it disappeared from the front pages and, finally, even from the back pages. The final article to deal with the disappearance at length linked it to other disappearances around the same time: a young couple (though many thought an elopement was likely in that case, given the young people's problems with both families) and a pawnbroker whose downtown shop was found unlocked, cash still in the register, nothing missing except the proprietor, Edward Arany, also of Hungarian descent.

The author of the newspaper article pointed out that over the preceding years there had been a number of other disappearances, in which people seemed to drop off the face of the earth. The reporter had discovered that a significant number of them came from Eastern Europe—primarily Hungary and Romania. But he was at a loss to explain the significance of this fact. Nor did he hazard a guess, leaving the question an open one for his readers.

Weird, thought Tony. *But then, everything even slightly connected with Lili seems to be loopy.*

He glanced at his watch and decided he still had enough time to go through the last two spools of film.

Nineteen thirty-seven was a bonanza year for national and local news, and disasters in particular.

On March 17, an airliner bound from New York to Kansas City crashed in the Pennsylvania mountains, killing all thirteen people aboard. On May 6, the German dirigible *Hindenburg* was destroyed by fire and explosion as it was landing at Lakehurst, New Jersey; thirty-six of the ninety-seven people on board were lost.

On October 21, the Hotel Bethel caught fire shortly before midnight. The fire apparently started near the boiler room, in the basement. Flames swept through the east wing, routing guests and gutting numerous rooms and suites. By the time the blaze was under control, thirty-three people were dead, scores were injured, and the damage was estimated at over $200,000.

Eyewitnesses who were hotel guests and staff, as well as several bystanders attracted by the flames and sirens, reported seeing a thin, coatless man, the front of his shirt scorched and smoldering, fleeing from the scene. This, plus the fact that investigators subsequently found the remains of several canisters of gasoline in the wreckage, led to a verdict of arson, by person or persons unknown.

Most of the damage was confined to the interior of the east wing; the shell of the building remained intact. When the place was closed up and the windows boarded over, an observer could not, casually glancing at the hotel from the outside, guess just how extensive the internal damage was.

But the place never reopened. Lawsuits were filed on behalf of many of the victims, living and dead. The Bethel became the symbol for hard luck, and plans to restore and refurbish it evaporated.

An era had passed, and the Bethel remained an extravagant, lifeless souvenir of Stigesville's once-upon-a-time glamour and vitality.

Tony shut off the viewer and rewound the last spool. As he surrendered the microfiche to Harry Poundstone, he asked, "Did they ever find out who set the fire at the Bethel?"

"Never. It was never solved."

"There were a bunch of people who disappeared around the same time . . . ?"

"Another mystery. Maybe UFOs got them. More likely they were ducking out on the bill collector."

"Yeah, well, thanks. Oh, one other thing . . ." Tony dug into his hip pocket and fished out the scrap of paper on which he had written the message from the Ouija board. He pointed to the word *Mpusa*. "You recognize that word?"

The archivist looked at it closely. "Doesn't mean a thing to me. You might try looking in the dictionaries over there."

"Nah, I already looked through some at school earlier. I just thought it might ring a bell with you."

Poundstone scratched the side of his head. "Might be some African language."

"Well, I gotta run. I'll see you again, since I'll be working on the yearbook a lot."

But the man had already turned back to his files.

When he saw how late it had grown, Tony began walking rapidly toward the stairs leading to the street door. He prayed for a bus, and for once the god of municipal transportation granted him his wish. A blue-and-orange coach was just pulling up to the bus stop as the boy reached it.

# Nine

LATER THAT NIGHT, sitting in the Pizza Mia in the Four Corners shopping center, Tony smiled at Janet Dillon across the table they were sharing with Ted Davis and Sandi Hall. A jumbo pizza plate, with half a dozen slices of cold combination pizza, sat in the middle of the sheet of greasy glass protecting a red-and-white-checked tablecloth. Janet, sipping the last of her Pepsi, looked back at him with her I'm-goddamned-angry-but-I'm-not-going-to-make-a-scene-(just-wait-until-later) look.

So far the evening had been less than terrific, though Ted and Sandi were enjoying themselves. Ted had just interrupted a mildly obscene joke to belch softly; Sandi, seeing how far she could stretch a strand of still warm mozzarella cheese, said, "Oh, *gross*," and began to giggle.

Tony knew that Janet was mad because he'd been ignoring her so much of the evening. He hadn't meant to; there was just so much on his mind. He felt tired, his head ached, and his left arm felt sore from his wrist to his shoulder. He suspected he might have pulled a muscle in it; he was afraid that the bruise in the crook of his arm was only the outward sign of a more serious problem. Without going into too much detail, he had sketched in all the hassles at home and his other problems (leaving out the matter of Lili).

When they were driving over, everyone had pumped him for details of the assault on Saturday night. When that topic had been exhausted, there was some discussion of just how off-the-wall SoHo and his punk friends were. That carried them through salads and as much pizza as they could manage. After that Ted had launched into a stream of steadily raunchier jokes; Sandi investigated the tensile strength of Italian cheeses; and Janet set to work spelling out in body language just how bored she was with the evening in general, and Tony's preoccupations in particular.

Several times he had tried to muster the energy to smooth things over, but Janet didn't respond to these halfhearted attempts. She laughed loudly at Ted's lousy jokes and chattered endlessly with Sandi about her trip into New York City over the weekend for a shopping excursion highlighted with lunch at Trump Tower on Fifth Avenue. She ignored Tony except for the stare-and-glare silent treatment.

Ted lowered his voice. "I've got two six-packs in the car. Let's drive out to Pook's Hill and kick back—wink-wink, nudge-nudge."

Giggling again, Sandi tossed the bit of mozzarella she had rolled into a ball between her thumb and forefinger onto the pizza plate. "Sounds great to me."

"Anybody want any more of that?" asked Ted, picking up the grease-soaked tab. When his companions shook their heads, he said, "Let's see what the damage is."

They had agreed to go Dutch, but Tony insisted on paying for Janet's share, trying to make up for his inattention. At first she refused, then she shrugged and said, "Okay—if you really want to."

He pulled out the twenty-dollar bill he had borrowed from his mother against a promise to repay her by the following Saturday, when he and Ted were going to work all day at Ted's father's hardware store rearranging the stock room. Mr. Davis always paid top dollar, and in cash, at the end of the day. Since his mother saved most of her grocery shopping for Sunday afternoon, the arrangement had worked out fine.

Ted took the twenty, added it to his own money and Sandi's, and headed for the cashier. Everybody else seemed to have forgotten about the waitress, so Tony dug out a single and left it in the middle of the table.

"Here's your change, big spender," said Ted, handing him some crumpled bills and loose change. Tony stuffed it in his jeans pocket without bothering to count it. "The girls wanted to make a pit stop before hitting the road,'' Ted explained. As he and Tony were zipping up jackets and wrapping mufflers tightly around their throats, Ted asked, "Something wrong between you and Janet?"

"No," said Tony. "It's just . . . some of the stuff I was telling you about yesterday. I'm just . . . I don't know—tired, I guess. And Janet can be a pain in the ass when she thinks she's not getting one-hundred-percent attention from me."

"If she was my girl, I'd give her plenty of attention, every chance I could get."

"Better not let Sandi hear you say that." Tony laughed, trying to lighten up the conversation.

"Oh, we have a very open relationship."

"Since when?"

"All along. It's an open-and-shut case. It's open as long as I keep my mouth shut. Sandi finds out, I lose her and probably one of my balls."

"How much is it worth to you to keep my mouth shut?" asked Tony.

"How much do you want to walk home?" countered Ted.

Then Sandi and Janet returned, and they dropped the matter. Janet hooked her arm through Tony's, snuggling close in the blast of cold air as they pushed outside. He knew all was forgiven—for the time being, at any rate.


Pook's Hill was out East Mather Road, beyond the old cemetery. A badly rutted, single-lane country road ran back through thick woods, then climbed to the top of a rocky outcropping that had been struck by lightning years before and burned clear of trees. From the circle of bare earth at the top, one had a view northeast to the lights of Stigesville, and west, past the light of intervening towns and farms to the pale smudge of Pittsburgh's skyglow.

The place was the local lovers' lane. On warm summer nights cars would be parked every which way at the top, and backed up along the access.

Tonight, however, the beginning of a work week, and the autumn cold snap and threatening rain, left the place to the foursome. Ted parked his car aimed toward Stigesville and retrieved a six-pack from the ice-chest in the trunk of the Ford

Fairmont. He and Sandi sat nuzzling and sipping Coors in the front seat, while Tony and Janet snuggled in the back.

The beer, the quiet, his hand resting on Janet's thigh, all relaxed Tony. He was able to push his problems to the back of his mind and focus on letting his hand slide a little farther up Janet's leg. The soft material of her skirt clung to the side of his hand, as though it had a faint electric charge. Janet offered no objections; she shifted a bit on the seat to press her hip closer to his. He was getting hard and enjoying the pressure. Sex is the best therapy in the world, he reminded himself. He edged his hand a bit farther; the girl beside him sighed softly. Good therapy for everyone, Tony thought, happy to think that the evening wasn't going to be a total disaster. Not by a long shot, he decided, shifting himself to accommodate himself. Not by a very long shot.

"Hey," said Ted, sounding thoroughly contented himself, "remember all those stories you'd hear when you were a kid about what happened to people parked out in the middle of nowhere like this?"

*"Ted!"* Janet cried. "Don't talk about stuff like that."

"Yeah," said Tony, shifting his hand again and stretching out his little finger so the tip of it just brushed the edge of Janet's panties. "Put some music on the radio and don't wreck the mood."

"You're weird." Sandi giggled. "But I know the kind of stories you mean. Like the one about the guy with the hook."

*"Sandi!* Don't *you* start!" warned Janet. She gave the other girl a poke on the back of her head.

But Sandi just laughed and turned around to stare at the couple in the backseat. "Forget your mittens, Tony?" she asked.

"Jealous, Sandi?" asked Janet.

"No," she said. "Ted forgot his too." She turned to look out the windshield again. The moon was hidden behind the clouds, giving the sky a soft, misty silver sheen. Tony's little finger began probing the elastic of Janet's panties. The moment was perfectly romantic to Tony's way of thinking. He felt a vague sense of disloyalty to Lili, but that whole fantasy scene seemed light-years away from the feel of Janet's thigh under his hand. The other girl had no claim on him, he told himself. And if he wasn't totally convinced, Janet's tongue tip in his ear was a strong enough argument for the moment.

"The story about the hook was the best," Ted went on, reflectively popping the top on a fresh beer. In the backseat, Tony and Janet groaned, mostly in protest. But Ted, the hand with the beer resting lightly on the steering wheel, his other hand on Sandi, ignored the critics, saying, "That was the one where that couple was dating and they'd parked somewhere out in the woods *just like us.*"

"Gimme a break," said Tony.

"And they heard on the radio that a murderer with a hook instead of a hand had escaped from some prison not far away. And the girl gets real nervous and makes them lock the doors. And then they're getting it on hot and heavy, but she thinks she hears someone outside. Then she hears a sound like some-one's fooling with the door handle. So she makes her boy-friend drive them back into town, even though he's pissed off because he thinks she's being silly." He took a long swallow of his Coors and finished, "But when they get back to her house, they find a hook caught in the handle of the door."

"Gosh, wow, that's really a scary story," said Tony in a totally bored tone of voice.

"It creeped me out when I was a kid," said Ted.

"I liked the one best about the woman who pulled into a gas station and the gas station guy said there was some problem with her credit card. So he took her into the office and told her there was a guy scrunched down in the seat behind her. Then they called the police and they caught the guy. He had all kinds of knives and was a psycho from the mental hospital. I never get into my car without looking in the backseat first," Sandi said.

"Take my word, Sandi," said Janet. "There's no killer back here. Just a *pervert!*" She began to laugh as Tony began to tickle her sides. "Don't, oh, don't!" She giggled, twisting all around in the seat.

"Jeez, you guys must've really been horny," commented Ted. "I'm surprised you didn't just climb onto the table at the pizza place and have at it in the leftover pizza."

"Oh, *gross!*" said Sandi.

Tony released Janet and put his hand on the door to the backseat. "Sorry, nature calls."

"I thought it just did," said Ted.

"Back in a minute," said Tony, climbing out of the car.

"Aren't you scared there might be a killer out there?" teased Sandi.

"I'm more scared of being bored to death with your stupid ghost stories," he said.

"Bring that second six-pack out of the trunk when you come back," Ted suggested.

"Don't get lost!" said Janet.

"And don't take any wooden hooks!" yelled Ted as Tony let the door slam back into place.

He walked a short distance back down the road, to a clump of pine trees.

He had just zipped himself back up when he heard something high overhead. He paused, listening. The sound was repeated an instant later. Now he recognized it as the sound of a night bird fluttering its wings. He imagined an owl perched on a branch, riffling its feathers impatiently while it waited for an unsuspecting rodent to provide it dinner.

He took a step back toward the car, then stopped.

Something large was stirring in the underbrush that spilled from under the sheltering trees onto the road's edge. He could hear the soft *popple* of rain-soaked branches breaking under a heavy-moving creature. Staring into the night, he became certain he could see a darker shape behind the screen of wet leaves gleaming pale in the diffused moonlight.

He couldn't be certain, but it seemed as large as a big dog. Or larger. He tried to remember if any bears or wolves had been sighted in the area recently. He couldn't remember any newspaper accounts.

Something growled softly. Instinctively he raised his hands to ward off a sudden attack. He felt the same helpless terror he had felt that night, unable to tear free of the fence surrounding the Hotel Bethel, and hearing the watchdog bounding across the grounds at him.

He took several steps backward, trying not to move too quickly. He was sure he had read somewhere that sudden movements were apt to provoke an attack from an animal that might just be checking him out and would, if not startled, go its way and leave him alone.

Tony debated saying something, to try to reassure whatever was crouching there in the dark that he meant it no harm. But his throat and mouth were so dry, he was sure all he'd be able to force out would be a squawk that would be not in the least reassuring.

They must be beginning to wonder back in the car what had happened to him. He listened for the sound of the Ford's doors opening, knowing he would have to shout a warning if one of his friends came looking for him. But for the time being they continued to sit tight.

The thing in the shadows growled again; it seemed more menacing this time. Tony backed off several more steps. He was standing in the middle of the road now. He debated making a run for the car, hoping to scoot past the lurking shape before it had time to realize what he was up to. But that struck him as likely to provoke an attack. The other options— standing his ground or retreating back down the road—didn't seem much better. The only other possibility was working his way through the trees and brush on the opposite side of the road.

He heard the flutter of night wings high above. Then the rhythmic beat-beat of the night bird taking the air. He saw a curious silhouette against the silvery sky but decided he was just looking at the winged thing from an odd angle.

The creature in the bushes hissed. The sound was unexpected and startling. *What the hell is in there?* he wondered. It sounded more like a snake than any mammal.

It was moving through the underbrush on his left now, circling him. He edged across the road, until his boots crunched on the gravel of the shoulder. Whatever it was, it had stopped directly opposite him. His skin prickled as he felt the unseen eyes fixed on him.

One of the car doors opened. Janet called, "Tony, are you okay?"

Then there was a sudden scream from the parking area.

Something sprang at him, snarling, gleaming white teeth snapping the air right behind him as he sprinted for the car. He rounded the clump of pine trees, not daring to look over his shoulder. Behind him, he heard the sound of something loping right behind him, inches behind his pumping legs.

He saw the car. Janet was standing beside it.

"Get inside!" he shouted, waving frantically to her.

Then he saw it wasn't Janet at all—it was Lili. In the instant that he recognized her, the sounds of pursuit vanished. He wheeled around and saw the empty bit of road curving around the pine trees. Whatever had been hot on his heels had melted into the shadows or been swallowed by the earth.

He turned back.

Lili was still there. She was dressed in her black lace shawl draped over a white shift. There were red slippers like ballet slippers on her feet. Her long hair fell in equal parts over her shoulders, framing the pale oval of her face.

Her hand was upraised in the gesture he had seen her make before, with her hand closed, the thumb protruding between the fore and middle fingers. She was pointing back the way Tony had just run. After a moment she lowered her hand and pulled the shawl more tightly around her.

The car was silent. He couldn't hear any talking or laughing from its interior. Taking a step closer, he realized the windows were black, as though someone had painted the inside of the glass.

*Something is very wrong here,* he thought. To the girl, who had taken a step toward him, he said, "Lili, what's going on?"

She ran to him then, and put a slender finger to his lips. "Don't ask questions, just listen. My time is very short here. I don't have the power *she* has."

"Lili, you're not making any sense—"

But she pressed the fingertips of both hands to his mouth. "You're in danger—very great danger. Her dreaming has snared you the same way it's snared so many others. The way it caught me a long time ago. You and your life are becoming a part of her dream. *This* is a piece of that dream I've stolen."

*Loony tunes,* he thought desolately. *She's out of her gourd. But how did she know I'd be here? Has she been following me?*

None of it made any sense. It was like a nightmare in which he suddenly realized that what seemed familiar was suddenly utterly strange.

"But the two of us—we're only channels to the one *she* really needs. You have to run away, Tony. She's only strong near her place of power. Take this"—she pressed something into his palm—"it will help a little. But go, and take—"

Suddenly the girl began to scream. He grabbed hold of her, shaking her, but she only screamed more loudly. He hugged her to him, trying to muffle her screams in the softness of his down jacket. But she broke free and stared wildly all around at the dark trees and boulders ringing the parking space. Her screams turned to despairing moans as she seemed to discover that her every avenue of escape was cut off—though Tony could see nothing except shadows.

"Lili," he whispered, gathering her to him, feeling how she trembled in his arms. She was sobbing now, mumbling incomprehensible things into his protective shoulder. He felt his own heart breaking at the proof of just how mad she must be. Suddenly she fainted, slumping so quickly, he was barely able to support her before she sank to the pitted and cracked asphalt.

Half carrying, half dragging her, he approached the car, wondering why none of his friends had climbed out to help. They *must* have heard the screaming and shouting not ten feet from the car. The beer couldn't have wiped them all out, could it? he wondered. And what's wrong with the car windows? They were still jet-black; it didn't seem to be any trick of the uncertain moonlight.

"Ted. Janet. For chrissake, gimme a hand, will you?" he called.

No answer.

Now he could see something hanging on the door handle of the right front door. A curlicue of metal shining dully in a stray moonbeam. There was something oddly familiar about it that sent a chill through him.

Unable to maneuver with the fainting girl in his arm, he gently lowered her to the pavement. Then he rapidly walked the last few paces to the car.

It was a huge hook, the size of the ones Tony saw sides of beef hanging from in MacDonald's Meat Market. The vicious metal curve ended in a stump of twisted red flesh—as though it had been torn from a living body. It was dripping blood. As Tony looked closer, he saw that the whole point of the hook was slathered in gore. *Oh Jesus, oh Jesus . . . what's going on?* It was a nightmare. It made no sense. It made horrible sense. He felt his head spinning, and his legs grow so weak, they threatened to buckle under him. He stared frantically around the parking area, searching for the hook's owner. *Was that what I saw crouching in the bushes? A psycho? And what happened to the others?*

The windows were not painted black, he could see now; they were smeared with blood.

*Jesus oh Jesus oh Jesus!*

But he had to know, he had to risk it. He stretched a trembling hand out for the right rear door handle. But first he looked all around the encircling trees. Nothing. A few feet away, Lili was a crumpled shape of black and white. Her face was turned away from him; a breeze tugged at strands of her long black hair; he thought he heard her groan softly to herself.

Trying not to look at the hook, Tony took a grip on the car door. *What if he's hiding in there? Like the black goblin in that fairy tale? Waiting to spring out and grab me?*

But his friends were in there. He had to know.

He wrenched open the door, jumping back as part of the same motion.

For an instant nothing happened. Then someone started to climb out of the car.

"Jan—" he started to call, then the words turned into a strangulated gurgle.

The body of his girlfriend pitched forward onto the asphalt with a wet *tunk.* Her body had been repeatedly gashed by something—the hook, Tony guessed. Her down jacket was a ruin of blood-soaked material and padding. Her head had been nearly severed from her body, hanging by a few strips of muscle tissue.

In shock, Tony began to giggle. *This is a scene from* Friday the 13th, *and it's only Monday!* Now he was laughing out loud as he moved away from the car. He kept his eyes on the open door, still half expecting Janet's murderer to climb out.

He reached Lili's prone form and knelt beside her, eyes still on the Ford. "C'mon, Lili, wake up! Wake up, dammit!" He took her by the shoulder and shook her.

She groaned and stirred, weakly protesting his rough treatment. "Wake up," he pleaded. *Or wake up yourself,* he told himself. *This is a slasher movie, this is a nightmare, this is too fucking unreal to be happening.* What was it Lili had said? *This is a piece of some dream.*

"Lili, you've got to wake up. If you're dreaming this, you've got to wake up and end it!"

*Am I really saying this? I'm as crazy as she is.*

But she was coming around. Her eyes popped open; for a moment she seemed to have trouble focusing. Then she saw him and whispered, "Tony." There was a rasp to her voice; he guessed it had come from all her screaming earlier. He helped her to her feet.

"We've got to get out of here right away," he said. The car, Janet's body, the gory hook were all indicators of how dangerous their situation was. There was no time for thinking about how insane it all was; they had to get away before the owner of the hook came back for it . . . and *them*.

"I'm going to try to drive the car. We'll have to—to—" He shrugged, indicating that what had to be done was only going to seem worse if they had to talk about it too. "Can you stand up all right?"

"I think so," she said huskily. He helped her get to her feet. She swayed unsteadily for a moment, then said, "I'll be fine."

He doubted either one of them was going to be fine. He only hoped they'd be *alive* to see the next morning.

He moved warily back toward the car, then turned, realizing Lili had made no move to follow him.

She was standing where he had left her. She had pulled the black lace shawl tighter around her, and her head was angled forward, so all he saw was a cascade of glossy black hair.

"Are you okay?" he called in a nervous whisper.

No answer.

"Lili . . ."

She remained rooted in place, still in the same pose. He walked back, saying quickly, "If you're going to be sick, let me help you."

Her head snapped up. The face wasn't Lili's.

The face was barely human. It was too long and narrow, with piercing red eyes and fanglike teeth. The mouth was drawn back into a snarl. The creature threw back the shawl to reveal her nakedness. Tony saw she had the breasts of a woman, but they were covered with pale green scales that extended down to hooves like those of an ox. The shawl itself, fluttering in the pewter-gray light, became the huge, dark wings of a night bird. Her hands were now crooked claws tipped with razor-sharp talons. The horror screeched at him, making a sound no human throat could have made.

Tony ran like he had never run before, away down the road from Pook's Hill.

Behind him, he was certain he heard the beating of heavy wings taking the air.

He was some fifty yards past the stand of pine at the bend in the road when the night-haunter slammed into his back with a triumphant screech. The impact sent him spinning into a clump of grass and weeds beyond the shoulder of the road. He lay blinking up at the tree branches above him, too stunned to move.

A shadow fell over him. He heard the sounds of a large creature moving over the loose gravel toward him. But he was so dazed, he wasn't even afraid.

Then Lili was bending over him.

Only it wasn't really Lili, because her eyes were red; and it wasn't a shawl but an immense pair of wings, folded around her. Still, it was enough Lili that he didn't object when she knelt down beside him and turned his head to one side. He saw that some of her gleaming white teeth were as sharp as the point of the hook he had seen earlier. *Grandma, what big teeth you have. All the better to—*

"Lili?" he asked, afraid now.

But she just put the fingers of her left hand to his lips while she stroked the right side of his neck with the long fingers of her right hand. Her fingertips were cool, hypnotic. His fear dissolved. Then she leaned down, and he couldn't find the words or the will to protest the sudden stinging in the side of his neck.

It was gone in a moment.

Then he fell asleep.

"Jeez, what happened to you?" asked Ted, who was kneeling beside Tony and sprinkling Coors in his face.

Tony woke up and stared at Ted, then at Janet and Sandi, who were standing behind his friend.

"I—" he began, then stopped. He wasn't sure what he could tell them. He'd been asleep. He'd had a dream. Then a nightmare. But they were a clutter of images that he couldn't begin to sort out.

"I don't know," said Ted. "I mean, if you can't even take a leak by yourself. . . ."

"There was . . . something . . . in the bushes. It . . . chased me."

The girls moved a bit closer together. Ted glanced quickly

around, then said without much confidence, "Well, there's nothing there now. But I think we'd better get you back to the car. C'mon, let me help."

As they trudged back to the car Tony, supported by an arm around Ted's shoulder, kept swiveling his head from side to side, looking for something, though he wasn't sure what, exactly. The others began doing the same.

"Something must have spooked you good," said Ted as he helped settle Tony in the backseat of the Ford. "You ran right into a tree branch and went down for the count."

"Oh," said Tony, willing to accept the explanation since there seemed to be far too much confusion in his mind for him to suggest a better explanation.

"Your ear and the side of your neck is bleeding," said Janet. She took a bit of tissue out of her jacket pocket and began dabbing at Tony's injuries.

"Next time," said Sandi as Ted drove them back toward East Mather Road, "let's go to the movies."

Tony was sound asleep before they passed Four Corners.

They dropped him off at home first. Janet gave him a quick peck on the cheek. He couldn't decide if she was angry or merely tired. He didn't really care.

The household was asleep, which suited him fine. He didn't have the energy to talk to anyone.

Just climbing the stairs seemed a major ordeal.

On the second-floor landing he paused. An idea occurred to him, and he walked to the end of the hall.

Outside Leslie's room he paused. It was freezing there; he glanced at the window at the end of the hall, but it was shut tight. The doorknob felt like ice—cold enough to burn.

The minute his fingers circled the knob, he felt a sudden wave of familiar fear. The bits of his dream on Pook's Hill that he least wanted to recall came flooding back in graphic detail. It was only with an effort that he was able to shunt them off his main line of thought. Concentrating on moving quietly enough not to disturb his niece, he opened Leslie's door.

But as soon as he stepped inside, she gasped and sat up suddenly in the bed.

"Easy, pumpkin, it's only Uncle Tony," he said.

"Oh, you scared me. I thought it was *her*. She was out there, you know."

"Well, there's no one out there now."

"No, she's gone now. But she'll come back. She *always* does."

"You were just dreaming again, sweetheart."

"No. Or if I was, are you part of my dream?"

"Ask me tomorrow. Right now I'm so tried and mixed up, I just might be a piece of your dream. Or is this a nightmare?"

"If you're here, it's not. If she was here, it would be a nightmare." She whispered across the darkness, "What did you come in here for, Uncle Tony?"

"I want to borrow your Ouija."

"You can't."

"I'll give it back. You always let me borrow your stuff before."

"It's not *me*, it's Daddy," Leslie explained. "He threw the Ouija out today. I'm mad at him. But I'm more mad at Nona, because she's the one who told him to."

"Maybe it's better that way," said Tony, turning to go. "Now that I think of it, messing around with ghosts is the *last* thing I should be doing."

"But what about Rose? And what about Lili? Who'll talk to them now?"

"Rose has all those other kids in heaven, remember?"

"Oh, yeah," the little girl said, snuggling back down under the bedclothes and yawning.

"And Lili isn't a ghost."

"Oh, who is she?"

But Tony had no clear answer for that. "Just someone I've met a couple of times."

"I don't want to talk anymore," Leslie said drowsily.

"Good night, pumpkin," he said, closing the bedroom door softly.

# Ten

IN THE ATTIC room Tony sat on the padded ledge that served as a seat in the dormer window nearest his bed. He was perched with his back resting against one alcove wall, the toes of his stockinged feet pressed against the facing wall. Across the room, Vic slept soundly. His fever had broken, and he was mending. Below the third-story window, Kossuth Street slept, too; there were few lights on in any of the houses, except for an occasional porch light; Tony could have counted the cars that had passed in the last hour on one hand and still have fingers left over.

*No way* could he sleep. The bizarre dream out on Pook's Hill had unnerved him—it had seemed far too real. But the grotesque vision of murder and monsters had not frightened him nearly as much as the little silver charm he kept turning around in his fingers. It was tarnished and pitted; it looked as old as the hills; and it scared the shit out of him.

"What's in your hand?" Janet had asked. She had shaken him awake when they were getting near his house. Now she was staring at his fisted right hand.

"My hand?" he mumbled, still fuzzy.

"Well, the way you're holding it, it looks like you've got something there. Let's see."

Like a dutiful child, he had held out his hand and un-

142

clenched his fingers. There, in the sweaty palm of his hand, was a silver representation of a hand. The little finger and ring finger were folded into the palm; the other fingers and thumb were upraised. A tongue of sculpted flame danced on the tip of the upraised middle finger. There was a loop at the end that suggested it might have hung from a necklace or bracelet. It reminded him of something, though he was still too woozy from all that had gone down to piece it together.

"That's weird," said Janet. "Where did you get it? It looks like real silver."

Sandi reached her hand over the front seat, saying, "Let us see what you're talking about."

Tony wasn't sure he wanted to let it out of his keeping, even for an instant—though he couldn't say why he felt that way.

But Janet snatched it and gave it to Sandi, who held it up so that at the first convenient stoplight Ted could study it too.

"Looks like an antique," Ted said as the light changed to green. "Where'd you find it?"

"In the woods," said Tony.

"It might be an heirloom or something," said Sandi. "Maybe you should try to find the owner."

But Tony already knew the owner.

"Finders keepers," sang Janet. "If it's worth anything, Tony's in luck. Give it back—" Sandi did so, and Janet held the bauble up in front of her face. "Wonder if it's worth enough to buy at least a secondhand car?"

"You may really have lucked out," said Sandi.

"It's probably something some kid threw away from a box of Cracker Jacks." Ted laughed.

Tony wasn't about to tell them what an extraordinary thing the bit of silverwork was. He wasn't sure he believed it himself. But there it was, in front of his eyes. He reached out and took it back from Janet. It was real. It had weight; he could feel the coolness of the metal when it lay in his palm; he could feel each gracefully sculpted detail under his fingertips.

It scared him like nothing had ever scared him in his life, because *Lili had given it to him. In a dream.* But this silver bit of dream hadn't dissolved when he woke up. He could touch it; so could his friends. It had no business existing, *but it did.*

He tried to explain a way for it to have been in his possession after dreaming Lili had given it to him, but none of his explanations worked for him. He had dreamed her giving this to him, before she had become that other creature; and now he was holding it. He remembered how disappointed he would sometimes be as a kid when the dream of a wonderful toy or treasure had evaporated with the morning light. This time, he thought grimly, he would love to see the persistent bit of dream go *poof*.

But it remained stubbornly in hand, signaling the overlap of his dreams and scaring him with all that that implied. Up to now, he thought, life in Stigesville hadn't been exactly a party, but it never left any doubts about where imagination ended and hardass reality began. Now, suddenly, reality had been re-zoned, and ghosts and goblins were setting up housekeeping in everyday, dull Stigesville.

Unless, of course, he *really had* found the charm somewhere else and had only imagined Lili had given it to him on Pook's Hill. But he believed so utterly that it had come to him in his dream that the only alternative was that he was crackers himself.

Neither possibility had much appeal.

*Take this,* she had said while handing him the trinket in his dream. *It will help.*

*Yeah,* he thought to himself. *Help get me a one-way ticket to the funny farm.*

He sighed and dropped the charm into his shirt pocket. *There had to be a logical explanation,* he decided. *I'm just too friggin' tired to see it.*

He stared out the window. Then he looked closer at the black van parked across the street. It hadn't been there the last time he looked. It must have parked within the last few minutes. He could see from the steam pouring from the exhaust that the driver was idling his engine. The van's lights were off; Tony had the uncomfortable idea that he was watching a getaway car primed and in position at what was soon to be the scene of some crime.

He had a pretty good idea who that driver had to be. The line of skulls, like a racing stripe down the side of the vehicle, instantly identified it as SoHo's. But what was that guy doing on Kossuth Street? Tony wondered. He lived on the other side of town, in the Forest View section.

He was instantly alert to the possibility that SoHo was scoping out the house to make some trouble for Vic. Their run-in at school was still fresh in Tony's memory. Maybe SoHo was just satisfying a perverse bit of curiosity, Tony tried to tell himself; but remembering the glint of SoHo's switchblade reminded him that SoHo was not a threat to be taken lightly.

Tony had half decided to pull on his shoes and jacket so he could go down and confront the turkey when the van's running lights were switched on. A moment later the vehicle pulled out and was off down Kossuth, burning rubber enough to raise half a dozen lights in adjoining houses.

Good, Tony thought. He really didn't have the energy to deal with another crisis. His left arm and the right side of his neck were throbbing in tandem. All his muscles ached. He wondered if he was coming down with the flu. Maybe he'd caught whatever had knocked Vic out for two days.

He pivoted on the window seat, setting his feet down on the floor—

—and jerked backward with a sharp cry when he found himself confronted by a tall, angular figure in white.

"Sorry," said Vic, who was standing a few feet from his nephew, swathed in a peach-colored blanket. "I didn't mean to freak you out."

Now that the ghost was clearly not a ghost, Tony began to laugh at his nervous-nellie reaction. "Sorry, I've had a rough day. It wouldn't take much of anything to send me up the wall at this point."

"Tell me about it," said Vic in a tone of voice that implied he already knew all there was to tell because he was going through the same thing. Now Tony could see that his uncle was looking past him, through the window, and deep into the night. He was surprised at how lucid and even friendly Vic sounded. Usually what he wanted to talk about had no bearing on what anyone else was interested in; and he was so preoccupied with himself that he often seemed unaware that anyone was around—unless, Tony reminded himself, it was one of his buddies. It seemed oddly fitting that Vic would begin going sane at the exact moment Tony's world was on a collison course with the Twilight Zone.

But he quickly understood that the difference was purely on the surface. Vic's next words set off an alarm in his brain.

"The war's come home. *My part,* anyhow."

"What do you mean?" asked Tony, hoping to humor him

and talk him back to his bed so they could both get some sleep.

"Nham Diep. Mosquito Ridge. I thought that was over a long time ago, but now I see it was never finished. Now *she's* got my buddy Pat."

"No one's 'got' him, Vic," Tony said as reasonably as he could. "He . . . wandered off," he finished lamely, suddenly coping with the fact that he knew nothing, really, about what had happened.

"*She* took him," said Vic. Still draped in his blanket, he sat down cross-legged on the floor and looked up at Tony. "See, Pat was the one who rescued me. He was the one who got them to agree to a commando raid on the Ridge. It was Pat's machine gun I heard blasting into the tunnels. I thought I was going to buy it in there— *Shit!* By the time they'd kept me blindfolded back in some corner, my hands and feet tied, and *things* crawling on me—" Vic nervously began brushing at his face and neck with the memory; watching him, Tony felt his own skin begin to crawl. "I'd scream my throat out into my gag, but if they even noticed, they'd laugh or kick me in the face or balls. Sometimes they'd piss on me. I was buried in that hillside," said Vic in a very small voice, "only I didn't have the smarts to be dead."

He paused. Tony could almost sense the waves of cold terror, hopelessness, and anger breaking over the man. He wanted to say something comforting, but the only words that came to mind sounded inadequate, even idiotic.

"Pat saved me. He believed I was still alive. He wouldn't let *her* keep me."

"Who's this 'her' you keep talking about?" asked Tony, puzzled.

Vic didn't answer directly; rather, he began in a round-about fashion. "When you looked at Mosquito Ridge from across the valley, you'd see the outline of what looked like a woman lying on her side sleeping. The locals had a lot of dirty nicknames for that. But it was the fact that the mosquitoes were worse there than anywhere else I saw during my hitch—and I saw a lot of that fucking country, you better believe." Tony saw his Uncle's fingers clench angrily on the blanket edges, then relax slightly.

He went on. "The mosquitoes were a bitch to the farmers in that area—before they got moved out to a relocation camp.

The name Nham Diep came from a legend they had. Nham Diep was the name of a farmer's wife. But she died. Her husband—I can't remember the name—went to a holy man on a magic mountain. This old guy told the farmer to make a small cut on his finger and let three drops of blood fall on his wife. He did this, and she woke up, like she'd been sleeping all along—not really dead.''

''Ummmm,'' said Tony, hardly able to keep his eyes open, barely following Vic's apparently pointless rambling. ''I think maybe we'd better crash now.''

''You don't see what I'm getting at,'' said Vic, sounding both disappointed and angry.

''Vic, I'm so tired, I can't see straight.''

''*Fucking-A!*'' shouted Vic. ''No one would listen then—no one except Pat. Not the fucking doctors or fucking nurses or fucking shrinks or—''

''Easy, easy,'' Tony said quickly. ''I'm listening! I swear to God, I'm listening.'' The last thing he wanted to do was send his uncle into a rip-roaring rage in the middle of the night. He'd *never* get any sleep if Vic woke up the whole house. ''*I'm listening.*''

Mollified, Vic took up the thread of his narrative. ''But then the farmer's wife—the one who had been dead and was alive again—ran off with some rich guy. But the farmer found out where they were living and followed them. He found her in the rich guy's garden, cutting flowers with a knife. She was afraid he was going to drag her away or hurt her, but he just said, 'Give me the three drops of blood and I'll go away.'

''She thought she was getting off easy, so she nicked her finger with the flower knife and squeezed out three drops of blood. Her husband held out his arm, and she let the drops fall onto it one-two-three.

''But when he got the third drop back, she turned ugly and began to shrink to the size of a mosquito. She buzzed around him and tried to get the blood back, but he ran away. It's only the female mosquitoes that bite, you know. Since that time, the female mosquitoes who came after her keep searching for the three drops of blood that will turn them into a woman.''

He shifted uncomfortably on the hardwood floor. Tony hoped this signaled an end to the lecture, but Vic stopped fidgeting after a minute.

"When I was lying in the dark, in the mud and stink of that tunnel, I thought about that story a lot. Those tunnels were swarming with mosquitoes. I never could figure out how Charlie could stand it there, but whoever held the Ridge held the whole valley.

"I thought, if there were so many mosquitoes in one place, maybe there really was something to that old story. In that case, being inside Nham Diep, I was in the belly of the bitch. And those mosquitoes were draining my blood, bit by bit. And when they took enough, she was going to be alive again. Because we have the gift in our blood. Grandma Eva used to tell me that when I was growing up. Sometimes I'd see her in the dark—"

"Who?" snapped Tony, now at the edge of nervous exhaustion. "How could you see anyone if you were blindfolded?"

"I don't know. But she was there. Old and ugly and hungry for my blood. Just like I've seen her in my dreams these last weeks."

"You were dreaming it then, the way you're dreaming it now," said Tony, forcing himself to keep his voice level.

"You don't believe me," said Vic. It was a statement, not an accusation. He shrugged. "But she's come back for me. She took Pat, but it's *me* she really wants. My blood. She took Pat to get at me, because I *know* her. I know her well enough to know what she's up to. I can fight her. I fought her off in the dark under Mosquito Ridge, and I can still do it. But now she's got Pat, and she knows I'll go after him."

"Where has she got him?" asked his nephew wearily.

"The hotel. That big empty one on Dreamers Hill."

"*How* do you know that?" asked Tony, suddenly alert.

"I dreamed it. But I learned the hard way that some of what you dream is true. Mosquito Ridge and Dreamers Hill are the same place in my dreams. And *she's* inside them both."

After a moment he added, "And I'm going in there to get Pat out."

"There's no one there," said Tony. "Just a girl I met who's using the place as a crash pad. I've been in there. It's an empty shell."

"Pat's in there. I know in my gut he's in there. I owe him a big one. I've got to get him out, the way he got me out of that hellhole in Da Trang."

"I've been inside. There's nothing for you there. Whatever happened to Pat, he's not in what's left of the Bethel."

Vic just stared at him. "I'm going to check it out tomorrow. Hit them fast and bring Pat out."

*Now what do I do?* Tony asked himself. Vic would probably get himself busted. And he might get Lili arrested for trespassing, if he managed to attract the police to the place. He might even hurt Lili, since he was sounding more loony tunes with each word.

*Simplest solutions are usually the best.* "I'll go with you. I'll prove the place is empty. You can see Lili and find out she's a nice person—just a little mixed-up. Maybe I can get the answers to a few of my own questions."

"Like what?"

"Nothing very important," Tony said, temporizing. "But we'll have to go in late at night. We're going to be trespassing— maybe the police would even call it breaking and entering— and I wouldn't want them involved." He didn't elaborate, but Vic seemed satisfied. "The commandos strike at dawn," he said, then began to laugh as if he'd made a rich joke.

"The commandos crash and burn tonight," said Tony, unable to stay up any longer. He padded over to his bed, shucking his jeans along the way, letting them fall in a heap on the floor, too tired to bother picking them up.

He was asleep almost the minute his head hit the pillow. He had one final impression of Vic standing by the window, staring out in what would be the direction of the Bethel, if the place wasn't too far away to see. Tony wondered briefly if he was going to play sentry all night; then he was out of it.

Vic was awake and dressed before Tony was aroused by the clock radio with the Bangles rocking out "Walk Like an Egyptian." While he fumbled to shut off the blare, Vic shrugged into an overcoat and said, "I've got to go out and talk to my buddies. Take care of some business. Don't forget about tonight."

"No," said Tony, wishing he could forget about every crazy thing that was going on and just sleep for a week. But if he didn't get a move on, he was going to be late for his first class. At least the overall ache had subsided enough so he didn't think he was coming down with the flu.

"See you," said Vic as he left.

"Aye, aye," Tony answered, with a mock salute to the closing door.

Downstairs, Daniel Kovacs sat with the inevitable sports section spread out in front of him. He looked up as Tony entered the dining room. "You got in pretty late last night. Have your grades gotten so much better that you don't have to study anymore?"

"I had a date with Janet," said Tony, "and it wasn't that late, anyhow." He glanced around the table. "Where are Jerry and Elene?"

"They had an appointment to talk with a loan agent this morning," Daniel said. "But don't change the subject. If I was out running around like you do, my father would thrash me to within an inch of my life. He knew how important schooling was."

*Yeah, look where you've gotten: out of work and living in the same house you were born in,* thought Tony. "Things are getting better at school," he said vaguely.

"You left that book you got on Army enlistment in the living room," said Daniel. He sounded approving. "The Army might be a good idea. Toughen you up, give you a little nest egg. Then, when you come home, you could get a real job. Work in the mills. There's talk of an outside investor buying the plant; they're talking about going back to eighty-five percent production within two years."

Tony poured himself a glass of orange juice. "That's a pipe dream, Dad. It's never gonna happen. The mills are going to shut down completely, and all the wishing in the world isn't going to change that fact."

"Since when did you become an expert?" said his father, clearly stung. "You kids are all so goddamn smug and negative these days. You'd have been taken down a peg or two in my father's day, you can bet your ass."

"Daniel," said Maria Kovacs with a sidewise gesture of her head toward Leslie, who had stopped eating her cereal in mid-bite to take in the debate at the other end of the table.

"Finish your breakfast, Leslie," ordered her grandfather. "You're going to miss the school bus, and I'm not about to run you over to class. It's a long, cold walk."

Leslie began chewing her cereal with rapid crunching sounds that filled the sudden silence at the table.

Finally Tony said, ''Taking me down a peg or two isn't going to change what's happening.''

''Ahhhh!'' said Daniel Kovacs disgustedly, swiping dismissively at the air in front of him. ''You kids today aren't worth the power to blow you over the hill.''

''At least we'd have the sense to know when we *are* over the hill,'' Tony retorted.

''I won't have this bickering at the table,'' snapped his mother angrily. ''It wears me down. Leslie, if you're finished, go brush your teeth.''

Leslie took the hint and ran upstairs to the bathroom. As soon as she was gone, Maria spoke rapidly to her husband and son, swiveling her head from one to the other. *''I won't have this anymore.* If you can't be civil to each other, then you sit, you eat, you don't say a word, and you go on about your business as fast as you can. But stop making everything so unpleasant for everyone else!'' She got up suddenly and walked angrily toward the stairs to check on Leslie.

His appetite suddenly gone, Tony stared across at his father. Daniel was staring back at him. He shrugged. ''Truce?''

The man just stared at him. Finally he said, ''Your mother's been edgy lately. I think Vic's really got her worried.''

*No use,* thought Tony, *he never sees what he doesn't want to see.* ''Vic will be okay,'' he said, just to be saying something.

''I don't understand, though, why you hate the steel mills so much. They gave my father a good living. They kept a roof over *your* head until all that Korean and Japanese product took away the market. Hungarians have always worked in the mills,'' he boasted, as if that clinched things.

''It's not the mills, don't you see? It's just that I want to do something different with my life.''

''Hunh! The greatest steelworker of all was Joe Magarac, a Hungarian. He could squeeze out steel rails bare-handed. And he lived right here in Pennsylvania. He finally had himself melted down in a ladle of boiling steel so his mill could have the finest steel in the world and they could build a new mill.''

''That's a legend, Dad,'' said Tony wearily.

"Oh, some of the stories aren't true; I know that. I'm not as dumb as you think. But Magarac really existed. And he stood for a tradition that you should be proud of."

"Sorry, Dad, all the traditions in the world aren't going to make me jump into a pot of boiling steel. I never want to owe my soul to a company that way."

"You'll be a bum, a drifter. If you don't stay where your roots are, you're nowhere."

"Grandpa Kovacs came here from Hungary. He didn't exactly stay put."

"He put down roots here."

"Then maybe I'll put down roots somewhere else," said Tony, getting up from the table before the disagreement got out of hand.

"You're like Magarac one way," Daniel Kovacs said darkly.

"Which is?"

"In Hungarian, *magarac* means a donkey or jackass. A damned fool. On him, it was a compliment. On you—" He made a deprecating gesture with his hand.

Tony shrugged. "I'll tell you one last thing. Vic's friend Pat McKenna—he's Irish—said they've always known Joe was Irish, and his real name was Joe *McGarrick*."

He left the room before his father could respond. His momentary pleasure at getting in the last word disappeared as he hurried to the SMT bus stop. His mention of Pat McKenna brought the whole problem of Vic's delusions about the hotel to mind. And the problem of Vic brought up the question of what SoHo had been doing parked outside the Kovacs house the night before.

Tony decided the first order of business was to confront SoHo—but at a time and in a place where the latter wasn't about to get knife-happy.

*Gee, the days get better and better,* Tony thought miserably to himself. *If they get any better, I'll wake up dead.*

But the meeting with SoHo never came off. The skull-decorated van wasn't in the school parking lot. When he asked where SoHo was, one of the guys who hung out with him shrugged and said, "He cut school. I saw him early this morning with Trick and Razz—"

"You mean, those friends of his who disappeared?"

His informant looked blank. "How could they disappear if I saw them this morning?"

"Never mind," said Tony quickly. "Uh, thanks for the help." He felt the morning was a little less bleak. At least the bone of contention between SoHo and Vic was gone. And one less thing to worry about was a blessing at this juncture.

The morning really improved when Janet Dillon greeted him as he settled into English class. She seemed genuinely concerned that he was feeling all right; and, better yet, she seemed to have forgotten she'd been angry at him the night before.

Maybe, he promised himself, once he'd proven to Vic that there was nothing in the hotel, things could get back to normal. *Whatever "normal" means in my life these days,* he added on reflection.

The rest of the day went smoothly enough. Ted had promised him a ride home, which he appreciated.

But when he was walking toward Ted's car, he suddenly spotted the old man who had helped him on the night of his mugging. The old guy—same thatch of white hair, same rimless glasses, same burn scar—was tapping the steel tip of his cane impatiently on the ground beside the left rear wheel of Ted's car. Clearly he was waiting for someone. Tony glanced around to see if anyone else was in the vicinity, but the lot was pretty quiet. Ted had stopped near the lockers to talk to Sandi in private, giving Tony the keys to the car.

He hesitated. *Could he be waiting for me?* he wondered. *But how would he know I was getting a ride with Ted? I just found out an hour ago.*

"Hi," he said, approaching the old guy slowly. "We met before. You helped me when I got in trouble last Saturday. How come you didn't hang around to tell the police what you saw? I know they'd like a statement from you."

The cane stopped moving under the guy's right hand; with his left he made a dismissive gesture. "The police can't help. They only see what they're supposed to see. And time is running out."

Tony glanced back toward the main entrance to the high school, but Ted was nowhere in sight. "Were you waiting to talk to someone?" he asked cautiously.

"You, of course," said the old man in the tone of voice of

a teacher explaining something for the umpteenth time to the class bonehead. "There's very much I have to tell you, and very, very little time. Come with me." He pulled on Tony's sleeve, but the boy shook free and stepped back out of reach.

"Look, I don't want to be rude, but I haven't got the time—"

"Time"—the old man laughed mirthlessly—"is what *none* of us have to spare now." Then he fixed Tony with a stare that was so intense, the boy felt his objections crumbling. "We have to talk immediately," the man insisted.

"If you won't go to the police—" Tony began again.

The man's gesture of irritation made it abundantly clear that Tony was playing the fool and wasting valuable time. "What I have to say is about that girl in the hotel. Among other things. She's not what you imagine."

"Have you been spying on her? On us? Who *are* you, anyway? What is any of this to you?"

"A matter of life and death," he said with frightening intensity. "But not just for me. I'm pretty unimportant in the scheme of things. *You're* in danger. And the girl. And Vic."

*Loony tunes time on the Wonamey*, thought Tony. *Every wacko in town is determined to drive me crazy.*

"Uh, maybe some other time," he temporized, seeing Ted running down the school steps, two at a time, toward the parking lot.

The old man grabbed his wrist suddenly and pressed his face close to Tony's. "I'll tell you about the silver charm in your pocket," he hissed. "I'll tell you about the words you've got written on that scrap of paper along with it."

Startled, Tony touched his left breast pocket, feeling the bauble he dreamed Lili had given him there, and the folded sheet of notepaper.

Ted, glancing curiously at the old guy, said to Tony, "Man, what's the matter with you? You look like you've seen a ghost."

"Um, this is an . . . an old family friend," Tony ad-libbed. "I just ran into him. I said we'd give him a lift. He lives, um—"

"Over at the corner of Third and Mason," said the old man, smiling quite nicely at Ted. "I've known Tony's family for years. Tony's going to stay and chat a bit. I've got a lot to catch him up on."

Ted gave Tony a questioning look.

"Uh, that's right. If it won't be too much trouble."

Ted continued to stare at his friend. "I thought you said you had to get right home."

"I . . . you know, changed my mind. *Please,* Ted . . . I'd really appreciate it."

With a shrug Ted said, "It's not too far out of my way. Gimme the car keys, Tony, and let's get going."

# Eleven

"MY NAME IS JOZSEF Zagonyi," said the old man, settling into a threadbare armchair patterned in faded white and red roses and indicating that Tony should seat himself in its twin, facing him. Floor-to-ceiling bookcases, jammed with books set every which way, filled all the wall space in the room, except for doorways and a single casement window. The grimy panes, spattered and streaked with white paint from a lousy paint job, overlooked an empty yard.

He gestured toward the bursting bookshelves. "I am a scholar, with many fields of interest. At one time I was a teacher; I have not worked with students for over twenty years. At present my concern is the study of the occult."

"You study ghosts—that sort of thing," Tony said quickly, anxious to keep the man from a long rambling through his personal history.

"Among other things," said Zagonyi, "among other things."

The cottage he lived in was set behind a larger house fronting on Third Street. They had walked up a path alongside the main house; the backyard was surrounded by a high wooden fence. The old man had unlocked a narrow gate at the end of the footpath with a loose key fished from the pocket of his heavy tweed coat. He had insisted that Tony lock the gate once they were inside.

The cottage was tucked into the far corner of the yard,

surrounded by the remains of a long untended flower bed. It looked like it had once been a storage shed that had been converted to a mother-daughter unit years before.

The sweep of lawn between it and the main house looked like it hadn't been mowed in months. All the blinds were drawn at the back of the two-story house. A cracked and empty fish pond was protected by a cement frog seated on a concrete tree stump. It was leaning forward, forever posed playing a guitar to nonexistent goldfish.

The smell inside the house nearly did Tony in. It reeked of sour milk, stale air, and an overflowing garbage pail. The books, massed all around him, gave off an oppressive, dusty, mildewed smell. For all that Jozsef Zagonyi looked neat enough, himself, he obviously didn't pay much attention to how he lived. Tony wondered how anyone could live in such a way. To add to the problem, it was stifling; he wondered if the little wall heater was ever turned off. It had been going full blast when they entered. The man had turned on a dusty overhead light as soon as they stepped into the living room, but it didn't do much to relieve the gloomy feeling of the place.

Two doors opened off the compact living room. One led into a small, dark kitchen, where a single chair was pushed under a table littered with opened cans, a loosely wrapped loaf of bread, and several volumes stacked haphazardly. The other door—presumably to the cottage's only bedroom—was firmly shut.

Zagonyi continued. "I was born . . . a long time ago, at Szasz-Dalya, in the Transylvania region of Hungary."

"Vampire country," said Tony automatically, all the Dracula movies he'd seen leaping to mind. *Get to the point*, he pleaded silently.

"Yes"—the old man smiled grimly—"though things are not necessarily what the popular literature of this country or Western Europe has made them out to be. Vlad Dracul, the actual historical figure the author of *Dracula* drew on, was quite different from the creature of that distasteful bit of fiction.

"Vlad was named Vlad Terpes, or Vlad the Impaler, because of his method of executing his Turkish enemies—a horrible way of killing people, to be sure!—but he is still regarded as a hero in Eastern Europe. He was popular because he was a relentless enemy of the Turks, who were hated throughout Europe. In the end he was killed by the Turks. It was the Irish writer Bram Stoker who first suggested he was a vampire and turned him into Dracula.''

The old man paused, then went on. ''But if the stories of vampires who run around in capes and talk like that actor Bela Lugosi—a respected Hungarian actor who should have known better!—are so much foolishness, the idea of supernatural evil isn't.

''There are entities of unbelieveable perfidy who sometimes reach through into this world at a point—mercifully, rare—where life and death, reality and dreaming intersect. They usually come no closer to us than our nightmares,'' said the old man with a shudder, ''but sometimes they come much closer. . . .''

*Loony Tunes meets Creature Features,* Tony thought. *My brain is going into overload in about thirty seconds.* He didn't understand everything that Zagonyi was saying, but that didn't matter so much. He wanted to know what the man could tell him about the silver charm and the folded bit of paper in his pocket. Taking advantage of the man's pause, the boy drew them out and held the tiny sculpted hand and arm out to the old man. Jozsef took it with a nod.

''You said you knew something about that,'' Tony reminded him. ''And about Lili. And you were going to tell me what this meant.'' He opened the square of paper and handed it to the old man as well.

Zagonyi set the paper in his lap. Then he held the charm up to the light. ''This amulet is an old protection against the evil eye, witches, or harm of any sort. I have seen it worn very often among the Gypsies who lived in Hungary. This has an eyelet at one end; I would guess that it came from a necklace.''

Tony nodded, remembering in a flash the silver necklace Lili wore, which looked like it had lost a pendant. ''What do you know about Lili?''

''Everything in its place,'' the old man said firmly. ''Our next order of business is the message you've written down. *Danger. Sleeping now. Dreaming. Waking soon. Danger. Lili the Mpusa.*''

''Most of it's pretty clear,'' said Tony. ''It's the last word that doesn't make any sense. I'm pretty sure I wrote down exactly what the message was.''

"Then we'll start there. You wrote the letters down correctly. You just didn't arrange them properly. The transcription should be, Lilith. Empusa."

"What does that mean?"

"*Lilith,* or Lilitu, according to ancient legend, was the first woman on earth, even before Eve. She gave birth to demons and spirits. Even in olden times, amulets—like the one your friend gave you—were used as a protection against her and her demon offspring. She continued to haunt people's dreams throughout the whole of recorded history. She is the mother of Western belief in vampires.

"Much later the Greeks called her the *empusa.* According to them, she had no shape of her own but appeared as a horrible phantom. She was able to take any shape that suited her. A vampire demonic spirit, she could, under certain circumstances, enter and take over a living body. Or reanimate a corpse, if it suited her purposes.

"She would usually appear as a beautiful woman, seducing men so she could eat their flesh and drink their blood. But underneath the surface glamour was what Aristophanes, the playwright, described as a 'a hellish vampire, /Clothed all about with blood, /and boils and blisters.' This monster is well known to people through history under a variety of names. *Ekimmu. Lamia. Succubus. Vampyr.*"

"*Lili. Lilith,*" Tony repeated. "You're saying that Lili is one of—one of *those?*" The idea chilled him at some gut level, even though common sense said what he was being told was a crock.

"No—not in the way you're thinking. She is a *victim* herself; in the toils of the monster. The similarity of names is merely . . . coincidence or synchronicity—it doesn't matter," Jozsef said hastily, seeing he was losing the boy. "What matters to you is that she gave you this amulet"—he handed the charm back to Tony—"precisely because she's *not* wholly under the sway of the *empusa.* Nevertheless, the creature controls her most of the time. Her will can only break free for isolated moments. She gave that to you during one such instance."

"I dreamed she gave it to me," said Tony, staring at the bit of sculpted silver as though it, not Zagonyi, held answers to the questions crowding into his mind.

"Dreams are the place where the *empusa* exists," said the

old man. "They're the point at which our world and another overlap. They are her gateway to us. But only certain people have the gift of reaching through to that other place."

"Some gift," said Tony sarcastically.

"There are other beings who can cross over and bring healing and guidance, using the same avenues. It's a two-edged sword," the old man said, "as is most involvement with—call it the 'spirit world,' for want of a better term."

"If what you're saying is true, it seems awfully risky. Like nukes."

"A good analogy," said Zagonyi with a little smile.

"But whose side is Lili on?" he asked, desperate for a clear answer.

"She wants to help, but the *empusa* is strong enough to control her most of the time. She has had the girl in her power for years—"

"Since 1936," said Tony.

"Yes," said the old man, who seemed surprised by Tony's knowledge. "How—?"

"I read about her in a newspaper article," the boy said. "But you're telling me that she was the girl who disappeared *more than fifty years ago?*"

Jozsef nodded.

"Then why doesn't she look older?" Tony challenged.

"She's been in the creature's . . . keeping. She's been kept, unchanging, in a corner of the *empusa*'s dream. Until her services were needed. Then she was awakened."

"Like Sleeping Beauty?" Tony laughed. "You don't *really* expect me to *believe* all this stuff, do you?"

"Just listen a little longer, then make up your mind." Before Tony could make any further objections, the old man pushed on. "Lili has a gift. That's why the creature took her. But she hasn't the special gift that the creature needs. The *empusa* wants to cross over into this world where her powers would assure her an unlimited source of what she hungers for—human flesh, human blood, the *life* they contain."

"But if she's existed in our world before, why didn't she stay?"

"She and her sisters—oh, there are many such creatures on that other plane of existence—rarely find the right circumstances to do more than rip a little way into our world. They can exist among us briefly, sustained by a vital energy—what

I call *mana*—they steal from the living. But most people have only a small portion of this. And the vampire must replenish its supply frequently. When they can't absorb enough, these creatures must return to their proper realm with their lust for the *mana* in blood and flesh unsatisfied.

"It's not the blood or flesh as such they crave, it's the *mana*, the life force that sustains all living things in the universe. The Hindus call it *prana*, the Chinese *ch'i*, and the Japanese *ki*. When a body—living or dead—controlled by an *empusa* sucks a person's blood or eats the still warm flesh, the creature within is really ingesting the life essence of its victim. The *mana* courses through a person's veins, steeps the muscle and nerve tissue, though it is always separate from these, the way that electric energy remains distinct from the wires it passes through.

"You said most people only have a little of this *mana*," Tony said. "Do some people have more?"

"Yes. Certain people carry vast reserves in their being. Why this is so, why certain people or certain racial stocks have a disproportionate share of *mana*, I can't say. But it is a fact. In individuals it is often manifested as mediumship—the ability to contact the spirit world. In a rare number of cases mediums can actually provide a spirit with a material existence, through the transfer of *mana* in the form of ectoplasm drawn from the medium's body.

"Gypsies are one such people heavily blessed—or, in some cases, cursed—with *mana*. Their bloodlines go back to ancient India and Egypt. The word *Gypsy* itself derives from the world *Egypt*. They have always been people with a 'gift,' and Hungary has always been home to many of them—more so than any other country in the world.

"As they intermarried with Eastern Europeans—Hungarians in particular—they bequeathed to them—*to us*—the power in their blood. Before I left my native land, I witnessed many instances of enormous occult powers among people who were natural mediums. Often they were confused and frightened by their gifts. They were as apt to think it the work of the devil.

"One of the most common manifestations was the frequent number of documented hauntings I investigated as a young student. I very quickly concluded that many people in the old country had enough *mana* to keep their astral bodies—their ghosts, if you will—from disintegrating for a time after the death of the physical body.''

"I don't see how this all connects," said Tony wearily.

"When a creature like the *empusa* can drain the *mana* of such extraordinarily gifted persons, its own power grows accordingly. And so does that threat to all life.

"It's significant that the earliest mentions of Lilith refer to her as vengeful, hostile to childbirth, and demanding of human sacrifice. The name means 'night monster.' She represents a dark force utterly antithetical to life. References to her in certain old books I've studied suggest that she would, if unchecked, drain the universe of all other life, *then, in her greed, feed upon herself.*''

"Why Stigesville? Why now?"

"There has always been a place of extraordinary power here. Such places draw the darker spirits because the boundaries between the spirit world and our own are at their most fragile at these points. In Hungary, the Transylvania region was one such 'borderland.' This region is another. The Indian peoples who lived here long ago knew this. Some tried to draw on that power; most shunned it. The tribe that boldly tried to turn the power to its advantage vanished—not even their name survived—long before the Vikings first reached these shores.

"Later, before the Revolutionary War, there was a misguided group of worshipers—they called themselves the Dreamers—who emigrated from Eastern Europe and came to this place so they could use magic to draw upon the elemental power of the earth. Instead, to their everlasting grief, they summoned something far more powerful and dangerous. Something that promised them the sun and the moon but only wanted to use them to reach through to this world and the teeming life it holds.''

"The *empusa*," Tony said.

The old man nodded. "History books say the Dreamers were massacred by Indians. Rumors at the time suggested their neighbors murdered them because they couldn't abide devil worshipers—who were also reputed cannibals and blood drinkers—so near 'proper Christian' towns. I'm inclined to think that the Dreamers destroyed themselves when the creature's hunger went out of control. My guess is that the first outsiders on the scene burned the town down just to spare anyone else the sight.''

Tony had a sudden, horrifying image of sharks in a feeding frenzy. Or the worst sequences of *Night of the Living Dead.* "We talked about the Dreamers in history class. I can't believe what you're saying could have happened."

"There are other historical instances that parallel what happened here," Jozsef said. "In the sixteenth century our own Hungarian countess, Elisabeth Bathory, butchered six hundred and fifty young girls, in order to bathe in their blood. She was called the Bloody Countess and the Tigress of Csejthe, the name of her castle; she believed bathing in blood would keep her young and beautiful. Relying on three female servants to help her, she lured a steady stream of virgins to her service.

"Initially these sad young women would have their lives ended while they were suspended in an iron cage. Iron hoops would contract and slash the victim inside to death, showering the countess, who was seated beneath, draped in a gown of immaculate white, in a shower of fresh blood."

Tony shuddered.

"Later," Jozsef went on, "she had a German clock maker design an 'iron virgin,' which victims were forced to hug. The poor creatures would suddenly find themselves locked in an iron embrace, while hidden blades impaled them. Elisabeth's servants would catch the blood in basins and take these to the countess's bath chamber in time for her grisly baths at four o'clock each morning.

"In 1611, she was tried, and imprisoned for life in her own castle, the very place where she had committed her horrible crimes. There she died, three years later. The whole hideous incident was looked on as a human aberration. An aberration, yes," said Jozsef with a sharp nod of emphasis, "but not of *human* origin.

"I think this was an instance of the *empusa* reaching through into our world. There was a power in the countess's blood—in all likelihood a Gypsy strain—that attracted the creature. And the region was one of those 'supernatural borderlands' that are scattered over the face of the earth.

"But the Bathory clan also had a strain of madness in its genes. A look at the family tree reveals eccentrics, psychotics, and murderers. In the end, I think that was what defeated the most recent attempt of a 'night monster' to gain a permanent hold on our world.

"Elisabeth was the focus of the *empusa*'s attempt to reach

through to our world; in her demented state I suspect she welcomed the creature and surrendered a part of her being to it. But her mind snapped under the burden. The creature's lust for blood and life became entangled with the countess's own fears of aging and death. In her increasing confusion, blood became the key to prolonging her own youth, as well as feeding the hunger of the being who must have raged in her dreams. The twin drives pushed her to blood orgies and excesses that alerted the authorities, who put an end to her crimes before the *empusa* was strong enough to cross fully into our world. And when Elisabeth Bathory died in her tower prison, what the creature hoped to achieve died with her."

"Then why didn't killing off the Dreamers put an end to things here?"

"It did, to some extent. But the violence and horror added to the negative power of the place. And I think there was enough power here to start with for the creature to . . . linger in this world. Though it went into a kind of . . . hibernation, when the Dreamers were exterminated. Or destroyed themselves."

"What you're saying," Tony said carefully, "is that when they built the hotel on Dreamers Hill, they woke it up, right?"

"No—the hotel didn't really become a focus until later. Other circumstances—a one-in-a-million chance—brought another crucial element to bear. The steel mills of Pennsylvania began attracting thousands of émigrés from Eastern Europe. People in whom the strains of Gypsy blood run truest. People gifted with *mana* in large amounts."

"My family has Gypsy blood," said Tony. "My grandmother is always talking about our 'gifts.' " If he let his mind free-float a little, Jozsef's insane story began to make a crazy kind of sense. "Lili said her family was Hungarian. The other people I read about who disappeared—a lot of their names sounded Hungarian too."

"Exactly," the old man said. "So many people of Gypsy descent moving into this area brought enough energy to wake the creature. The power of such blood isn't diluted with the passage of time: it is reborn once each generation into those families that have been vessels of the power since time immemorial. Such persons have the power to bring great good into this world; they can also serve as the unwitting conduits for vileness."

"I would guess that the first people to migrate here from Eastern Europe had only small 'gifts' of power when they settled here. But as more and more of them arrived, the power began to accumulate. And others arrived whose bloodlines represented an even richer purity and power. Like a vast, dark moth to an irresistible flame, the creature came, and fed, and grew, and dreamed again of ravaging this world to satisfy its hunger, which will never be satisfied until all life has been consumed, including its own.

"It moved through the dreams of those settling in and around Stigesville. It fed on their energy, taking possession of the occasional unfortunate, sending the benighted creatures out into the world to drink human blood and eat human flesh in order to provide the life energy their invisible mistress craved.

"When the *empusa* was strong enough, it began reaching out to others, invading their dreams, draining their power, drawing more of them to this place of power and death. Always, it was searching for the ones who had the strongest 'gifts'—the ones who had the potency to let it cross a final time. To let it break free from the dream and touch our waking world for an unlimited time.

"At present, the creature is still, in a sense, sleeping. But it is waking up. It exists in the collective dream of those it has already gathered in the ruin of the hotel. For a long time it fed off them just enough to survive; but now it is waking up and hungry enough to drain the life energy out of the most expendable. And it has begun to wake up a few to carry out special assignments. Some bring in more victims to add to the collective dream and the energy pool that sustains it; a few others"—here the old man hesitated—"like Lili, were awakened to bring to it those with the strongest 'gifts' of all. With these in its power, the time of dreaming will end for it. Then the nightmare begins for the living."

"Who does the creature want now?" asked Tony, though he already knew the answer.

"*You,* for a certainty. Others in your family, perhaps. But you seem to be the focus."

Tony shook his head. "I can't believe what you're telling me."

"Look at what's happening to your life," Jozsef insisted, "just in these past few days. *Can you be certain any longer*

*where reality stops and the dream begins?* You can't, can
you?''

"How do you know? How do you know so much?"

"I have my own . . .'gifts,' " said Jozsef softly. "I can
. . . see things."

"If you've known what's going on, why didn't you do something before now?"

"Once, when I had . . . more power, I tried to stop what
was happening. I knew that the hotel was the physical place
where the entity's power was strongest. It was there that it
drew people who were never seen again. They would wander
in and become lost walking down corridors that never truly
existed in this world. They would fall asleep in rooms that
occupied the same space as the familiar rooms in the hotel but
were never seen by any except those who were already pris-
oners of the *empusa.*"

"I don't understand," said Tony, shaking his head helplessly.

"There was the real hotel, and a *dream* of that hotel." The
old man cut off Tony's next objection, adding hastily, "I'm
trying to make this as simple as possible. In one sense, the
two structures exist in a single spot, but, in fact, they're parts
of two very different orders of existence."

"You're still losing me. . . ." Tony complained.

"It doesn't matter. What matters is that as the creature
stirs, the hive of dreamers it has built around it is becoming
more real. It looks like the old Bethel, but it's a part of
another world *taking its place.*"

"You said you tried to stop the thing," Tony said. "How?"

"When I realized—years ago—how strong it had become,
I—" The old man's head drooped; he shook his head at the
bitter memory. "I tried talking with the authorities. They
thought I was mad. Then the thing began coming to me in my
dreams, taunting me because I was so ineffectual, promising
me that my time was running out. The *world's* time was
running out. I was frantic. I—I like to think that my mind
slipped under the pressure; it makes it easier to bear the guilt
for what followed. I—I knew that evil could often be cleansed
by fire. And I—" He sighed, unable to continue for a moment.

"You set fire to the Hotel Bethel," whispered Tony, "and
all those people died."

"My efforts were no more than an annoyance to it. In the
end, it left me with a burden of terrible guilt. And the

creature would use that to turn my every dream into a nightmare of flames and choking smoke and charred bodies and screaming people. Always that terrible screaming—''

''It was a long time ago,'' was all Tony could think to say.

Jozsef Zagonyi looked across at the boy and shook his head. ''In your dreams everything is happening for the first time. Every night I relived those horrible minutes as though I were going through the ordeal once again. I was badly burned for my efforts''—here he touched the scar on the side of his face and neck—''but I welcomed the suffering as a small way of offering penance for my folly.''

''If I got Lili out, why couldn't you call the police and make up some story so they'd *have* to check the place out?''

''Even if they went inside—and as the creature gets stronger, as the power of its dreaming seeps into every corner of the city, it's hard to imagine police not suddenly finding themselves with a thousand reasons *not* to go near the place—even if they did search the Hotel Bethel from basement to attic, they'd never see anything suspicious. They'd find empty rooms and dust. No dreamers. No *empusa*.''

''But if it has that much power, why hasn't it just taken''—he paused—''whoever it wants?''

''Because those with the power it most needs are those with the greatest ability to resist it. Even if it's subconscious. There is an old idea that a vampire could only go inside a house *if it was invited in*. I think there's a similar principle at work. The *empusa* can't *force* some people to its will, but it *can* seduce them. Your blood holds the *mana* that it needs; your blood holds the power to deny the creature what it wants. So it works its wiles on you in other ways.''

''Lili?''

Zagonyi nodded. ''She's stolen a little blood from you; at the same time the *empusa* has taken a bit of your life force through her. But some part of your *mana* has protected you from worse, even when you're seemingly at the creature's mercy.''

''You're saying Lili's a *vampire?*'' Tony cried, suddenly understanding what the old man was telling him. ''You're crazy!'' He started to rise from his chair.

But with surprising agility the old man hobbled across the intervening space and restrained him, forcing him back down into the chair cushions.

"She's not such a creature by choice. And you must always remember, she's fighting back with all the resources she can. She's in the belly of the beast, where maintaining a shred of her own will must be the hardest battle of all. She gave you that charm *to help you.* Don't hate her," said Jozsef with sudden ferocity. *"Help her. Help us all fight back."*

"But even if what you're saying is true, what could anyone do?" He felt angry at the old fool for even suggesting what he had suggested; and he felt angry at himself for betraying Lili by listening to such crap. "You're saying the situation is hopeless, and I'm saying this is all a load of bull."

He climbed to his feet. This time the old man made no effort to stop him.

"I don't know how you know so many things about me. But what you're saying is crazy."

Tony took a step toward the front door of the cottage.

"Please . . ." Zagonyi began. He held out his hand to the boy.

"You don't have to worry," said Tony. "I'm not about to tell anyone what you told me." *Who'd believe any of it, except maybe the part about setting the fire? And he looks like he's suffered plenty for that. If he didn't make the whole thing up,* he told himself.

"Oh," the old man cried. It was such a lost sound that Tony stopped indecisively, his hand on the doorknob.

"If you could give me some proof . . ." he began.

"There isn't the time; I haven't the strength." Zagonyi shook his head sadly.

"I'm sorry," Tony interrupted, "but I just don't have time for any more ghost stories. And don't bother me or my friends anymore. I—I'm sorry," he said again, and pulled open the door.

He walked rapidly down the street, welcoming the cold, clean air that cleared his nose of the sour smell of the stuffy cottage. With every pace he took away from the place he felt more assured that the old man was senile.

*But he knew so much,* a part of his mind protested.

*Carnival tricks. Who knows how long he's been spying, who he might have talked to, what he might have seen? Maybe he does have an ability to read minds: I've heard that's been scientifically proven,* Tony rationalized. *But it doesn't make me believe for one minute that bullshit about Lili being a vampire, and monsters hiding in a burned-out hotel. Guy's as far gone as Vic—*

He glanced at his watch. It was nearly six o'clock. *If Vic thinks I've forgotten—shit!*

He was running down Third now, frantically looking for a phone booth. The first one he spotted was missing the receiver. A length of metal-wrapped cord ending in a tuft of tiny torn wires dangled in front of a metal panel covered with felt-tip marker graffiti. Wishing he could strangle the vandals in what was left of the phone cord, he ran two more blocks before spotting a phone booth at a corner service station.

Leslie answered the phone. "Mom and Dad didn't get the loan, so they're fighting. And Grandma and Grandpa are still mad because of what happened at breakfast. I'm watching TV with Uncle Vic. We're watching *Gimme a Break*, and we're the only ones who aren't mad."

"Thanks for the news update, pumpkin. Would you let me talk to Vic?"

"Just a minute."

There was a long pause before Vic came on the line.

" 'Lo," he said. "Where are you?"

"I got held up. At school. I'll be home in twenty minutes or maybe half an hour."

"Fine." Another pause. "You haven't forgotten what we've got to do tonight?"

"No, I haven't forgotten."

"Good, because I've got just the ticket for getting Pat out of there."

"What do you mean, Vic?" asked Tony, feeling his stomach muscles tighten.

"You'll see. I can't talk about it. See you later, bro."

"Vic—" Tony began. But the dial tone told him he was talking to a disconnect. "See you, bro," he said, hanging up the phone.

# Twelve

"WE'RE GOING TO shoot pool with some of Vic's buddies," Tony said when his mother asked where her son and brother were headed.

"Don't you want to wait and have some dessert?" Maria Kovacs asked.

"I'm full," Tony said. "Vic?"

"Couldn't eat another mouthful," said Vic, who was rocking impatiently back on his heels. His hands were buried in his army fatigue jacket. He was wearing a blue-black wool sweater underneath it.

"Don't you have homework?" Tony's mother wondered.

"Not tonight—just some reading. We won't be back very late. Thanks for the car. We gotta go. Jack and the others are waiting, right, Vic?"

"Sure," Vic responded, following his nephew's cue.

"See you," said Tony, kissing his mother lightly on the cheek. His father called from somewhere at the back of the house. With a sigh Maria went to see what her husband needed.

Tony and Vic stepped out on the front porch. Leslie, wearing a red pullover sweater, was sitting on the porch waiting for them.

"Take me with you, Uncle Tony," she asked.

"I can't, sweetheart. Men only. Besides, isn't tonight your night for watching *Moonlighting?*"

Leslie shrugged. "I'd rather go with you guys."

She looked so sad, Tony reached down and gave her a hug. "Look, next Saturday I'll take you for pizza, okay?"

"Okay," she responded, clearly not happy to be left behind.

"We gotta get *going,*" Vic called impatiently. He was already standing at the foot of the front steps.

"In a minute," Tony yelled. To Leslie he said, "Is something bothering you, pumpkin?"

"Well, I don't like it that everybody else here is mad at everybody. Except you and Vic. But that's not *really* it."

"What is it, *really?*"

"I'm scared to be alone in my room upstairs. I have these really bad dreams, and I try to wake up but I can't. Even if I do, the lady who's in them is sometimes in my room. She looks sorta pretty, but then I see she's got funny teeth and funny eyes—like Red Riding Hood's Grandma when it wasn't her Nana at all."

"*Tony*—" Vic drawled.

"One second!" Tony called over his shoulder. "You're just having bad dreams—honest, I wouldn't lie to you, would I? Be careful how you answer that!" When she smiled, he said, "There's nothing to hurt you. But tell you what—I'll look in on you when I get back, just to be sure everything's okay. Okay?"

"You won't forget?"

"Cross my heart. Now go on inside; it's pretty cold out here."

She scooted through the front door as Tony hurried to join Vic.

They had parked on Hudson Street, just past the intersection of Stanwix. The car was facing toward the hotel, catty-corner to them.

"That's the corner I climbed over," said Tony, pointing through the windshield.

"There's no other way in?" Vic asked.

"Not that I've been able to find. The girl inside has a key to the side gate, halfway up Stanwix. But she keeps it locked."

"She work for them?"

"No," said Tony, not really clear who "they" were. "She's

just a kid. She uses the place as a crash pad. Vic, she's the only one living there, swear to God. Won't you take my word for it so we can go home?''

"Pat's in there," his uncle said, staring at the brick pier at the angle of the fencing around the Bethel. "I owe him one.''

Tony sighed. Vic wasn't going to be satisfied until he'd rambled through the partially burned structure. For a moment Tony thought of Jozsef Zagonyi and his confession. He sure wouldn't want to live with *that* on his conscience, he knew.

"Anybody tries to mess with us, I've got a little surprise for them," said Vic softly.

"What surprise?" Tony had forgotten Vic's words over the phone earlier.

From the pocket of his fatigue jacket Vic produced a snub-nosed revolver, taking careful aim with it at the hotel's brick pier.

"Jeez! Where'd you get that?" Tony asked. With the gun Vic kicked the already loopy adventure into a dangerous new gear.

"One of the guys," said Vic, deliberately evasive. "It's a .357. Designed for close range—not more than five yards.''

"Is it, you know, *loaded?*" Tony knew the question was idiotic, but he had to ask, anyway.

"Does a bear shit in the woods?"

"Leave it under the car seat, Vic. Otherwise someone might get hurt. There's a girl—a *friend of mine*, for chrissake!—in there. I don't want you fuckin' blowing *her* away.''

"If anybody gets wasted, it's not going to be a friend. I'm taking this with me—just for insurance," the man replied stubbornly. He slipped the handgun back in his jacket pocket.

"What if I say I won't go?"

"Suit yourself. I'll find my own way up and over," said Vic, pushing open the door of the station wagon. He climbed out, then stood beside the car, watching Tony.

After a moment of indecisiveness the boy sighed and climbed out the driver's side. The evening smelled of disaster already, but letting Vic go off half cocked, carrying a loaded .357, was begging for it.

Tony opened the back door of the car and took out two flashlights, handing one to Vic. They slipped these into their belts. Then he removed the coil of rope Vic had taken from the family garage. He had put knots all along its length, for use in scaling the Bethel's fence. The plan was for Tony to climb up and fasten the rope at the top of the fence so they could use it for getting in and out. With Vic's help he quickly looped the rope around and around his waist and stomach so it wouldn't be in the way. "All set," he said when the rope was secured.

"Let's move out, soldier," said Vic.

When they crossed the street and stood at the base of the brick pier, they discovered a guy walking toward them down Hudson with a German shepherd. They turned abruptly and made a show of casually strolling up Stanwix. When they were almost to the side gate, Tony glanced back. Man and dog apparently had continued on their way.

"Since we're here," said Tony, "let's try the gate on the off chance she may have forgotten to lock it." He was stalling now; he hadn't the least desire to scale the fence that night. But there was nothing else to do.

Vic shrugged and followed him to the side gate. Tony hastily checked out the street in both directions, as well as the grounds beyond the fence. He saw and heard nothing. Expecting no results, he took hold of the gate by the nearest picket and rattled it.

The gate swung inward so abruptly, he nearly tumbled through onto the gravel path inside. "Well," he said when he'd regained his balance, "that sure simplifies things."

"Could be *too* easy," said Vic, his hand jammed into the pocket with the revolver. "Could be a trap. *She*'s no fool."

"Be cool," Tony urged. "There isn't going to be any trap. We'll see if Lili's around, so we don't frighten her. Then you can search the place to your heart's content."

Vic relaxed slightly, but he kept his hand in his gun pocket. When he was standing on the gravel path, Tony shut the gate behind them, aligning it so it would look locked to any casual passerby. "I'll go first," said Tony. "I'm the one Lili knows."

"I'm right behind you, bro," Vic said. Tony thought he was being funny, but with Vic he never knew.

He decided to try the back entrance, since that was the one Lili used. She might be in the kitchen having tea. He hoped he'd find her before he had to go up the main stairs to the second floor. He remembered her saying her room was up there somewhere.

He also vividly recalled his feeling of terror when he had
looked up at the shadowy gallery at the head of the stairs. If
they found Lili downstairs, he was inclined to let Vic do his
own exploring. He'd keep Lili safely away from Vic's handgun while he asked her some questions about the charm, and
maybe about the words that had come from the Ouija board.
But that part was so crazy—and, in his mind, was now
compounded with old Zagonyi's ravings—that he wasn't sure
he wanted to bring it up at all.

They passed by the drained swimming pool. Again Tony
had the impression of something huge with black, oily skin
hiding under the leaf litter in the deep end. He felt particularly edgy. Behind him, Vic glanced around, only mildly
curious about his surroundings, keeping his hand in his gun
pocket.

Their luck held. The back entrance was unlocked. With
Tony as their guide, they passed the solarium, the dining
room, the ballroom—all were empty. Tony was glad he'd had
an earlier walk-through, since the place seemed much darker
than he remembered it, though there had been about the same
amount of moonlight outside. They used only Tony's flashlight, keeping the second one as backup. Somehow the flashlight beam made the darkness it bored through more intense.
He wondered how he and Lili had managed to wander about
without even a candle to light their way.

When the flashlight beam hit a window, the boards outside
looked like sections of dark, segmented skin. Tony had a
curious mental picture of the hotel, coiled around and around
with the body of a huge, dark-scaled snake that would at any
moment begin to crush the building—and the two of them in
it—like a giant boa constrictor.

They went into the kitchen. The candle holders, stubbled
over with wax, were still sitting on the little table near the
boarded-over window. The counter nearby was empty. On
impulse, Tony pulled open the topmost drawer and found
Lili's stash of tea and several Sterno tins.

The building felt emptier than it had the night he and Lili
had sat drinking her weird tea. He was beginning to wonder if
she had gone out somewhere. More likely she was sleeping
upstairs.

"They knew how to live," Vic said, glancing apprecia-
tively at the dusty chandelier overhead, momentarily caught

in the flashlight beam as they recrossed the dining room to the lobby. In the vast, shadowy waiting area, he leaned back against the long abandoned registration desk and surveyed the place. Sliding doors at the east end opened onto an auditorium, and a pair of matching doors at the west end gave way to a second dining room, the sealed front entrance, and the sweep of staircase. "There was a place like this in Saigon," Vic said finally. "It was firebombed because so many GIs hung out there."

The thick gloom in the lobby area seemed to have grown worse; Tony wondered if the moon outside had disappeared behind a cloud. Very little light filtered through the slats over the generous windows.

"Basement next, I think," said Vic. "If they're running true to form, they've got him underground."

"Let me see if Lili's around first, okay?" Without waiting for his uncle's response, Tony went to the foot of the stairs and called, "Lili?" When there was no answer, he called more loudly, "*Lili!*"

Silence.

He called several more times, to no avail. He was pretty sure she was gone, at least for the time being. Maybe that was why the outside gate was unlocked. She could be running an errand—say, getting food, he told himself. But he was afraid she had gone as suddenly as she had turned up.

Maybe something frightened her away, he thought. In the dark of the deserted lobby he found the idea easy to accept. And unnerving. He took a step closer to Vic, glad for the man's company. One last shouted *"Lili!"* then he said to Vic, "Let's finish looking and get out. This place is beginning to give me the creeps."

"Don't worry, bro. You've got someone who's taken the course to keep an eye on things." To demonstrate, Vic pulled the .357 out of his pocket, released the safety, and held it at the ready as he motioned with his free hand for Tony to follow. Not about to be left alone in the shadows at the foot of the stairs, the boy followed.

Behind the registration desk, Vic pulled open a door that gave onto a service hall. A door labeled BASEMENT was partially ajar at the end of the hall. Unhesitatingly Vic headed toward the door as Tony, a few paces behind, lit the way for them both.

The stairs made three right-angle turns before leading to an open door at the foot of the stairwell. Beyond the door, they found a short passageway ending in a blank stretch of cement wall on their right; on their left it ran a short distance, forming a *T* with a wider corridor at its terminus.

The blackness around them was absolute; the light from the single flashlight seemed compressed by the weight of darkness. There was a pervasive smell of earth and damp; the chill of the place quickly seeped through Tony's coat and shirt and his heavy woolen socks.

Even Vic seemed intimidated. He tightened his grip on the revolver.

"Easy," Tony said. "Don't start shooting up the place the first time you hear a . . . mouse." The naked-tailed, red-eyed image that came to Tony's mind was hardly a field mouse, but he was superstitious enough not to want to voice his real fear aloud. He remembered his mother telling him, when he was a kid, that goblins hid just out of sight, spying, ready to send whatever you least wanted your way, if you made the mistake of naming fears aloud. He could almost envision one squatting around the corner, giggling to itself, holding a rat at ready to send in Tony's direction. *Say the secret word and win a rat*, he thought, kidding himself, trying to exorcise his unease with humor. But he felt uncomfortably like he was whistling in a graveyard.

Vic was rattling the closed doors that lined the short stretch of corridor—two on the wall with the stairwell entrance, four on the wall facing.

Only one opened, revealing a shallow closet filled with mildewed samples of what must have once been expensive luggage. Vic nudged one valise on a stack, and it fell to the ground, the corroded clasp bursting when it hit the floor. "Empty," he said, giving it a disgusted kick.

"These must all be closets," said Tony. "Let's not waste time."

But Vic insisted on checking out each door. When none of the others would open, he shrugged and walked on to the main corridor. They decided to head right.

They walked along side by side, Tony sweeping the light left to right and back, Vic keeping the gun aimed into the darkness ahead. The poured concrete walls wept slime and fungus. They discovered a stack of two-by-fours on one side, and aqua tiles, apparently for the swimming pool, stacked along the opposite wall. Shattered light fixtures appeared at regular intervals overhead; standing water gathered in puddles along the uneven flooring.

Smaller corridors and chambers opened off the main passage at regular intervals. Exploring these, they found a laundry room with rows of gray cement tubs; food-storage lockers with a few rusting tins, the labels long since rotted off, some broken crates and Mason jars filled with time-blackened, unguessable contents. A large room filled with broken furniture contained chairs with splintered legs, a smashed table, and a dresser surmounted with a circular metal frame that must have once held a round mirror.

One door they passed on the left was sealed fast. A frozen cascade of black fungus half hid the red-painted letters EMP.

"Empty," Vic read. "Wonder why they kept this vacant?" On impulse, he lifted his right leg and slammed his boot heel against the thick door. It held. All he got for his efforts was a smear of black gunk. Cursing, he scraped his boot off on a relatively dry patch of floor.

Suddenly he slapped at his neck. A minute later he held out the palm of his hand to show Tony. "Mosquito," he said with satisfaction. "Got the mother."

*Shouldn't be mosquitoes this time of year,* thought Tony. But now he could hear them buzzing near his own ear. And the air seemed warm, almost humid. He wiped his forehead.

"Fucking monsoon weather," said Vic.

Tony went a little farther down the corridor, stopping at a massive, metal-sheathed fire door that blocked any further movement.

"Don't take all the light away," Vic yelled.

"Use your own flashlight for a minute," Tony said. He had found the door could be pushed inward. "I want to see what's in here."

He glanced back and saw Vic had switched his flashlight on and was using it to check out the damage to his boot. Tony entered the chamber beyond and discovered it was a boiler room. The center of the huge area was dominated by an ancient furnace, its steam mains branching in all directions like the tentacles of some monster from the ocean floor. It was caked with dirt and dust, giving it a furry look.

As everywhere else in the cellars, the floor was damp, and

the air musty. But there was a different smell: the mingled
odors of charred wood and burned rubber. It reminded Tony
of the smell that had lingered long after the fire was extinguished in a small, fire-gutted grocery store. Running his
flashlight across the roof of the boiler room, he saw that it
was blackened, as though fire had geysered up from the far
side of the room, beyond the furnace itself, and poured across
the ceiling.

Moving closer, he saw that much of the boiler itself, as
well as its exhaust duct and chimney, was also blackened. A
pressure gauge and thermometer had been shattered by a blast
of heat. In the far wall, double metal-sheathed doors were
twisted to either side, as though the force of an explosion had
ripped them open and nearly torn them from their hinges.
What was left of the doors was scorched; the metal sheathing
was blistered and blackened—it looked like it had melted.
The surrounding walls, the floor, and the ceiling were
soot-black.

The fire that had wrecked the hotel must have started
inside. Whatever Jozsef Zagonyi had done—a bomb or a fuse
set to gasoline canisters or whatever—must have been set off
beyond those doors.

Something kept him from going too close to the burst
doors. Standing under a network of steam mains, Tony shone
the flashlight into the darkness beyond.

And the dark ate the beam—swallowed it completely. He
had a sudden impression of vast distances just beyond the
ruined entranceway.

Something moved in the darkness, shifting slightly, like the
flank of a hibernating creature stirring in its wintry sleep.

*You're imagining it*, logic told him. *You stare long enough
at any one spot and your eyes are going to get tired. They
adjust. There's nothing there.*

All the same, he decided, the whole room was getting to
him. An overpowering smell assaulted his senses under the
mustiness and the tang of burning—a rotten door. Like something had been dead a long time. A rat, maybe.

The stench was growing stronger, and it was coming from
the black gap in the wall.

Tony backed away; he was afraid to turn his back on the
dark within the darkness. Vaguely he wondered why Vic

hadn't followed him into the boiler room, but at this point, all that mattered was getting *out*.

The stink was thick in the air now. He put his free hand across his mouth and nose while he kept the flashlight aimed beyond the furnace, as if it were Vic's .357 he was holding.

Only when he reached the first fire door did he dare turn around. "Shit!" he said, pushing the door shut behind him. "Vic, where the—"

The corridor was dark outside. "Hey, Vic! Did your flashlight go out?" Tony called, shining his light as far down the raw concrete passage as he could.

No answer. No sign of Vic.

"Oh, Jee-sus!" he whispered to himself. For a moment he felt smaller and more terrified than he had ever felt in his life. The fear paralyzed him for a moment. He recognized it as the kind of fear a climber can get when he becomes afraid of climbing any higher but is just as afraid of climbing down, because of the drop below him. Facing the darkness of the corridor ahead alone was as unthinkable as reentering the room he had just fled. But standing still, waiting until the flashlight batteries gave out and trapped him utterly in the dark, was the most frightening thing of all.

He wiped his face free of sweat and called again, "Vic?"

No answer. He assumed his uncle had gone off to explore another part of the cellar.

He *hoped* that was all.

The dark was disconcerting enough, he thought, without filling it full of maniacs and monsters. *Get your ass in locomotion, boy,* he ordered himself.

Slowly, alert for any sound, he advanced along the passageway. Once he nearly bolted, thinking he heard the scrape of the fire door opening behind him. But he shot the flashlight beam back and found it as firmly shut as he had left it.

His flashlight beam glanced off the puddles of brackish water. "Vic!" he called in a hoarse whisper.

The door marked EMPTY was wide open. Shining his light in, he saw a rubbish-littered stretch of damp concrete flooring. Vic must have forced the door open while Tony was in the boiler room. That surprised him when he remembered how it had resisted Vic's first kick.

From where he stood, one hand resting against the doorjamb, he couldn't gauge how deep the room was. The beam of light didn't reach all the way across the space. He had the impression that it might be as big as the boiler room. He wondered what it could have been used for, then the flashlight caught the corner of a wooden wine rack. So this was the Hotel Bethel's wine cellar.

The light glinted off metal. Beside the wine rack, lying half sunk in muck, was Vic's .357.

Vic went in there, Tony thought frantically, but something happened to him. The most frightening thing of all was that he hadn't heard any shots, suggesting that whatever had happened to the man had happened so fast, he hadn't had a chance to get off a single round.

Tony stood stock-still, listening for any sound of movement. *Anything.*

Darkness and silence. *Where is Vic?* he wondered; then, *Am I next?*

*First things first,* he cautioned himself. He made a lunge for the revolver. *It may not have helped Vic,* he reasoned, *but it's going to help me feel a lot better.* He scooped it out of the oily gunk.

Behind him, the door to the corridor slammed shut.

Startled, he swung around and fired. The roar of the gun in the enclosed space nearly deafened him. Faintly, as from far away, he heard the *chunk!* as the slug embedded itself in the heavy wooden door.

Shaking, his ears ringing, he went to the door and tugged on the corroded handle. It was locked tight.

For a moment he went crazy, imagining what it would be like to be trapped in the hotel ruins while he slowly suffocated. Or starved to death. Or went totally insane. No one knew they were here at the Hotel Bethel. People would think he'd dropped off the face of the earth. The batteries would go quickly, then he'd be alone in the dark until he died.

Or maybe *not alone.*

*Wait! Now wait!* he commanded himself. He still didn't know what had happened to Vic. *Maybe the guy just spaced out for a while . . . dropped the gun and wandered away. He could come back looking for me.*

Another thought struck him. *Lili. If she hasn't left for good.*

*But who—or* what—*shut the door? The person is out there*

*now. He could hurt Lili. If it's that psycho who tried to off
me, he could kill her. Or Vic.*

He gave another tug on the door handle.

Zip.

For now, he decided, his best—his *only*—course of action
was to check out his prison. There might be another door, a
window, a ventilation grate he could pry off. He started
walking the periphery of the wine cellar, finding nothing but
some built-in wine racks lining the wall.

Then, almost to the back wall, he discovered a trapdoor in
the floor. It was metal, surrounded by raised wooden framing, with a ring in the center. Since it obviously led down,
rather than up or out, it wasn't terribly promising. Still, he
considered, it could be part of some extra storage or plumbing
system, with other exits. *Got nothing to lose*, he decided.

He pulled back on the ring, and the solid square of metal
came up with surprising ease.

He flashed his light into the space below and yelled.

A human form writhed on the floor. His light picked out a
ghastly expanse of white where a face should be.

He scrambled back from the horrible sight, ready to slam
the trapdoor back into place, when he heard a muffled, *"Toey
. . . Toey."*

"Vic?" he cried. His hand still shaking, he peered into the
space again. Now the flashlight beam revealed Vic's fatigue
jacket, slathered with the oily black mud. His hands were tied
behind him; his feet were lashed together. His flashlight lay
in the muck near his hip.

Enough light from the flashlight must have seeped through
the sack over Vic's head to let him know help was near. He
began thrashing around like a freshly caught fish.

"Stop it, Vic!" Tony shouted. "You'll hurt yourself." But
he could all too vividly imagine the man's frantic horror at
finding himself trussed up like a pig, blindfolded, and left to
rot under the floors of a godforsaken ruin.

Before he lowered himself the five feet to the packed-earth
floor below, Tony did a quick check of the room to be sure
no one was hiding, waiting to slam down the trapdoor on
him. As an extra precaution, he jammed part of a wine rack
between the upraised trapdoor and the rim of the opening. It
would prevent a surprise imprisonment; and, Tony guessed,

give him a chance to get off one or two shots to scare off any ambusher.

The revolver clenched tightly in his fist, he dropped down beside Vic. The first thing he did was remove the white sack that covered the man's whole head.

Vic had been gagged underneath the covering. Tony had to set the gun aside momentarily while he worked loose the thin strip of dirty gray material that had been wound several times through Vic's mouth, before being clumsily tied off at the back. When it was removed, Vic said, "Tony—shit! *Tony!* Oh, man, it's 'Nam again. It's fuckin' Mosquito Ridge. *And she's here, Tony!* I heard her laughing, in the dark, near me."

"A woman, Vic? Did you see who did this to you?"

The man rolled his head side to side. "No . . . too fast. But I *heard* her. I *know* who it was. It's 'Nam all over." He kept on babbling while Tony untied his wrists and ankles. Tony tried unsuccessfully to shut him up so he could listen for any sounds of footsteps sneaking up on them, but Vic was too strung out from the replay of his Vietnam ordeal. He just kept rattling on: "She's got Pat. She told me"—here his voice dropped to a frightened whisper—"the bitch told me she'd rip out his liver and make me eat it if I didn't—didn't—"

"Didn't what, Vic?" asked Tony, chafing the man's wrists and ankles to get the circulation going.

"Don't remember," Vic said. He brushed his hands in front of his face. His sweat-outlined face caught the flashlight's glow. His eyes had a sudden, faraway look. "Pat?" he asked suddenly. "Did you really come? Or is this some kind of a trick?"

"It's *Tony.* And we're going to be fine. Let me help you to your feet."

Vic nearly stumbled when he put his weight on his feet, to which the circulation had not yet fully returned. He grabbed the sides of the trap for support. Clumsily he began to pull himself out; Tony locked his fingers and gave him a boost the rest of the way. When Vic was sitting on the rim, his feet still dangling into the opening, he reached down for Tony. But his nephew shook his head. "I've got to see if there's another way out through here; the door is locked up there."

"No, man, I couldn't go back down there. Ever." Vic

began to shake like someone with palsy. "If you find a way out, you come back for me."

"Let's deal with that when we have to," said Tony, handing up the other flashlight. "See if this works."

It did. After a moment he handed up the revolver. "You're probably in more danger up there than I am down here," he said with no real certainty. "And I want to be damn sure that trapdoor is open when I finish looking around down here."

"You got it," said Vic, flashing a mock salute.

Stooped over to avoid hitting his head on the floor joists and girders above, Tony began picking his way among thick wooden posts set on concrete footings. Again and again he raked the supports overhead with his light, but he could find no sign of another exit.

Suddenly he stopped on the edge of a depression into which he had almost stumbled. It lay like a mortar crater in the middle of the endless forest of floor posts. Several concrete post footings had been undercut by the force of the blast that had caused the hole. They were within inches of having no ground support at all.

A curve of gray-green metal was embedded in the side of the pit. Curious, Tony began working it free.

It was an Army helmet. He'd seen pictures of Vic wearing the same kind during his hitch in Vietnam. After a moment's resistance it came free, carrying a skull, still held in place with a chin strap, with it.

Tony gave a screech and dropped the thing. It rolled to the bottom of the crater. He stood up suddenly. From the same section of wet earth, hidden underneath the helmet, something white and sluglike was poking up from the dirt.

Maggots, thought Tony, thoroughly grossed out.

He backed away from the crater's rim, disgusted and confused by the whole scene. What he was seeing was a leftover chunk of wartime horror; he couldn't imagine what it was doing under the sub-subflooring of the Hotel Bethel. It was like one of Vic's nightmares brought to life.

*One of Vic's nightmares . . .*

He flashed his light on the maggots.

They had been joined by two others.

But they weren't maggots.

*Skeletal fingers. Something very dead. But something that*

*didn't want to stay buried, was working its way out of the
earth.*

Any thought of investigating the packed-earth-and-floor-
post wilderness vanished in an instant. Tony had only one
thought. *Get the fuck out!* It didn't matter that it made no sense
when a mud-clotted, fleshless fist was suddenly thrust into the
air, the fingers clutching spasmodically at the air.

He ran as quickly as he could, dodging posts, ducking
girders. Afraid of losing his bearings, he began to shout,
"Vic! Turn on your flashlight! Let me see it!"

Behind him he thought he heard a wet, sucking sound as a
large object was extracted from the moist earth. *Maybe he
won't come after me until he finds his head,* he thought
giddily. Then he screamed, "Vic! Where's the fucking light?"

From far away to his right he heard Vic's answering call.
He was in danger of losing himself. There were no points of
reference, he now realized, for orienting himself. He had
gone off without blazing a trail behind him, and he was
paying the consequences of his carelessness.

When he heard Vic shout a second time, Tony shut off his
flashlight for a minute. To his relief he saw the glow of Vic's
flashlight closer than he dared hope. In the dark, several
small living things scuttled away from him. *Maybe the skull is
rolling along by itself, like in that story. . . .*

Turning on his own flashlight again, he made for the spot.
Whatever had been near his right foot a moment before had
vanished. He was panting too hard to hear any sounds of
pursuit—and he hoped to God there were none to hear.

Then he was under the open trapdoor, dancing up and
down in his fear, shouting for Vic to help him.

Vic lay full-length above him. He reached down, and with
surprising strength, he hauled Tony up. Each second that
passed, the boy expected to feel his ankles encircled by bony
fingers. But Vic pulled him up, free and clear.

The minute he felt the floor of the wine cellar beneath him,
Tony half crawled, half rolled to the edge of the trapdoor. He
knocked the broken wine rack out of the way and slammed
the door into place.

A moment later Vic and Tony heard a loud *thank!* on the
underside of the metal plate. The noise was repeated at
regular intervals.

"What the hell is that—?"

"Don't talk, Vic. Help me bury this door," said Tony, dragging a freestanding wine rack across the floor. When it was close enough, he tipped it over, watching with a small sense of relief as the heavy wooden frame fell across the trapdoor. Together he and Vic hauled several more frames over and tumbled them onto a pile, until the door was completely hidden from view.

"You saw her, didn't you?" asked Vic when they took a breather from their labors.

"I saw something—but I don't think it was a *her*. What I saw . . . Shit! It didn't make any sense at all. Not a bit!"

"She can do that," said Vic. "She can take your worst nightmares and drop you into the middle of them. Whether you're asleep *or* awake."

"There's got to be an answer," said Tony. *Here come the Hardy Boys,* he thought, mocking himself. *They'll find out there isn't really a ghost—that it's just someone playing a trick. I used to feel cheated when I found out the haunting wasn't real; now I'm praying it ain't so!*

"Let's try the door again," said Vic. "Maybe it was just stuck when you tried it before."

Tony shrugged. Using a single flashlight to conserve batteries, they found their way back to the door. It was still closed tightly. But when Vic put his hand on the knob, the door suddenly swung into the chamber.

Lili, holding a candle in an old-fashioned pewter holder, stood framed in the doorway.

# Thirteen

"LILI!" TONY CRIED. "Jesus, are we glad to see *you!*"

She was wearing a dress similar in style to the dresses Tony had seen in pictures of his mother when she was a young girl. It was made from some soft, filmy, pink material, and it looked several sizes too large for her. The slippers on her feet were stained with black mud. The Spanish-looking shawl was thrown over Lili's shoulders and held in place with an old-fashioned brooch of ivory, sculpted in the shape of the head of some Greek goddess.

"You know her?" asked Vic suspiciously. Tony saw that he had slipped his hand into the jacket pocket where he had stowed the .357 a few minutes earlier.

Tony put a gently restraining hand on Vic's arm. "Very well. We're . . . good friends."

Vic shrugged and let his empty hands dangle at his sides.

"Look," Tony said to Lili, "could we get out of here *real fast?*" He thought he could still hear the *thunk! thunk!* from far back across the wine cellar.

"Of course," she said. She turned to walk down the corridor, but Tony paused to draw the door shut. An ounce of prevention . . . he told himself. Aloud, he asked Lili, "Did you see a key? You must have, since you let us out. I'm sure someone locked the door on us."

"There's no one here," she said in a vague way. "But

there *is* a key." She fumbled with the pocket of her dress. To Tony she seemed to move with the deliberateness of someone who has had too much to drink, or maybe wasn't fully awake. "It was in the door," she said. "I suppose I should have left it there."

"It doesn't matter," said Tony, turning the key in the lock. He breathed a sigh as he heard the heavy bolt slide into place. He removed the key, thought a minute, then dropped it into his hip pocket. "But didn't you see anyone?" he asked. "Someone trapped us in there not long ago."

"There's no one here but me," she said, repeating what she had said earlier. She led the way back to the stairwell. The wavering light from her candle and the bobbing and darting flashlight beam made their shadows flicker and dance along the walls like a demented escort.

*Could I have imagined everything back there?* Tony asked himself hopefully. *That stink in the air in the boiler room could have been spilled chemicals. Maybe the fungus down here gives people visions.* With each step he found another way of discounting the nightmare under the cellar floor.

But who had tied up Vic and locked them both downstairs? *Lili?* But, looking at the frail, dark-haired girl, drifting along like some soft, pink ghost in the candlelight, he couldn't imagine her overpowering Vic, tying him up, and lowering him into the pit—all inside the short time that Tony was investigating the boiler room.

No, the more he thought about it, the more unlikely it seemed. Which left only the possibility of some midnight prowler—someone very likely hidden in some corner of the hotel at that very minute—or . . .

*Or what?* Unless someone wanted to go off in nonsensical (to his way of thinking) directions and talk crackpot theories of vampires and demons like Jozsef Zagonyi, there was only the prowler to consider. Dangerous, yes. Unbalanced, in all likelihood. But a flesh-and-blood man. Not a monster from some wacked-out Creature Feature.

As they started up the stairs leading back to the main floor, Tony said to Vic, "Maybe you should keep the revolver handy. Just in case."

"I read you loud and clear," said Vic, pulling the gun out of his pocket. "She's not going to get the drop on me a second time."

Tony didn't have the energy to argue the sex of the midnight prowler with his uncle. If things went according to his plan, none of them would stick around long enough to settle the matter one way or the other.

They reached the lobby without incident. There, Lili went and sat on the third step of the main staircase, setting her candle on the step above her. Tony walked over and stood beside her.

Vic, impatient to carry the search to the guest rooms and servants' quarters upstairs, had reluctantly agreed to let Tony first have a few words with Lili. Bored, he wandered around the hotel lobby, using the beam of his flashlight to pick out the exquisite plaster rosettes and moldings of the lobby's high ceiling, the beautifully decorated window casings, and the burnished walnut paneling. Everywhere the light would go, the muzzle of the .357 would follow. Vic wasn't about to let his time-killing and Tony's preoccupation with Lili set them up for a surprise attack.

Tony, looking down at Lili, said, "Thanks for rescuing us. But how did you know we were in there?"

She shrugged and gave him a vague smile. "I suppose I heard you calling for help."

"We didn't do much of that—mostly a lot of yelling to each other."

"Well"—she smiled brightly—"*that* must have been what I heard. Anyway, what does it matter? You're safe now."

"I don't think any of us are safe, Lili," Tony whispered urgently. "Whoever nailed Vic and me is still around. We've got to get out of this place."

"Not before we find Pat," Vic interjected. Tony hadn't realized his uncle had wandered close to the staircase.

"Vic, Pat's not here. But someone who's pretty dangerous *is* hiding out here. I can *feel* it. We're pushing our luck every minute that we stay here." To the girl he said, "Tell him there's no one here."

She looked down, adjusting her brooch. "Of course there's no one here. Not your friend. Not your prowler, either." When she was satisfied with the way the pin looked, she smiled brightly at Tony. "I couldn't possibly leave."

"Why not?"

"Because—well, I *belong* here," she said. She looked very fragile in the candlelight; what little color her pale skin picked up came from the golden glow of the candle's flame. Tony felt she might vanish when the flame was extinguished. Unable to help himself, he suddenly leaned forward and gently touched the skin of her left cheek with one finger. He traced the line of her cheekbone down to the corner of her mouth.

"That tickles," she said with a small laugh, pulling her head away, just out of reach.

She seemed as childlike as Leslie in many ways, yet she aroused in him a sexual hunger that his aborted couplings with an enthusiastic, if not very imaginative, Janet Dillon never had hinted at. Tonight there was a scent of roses about her, as if she were wearing some expensive perfume.

"Pat could be in one of those rooms upstairs," said Vic, "and no one would know it. You can't tell me that *she*"—he jerked a thumb at Lili—"knows everything that's going on in every corner of this wreck."

"I know enough to know you'd be wasting your time looking through the rooms upstairs. Go ahead, if you feel you have to. But you won't find your friend in any room in this place."

"Vic, there's a loony tune running around this place. Use some common sense," Tony pleaded. "You almost bought it once. You may not be so lucky a second time."

"I've got to risk it," said Vic, starting for the steps. Tony made a grab for him, but Vic shoved him out of the way. "If you won't help me, I'll do it alone." His boots, slamming up the polished mahogany staircase, ricocheted in the silence around them.

Tony started after him, then stopped indecisively. Vic stood for a moment at the head of the stairs, staring to the right and left, before heading down the west wing. He disappeared into the shadows, which seemed to have grown denser.

"I shouldn't have let him go," said Tony miserably. His hand, resting on the ornate carved cap of the wooden newel post at the base of the stair railing, was sweat-slick. His whole body was trembling. He couldn't bring himself to set foot on the staircase. *What's happening to me?* he wondered. *I'm turning into Jell-O.*

"There's nothing you can do," said Lili simply, sadly. "I thought there was, once; but I don't think so anymore."

Feeling wretched, he turned to her. "I swear, I don't know

what's wrong! I'm not—I can't—" He fumbled for words, feeling his mind turning to mush. "I want to be strong for you," he said, but the truth was that he felt ready to curl into a ball at her feet, sucking his thumb like a child and making the things that scared him so—things he could feel but not give a name to—go away.

"You *are* strong, Tony. You're stronger than you dream," she said, staring toward the place where faint threads of gray light outlined the hotel entrance and hinted at the shape of a window. "But don't you see? *She's* stronger. And it's the hour of the wolf."

"What do you mean, Lili?" he asked, afraid that she was going to run away from him into some shadowy fantasy world of her own, where he could never reach her again. "Talk sense."

She spoke to the darkness rather than to him. "My mother used to tell me the hour of the wolf was the time between midnight and dawn, when you sleep the deepest, when your nightmares become most real, when ghosts and goblins have their greatest power for hurting us. Oh, Tony," she said, turning to him suddenly, her voice shrinking to a whisper, "that time is *right now*. And the nightmares—they're *real* now. And we're not asleep, Tony, *we're not asleep*." He could feel her fear break over him like an icy wave.

"It's this building," he said, groping for something to say that would explain their fears away. "There's something in the air—"

"Oh, Tony, you can't believe that!" she cried, interrupting him. "*She* isn't something you can wish away. Or pretend doesn't exist. *She's real!*"

"You're not making sense." Tony refused to buy into her fantasy trip. "You're sounding as—well, *like Vic*." His disappointment was turning into anger, and the anger freed him to think clearly. "I'm going up to get Vic. Then we're leaving. I want you to come with me. But if you won't, then—then—that's up to you!"

"I can't, Tony" was all Lili said. There were tears of hopelessness in her eyes. "I don't think Vic can any longer. But you might still be able to, if you go this minute." For a moment she seemed to be listening to distant sounds only she could hear; then she said tonelessly, "Even if you run away now, I don't think it will matter much."

"I'm not going to run away yet. There's Vic—and there's *you*. We're walking out of here together."

Her shoulders slumped; her head drooped. She sat, not making a sound, like a marionette whose wires had suddenly been severed. Tony knelt beside her and took her by the shoulders, shaking her gently. "Lili! What's the matter? Are you sick?"

"She's just . . . resting," said a man's voice from the darkness behind him.

Spinning around, Tony shot his flashlight beam in the direction of the sound. In an instant it had illuminated the form of a dark-haired, husky man in a gray trench coat. In the light his eyes glittered; he was grinning mirthlessly. Tony recognized him at once as the man who had attacked him several nights before. The only thing missing was his hat.

"You don't sound very afraid," the guy said in a throaty whisper. "And you *should* be frightened. There's so very much to be frightened of, if you only know where to look."

Tony backed up a step, nearer Lili. The girl sat like a broken doll. She was humming tunelessly to herself like a child, the way Leslie did when she was engrossed in a project of some sort.

"Lili!" the man barked.

The girl raised her head obediently, but her eyes still had that faraway look.

"Lili! Tell Tony why he should be afraid," the man ordered.

"Please—I—*no*," she begged. She shook her head, but it was an empty gesture, Tony realized; there was no real resistance in her.

"Leave her alone," he said, deliberately shining the light into the man's face.

He didn't move. "It's for your own good, sport. You need to have all the facts in the case." Then he shouted, "Lili! Tell Tony about Mickey."

But all she did was to start twisting her hands around each other in her lap and moan.

"I don't know what you're doing to her, but *stop it*."

The man ignored him. "Mickey, Lili! Tell us about Mickey."

This time his voice cut through her growing distress. Her hands were still. Her voice was a monotone as she said, "Mickey was five when we came to the hotel all those years ago. I didn't want to go. Neither did Mickey. But Mama and Daddy said, 'We have to go there.' When I asked them why, Daddy said, 'We have to meet someone.' 'Who?' I wanted to know. 'Don't ask so many questions,' Mama told me.''

She paused a moment, as if gathering together the threads of a long forgotten story. When she spoke again, there was some animation in her voice, as though she had discovered an unexpectedly pleasant memory among the distressing ones.

"I had seen the hotel from outside lots of times when we'd drive past it in Daddy's Studebaker.'' Here she gave an affectionate laugh. "Oh, he was so proud of that car, even though he got it secondhand and it didn't run very well. To him it looked every bit as grand as the brand-spanking-new Hudson he parked alongside that Sunday.

"The hotel was bustling that afternoon. Bellhops in their funny little monkey suits with shiny buttons were running everywhere, hurrying to answer the bells that kept ringing at the desk, carrying luggage and packages up and down stairs. I wanted to look in the gift-shop windows, and Mickey wanted a comic book from the newsstand. But Mama took his hand, and Daddy took her arm, and he walked us upstairs. We had dressed in our very best Sunday clothes,'' she said with a sad little sigh, "but even so, I think we must have looked like someone's poor cousins. I remember some people staring at us as we went up the stairs—these stairs,'' she added, patting the dusty step beside her. "I knew we didn't belong here.''

This time she paused for such a long time that the man said warningly, *"Lili.''*

Her voice had turned lifeless again. "When we got to the second floor, we walked down a hall. Then we walked farther, until we found another hallway. After a while I was so turned around, I didn't know what direction I was walking in. I knew the hotel was big, but it still didn't seem possible it could have *so many* halls and rooms in it.

"We just kept walking. When Mickey got tired, Daddy carried him. When I complained to Mama, she just told me to hush, that I was going to meet someone very important.

"So I went along. I wondered how Daddy was so sure of where he was going, because the halls kept twisting and turning until I felt I was going in circles. I tried looking at the metal numbers on the doors of the rooms we were passing, but they didn't make any sense—they were all jumbled up, or missing, and some didn't even look like real numbers.

"When we first walked in, there were windows at the ends of the hallways, so you could see the sunshine outside. But after we'd been walking a long time, there were no windows at all. I noticed that the halls began getting shorter and shorter after each turn. When I thought about it, I imagined all the hallways looped in, like an old watch spring. It seemed like we were gradually working our way deeper and deeper into the middle of the hotel.

"Then we turned the last corner and found the shortest hallway of all. At the end was a single, open door. Daddy told us to walk right in, though I thought we should knock first."

Though Lili's voice was emotionless, Tony saw out of the corner of his eye that her fingers were anxiously twisting the material of her dress. He wanted to reach down and comfort her, but he didn't dare take his eyes off the man, who hadn't moved a muscle during Lili's recitation.

"It was very dark inside," the girl continued. "The light from outside didn't come through the open door. If there were any windows or skylights, they were covered in layers of silky black stuff—almost like black spiderwebs.

"There was a lady in the room; she was wearing a robe of the same black, gauzy stuff. I really couldn't see her very well, but I remember saying to her, 'I *know* you. You've come into my dreams lots of times, haven't you?'

"She didn't say anything. She just nodded. No one else said anything, either. Mickey was making those soft little noises he always made when he was just falling asleep or waking up. When I looked at Mama and Daddy, their eyes were closed. I thought, 'Why, they're so tired from all the walking, they've fallen asleep standing up.' I thought that was very rude of them. But then I realized I was beginning to fall asleep, myself. 'Oh,' I told myself, 'we really *don't* belong here if we haven't got the good manners to stay awake when meeting—' But I hadn't any idea who the woman was, even though I had dreamed about her. I felt more and more like Alice in Wonderland, floating down the rabbit hole. But I knew I was going to be asleep long before I reached the bottom."

She clasped her hands together suddenly, almost as if she

were going to pray. A strangulated groan escaped her, and she swallowed several times before she went on. "Just before I—I fell asleep, I saw the woman come forward. She buried her face first in my father's neck, and then in my mother's. Then she held out her arms and—and my father—he—he was carrying, Mickey, you see—and he just—gave him over to her. And she—she—she looked down at him—like my mother did when—when he'd b-been christened. And then she—the woman—just smiled—and bent down—and bit a bloody chunk out of his neck and—chewed—and someone—it must have been Mickey—could it have been me?—began screaming—but then I got to the bottom of the rabbit hole and the room and everyone in it was gone—"

She stopped suddenly. She stared wildly about her for a minute, then collapsed onto the stairs, unconscious.

*"Bastard!"* yelled Tony, lunging for the man, swinging his flashlight. The man twisted to defend himself, but the head of the flashlight crashed into his upper right arm, causing him to bellow in pain, just before Tony hit him in the gut, sending them both sprawling across the grimy floor. The impact shattered the glass in the flashlight, plunging them into near complete darkness, except for the glow of Lili's candle, which was beginning to gutter out. The wildly gyrating shadows it cast added to the confusion as Tony and the man rolled across the floor. Furious, the man wrenched the flashlight tube out of Tony's hand, flinging it into the shadows. Then he was going for the boy's throat.

Tony knew that this time one of them wasn't going to come out of it alive. He fought with the fury of a cornered animal against the greater bulk and strength of his opponent. As they pummeled each other and rolled across the floor, he heard glass fragments from the broken flashlight crunching under them. The two of them grunted and gasped as they alternately tried to grab each other's throat or break a sudden stranglehold. Tony kicked wildly, feeling small satisfaction as one or two kicks connected, forcing gasps from the man. He tried to knee his opponent in the crotch, but the guy was alert to that and kept Tony from positioning himself to deliver the painful thrust.

Unless something happened to break their momentary stalemate, Tony knew, the other's greater strength was going to wear him down sooner or later. He needed a weapon to equalize things. But the gun had disappeared upstairs with Vic—*Jeez! Why doesn't he come back? Is he deaf?* The flashlight casing vanished into the shadows near the hotel entrance.

Tony broke free for a minute and began scrambling for the stairs, where Lili still lay slumped in the dancing candlelight. He was scrambling on his hands and knees, trying to get to his feet, when the man floored him by grabbing his ankle. Within seconds Tony felt himself yanked back and hauled to his knees in a deadly bear hug. Arms like a vice encircled his ribs and began squeezing the air out of his lungs.

Frantic, he jabbed back into the man's own rib cage, hearing a roar of pain at the instant that the death hold loosened. Tony jammed his elbows back again and was sure he felt a snap. A third thrust and a sudden upward slam with his fists broke him free. He carried the energy forward in one continuous motion, heading for the stairs.

The guy was after him an instant later, but lumbering with one arm held tightly across his rib cage. He was wheezing loud enough for Tony to hear as he dashed up the steps. The guy, ignoring Lili, came raging up after him, but Tony thought he had enough lead, given the guy's injury, to stay out of reach, until he found Vic or one of the other stairways he knew existed in the Bethel.

But when he was almost to the landing at the top, and his pursuer had only climbed a few stairs, a flashlight beam suddenly speared down from the gallery. The man in the gray coat threw up an arm to block the light. "Back off!" Vic shouted from the shadows somewhere above Tony. "Hold it right there."

The guy was having none of that. With a roar he charged up two more steps before Vic fired. The first shot went wild, but the second tore into the man's left side, spinning him around so that he slammed into the balustrade. The impact of his weight sent him crashing through the elegant wooden railing, and he fell heavily to the floor below.

Tony grabbed Vic and hugged him for a moment, sobbing for breath. "I have nev-never been so *glad* to see anyone in my life."

"Easy, bro," said Vic, patting the boy's shoulder reassuringly. "Everything's fine. Just fine."

"That guy—"

Vic released him long enough to lean past the broken

railing, shining his flashlight into the blackness below. After a moment he returned and put his arm across Tony's shoulders again. "He's dead," said Vic. "I saw enough of that in 'Nam to call it when I see it. But the sucker earned it."

Listening to his uncle, Tony *wanted* to believe everything was fine. It all had the shape of a neat, things-come-right-at-the-end wrap-up. *If only I* could *believe it*, he thought.

*We just gather up Lili and ride off into the sunset—or sunrise—I guess* was what Vic's nick-of-time appearance seemed to suggest. Only there were far too many loose ends and missing pieces to tie life up into that particular rose-colored bow as far as Tony was concerned.

He was too tired to deal with it all. He gently shrugged free of Vic's supporting arm. "I'm okay," he said. *"Really."* He hurried down the stairs to where Lili lay sprawled. Kneeling beside the girl, he massaged her wrists, trying to bring her around. He refused to accept the details of her grotesque story, preferring to dismiss it as merely the product of an overwrought imagination. Lili was a beautiful, delicate person; he had fallen under her spell; he needed to believe that her fantasies left some room for him and the real world.

*"Hey!"* Vic bellowed down to him, "you didn't hear the good news yet. *I found Pat.*"

The news should have cheered Tony, but for some reason it sent a negative jolt through his already overloaded mind. Good news, bad news, *any* news at this point, was too much to deal with.

"Great," he said with no enthusiasm. His attention was focused on Lili. She was regaining consciousness, murmuring softly to herself, though her eyes remained closed.

"Yo!" roared Vic—

Tony looked up toward the top of the steps.

"Heeere's Pat!" Vic finished. He aimed the flashlight like a theater spotlight at the ornate balustrade that ran back into the shadows of the second floor. A haggard Pat McKenna, his red hair and beard leached orange by the flashlight's glare, leaned heavily on the mahogany railing. He waved weakly down at his buddy. "Yo, Pat! C'mon down. Join the fun," Vic invited.

*Jeez, some fun!* Tony thought, returning his full attention to reviving the girl. Behind him, he could hear Vic hurry back upstairs, presumably to help Pat, who looked like he'd had a rough time of it. The boy was curious to hear his story, but not until more pressing matters were settled. He could hear the two men talking softly to each other; whatever had happened to them on the floor above, *he didn't want to know—at least, for a while.*

Lili's eyes were open. She whispered something.

"I can't hear what you're saying," he said gently, leaning his ear close to her mouth.

"It isn't—" she managed to say, before her voice failed.

"What isn't it?" Tony asked. "Everything's fine now."

"Him." Every word she spoke was clearly an effort; Tony felt the effort behind each. *"Me,"* Lili said. "We're part of her dream. *Part of her."*

Suddenly she screamed, twisting so violently in his arms that he could barely restrain her from throwing herself down the stairs. "Don't," he begged. "You'll hurt yourself."

"Run, Tony," she said, clutching the front of his jacket. "Run away *now!"*

"Easy, easy," he responded. "I can't leave without you. I think"—he laughed self-consciously—"I think I'm falling in love with you."

"If you love me," she whispered, *"run away!"*

"Looks like we've got the walking wounded here," Vic said with exaggerated cheerfulness. She was helping Pat, who seemed to have an injured leg. They had almost reached Lili and Tony.

"Oh, Tony, I'm so afraid for you. For us." She began to cry.

He held her to him, as though he could keep her safe from her nightmares in his embrace. She felt as fragile as a bundle of dried reeds in his arms; he was afraid of hugging her too tightly, for fear he would snap her in two.

She surrendered whatever fight was in her. She melted into a wonderful softness and warmth in his arms. Lili was a mystery at the heart of mysteries, he thought dreamily, the most perfect woman he could imagine. He knew he was falling asleep; the effect of everything he'd been through the last several hours was suddenly catching up with him. He wanted nothing more than to curl up in Lili, and he wanted to wrap himself around her like the shawl she was wearing.

She drowsily nuzzled his neck. The tip of her tongue flicked across his skin. He felt a sexual thrill from the crown of

his head to the soles of his feet. The scent of roses that clung
to her was intoxicating. . . .

He could feel the kiss of her, drawing gently on his skin,
her teeth just touching his flesh playfully, as though she were
going to—

*"No!"* she screamed, suddenly flinging herself backward
with such force that she hit the balustrade with a loud crash.

"Lili, what's the matter?" he cried, reaching across for her.

But she pushed his hands away and screamed, *"Leave me
alone! Oh, please, Tony, don't come any closer."* She tried
to scramble up the stairs. Then, abruptly, she stopped. A
change came over her, so startling that Tony, who had ignored her pleading and was coming after her, stopped, then
sank to his knees, feeling sick and weak.

The Lili who glared hungrily at him with a feral expression, whose eyes blazed red in the sputtering, ending light of
the candle, was no longer anyone he knew.

"You have so much life in you," she pleaded. "Give me
just a little." But it was a stranger talking to him. The words
were spoken in soothing tones, completely at odds with the
desperate hunger that flared in the eyes.

Vic, supporting Pat McKenna, watched the odd performance on the lower steps for a few minutes, then asked Tony,
"What's wrong with her? Is she on something?"

In that moment Tony felt his own mind was on the verge of
cracking. He saw before him, crouched on the step just out of
reach, the proof of what he had been denying all along.
"Give Lili back to me!" he raged at the darkness pressing in
all around him.

Lili-who-wasn't-Lili-any-longer held out her hand to Tony
and pleaded with him. "Tony, I'm who I've always been."
In the light of the bobbing and darting candle flame, her lips
were flecked with spittle. The scent of roses had become
cloying; the fragrance turned from sweetness to poison.

Gagging, Tony backed away. "Liar!" he shouted. *"You're
not Lili!"*

Vic, who had been watching all this exchange with an
increasingly puzzled expression, while Pat hovered uncertainly on the step above him, started toward the girl.

Lili had begun to tremble; she tried to say something, but
the words were only strangulated gurglings in her throat.

"Tony, I think she's sick. You'd better help me," Vic said to Tony, who had remained rooted in place. "She's sick."

But Tony could only shake his head. He was trembling almost as much as Lili.

When Vic tried to take hold of the girl's hand, she pushed him away. "Go," she pleaded, managing to force the few words out. "Both of you, just go." She sank back against the balustrade, hanging on to two fat balusters while her body was swept with tremors as though jolts of electricity were coursing through it.

But Tony grabbed her and hugged her, trying to calm her violent trembling in his arms. "Lili," he said, then he repeated her name over and over, as though this might keep at bay the demon that was making her suffer so much. He could feel tears on the back of his hand as she pressed it to the side of her face. "Oh, Tony," she said, sobbing miserably, "she's so strong. She's almost awake, and she's so very strong."

"Lili, you've got to run away. It's this place. Someone told me it's this place that's making her so strong."

"And the others," she said in a whisper, "all the others asleep upstairs. They're feeding her, too, with their dreams and their blood." Another spasm shook her. "Sometimes I can break free of her for a little while," she said, her voice growing so weak that he had trouble understanding her now. "But she always pulls me back into her—*No!* Oh, Tony, she's very near us. She's—*I won't let you!*—oh, sweet heaven, go, just go, Tony! *Not! Not! Can't. Won't—I—*"

"Fight her, Lili," he screamed. "Don't let it get inside you again." He pulled her to her feet, hanging on to her because she seemed unable to support herself.

But Lili shook free of him with surprising strength. She threw back her head and howled like some mad animal under a full moon. It was a scream of pain and a howl of triumph at the same time.

"What the fu—?" Vic began.

"Vic! Help Pat get out, *now!*" But Vic hesitated, still staring in surprise at the girl who leaned against the banister, her back arched so sharply that she was staring directly up at the carved ceiling overhead. She worked the fingers of both hands spasmodically, clutching at the empty air. Her mouth was moving, she was swallowing compulsively, but the only sound issuing after the scream was a rasping, as though the cry had scraped her throat raw.

Tony yelled to his uncle, "Move it, soldier!" He gave Vic a shove in the direction of Pat, who had begun hobbling solo down the stairs, using the opposite railing to steady himself. Vic kept glancing back at Lili as he went to help his buddy.

Tony, in the meantime, had grabbed Lili's wrist; and she relaxed a little at his touch, shaking her head like a punch-drunk boxer. She let herself be led down a step or two as Tony followed Vic and Pat and the flashlight beam.

Suddenly she turned and stared into the thick shadows at the head of the stairs. She shook her head wildly from side to side, then, apparently with tremendous effort, she raised her hand and made the sign against evil with her right hand. With her left hand she grabbed for Tony, saying, "Give me your strength, Tony! Help me."

They interlaced fingers. He felt her skin tingling, as though an electric current were running through her flesh. A mosquitolike humming near his ears grew until it filled the air all around them.

"What's that?" asked Vic, turning a frightened face to Tony and the girl.

Something huge and black was filling the shadowed gallery at the head of the stairs. It boiled like trapped thunderheads; it gleamed like oiled black skin.

A stench like rotting flesh poured down from the darkness; it was the carrion smell Tony had discovered in the fire-damaged boiler room. He felt himself gagging, but he stood his ground, supporting Lili.

Something raged at the top of the stairs. Tony heard a confusion of sounds, each amplified to ear-shattering volume: insect chittering, reptilian hissing, the shriek of a night bird, the roar of a hunting predator, and other sounds, all the more frightening because he *couldn't* give a name to them.

"Sounds like all hell is breaking loose up there!" Vic shouted. "Let's get out of here!"

He turned to Pat as a second, nauseating blast of foulness rolled down the staircase.

At that instant Pat clasped his hands together into a fist and, holding his arms at full length, swung them like a club, hitting Vic in the stomach, doubling him over with pain. Tony, still holding Lili's hand, struggled to reach his uncle, who lay groaning across the steps, his hands clutched to his gut. The flashlight rolled *clunkclunkclunk* down the last steps and came to rest on the lobby floor, its beam angling across the rubbish-littered floor toward the entrance, hidden in shadow.

"You crazy bastard!" Tony yelled.

"Tony!" said Lili over her shoulder, her hand still upraised against the dark. "It's *her*."

Pat, his eyes fixed on Tony, snarled. Then the man's familiar face was melting away; it was being reshaped into the most hideous face Tony had ever seen. His eyes glinted red and vicious, like those of the jungle rats that had haunted Tony's nightmares when Vic once told him how they plagued the bunkers in Vietnam. The skin of his face was dried and yellow, flaking away. Blackened lips peeled back from jagged teeth and desiccated gums in a rictus that was sickeningly like a smile. The creature's mouth moved as though trying to form words, but all that came out was a hissing noise and a sewerlike stench.

Then the living corpse that had been Pat threw itself at Tony. Straddling him, it clawed clumsily for his throat. Lili, not daring to lower her right hand, pounded ineffectually on the back and side of the skull-like head with her left. But the skeletal hands kept coming at Tony's neck. When the boy beat aside its flailing hands, the thing suddenly sank its teeth into Tony's wrist. The second jolt of pain as he wrenched free made him scream; a bit of his skin remained caught between the moldering teeth. And the creature was chewing greedily on it.

Then Vic's boot slammed into the thing's chest, sending it spinning down the last few steps, where it fell near the flashlight.

"I don't know what the fuck's going on," yelled Vic, "but we're getting out now!" He jerked Tony to his feet.

There were explosive sounds from the head of the stairs; the sound of wood cracking; somewhere glass shattered.

The darkness was moving down the stairs, a stinking cloud that swallowed the light.

At the bottom of the stairs the Pat-thing was awkwardly picking itself up, its eyes fixed greedily on Tony's left wrist, which was sticky with the boy's blood. But Vic had his gun out now. Tony stared in shock at his injured wrist for a minute, then he took a step toward Lili.

"*Run,* Tony," she begged. "There's no time left."

The Pat-thing, face frozen in a corpse-smile, its mouth making obscene chewing and sucking noises, reached out for Tony. Vic fired one, two, three shots. One shattered the creature's shoulder so that its outstretched arm jerked wildly away from Tony; the second went wild; the third shattered its forehead with a wet, pulpy sound. The thing dropped in place; Tony looking down, saw only Pat McKenna's blood-soaked corpse.

The sound of the gunshots blended with the thunder of the advancing darkness. The stairs were shaking underfoot.

Vic, seeing Pat's body, gave an anguished cry. He looked at the gun in his hand as if it were to blame, and flung it into the darkness. Then something seemed to snap in him; with a bellow he broke for the front door of the hotel. Tony, grabbing Lili, ignoring her screams to leave her there, ran toward the door that Vic had flung open.

Blundering through the litter, he dragged Lili behind him as the darkness raged to the foot of the stairs. Then they were outside, stumbling through night, while the hotel doors crashed shut behind them.

# Fourteen

THEY WERE ALMOST to the side gate when Tony stumbled over a shattered bit of statuary in the weed-choked garden. Together they rolled through brambles and rotting leaves. Tony started to scramble immediately to his feet, but Lili placed a restraining hand on his, shaking her head, trying to catch her breath.

"She's not going to follow. There's something—" Lili gasped, catching her breath. "I think she's afraid. *Of you.*"

Tony, who lay on his back, his chest heaving, laughed bitterly. "Why?"

"Something inside you. The reason she wants your blood. She needs it, but she's afraid of it too."

"What does she do when she's *not* afraid?" asked Tony, trying unsuccessfully to make light of the situation. But his own fear and horror were so overwhelming that he began to shake. He could hear his teeth chattering. As soon as he could move again, he was determined to put as much distance as possible between the hotel and himself.

Beyond the shadowy gardens and occasional tree, the dilapidated building bulked against the night. He felt it watching him, hating him, like a wounded animal that had returned to its den to lick its wounds and dream of hunting down the prey that had escaped its claws.

*The prey. Him. Lili. Vic . . .*

203

"Where's Vic?" he asked, heaving himself into a sitting position.

"I caught a glimpse of him just ahead of us," said Lili. "He must have escaped through the gate by now."

"I hope so," Tony said. "Come on, let's get out of here ourselves."

She said nothing as he helped her to her feet. She was lost in her own thoughts. Probably in shock, he thought. He felt woozy enough himself, though the fit of shaking and feeling sick to his stomach had subsided.

Glancing frequently back at the darkened building, Tony picked his way carefully among the overgrown paths and gardens back to the gate.

He was surprised to find it still closed, exactly as he had left it.

*Then Vic . . . ?*

But the man was crouched beside the gate, his back supported by two of the rusty iron pickets. He was rocking back and forth on his heels, moaning softly to himself. His arms were draped over his knees; his head drooped between them.

"Hey, Vic—" Tony called in a hoarse whisper.

With a small cry of pure animal fear, Vic stood up, still with his back to the palings. He stared wildly at Tony and Lili, as though he didn't trust what his eyes told him.

"Easy, Vic, easy," Tony said. "It's just me. We all made it."

He stretched out his hand to touch Vic's arm, but the man backed away, shaking his head. "It wasn't Pat inside. It looked like him, but it wasn't. It was a trick."

*He's over the edge now,* thought Tony, *and I can't blame him.* "This isn't a trick," he said reassuringly. "But we've got to get away before something more happens."

"I couldn't leave you," said Vic miserably. "But I couldn't go back. *I couldn't.*"

"I know you couldn't. I'd never be able to go back there myself. But it's over now."

"I shot Pat. It wasn't Pat in there, but then it was. I saw him. *Oh, Jesus, Tony—Tony, what do I do? I killed him. I killed my buddy who got me out when no one else would believe I was alive!*"

"That wasn't Pat in there. Pat would never do . . . anything like that."

"Do you really think so?" Vic asked eagerly, like a child needing comfort.

"Yes. Whatever happened in there, it wasn't Pat. Pat was your friend. That—in there"—he gestured back toward the dark and silent building—"*that wasn't even human.*"

"In 'Nam the enemy was invisible," said Vic, suddenly going off on another tangent.

"Later, Vic. We can talk about it later," said Tony with another nervous glance at the Bethel. Though it had stopped bleeding, the wound in his wrist was throbbing. He was afraid of infection. "We've got to go now. Lili?" But she had wandered off a short distance, to sit on a stone bench. She had her arms crossed over her breasts, with each hand holding on to the opposite shoulder. She was staring back at the hotel. She didn't acknowledge him when he called her name a second time.

Have they both freaked out? he wondered. It was frustrating that they were falling apart with safety so near. For all of Lili's reassurances, Tony wouldn't believe that they would be safe for even a moment until they were off the hotel grounds. He dropped down onto the bench beside her. "Lili," he insisted, "we can't stay here."

"I can't go," she said despairingly. "If I go outside, I'll die. I'll just . . . stop existing. Even if I *could* go out there, I wouldn't belong. I've been locked away from it too long. It's not *my* world out there any longer. But—oh, don't you *see,* Tony? I'm a part of *her.* I feel it. I've wandered around in a corner of *her* dream so long, living in it, that I *can't* live outside of it. Every minute I'm awake, I feel her in my soul, in my brain. Right now she's just a distant whisper, but soon"—Lili shivered and drew her shawl more tightly around herself—"she'll come roaring up inside of me, until my head is ready to burst, until I—I'll do anything—*anything*—to please her and make her stop hurting me."

She was sobbing now.

"Walk through that gate, Lili. With me. The world out there isn't so terrible." He tried to smile, but her grief made him incapable of doing anything more but cupping one of her hands in his own and patting it. "Please, Lili! Won't you try?"

She shook her head. "What happened inside to that friend of yours would happen to me. If I ran away, she'd stop giving me the power to make me alive. You know''—she wiped tears away from her eyes—''sometimes I think *I'm* only a dream of hers. That the real me died a long time ago, and what you see here—what I think I'm feeling—is all just—*empty air.*''

''You'll never convince me of that,'' he said. ''Never.'' He leaned across and kissed her. It was a clumsy kiss, but she threw her arm around his neck and kissed him back with all the need in her. ''Now come with me,'' he said, holding her hands firmly in his own.

But she kept on staring at the hotel. ''I'm so afraid, Tony. I don't think I can.'' She tried to pull away from him, but he wouldn't release her hands.

''She's doing this to you. She's making you imagine all sorts of terrible things. Here you are, the *way* you are. That isn't going to change when you walk out the gate.''

''You don't know her. You don't know the kind of power she has. *And . . . she's getting stronger.*''

''This is a bad dream, but we're waking up now.''

''*So is she. But she's making the nightmare stronger.*''

Vic came over to them. There had been a change in him in the past few minutes; now he spoke like a man who had lost his way but was beginning to find it again. ''In Nham Diep the enemy was invisible. You'd look around and all you'd see were smiling yellow faces. No enemy. The countryside would look empty for miles. But they were around. Your buddies would get killed by land mines or booby traps or sniper fire or taken out by a mortar attack. Then you'd suddenly be hit with human waves, screaming like banshees. But you never really saw *the enemy.*''

He gestured with a closed fist at the hotel. ''*She's* like that. You don't see her, *but she's there.* She killed Pat, not me. But I'm not going to run away. Not this time. I've spent too many fucking years running away. Now I'm ready to fight back.''

''Vic, you saw what happened in there. You can't go back. Let it rest.''

But Vic just shook his head and grinned. ''When I go back, it'll be in my own time. *And I won't be alone.*''

''Vic—''

''You'll see,'' Vic said, then added with grim satisfaction, ''*And so will she.*''

His boots crunched rapidly over the gravel. A moment later

Tony saw him pull open the still unlocked gate. Vic slipped through and was gone, hurrying toward Cabot Street, while the gate came to a standstill, half open.

"We've got to go, too, Lili," said Tony. *"Now."*

This time she broke free and ran back a little way toward the hotel. "Don't try to follow," she shouted. "I have to stay here. She's telling me I have to. And I'll die anywhere else."

Then she was running again. He started to follow, but sudden laughter, growing into a howl, filled the gardens. The sound of it threatened to split his head in two. He pressed his hands to his ears, trying to drown out the sound, but it seemed to be *inside* his skull. It felt like it would swell in the core of his brain until his head burst like the watermelon Ted had cherry-bombed one summer.

Through waves of pain he saw Lili, her hands clasped to the sides of her head, stagger across the porch and through the doors of the hotel, which now stood open, giving on the absolute darkness inside.

Then he could stand it no more. He ran for the gate, practically falling through it. The minute he was outside, the mind-wrenching sounds stopped. But the experience had left him feeling so sick that he could only stagger to the gutter, where he fell to his knees, clutching his stomach and retching into the gutter.

A car roared by along Stanwix Street. Tony weakly lifted a hand for help, but the car only slowed long enough for someone to yell, "Fuckin' drunk!" then accelerate again.

In the silence, Tony got to his feet. There wasn't a sign of Vic or anyone else. He began walking unsteadily toward the car.

Lili was lost to him, unless . . .

A second wave of nausea hit him while he was in the car. He was doubled over with dry heaves for a few minutes. When his stomach had quieted and his hands weren't shaking, he started the Chrysler's engine and pulled cautiously into the street.

There was only one person who could help, he decided. *Jozsef Zagonyi.*

The main house at Third and Mason was deserted. The blinds were drawn; not a glimmer of light showed at any window. Just as he pulled to a stop, Tony saw SoHo's black van peeling around the next corner; there was no mistaking the huge, smiling skull painted across its rear doors.

But SoHo was forgotten as soon as he had the car door open.

The wooden gate to the backyard was ajar. That made Tony uneasy, remembering old Zagonyi's fetish for locking it behind him. Looking more closely, Tony saw that the wood was nicked and raw around the lock, as though it had been forced.

With a growing sense of dread he hurried past the fish pond, where the cement frog strummed its silent guitar by the light of the waning moon.

There was a light in the old man's cottage. Tony felt a surge of relief. But relief vanished when he pounded on the front door and Jozsef didn't answer.

Maybe he's gone, thought Tony.

Then he heard a faint, muffled sound from inside. He leaned his ear to the door, straining to hear.

Silence, then a *thump!* that certainly came from within the cottage.

"Jozsef! Mr. Zagonyi! It's Tony Kovacs. *I've got to talk to you.*"

Another *thump!*—as though someone were blundering around inside, upsetting furniture.

Burglars? Or could it be the old man himself—maybe sick or having a heart attack?

Should he call the police? But running to a neighbor's for a phone seemed a dangerous delay if Jozsef was in some life-threatening situation. And since the door and windows were securely locked, it didn't seem likely burglars were inside. Nor did Tony think they'd have gone on making noise if they knew someone was outside.

Tony threw himself against the closed door, surprised at the unexpected pain. The door at first refused to give an inch. He kept calling Jozsef's name, but there was only silence now.

Frantically he slammed himself against the door a second and third time. On the third attempt wood splintered somewhere. Then the door flew open, slamming into the wall behind it.

The room inside was a shambles. One of the old red-and-white patterned armchairs had been overturned. Books were scattered across the floor. A floor lamp in one corner lay tilted into a bookshelf-lined wall.

The kitchen was empty and dark. The door to the bedroom was open. Now Tony could hear a steady, soft sound from inside. He crossed to the door, hesitating in the doorway for a minute, surveying the room beyond.

Jozsef Zagonyi had fallen or been pushed to the floor. He lay in a tangle of bed clothes that had spilled off the narrow bed. With one hand he was beating weakly with the heel of an old slipper against the base of a battered dresser; his other hand was pressed to his throat, trying to stanch a flow of blood. When he saw Tony, he dropped the slipper and put his other hand on his ruined throat, but the blood continued pumping out. It had already soaked the front of his shirt, his sweater, and the sheets and blankets underneath him.

Trying desperately to remember first-aid lessons from Boy Scouts, Tony knelt beside the old man. Zagonyi watched him with a mix of horror and hope. He tried to talk, but all that came out was a gurgling sound.

"Don't," said Tony, wadding up the pillowcase he had just stripped off the pillow wedged between the head of the bed and the dresser. "Don't talk. You'll make it worse," though it was hard to imagine it worse. The old man's throat had been slashed; Tony saw just how bad the damage was when he pried loose the old man's hands for a moment to press the folded rectangle of cloth against the wound. From that glimpse he doubted the old guy would make it. He found it hard to believe Zagonyi could have lost as much blood as he had and still be conscious.

He folded the man's hands back over the makeshift pad and started to rise. Zagonyi clutched at him with one hand, keeping the other pressed to his throat. The blood was already soaking through the pillowcase. Jozsef shook his head when Tony gently tried to free himself from the grasping fingers and replace the man's hands on the pad.

"I've got to call an ambulance," said Tony. "The phone . . . ?" he started to ask, then realized the absurdity of the question. He got to his feet as the old man continued to shake his head. He tried to talk again, but all he could do was make more of the horrible liquid sounds before he began to wheeze. Tony was sure he was drowning in his own blood.

He ran into the living room but saw no phone—not even a

jack. He hesitated on the edge of the kitchen, wondering for a moment if the old man's attacker was still hiding in the dark, waiting. . . .

Taking a deep breath, he flicked on the overhead light and looked rapidly all around the small room. No wall phone. No nothing. There wasn't a phone in the cottage.

"I'm going to call from somewhere else," he yelled, leaning briefly into the room.

But the old man was clutching wildly at him, trying to speak. "Don't! I'll get help," said Tony, kneeling beside him and forcing the frail, ice-cold hands tightly against the now thoroughly blood-soaked bandage.

But the man suddenly arched his back so that only his heels and the back of his head rested on the floor. He made a terrible sound, drawing blood and air into his lungs in a last desperate hunger for life.

Then his whole body relaxed into the bloody bed clothes; his head slipped to one side, staring sightlessly at Tony; the pad slid away, revealing the cut from which the pumping blood had slowed to seepage.

His hands shaking, Tony attempted to find a pulse in the man's wrist. None. He didn't dare touch the bloody throat. But he was certain the old man was dead.

Unable to remain in the room any longer, Tony returned to the living room, wondering if the police, when they came, were going to make him a prime suspect in the murder. There seemed no way it could have happened accidentally. And he didn't believe the old man had harmed himself (though Tony did have to admit to a feeling of guilt when he remembered how hopeless the old man had sounded at the end of their last meeting).

*Jozsef Zagonyi was standing between Tony and the front door of the cottage.* He was dressed just as he had been when Tony had discovered him bleeding to death, wearing an old brown sweater and worn gray trousers. In a panic, the boy turned and looked behind him. The old man's body was just as he had left it.

"Don't be afraid," the old man said. "I can linger in this form for the briefest moment only. That"——he nodded his head toward the bedroom door—"was *her* doing. She has extended her influence over many more persons than I imagined. She is very strong now. But you, *you* have the power to challenge her.''

"No." Tony shook his head. "She's already shown that she's too strong.''

"Not yet. She needs the blood. You are strong enough to keep it from her. But there's another. She will take the girl.''

"Lili?'' asked Tony. "But Lili said—''

"Not her. The other—''

But the image of the old man suddenly turned to blinding white light, became a ball of glowing fire, then burst apart soundlessly. With a cry Tony threw his hands across his face, but the fiery droplets had no more effect than the sparks from a Fourth of July sparkler.

Then he was alone.

Dazed, he walked through the house, carefully turning out all the lights. He could not make himself look down at Jozsef Zagonyi's body when he snapped off the bedroom light. Going outside, he drew the door shut, rattling it until a bit of the smashed lock caught—enough, Tony hoped, to keep the wind from blowing it open.

*In the morning*, he promised, *in the morning I'll call the police. But I can't now.*

All he wanted to do was go home, curl up in bed. There was nothing he could do for Lili. There was nothing he could do for Jozsef Zagonyi.

There was nothing he could do for himself.

*Except sleep.* At that moment sleep seemed the most wonderful thing in the world. *Sleeping and forgetting and letting it all go away,* he kept repeating in his mind as he carefully tugged the outer gate closed behind him.

Dimly he was aware that this was some effect of shock, that his system was trying to shut down in self-defense for the overload on his body and mind that day.

His wrist still hurt, but he didn't care.

He only wanted to go home. Like a lost child, he only wanted to find his way home.

He drove slowly, fighting to keep awake.

But the nightmare wasn't over.

There were two Stigesville PD patrol cars pulled up in front of the house on Kossuth Street. Their radios were crackling; one officer, in a winter overcoat, was leaning in the window of the nearest car, talking into the microphone. Tony saw that it was the blond officer who had driven him to the hospital the night he had been attacked on the side street.

*Have they found Jozsef already?* Tony wondered. *Do they think I'm a suspect for murder one?*

He parked the car carefully a short distance from the house. He was too tired to run away. If they wanted him, they could take him. If only they would let him sleep somewhere. . . .

Bleary-eyed, he stumbled across the street.

"Hey!" the officer yelled. "You can't—" Then he stopped as he recognized Tony. "You live here, don't you?" He looked more closely at Tony, then asked suspiciously, "You okay there?"

"Just tired," said Tony. "Too tired."

"Do you know about what happened?" asked the policeman. "Inside, I mean?"

Tony's weariness vanished in a burst of fear.

"What!" he demanded. "What happened? Is anybody hurt?" He could only see Jozsef Zagonyi's lifeblood pumping out of his savagely gashed throat.

"Easy. The little girl—"

*"Leslie!"* Tony shouted, feeling a wave of sickness return. "What—"

"She's been kidnapped," said the officer, his voice a mix of solicitude and business. "We've got an APB on the suspect. A black van with skeletons painted on its side, belongs to—"

"SoHo." He saw the black van turning the corner as he neared Jozsef's cottage.

"Yeah," the officer said. "Real name: Sonny Hobbes."

*She's extended her influence over more people than I realized.*

Tony felt himself swaying; distantly he wondered if he was going to pitch forward onto his face. The officer gave him a steadying hand. "You'd better go inside and sit down. You might be able to help in there." He glanced up at the porch of the Kovacs house. "They're taking it pretty bad."

*Not Lili.*

*The girl.*

*Leslie.*

When the policeman was sure that Tony wasn't going to black out, he went on, "We've got a report that the van was seen heading out East Mather Road. We're checking that out now.'' He patted Tony on the shoulder. ''We'll get her back. She'll be fine.''

But you won't be looking in the right place, Tony thought. The van may be on East Mather Road, but Leslie won't be there.

The hotel. She would be at the hotel. But he knew enough by now to know that the police would never find her if they went looking there. She'd be in one of those rooms down one of those corridors Lili had talked about. Those places that didn't exist if *she* didn't want them to exist.

Tony plodded up the front steps. Two more officers were talking to Jerry and Elene in the front room. Elene was sobbing; Jerry kept slamming his fist into his left palm.

His mother sat at the dining-room table, flanked by two women neighbors who were patting her hand and making comforting sounds.

''Tony!'' his mother cried when she saw him.

He walked around the table and gave her a hug. She sobbed into his chest. ''Who'd want to *do* such a terrible thing? Who'd want to hurt her? Oh, Tony, you won't let them hurt her; don't let them hurt Leslie.''

''I won't, Mom,'' he said mechanically. ''She'll be fine.'' He disengaged himself, leaving her to the ministrations of the other women. ''I've got to take care of some things,'' he said vaguely. He left the room before she could say anything more.

His father was sitting on the top step of the third-floor landing, just outside Tony's and Vic's room. Tony had the feeling he was hiding from all the anguish and confusion downstairs. Daniel Kovacs was a great bluffer, Tony knew, who collapsed like a house of cards when any demand was put on him—especially an emotional one.

''How's your mother doing?'' Daniel asked.

''Okay, I guess.''

''Elene?''

''All right. Jerry's with her.''

''The police—they found that son of a bitch yet?''

''They've got a lead.''

''Jerry and Elene were asleep. Your mother and I were watching TV. Leslie couldn't sleep—more of those goddamn nightmares—so she was with us. The bastard cut through the screen door at the back. Your mother forgot to lock the back door. I've always told her to be careful, but—''

"It doesn't matter now," said Tony wearily. "Tell me about Leslie."

"He just *came into the room* . . . cool as you please. He had one of those pop-up knives—''

"Switchblades," said Tony automatically.

"And he kept jabbing it at us, forcing your mother and me back into the corner. We had Leslie between us, but he reached over and grabbed her. Then he put a knife to her throat and said he was going to cut it if we tried anything. Then''—Daniel Kovacs shrugged—''he dragged Leslie out. We couldn't do anything because he had that knife. He did say one funny thing, though—''

"Which was?"

" 'Battles and wars; mine and hers.' It didn't make any sense. The police can't make sense of it, either. But the guy's a fruitcake, so what do you expect?''

*And everything points back to the Hotel Bethel*, Tony thought numbly. To his father he said, "Go downstairs, be with Mom. She needs someone."

"You go," Daniel protested. "I'm no good with that sort of thing."

"I can't, Dad," Tony said decisively. "I've got something I have to do."

"What?" asked Daniel.

"Bring a war to an end if I can."

"What's that supposed to mean?" Daniel Kovacs sounded angry.

But Tony had no time for his posturing. "Go down to Mom. Your place is with her. I know where mine is."

He went into the bedroom and shut the door. He paused for a moment; then he heard his father descending the narrow attic staircase.

Sighing, Tony crossed to the desk by his bed. Vaguely he wondered where Vic was at that moment. Fighting his own war, probably. That was a side issue, as far as he was concerned.

From the top drawer he took the little charm Lili had given him. It felt warm in his hand; it felt reassuring. It brought into sharp relief his feelings for Leslie and Lili. And, by exten-sion, it made him think of the house around him, filled with

grief and love—and *life,* most of all. For all his disagree-
ments with his parents and other family members, he still felt
safe from the gathering dark inside these walls. The vitality
that filled the house stood in stark contrast to the emptiness of
the deserted hotel.

Somehow the tiny amulet brought that all into focus for
him. He would carry the little silver charm in his pocket; in
his mind he would cling to life and the good things his life in
this house had given him. He would wrap these around him
as a kind of armor, he decided.

*It isn't much,* he thought, *but it might be something.*

# Fifteen

THE HOTEL GATE was still ajar, just as Tony had left it. He paused momentarily; he could be walking into a trap. He touched one of the rusty metal curls of scrollwork gingerly but felt no betraying surge of power under his fingertips.

When he stepped through, he half expected it to *clang* shut behind him, but it remained as it was.

Everything whispered loneliness, desertion, harmlessness.

He felt the lie underneath.

Somewhere inside, he was certain, was Leslie. He had no clear idea of what he could do to help rescue her, but he was not going to fail for want of trying. Before he had left his family's house, he had taken one of the kitchen knives out of the drawer. Now he held it ready as he walked along the too familiar path to the hotel. He imagined eyes, flecked with red, following his progress from between chinks in the boarded-over windows.

Suddenly he was grabbed roughly and pulled into a clump of shrubbery. A meaty hand was clamped over his mouth. He took an ineffectual swing before he discovered Vic grinning down at him. "Easy, bro," his uncle said. "We're all friends in this operation."

Behind him, Tony could see Sag Miller, Jack Tandy, and half a dozen of the other vets who hung out with Vic in Skeffington Square.

"I told you I wasn't coming back alone," said Vic, grinning. "This is my elite corps. Vic's Rangers."

"Vic, Leslie's been kidnapped."

"When?" Vic demanded. "Who?"

"A few hours ago. The 'who' is a loony tunes from my school. One of those punks who hang out around the square. The guy called SoHo. But, Vic—I think Leslie's here. I'm *sure* she's inside the hotel."

The other man just nodded, not questioning the fact at all. "Then we've got even more of a score to settle," he said grimly. "We're going in. Are you with us?"

"I'd sure as hell rather go in with a bunch of you guys than face whatever's in there alone," said Tony. "I don't know what we'll be able to do, though. You saw what it's like in there. It's *insane*."

"So was 'Nam, as it turned out," said Jack Tandy.

"Buddies stick with buddies," said Sag Miller. "That's the only way any of us got through."

There were murmurs of agreement from the others assembled in the deserted garden. Looking at them, Tony saw that, even though these were all the Skeffington Square regulars he'd seen day in and day out, there was a difference in them now. They were men with a mission—no matter *how* insane it was. There was an *aliveness* in their eyes, a *wakefulness* that had replaced the vacant gaze of men who had been reduced to sleepwalkers amid the wreckage of their dreams.

"Have you told them that it's *Night of the Living Dead* in there?" Tony asked Vic.

"We lived it once," said a soft-spoken man with spaniel eyes, large and sad, whose name Tony couldn't recall. "A second time around doesn't scare us. We've all got business to finish—maybe we can each settle a piece of it here."

"We've got two revolvers, a shotgun, some knives, and a few lengths of good old-fashioned lead pipe," Vic boasted.

"Plus a couple of Molotov cocktails for good measure," added Sag Miller, opening his camouflage jacket to reveal four Jack Daniel's bottles filled with gasoline. Bits of rag had been stuffed into the necks as fuses. The man reeked of gasoline.

Tony whistled. "Just hold off until we get some people out, okay? There's a little kid—Leslie, my niece—and a girl about my age inside. Don't torch the place until they're safe, then you can burn it to the ground for all I care.''

"You got it," said Sag, who seemed to be Vic's second in command of the motley crew.

"The strategy is to split up," Vic said quickly. "Some go through the front, some through the back. Since Tony and I have been inside, one of us should go with each group."

They made a few more plans, keeping an eye all the time on the dilapidated structure. But nothing moved; no light could be seen around the place. It was decided that Tony would go around the back with Sag Miller, John Tandy, and the sad-eyed man, Stewart Kent. Vic would take the other four "commandos" in through the front.

Tony and Vic shook hands. Tony felt an exchange of energy between them—unexpected and welcome—as though they each were giving the others a reserve against the night ahead.

Then they separated. Tony and company, crouched low, circled around the back, using the shrubs and infrequent trees to screen them from anyone inside.

This is crazy, Tony thought. But it was exhilarating at the same time. He felt like he had stepped into some late-night war movie. *Or horror flick. Leathernecks Meet the Bride of Frankenstein.* What made it even weirder was that the men around him were still fighting, in their minds, a war that had been over since almost before Tony was born.

He was becoming as well acquainted with the hotel grounds as if he lived there. Though the moon had long since set, there was enough starlight and city glow for him to get his bearings. The men moved in single file, with Tony at their head.

They were circling near the pool when Sag, who was right behind Tony, suddenly signaled everyone to freeze.

"What is it?" Stewart whispered, hefting his lead pipe in his hand.

"Sounds like something *big* moving around over there." Sag gestured toward the pool.

Now they were all listening. They heard a sound like a heavy, wet mass being dragged over rough concrete. Jack Tandy, leveling his shotgun, took a step closer, then—

"Oh, my *God!*" Even as he spoke, he was backing away from the cracked cement apron around the north end of the pool. Something huge, gray-green, and slimy, its segmented skin glistening like oil, heaved itself up out of the pool. A triangular mouth, large enough to swallow a calf, opened to reveal triple rows of teeth. It's *Jaws* on land! Tony thought crazily, backing into Stewart, who was standing and staring at the thing, shifting his lead-pipe club from hand to hand.

"What *is* it?" he asked Tony.

But it was Sag who said—in a remarkably collected tone of voice, it seemed to Tony—"It's a leech. I picked enough of the bloodsuckers off me in 'Nam."

"You never picked one like that mother off you," Tandy said with a nervous chuckle.

The monstrous, wormy thing sensed the men were there. It rippled forward across the concrete with surprising speed. Tandy cocked his shotgun. But Sag shook his head and just waved the other three men back. "Best way to get rid of those mothers is with fire."

He untied one of the Jack Daniel's bottles from his jury-rigged utility belt, then lit the rag wick with a lighter from his coat pocket. The gasoline-soaked fabric flared so suddenly, Tony feared it would go off in the man's hand. But Sag merely held fast, his face tight-lipped in the orange glare, weighing his best advantage.

The leech lunged closer.

Sag hurled the incendiary device. It arced like a shooting star and shattered across the back of the creature, sheathing it in liquid fire. With a gravelly hiss—like a roar sucked backward—the monster leech writhed, reared to two thirds of its height into the air like a pillar of fire, then suddenly pitched itself back into the pool. Gold flecks in the tile glinted in the explosive firelight that suddenly filled the drained pool. Coils of thick, noxious smoke corkscrewed into the chill air.

*We can kill them*, Tony thought. *They've become that real. Or did we become part of the nightmare again when we came through that gate?*

"Was that someone's pet?" asked Jack Tandy, trying to make a joke. But his voice was so shaky, there was little humor in the remark.

"Whatever it was," said Sag Miller, "I have a feeling that we've got a few more surprises in store."

The back entrance to the hotel was locked, but it only took a few seconds for Sag and Jack to force it. Tony stood behind and between them, ready to thrust his knife forward at the first sign of trouble. Stewart, at the edge of the porch, kept looking back. The flames had almost died away, but curls of stomach-churning blue-black smoke continued to drift their way.

Beyond the burst door, the passageway was empty in front of them. Jack and Stewart had their flashlights on; Tony and Sag kept theirs in reserve.

They were just passing the back entrance to the solarium when Stewart paused by the open door, shining his light all around the room, picking out wrought-iron tables and the trunks of long dead trees in their ornamental holders. "I heard something rustling in there."

"Mice." Tandy shrugged.

"No, more like birds, up there somewhere—"

The probing flashlight beam swept across the withered branches, suddenly disclosing a cluster of what, at first glance, looked like curious black fruit growing *up* from one thick branch. But when the light touched them, the branch suddenly blossomed with wings. The ebony feathers were tipped with crimson. But the bodies to which the wings were attached were smooth—the pale pink color of a rat's tail—and the beaked faces were distressingly human. The creatures—there seemed to be six or seven of them—were about the size of large owls. They blinked painfully in the glare, shifted restively on scaly talons, and hissed menacingly at the men.

"We aren't in Kansas anymore," said Jack, his voice sounding hollow with shock.

"Shit!" whispered Sag. "This sure as hell isn't even *Pennsylvania!*" As the creatures grew more agitated, he added, "Whatever they are, they sound pretty pissed. Stew, kill that light and let's split."

But dousing the light was a tactical error. The flashlight beam held the monstrosities in thrall—like deer fascinated by the headlights of an oncoming car. When Stewart clicked it off, the tangle of snarling creatures were airborne. They dived at the men in a killing frenzy—screeching, snapping, slashing at them.

Through a mad dance of beaks and talons, beating wings, and shrill, near deafening cries, Tony saw Stew fall to the solarium floor, then roll onto his side, his knees drawn up to his chest and his arms locked behind his neck in the protective posture Tony had seen in civics class newsreels from the sixties war protests. The man had dropped his lead pipe; it lay near the extinguished flashlight. He was covered with the murderous things, thick as vultures on carrion.

From somewhere under the black-and-red seething of wings, Stew's cries were growing fainter by the second, degenerating into liquid gurgles. *"My eyes!"* the man screamed, then the sound became the terrified gasping of someone drowning in his own blood.

A second wave of feathered nightmares launched itself from the shadows.

Tony jabbed indiscriminately with his knife at the air around him, which seemed to have solidified into a mass of winged horror. His blade wounded one, then another, of the furies. Each time he had the grim satisfaction of feeling the knife point connect with a solid body of a creature. Both times the boy felt stinging pain. His fingers were slick with blood, though he wasn't sure whether it was his attackers' or his own.

Buried under the flailing wings, Stew gave a final, agonized bellow, then was silent.

*"No!"* Tony yelled. He lunged forward, determined to slice his way through the tumult to the fallen man's side. Then the knife was torn from his hands. Using one hand to shield his eyes and his other to batter at the creatures, he tried to fight his way to Stewart's still form.

But a pair of wiry arms were suddenly thrown around his shoulders, and he was pulled toward the door. "It's too late! Stew's dead!" Sag Miller shouted in his ear, "We're getting out."

Tony struggled to tear free of Miller's hold, but he was hauled roughly back toward safety.

"We can't leave him!" he shouted, twisting his head so he could see Sag.

"He's dead meat!" Miller yelled back.

Then Jack Tandy added his efforts to Sag's, and Tony was pulled the last few feet back and out through the door. He and Sag Miller tumbled into a heap, while Tandy, who had managed to retain his balance, slammed the solarium door shut. They could hear the screams of the thwarted creatures as they beat their wings against the far side of the panel, tearing it to pieces with their beaks and talons.

Sag got to his feet while keeping a restraining hand on Tony. "I won't let you go until you swear you won't do anything stupid," he said, tightening his grip on the boy for emphasis.

"But, *Stew*—"

"Write him off!" said Sag. "He's finished. If I thought— *hell!* I saw enough in 'Nam to know when somebody's bought it! Now, you gonna come along peaceably or—?"

Too exhausted emotionally and physically to do more, Tony nodded. Sag loosened his hold warily but didn't entirely release Tony. "Level?"

Tony nodded, feeling the fight drain out of him.

Sag watched him suspiciously for a moment, then smiled grimly. "You've got balls enough, boy," he said, "but let your brains have a say. Stew's dead, and all you'll do by going back inside is wind up dead yourself. And probably us too. Do you read me?"

"Loud and clear," said Tony.

"Let's move out, then," Jack Tandy urged in an anxious whisper. He used his flashlight to probe the shadowed hallway ahead. Sag snapped on his own flashlight. The twin beams revealed only dusty plaster, darkened ceiling fixtures, and warped flooring. This time Tony brought up the rear.

Something gray and furry scurried from a partially opened doorway through the intersecting beams. It paused to stare at the intruders, the light glittering sharply off its red eyes, before it darted through a hole in the molding.

"Shit!" whispered Tony. "Was that a rat?"

"I'm not sure," admitted Sag, "but my guess is an overgrown field mouse."

"Oh," said the boy, trying to sound cooler than he felt. He was grossed out by the rodent but not about to let his partners know just how unnerved the sight had left him. But he made a point of walking down the center of the passageway. Nothing interfered with their progress until they reached the entrance to the main dining room. Light, yellow as butter, suddenly spilled out of the doorway. Is it Lili? Tony wondered.

"Jee-*zus*," Jack Tandy said raspily. He was a little ahead of Tony and Sag, so they didn't see what he was seeing for a minute. They paused beside Tandy, staring into the huge room beyond.

Three men were sitting at a small table, hunched over

toward one another as though deep in conversation. They seemed oblivious to the intrusion. Sag and Jack turned off their flashlights as they peered at the seated threesome.

Tony could see that the table at which they were sitting was covered with yellowing linen, embossed with a fleur-de-lis pattern, the symbol of the Hotel Bethel. The head of the figure nearest them, seated with its back to the entrance, was covered with orange-red hair. It was streaked with ribbons of darker red—bright as poster paint.

With a sinking feeling Tony thought he recognized the thin figure. Then the man swiveled around, and Tony saw Pat McKenna's face—

—or what was left of it—grinning at him. His forehead had been shot away just above his eyes; bone fragments were embedded in the exposed brain tissue; blood streaked his face like war paint. Behind him, to the left, Jozsef Zagonyi nodded a head, which bobbed precariously on his neck, severed halfway through. On McKenna's right, Stewart Kent must have located the three newcomers by some sixth sense, since his face displayed mere bloody sockets from which his eyes had been torn.

"They should be dead with wounds like that," said Jack Tandy, his voice edging toward hysteria.

"It isn't possible." Sag Miller gasped. "We can't be seeing this—*not really.*"

But Tony said, "We're taking things on someone else's terms now. Whatever they are, they aren't who they look like."

Silently the three at the table rose to their feet and began moving toward Tony and his friends. Stewart, blind, walked with his arms outstretched, as though *feeling* his way toward his former buddies.

Tony saw Sag Miller reach instinctively toward his Molotov cocktail supply, and he quickly put a restraining hand on the older man's arm, shaking his head. He heard Jack Tandy cock his shotgun, then Tandy said shakily, "I can't shoot Stew—"

"That's *not him,*" said Tony as all three backed toward the entrance, being paced step for step by the ghastly trio. "It's just something that *looks* like him."

"He's right," said Sag. "We know Stew's dead. That's

*Charlie,* Jack—think of them as *Charlie.* Just another friggin'
*trick* to get close enough to—''

His words were cut off when the animated corpses suddenly rushed at them; to Tony the whole thing had the unreal
quality of watching a film that had suddenly lost its sound
track. The bloodied shapes opened their jaws as if they were
screaming, but no sound came out. Their feet made no sound
on the mildewed carpet. It had the disorienting effect of a
dream.

But whatever they were, they had substance enough to
react to a shotgun blast. Tandy got off two quick shots; the
image of Stewart caught most of both barrels in the chest.
The figure was flung backward by the first impact, then spun
around and knocked to the floor by the second. The sound in
the enclosed space was deafening; Tony felt his ears ringing
from the twin explosions. Incredibly, he saw the figure of
Stewart start to climb to its hands and feet—sluggishly, like a
mechanical toy whose wiring has been damaged.

Then the boy was slammed against the wall as the dead-
alive Jozsef Zagonyi barreled into him. He caught a glimpse
of Sag Miller using a series of rapid-fire karate kicks and
chops to short-circuit Pat McKenna's attack. Jack Tandy was
frantically trying to reload his gun; he looked like he was in
total shock, leaning against the doorpost for support.

These fleeting impressions were gone in a savage burst of
pain as Tony hit the wall behind him. He would have collapsed, but the old man's arms, as strong as an athlete's, kept
Tony's shoulders pinned to the wall, supporting him while he
caught his breath. The man's jaws flapped open and shut in a
silent parody of speech, though no sound came out. It was as
if the wound at his throat had damaged the muscles control-
ling his mouth. The head lolled from side to side; this movement frequently opened his neck wound like a second, larger
mouth smeared with dry blood.

With a sudden shift the hands released Tony's shoulders,
only to fasten themselves around his neck. He pummeled the
face and arms of his nightmarish assailant, but his blows had
no effect. He could feel his windpipe being crushed by fingers that were as cold and strong as tempered steel. Beyond
Zagonyi's blood-flecked shirt sleeve, Tony could see Sag
Miller and Pat McKenna rolling on the floor, locked in a
life-and-death struggle. McKenna was clawing and biting at

Miller, who had somehow managed to fend off any serious injury.

Jack Tandy, who had evidently reloaded the shotgun, was dancing around the edge of the fight, looking for a way to get a shot in at McKenna without hurting Miller. Suddenly he turned as the chewed-up body of Stewart Kent shambled into view. Startled, Tandy let him have both barrels again in the legs, shattering them. Like a puppet suddenly cut loose from its strings, the creature collapsed on the floor, where it stubbornly continued to try to get up. But it no longer had legs that could support it. After a few more useless attempts it began dragging itself by its arms toward Tandy.

Satisfied that the creature was effectively decommissioned, Tandy swung the stock of his shotgun at the side of McKenna's head. The impact knocked over the thing that had been straddling Sag Miller. Miller gave a kick and rolled free, while Tandy hooked a hand under one armpit and hauled him quickly to his feet.

Tony's vision was going as suffocating waves of black rolled over him; the ringing in his ears from the shotgun blasts was mingling with a ringing that came from lack of air and onrushing death. He was kicking feebly at Jozsef's legs, but he could feel himself losing control over his arms and legs. His universe was collapsing into the knot of pain in his throat, his desperate need to breathe, and the terrifying certainty that he was dying. He even tried biting the hands that were crushing his windpipe.

He heard Sag yelling something, but the sound seemed to come from far away, across a black ocean smothered in black fog. He was on the verge of sinking beneath that tide forever. He no longer much cared, as consciousness seeped away. . . .

Then Sag was yanking the nightmare Zagonyi off him, while Jack pried the viselike fingers from around his throat. Tony sucked blessed air deep into his lungs. When his sight cleared enough, he saw his two friends struggling to hold a furiously resisting Jozsef. They each had hold of one of the man's hands, but their captive was strong enough to force them all into a slow spin as it fought to break free.

Nearby, Pat McKenna's body twitched and shuddered, though his already damaged head had been reduced to an unrecognizable mass. The splintered stock of Tandy's rifle was mute witness to just how much force it took to subdue the zombie. Farther away, Stewart Kent lay like a turtle on his back, shattered legs akimbo, arms alternately flailing the air or pushing at the floor in a vain attempt to raise itself up.

Coughing, with one hand still rubbing his throat, Tony stumbled across toward his friends. He reached for the shattered gun stock, planning to use it as a club; but Sag Miller's sweating hands suddenly slipped free of the old man's right hand. Suddenly off-balance, Jack Tandy fell backward, dragging Zagonyi with him. They tumbled in a heap across the useless legs of Stewart Kent; Kent leaned toward them and grabbed a handful of Tandy's hair with one hand, causing the man to bellow, dragging him close enough so that he could reach his throat with the other hand.

The creature who looked like Jozsef tore free of Jack's grip, then turned to attack its former captor with such fury, that it was all Tandy could do to shield his face and chest from the clawing hands. Sag grabbed Zagonyi's arms from behind and twisted them up in a hammerlock, the two of them staggering back from Stewart.

"Hit this mother for all you're worth!" yelled Sag. "I can't hold him for long."

For a moment Tony, tightening his grip on the smashed shotgun barrel, was incapable of obeying. It would be just like hitting old Jozsef Zagonyi. *But it's not him*, he had to remind himself. *It's a lie.*

"He's wearing me down," warned Sag, breathing heavily. Turning his head so he wouldn't have to look into the hate-filled eyes that mimicked Zagonyi's, Tony swung the metal barrel. It connected with Zagonyi's skull so resoundingly that the *crack!* seemed as loud as a revolver shot. At the moment of impact Miller released his hold, giving the creature a tooth-jarring shove. Propelled by the double impetus, the old man's body staggered to the side, crashing into a crazily tilted table. For a moment Zagonyi just lay there, then they saw him begin to raise himself into a crouching position amid the ruins of the table.

"Let's get Stew and *get out ourselves!*" shouted Miller. Tony, still a little dazed by what he had just done, turned to follow. But at that instant Stewart Kent jammed Jack Tandy's head forward in a movement so sudden that Tony heard the snapping of his neck. Jack's body spasmed twice, then went limp.

"He . . . he fucking *broke his neck*," Sag said in a disbelieving tone of voice.

The broken thing on the floor shoved the body aside and tried to pull itself on its elbows toward Tony and Sag, its head angled around to them, bloody sockets fixed on them.

"We've got to kill it." Sag launched a kick at the creature's head. The boot connected solidly, the head flopped backward, bobbed into position again, and resumed its deathly crawl.

"No time," said Tony, pointing to where Zagonyi, using a bent leg of the table for support, had almost regained his feet.

Sag glanced one more time at the unmoving body of Jack Tandy, as if to convince himself that his buddy was really dead, then turned and followed Tony. Together they raced from the room.

Tony had lost his flashlight in the struggle, but Sag scooped up his where it had fallen just inside the entrance. He thrust it at Tony, saying, "You know the way, you lead."

The moment they stepped over the threshold, there was an ear-shattering screech, and the yellow glow was extinguished. In the sudden darkness and silence, Tony nervously clicked on the flashlight.

They were in the vast lobby area now. Tony swung the single beam of light in broad arcs, searching for any sign of an ambush.

"Where now?" asked Sag Miller.

"Upstairs," Tony answered, his mouth suddenly dry at the memory of the darkness that lay in the gallery at the head of the staircase. But he had the gut feeling that Leslie, and maybe Lili, and certainly that *other*, would be found above.

"Shit! I just heard something!" Sag said, rasping. "Behind us."

Tony turned and sliced the flashlight beam, expecting to pick out the figure of Jozsef Zagonyi.

But no one was there.

He started to breathe easier when he noticed the light was glinting off what looked like hundreds of tiny ruby chips scattered across the lobby floor. He lowered the beam to discover what was causing the strange phenomenon.

*Eyes.*

The floor was carpeted with rats—hundreds, *thousands*, of them—converging from the shadows all around. It was a flood tide of grayish-brown and black bodies, teeth bared, naked, scaly tails twitching.

With a groan Tony felt himself grow weak with horror. He almost dropped the flashlight. This was his worst nightmare come true.

The only hope was the stairway. Sag was already charging for the lower steps, shouting for Tony to follow him. Tony followed, hearing the sickening squeals and squeaks of the living tide surge after him. In one corner of his mind he wondered if Vic had made it past the creatures, or if they had forced him to retreat. He was sure, now, that he and Sag were going the rest of their way—short or long—by themselves.

Then he was bounding up the steps in Sag's wake, while the first furred wave boiled over the lowest step, and the rats began scrabbling up the staircase. Tony was sure he could hear every scrape of every single claw against the old mahogany. Panting, he reached the top of the stairs, pausing beside Sag. The flashlight beam revealed thousands upon thousands more of the rats pouring out of the shadows toward the stairs. They were a third of the way up, their teeth snapping at the humans the way Tony imagined piranha might when tasting blood.

Sag tugged one of his homemade firebombs free of his belt and fished out his lighter.

"No!" cried Tony. "You can't do that! We haven't found Leslie or Lili yet!"

He tried to grab the bottle out of Sag's hand, but the man shoved him away angrily. "Anything I can't stand, it's *rats*. I had my fill of jungle rats in 'Nam." Now Tony recognized the irrational fear in his voice: The man was even more terrified of the creatures than Tony was.

The rats were more than halfway up.

"Look, we can still get away from them."

"Bullshit! I'm just buying us some time. They'll be over us in a minute—and only too glad to pick our bones clean from the look of those mothers!"

Tony made another lunge at the hand with the lighter, but Sag's fisted hand smashed into his ear, sending him reeling back into the shadows. While he shook his head, Tony saw the man touch the tip of his lighter to the wick in the gasoline-filled whiskey bottle. The flare brought an angry hissing and chittering from the rats, a gray-black waterfall running uphill. Sag waved the flaming bottle overhead.

Suddenly, out of the high darkness of the lobby, one of the winged monstrosities flew directly at Sag's face. The man tried to use his free hand to shield his eyes, but the creature slashed furiously at the skin of his hand and wrist with its talons and beak, drawing blood again and again.

Tony scrambled to his feet to help Sag, who was trying to use the flaming wick to drive off the thing. But his efforts only seemed to infuriate the winged horror. It began tearing at his scalp. He tried to grab for it, lost his balance, and tumbled down the stairs.

The Molotov cocktail shattered, rolling down the stairs in a sheet of fire, igniting the fur of hundreds of the rats, which clambered all over each other in pain and a frenzy to escape the fire, tumbling off the sides of the stairs, plunging back into the midst of the unharmed animals behind them, and spreading the fire, already engulfing half the grand staircase.

Sag, still trying to beat off the murderous assault from the enraged winged creature, was unaware that his struggles were rolling him down toward the fire.

"Sag, don't move! I'm coming!" Tony yelled, pressing a hand over his mouth and nose against the choking billows of smoke pouring up the stairs toward the gallery.

Suddenly Miller tumbled down two more steps to the edge of the fire. His jacket dipped into the blaze. Tony had a sudden recollection of the reek of gasoline that steeped the coat. "Oh, Jeez—" he began.

Then Sag went up—*whoomp!*—like a human torch. Tony could only gaze horrified as the man became a figure of fire, head to toe. Now the thing that had attacked him was trying to beat free of the doomed man, but some last impulse made Sag hang on to the claws in spite of the creature's vicious efforts to break free. Tony could see the red-and-black feathers beginning to smolder. Then, incredibly, Sag staggered to his feet and started running *down* the steps, the flapping nightmare held like a bizarre prize.

An instant before he reached the bottom of the steps, the last firebomb at his belt exploded, and Sag became a gout of flame that splashed across the lobby, now empty of all but dead and dying rats. At that moment the winged creature, a mass of flame, detached itself and fluttered, like a clumsy comet, halfway to the hotel entrance before it tumbled to the floor, an unrecognizable mass of charred feathers and flesh.

The heat and smoke were growing unbearable. Choking, half blind, still in shock from the events of the last few moments, Tony stumbled down the corridor to his right. The cool darkness gave him momentary relief, but the smoke came rolling in right behind him.

"Leslie!" he called. "Lili!"

He was still holding his flashlight; the beam, though it seemed a bit weak, let him find his way easily enough down the deserted corridor. There was little time left to search, he knew, and nothing to guarantee he had even chosen the right wing to investigate.

But something seemed to be drawing him down this hallway; and, given the strangeness of the world inside the hotel, trusting to such instincts seemed his best course.

He plunged on deeper into the hotel.

# Sixteen

ALL THE DOORS that lined the passage were closed and locked. Tony pounded on them as he went past, but he heard nothing from inside. Once or twice he tried to force a panel, but each resisted his efforts, and he didn't have time for more than a brief attempt.

The smoke was following him, filling the hallway, forcing him to keep a hand over his mouth. The flashlight beam seemed even weaker in the thickening haze. And now he saw, amid the dust and rot of decades, unmistakable signs of an earlier fire. The ceiling was blackened, as though a sheet of flame had rolled across it. The wallpaper near the roof was charred.

He reached the *L* in the corridor and found that much of the passage opening off at a right angle was fire-scarred. The farther he went along the passageway, the clearer the signs became. Smoke and heat had discolored the papered walls and elegant plaster ceilings. The pale paint on doors and woodwork was browned and blistered. The remains of the carpet underfoot was singed.

Many of the fire's traces were hidden by mildew splotches, water stains, and general deterioration. But his flashlight beam picked out enough clues to know that this was the wing where the fire had done its damage.

Logic said it was foolish for him to be exploring this part

of the old building, but something deeper and more persistent kept urging him on. He called "Leslie!" and "Lili!" several more times, but he heard no response.

The smoke pursued him relentlessly. Far behind him, he could hear the distant roar of flames. The whole staircase—much of the lobby, too—would be in flames by now. He should be looking for a way out. There were alcoves that led to boarded windows; some of these bore the faint traces of *Fire Escape* legends; these would open onto the rusting balconies with fold-down ladders that should allow him safe descent to the ground. But he would have to break through the boards sealing each emergency exit.

He couldn't stop now. Something told him he was very near his goal. He was running on total intuition now, but his certainty was growing stronger every minute.

He was moving rapidly down the hall, where the fungus grew thick and pale, making the place feel cramped, diseased. Swinging the flashlight beam overhead revealed places where the ceiling had fallen or been chopped away; blackened beams looked like they might have been burned. Had the fire flashed through the spaces between the floors? he wondered. Or were the beams merely blackened by age?

The carpeting had been ripped up to reveal warped and stained parquetry underneath. Several holes, made by axes from the scarring around them, bore out the theory of a search judging to see how far fire might have traveled through the flooring, as well as the ceiling.

The place was steeped in heavy impressions of lost time and forgotten lives. The persistent smell of smoke from the new fire that clung to him seemed to link past tragedy with an insane present.

The smell of smoke was growing stronger. Tony looked back to the joining of the corridors but saw no glow to indicate the fire had reached that point. Still, he reasoned, the whole place should go up like a tinderbox.

He quickened his pace—

—and nearly stepped off into disaster. A huge hole, heat-blackened all around the edges, had been burned through the flooring. Only quick reaction on his part made him fling himself backward, landing on his right elbow with jarring impact. "Shit!" he yelled into the smoky dimness. When he moved his arm, the pain that shot from the point of his elbow to his wrist made him wonder if he'd broken something. "Way to go, Captain Klutz!" he said, berating himself.

Favoring his hurt elbow, he investigated the hole, approaching it with caution, afraid that more of the flooring might be burned through on the periphery. Getting as close as he dared, he shined the flashlight down into the opening. The weakening beam faintly picked up the walls and part of the floor of a fire-gutted room directly below. There was an even larger hole in the floor of the lower room; the darkness swallowed up the beam. Tony guessed the fire damage ran all the way through to the basement; he remembered what had happened down there. Shuddering, he pulled back the beam, as though afraid of disturbing anything below.

There was a narrow strip of flooring between the hole and the right-hand wall, just wide enough for him to cross. He inched across, listening for the least sound that would warn his bridge was giving way underfoot. Midway, he froze, hearing the sounds of something moving in the dark far below. He turned the flashlight beam down again but could see nothing.

Then he was on the far side. The smoke seemed denser now, a heavy fog coiling and billowing in the flashlight beam. And there was a flickering red glow backlighting it, as though the fire had broken through somewhere. For all he knew, the entire first floor was an inferno; but the faint, uncertain glow seemed to come from nowhere in particular. Curiously the smoke didn't bother him nearly as much as might be expected, given how thick it had become. He could hardly see more than a few feet in any direction, yet he still felt only a mild burning of his eyes, a steady irritation in his throat.

Tony saw someone blundering toward him through the smoke. He raised his flashlight threateningly, but the figure that materialized out of the billows was a middle-aged woman in a peach-colored nightgown, with a filmy robe of the same silky stuff pulled around her. The firelight lit her disheveled blond hair and revealed a look of pure animal terror in her face. She was shouting something over and over, but Tony couldn't hear any sound. It reminded him of the attack in the dining room, so he watched for any threatening movement from her when he called out, "Hey!" and grabbed for her arm.

She didn't hear him. She seemed totally unaware of his existence. Then his reaching hand slipped right through her arm, as though she were nothing more than a holograph projection. Still screaming soundlessly, she vanished into the black smoke, blindly seeking help. Tony's impulse was to follow her, to warn her of the danger that lay back along the corridor. But he knew that would be a wasted effort. She was part and parcel of the haunted world inside the hotel—mercifully for him, only a harmless bit of nightmare.

He pushed on. Now he could make out other shapes in the murk. Men and women and children (these were the worst for Tony) straggled by, their faces twisted in terror, coughing and choking, arms outstretched as they groped their way through the suffocating pall of smoke. For Tony, much of the smoke was as illusory as the stumbling figures trapped inside it. They were choked and blinded by it, while Tony still felt only mild discomfort.

With a cry he jumped back suddenly, startled to find he had put his foot through the back of an elderly man sprawled full-length across the hall. Most of the man's pajamas had been burned away; his skin, from his heels to the back of his head, was a mass of charred, oozing flesh. Insanely Tony thought of the pigskin cracklins Ted Davis was always munching on, and suddenly felt his gorge rising. He fought down the impulse to vomit his guts out. The heat had fused bits of scorched cloth to flesh. But the man was still alive—just barely. His unburned soles were arching and flexing; his fingers were twitching; Tony had the sense that this was all the screaming the victim's damaged body could do. Though he knew it was useless, he tried to grab the man's hand, do something to comfort him. But his fingers slipped through the other's fingers as through air. The man's agony was beyond any help Tony could offer.

He plunged deeper into the murky hell, trying to tune out the horrors that appeared suddenly, then receded again into the thickening black smoke through which the fiery glow cut like a knife. But still he felt no heat, and his discomfort remained minimal. There was enough light to see by, so he switched off the flashlight to conserve whatever energy was left in its batteries.

Everything felt increasingly unreal, though his horror at the human hurt and fear all around him was real enough. He began to think that he was crossing some nightmare boundary into the other reality both Lili and Jozsef had said lay at the heart of the Hotel Bethel.

The giant leech and the winged horrors, the living-dead assailants and the rat tide, he guessed, were sentries or outriders on the edge of the dream-space. He envisioned chunks of nightmare pushing out farther and farther into the familiar world, like the tendrils of some dark, diseased growth that had taken root in the fantastic soil of Dreamers Hill centuries before, had been unwittingly nourished for generations by the dreams and blood of the people who had settled in and around Stigesville, and was now coming to a deadly flowering.

He began to wonder if the failure of the town's spirit, its apparent willingness to turn in on itself and wither away, wasn't some larger manifestation of the leechlike growth that had been feeding off the place for the whole of its existence. As the town had fallen into decay and hopelessness, the unseen horror at its center had grown correspondingly stronger and greedier. He had a chilling image of the town, nearly as dead as the shell of the old hotel, like a seed husk ready to burst and be cast aside while a darkly fantastic new life, nurtured in sleep and darkness, laid claim to the waking world and the sun.

He forged ahead, convinced now that he had entered a dream-space beyond the pale of the world he knew, a dream-time where past and present mingled. Somewhere the Hotel Bethel was burning again, as it had burned in the past, but the heat from the present blaze couldn't touch him any more than the heat from the past that swirled all around him. He might have slipped into an eternity between one second and the next, where time as he knew it had no hold.

Here, in this nowhere, notime, he was going to have to challenge the ruler of shadows for the lives of those he loved most and the sanity of the world.

He stopped suddenly. A tiny figure stood unmoving in his path. It was the image of another fire victim—a young girl. She was rigid with shock. A blast of flame had seared the left side of her body. Her left cheek was a mass of blisters; her eye was swollen shut, weeping clear fluid that might have been tears. Her nightgown, patterned in forget-me-nots, was a smoldering rag; her left arm was charred to the bone, crooked around the still smoking ruin of a teddy bear. Half of her

long, dark hair had sizzled and melted like that of a doll
carelessly thrown into a fire.

*She looks like Leslie,* Tony thought, trembling as he reached
out to her—terrified that this time his fingertips would encounter real flesh and blood and torment.

To his relief his fingers touched nothing. Shaking with
relief now, he realized she was a ghostly bit of the past; he
only prayed that the child was no longer, in some other
dimension, reliving her dying at the same time he was en-
countering her disfigured likeness.

A scream tore him away from his morbid reflections. It
ripped through the smoke ahead. A child's cry.

It was repeated.

This time he was sure he recognized it.

*"Leslie!"* he shouted into the red-black obscurity that surrounded him.

There was a partial answering cry, choked off in the middle, as though a hand had been clamped over the girl's
mouth. *"SoHo!"* Tony bellowed.

This time there was no response at all.

Hefting the flashlight like a mace, he charged in the direction of the cry, no longer heeding the tragic figures that
flashed across his limited field of vision. His instincts had
been right: Leslie was somewhere ahead. And she was in
deadly danger. And Lili might be there too.

The smoke was thinning now. He could no longer taste or
smell it; his eyes were no longer watering. The red fireglow
suffused everything, but the signs of the half-century-old fire
were gone. The corridor along which he was running had
been miraculously restored to its former state. The red light
came from fanciful light fixtures glowing overhead at regular
intervals. The carpeting underfoot was thick and springy. Pale
wallpaper with rows of lilies and roses bordered by red-and-
gold strips met highly polished mahogany paneling that rose
chest-high along both walls. The cream-colored enamel on
doors and moldings gleamed as though it had just dried.

Each door was marked with a meaningless raised metal
symbol, where its identifying number should have been. *Now
I'm all the way inside,* thought Tony, remembering what Lili
had told him of how she had first entered the nightmare world
so many years before.

The corridors began to twist and turn, going sharply right,

then left, then right again. Sometimes they ran straight; just as often they curved. Sometimes the floors were true and level; sometimes they canted steeply right or left.

Each time Tony rounded a corner, he discovered another corridor lined with sealed doors bearing meaningless designations. There were no side alcoves here; no windows marked for escape. There was only forward and back.

The last traces of smoke were long gone. The air was cool and damp.

Suddenly, around a corner, he spotted a figure sprawled at the side of the hall, just outside one of the firmly sealed doors. Another illusion, Tony wondered, or a trap of some kind?

Tightening his grip on the flashlight, he inched forward, hugging the side of the passageway.

He crossed quickly and dropped to his knees beside the crumpled form. Vic's eyes were open and he was breathing, but he seemed unaware of Tony.

"Vic! Hey, Vic! What happened?"

He saw the answer to his question in a minute. His uncle's upper right arm had been slashed open. There was blood all over his combat jacket, soaking into the carpet below. Only the thickness of the material had prevented the wound from being much worse.

Tony quickly pulled out the tail of his shirt and ripped off a swatch of it. He eased Vic's arm out of his jacket sleeve and quickly bandaged the wound as best he could. The man neither helped nor hindered his efforts. He seemed to be in shock.

Once Tony had dealt with the wound, he began slapping Vic lightly across the face, trying to bring him out of his stupor. Gradually his uncle began muttering, then he raised his good arm weakly to fend off the blows. His eyes swam into focus, and he said hoarsely, "Tony?"

"Yeah, Vic, yeah—shit! Who did this to you?"

"That crazy son of a bitch. He's got Leslie," said Vic, trying to heave himself into a sitting position. Tony helped him up. "Go after him. I'll be okay."

"Where are the others?" Tony wondered, thinking of the four "commandos" who had accompanied Vic.

"Lost them . . . in the fire . . ." Vic gestured vaguely back down the corridor. "Listen"—he gripped Tony's shoulder with his good hand—"you gotta go *now* and get her. Before he hurts her!"

Tony climbed to his feet. "I will. You sit tight. I'll come back for you when . . . when I can."

Vic nodded weakly, and his head dropped down toward his chest. Anxiously Tony lifted his chin. He was breathing; he had just passed out. Not daring to delay any longer, Tony left him and ran on down the corridor. At the next junction he turned to glance back once more at Vic. The man still lay slumped against the door, like a child's rag doll. He seemed so vulnerable, Tony almost hesitated to let him out of his sight; but whatever hope there was of recovering Leslie sent him sprinting down the next passageway and the one beyond that.

Then, rounding yet another corner, he saw SoHo hurrying down the corridor, carrying Leslie's limp form. The punk was wearing his leather jacket and motorcycle pants. His spiked hair, thick with grease, glinted with red flecks from the overhead lights.

"Bastard!" yelled Tony. "Put her down!"

He was pounding along the corridor, swinging his flashlight like a battle-ax as he charged SoHo. The punk turned back, and a grin split his face. He lowered Leslie to the floor like so much dirty laundry, his real attention on Tony. In a flash he had pulled out his switchblade and snapped the blade into position. Now he stood with it extended, describing a small circle in the air at chest height.

Tony broke stride, coming to a halt several feet beyond the knife in its deadly holding pattern. "Back away," he growled, keeping his flashlight-turned-weapon at the ready.

SoHo only laughed. "You're too late, good buddy." He sneered. "She"—he nudged Leslie's foot with his boot—"belongs inside. Someone is waiting for her. Someone who needs her *very much*. Someone who's *dying* to meet her—or have I got that backwards?" He began giggling at his little joke with a high-pitched sound that grated on Tony like chalk screeching down a blackboard.

"Get away from the girl, asshole," warned Tony, taking a single step closer to the leather punk.

SoHo's grin grew broader still. "There was a time when *you* could have gone inside, bro. But you blew it. The lady doesn't like having you around. You . . . upset her. She needs a *real* man, like me. But she wants a little . . . *love offering* from me. The brat''—again he nudged Leslie with the tip of his heavy boot—''is my ticket to paradise.''

"It isn't heaven in there," said Tony, "it's hell. This is a friggin' *nightmare!* Can't you *see* how she's using you?''

"Any way she wants to." SoHo giggled. "She's the girl of my dreams—or nightmares. Have it your way! It doesn't matter . . . she's my dark lady, queen of shadows, and she can make me live *forever.''*

"You poor, crazy fool!" shouted Tony, suddenly swinging his flashlight at SoHo's knife arm. The head of the flashlight connected with stunning force. The switchblade flew out of SoHo's hand and struck the opposite wall, then dropped to the floor. Tony swung again, this time aiming for SoHo's head; but the boy ducked instinctively, and Tony's blow went wide.

The next instant, the punk plowed into him, locking his arms around Tony's shoulders as they both hit the floor. But Tony suddenly kneed SoHo in the crotch. Roaring in pain, SoHo released him, doubled over, hands cupped protectively over his injured groin. Tony scrambled on all fours for the switchblade, snagged it, and turned quickly back to face his adversary.

SoHo had made it to his knees, his hands still folded between his legs. His head was bent so far forward, the spikes of his hair were touching the floor. He had begun retching; Tony, keeping a wary eye on him, edged over to Leslie. Hunkering down, keeping the knife aimed in SoHo's direction, Tony began shaking his niece, saying, "Leslie, c'mon, pumpkin, get it together. Time's a-wastin'.''

The child groaned and started to come around.

SoHo, finished vomiting, got rockily to his feet. Breathing heavily, he half collapsed against the wall, glaring at Tony. "You wouldn't," he challenged, indicating the knife with a jut of his chin.

"Try me," said Tony grimly. "I'd really like you to try."

His tone of voice seemed to convince SoHo that the threat was a very real one.

"You can't escape," said SoHo. "You're a fool if you think she'll let you get out of here alive.''

"Shut up," Tony warned. Leslie's eyes were open now. "Uncle Tony?" she asked in a frightened whisper.

"Yes, sweetheart. Everything's fine."

At this SoHo began giggling again.

*"Shut up, scumbag!"* roared Tony.

SoHo stopped laughing, but he was still smirking. "You think you've won the game," he said, shaking his head like a wise man confronting the world's biggest fool. "Honey chile, *you don't even know the rules.*"

Abruptly SoHo clamped both hands to his forehead. For a moment Tony thought he was reacting to a sudden pain behind his eyes. Then the punk began drawing his hands down the length of his face. His sharp nails, painted red-white-blue-black-silver, dug into the rubbery skin of his forehead.

SoHo yanked harder. His skin began to peel away from his skull with a wet, ripping sound. Only it wasn't the white of bone that was revealed, it was the distorted, jet-black features of a monstrous parody of a human face.

SoHo tugged the flesh of his face to his chin. Now Tony could see clearly that the swellings the size of silver dollars were moist, lidless eyes as solid black as the leathery features in which they were set; nostrils and jaws like a gorilla's; the mouth a double row of obsidian teeth.

Leslie yelped and buried her face in Tony's side. Her uncle could only gape as SoHo fastidiously tore the last strips of human flesh from his throat and then set about ripping the skin from his fingers to reveal thick, knobby black hands tipped with wicked-looking black claws. With a sudden movement, what had been SoHo grabbed the collar of his jacket and ripped the thick leather apart as if it were just so much tissue paper. With equal rapidity he pulled apart the skin underneath, revealing a muscular, ebony torso that would have shamed any bodybuilder or football lineman. His sex would have made any stallion feel underendowed.

With a laugh like a male ape, the figure stepped free of the discarded clothing and flesh, kicking it carelessly aside.

Tony's raised knife seemed as ineffectual as a toothpick.

"The rules are very different here," rumbled SoHo.

*No,* thought Tony, his mind reeling from what he had just seen. *It isn't SoHo. It's the black goblin from the fairy tale.*

"One minute it's one thing, the next it's another," the creature went on in a taunting singsong. "One minute you're there, and the next minute—

*"—here."*

They were no longer in the corridor. They were in a vast room lined with softly billowing black silk, lit by a persistent red glow from unseen fires. Leslie continued to burrow into Tony's side. He put one arm around her shoulders, squeezing as hard as he could, trying to reassure her when he felt utterly defeated himself. He lowered his knife arm and climbed to his feet, dragging Leslie upright alongside him. When they were both standing up, she was able to look at her surroundings, but she kept her arms locked tightly around Tony's waist.

The goblin that had once been SoHo began an idiot dance around the foot of a little rise, also covered in black silk—or black mist, Tony realized. It was impossible to say, because his eyes could never bring the constantly rippling surfaces into clear focus.

"Enough," said a soft, feminine voice. "Sit still for a while, my lover and clown."

The goblin obediently dropped into a crouch, staring expectantly at the top of the hill. A ribbon of saliva dropped unheeded from its slack jaws.

As Tony and Leslie watched, the mist began to swirl faster and faster, rising into the air like a mini cyclone. As it spun, it took on density, like the cotton candy gathered around a cardboard spool that Tony had to keep buying for Leslie at the Stigesville High Fall Festival. It grew into a solid pillar of darkness, half again as tall as a man.

Then the whirling stopped. A tall, willowy figure veiled in black stood on the knoll; the hem of its ebony robe seemed to fuse with the dark mist flowing restlessly over the rise.

"Is this real?" asked Leslie in an anxious whisper.

"I'm afraid so, pumpkin," he answered, unable to take his eyes off the veiled figure.

"Then how do we get home?"

"I wish I knew," he said, hugging her again.

"Why would you want to go anywhere else?" the figure said, chuckling. "Everything you want is here. *Lili* is here."

Lili was standing in front of the creature now. She was dressed in the same white garment—an angel's robe or a corpse's shroud—that Tony had first seen her wearing. Her eyes were wide open, but she had the blank stare of a sleepwalker. Two hands, swathed in black gauze, rested on the girl's shoulders possessively. "She belongs to me. Now you do too."

"Never," said Tony with all the force he could muster. He was remembering now how Lili and Jozsef had told him that the creature was afraid of the *mana*, the power in his blood. And Leslie had the same "gift," which is why the creature had the child brought to this place, which was probably no more real than a dream. "Leslie, hold tight to me, *and don't let go*," he warned.

The girl obediently hugged him even more tightly.

His defiance angered the muffled figure. At the same time it seemed to awaken some glimmer of awareness in Lili's eyes. She looked down at him with an expression of fear and something else, something that offered a wisp of hope. But she was frozen in place under the touch of the mysterious figure. Her pale forehead gleamed with sweat; there was a desperate frustration in her eyes. He was certain she was struggling to break free of whatever force had her in its thrall. But only her eyes, locked on his, hinted at the rebellion in her. Her arms were rigid at her sides, though the fingers of her right hand moved slightly. Was she trying to send him a message? he wondered. The faint movement conveyed nothing to him.

"Bring the child to me," the dark figure whispered in Lili's ear; the sound carried clearly to Tony. He saw the look in the girl's eyes turn to horror, though her mouth remained a tightly set line. With the unsteady steps of a poorly controlled automaton, Lili awkwardly descended the black-misted hill. Now Tony could see tears streaking her face; the terror in her eyes was the look of someone trapped in a plummeting aircraft or a careening car—only what was out of control here, Tony realized, was her own body.

"*No!*" he yelled, and when she paused in midstep, he said gently, "*Lili, no!*"

"*Child—*" said the veiled figure.

Lili's head jerked a notch to the side. Tony thought she was trying to shake her head. He said, "Fight, Lili—you've fought before."

"Yes, Lili!" screamed Leslie, caught up in the drama of the moment. "Don't let her hurt you! She's mean!"

Lili was trembling now, but she refused to take a step. She fought the other's will.

A growling came from under the black veiling. Tony felt the hairs at the back of his neck rise.

"What *is* that, Uncle Tony?" Leslie asked in a tiny voice.

"I don't think I want to find out, pumpkin," he replied, his throat suddenly desert-dry.

"Why not?" roared the figure, throwing back the silky veils. "You'll embrace me soon enough!"

What stood revealed was as tall as a giantess. Wild, tangled hair, alive with maggots and vermin as big as mice, framed a skull-like face of taut skin as white as polished bone. Eyes, cold and glittering, black as a spider's, focused hungrily on Leslie. Withered black lips and rotting gums framed yellowing fangs. The body was so shrunken around its bones that Tony could distinguish each finger joint and exposed rib. A shroudlike garment, rotted and worm-riddled, was draped loosely around the horror; but this exposed one withered breast, black-nippled, dripping poisonous blood-red ichor.

"I'm thirsty, lover," rasped the horror. "I'm hungry, fool."

The goblin in repose quickly jerked to attention. In the same instant the four men who had accompanied Vic into the hotel materialized on the misty hillside, their heads near the monster at its crown. Whether they were asleep or dead, Tony couldn't be sure: their eyes were closed; he coudln't tell if their chests rose and fell or not.

The giant creature gestured impatiently at the four sleepers/corpses. Giggling, the ebony goblin capered toward the men, his claws now fully extended.

"No, you can't—!" cried Tony.

But his words had no power to stop the prancing servant of the animated corpse at the top of the hill. He tried to throw the knife he still held clasped in his hand, but it slipped from his numbed fingers. Sensing what was to happen, he grabbed Leslie's head and wrapped his arms around her, so she couldn't watch as the goblin danced and leapt over the prone figures, gesticulating wildly at them, then suddenly reaching down and ripping open the throat of each. Foaming red blood welled up from ravaged arteries.

Tony struggled to reach the carnage, but the beast on the hill waved him away, and he found himself powerless to move a step.

One by one the black goblin lifted the bodies up to his mistress, and she drank noisily, greedily, from the opened throats. Then she flexed her iron-tipped claws, ripping gobbets of flesh from one victim, disemboweling another to feed on his still steaming entrails.

Tony couldn't watch; he buried his head beside Leslie's, feeling as helpless as a child himself in the face of such overwhelming horror.

As if from a vast distance, he heard the hideous creature rumble, "I'm hungry yet; I'm thirsty still. *Bring me the child.*"

The creature was swollen like a blood-sated leech. The skin of its belly was as tight as a drum, and pink as though the blood it had ingested had leaked into its skin and bone. It pointed at Lili, whose tormented body jerked like the pair of dismembered frog's legs Tony had seen attached to battery wires in biology class.

Lili, resisting every step, nevertheless advanced closer to Tony and Leslie, who were clinging to each other. Tony tried to tear his feet free, but they were rooted to the spot.

Lili's hands reached jerkily out toward Leslie, then were just as suddenly pulled back.

"*Bring me the child,*" the thing on the hill commanded again.

"Nnnnnnnnn—" Lili protested, her erratic movements telling Tony that she was trying to force herself back and away from where he and Leslie knelt, locked in each other's embrace.

"You're mean!" Leslie screamed with unexpected power at the monster that manipulated Lili like a reluctant puppet. "*I hate you!*" She pointed her finger at the creature. The blood-gorged thing jerked backward and clawed at its chest as though an invisible arrow had suddenly struck it. The screech it gave was an unearthly mix of panther's roar and night bird's howl.

At the same instant Lili slumped forward, as though all the unseen rods connecting her to the hurt creature had been severed. She began to crawl toward Tony and Leslie. "Yeyesss," she gasped; she raised her right hand. Painfully, like a person with her hands crippled by arthritis, she folded her little finger and ring finger in toward her palm.

Tony understood. He fished the forgotten silver bauble out of his pocket. It felt warm to his touch. Holding it tightly in his left hand, he raised his right hand over his head, three fingers extended, two folded, as Lili had reminded him. "Do the same with your hand, Leslie," he told the child. Clumsily she mimicked his gesture, stretching her own right hand as high above her head as she could. "Now, hang on tight!" Tony told her.

Lili was still crawling toward them, her right hand steadfastly making the sign against evil, her left hand reaching out toward Tony. With a final effort she gripped his ankle. He felt power flowing into him from Lili and Leslie; he felt it unlocking the reservoirs of power in him.

The tip of his middle finger caught fire; it burned with a pure white light that lanced out in all directions.

The creature on the hill howled like a thousand furies. The goblin huddled at the foot of the hill, terrified of the darting white fire.

The thing on the hill summoned the black mist to rise in a swirling curtain around her; the blackness began to absorb the bolts of light that blazed from Tony's upraised hand.

"The talisman!" cried Lili. "Give it to me!"

Tony gratefully let the bit of metal, now almost white-hot, slip from his hand. Lili quickly grabbed it and wedged one of the extended fingers into the space where the blade joined the hilt. When she was sure it would stay in place, she handed it up to Tony. "Throw it," she whispered.

Their enemy was disappearing into black mist now. Only the outline of her could be glimpsed through the obscuring veils. Tony lowered his hand and grabbed the knife. "Hold tight, everybody, and give me all you've got!" he urged.

Then he flung the knife, which seemed to acquire a life of its own. It sped true to the mark, sinking deep in the blood-taut belly behind the swirling mists.

The creature gave a bellow that threatened to split their heads in two. Then its swollen body erupted like a pustulant wound pricked by a surgeon's lance, disgorging horrors as though a nightmare had been cut open. Gigantic two-headed worms, scorpions, snakes of every hue, cockroaches, beetles, maggots, and things to which Tony could not begin to give a name poured out. They spilled down the sides of the hill like a living, unending lava flow.

Tony, still staring at the havoc he had wrought, felt Lili take hold of his hand and begin tugging him away from the seethe of horrors that was heading toward them. "I think I can remember the pattern that leads out of here," Lili said. She had taken Leslie's hand in her free hand and was leading Tony and Leslie back into the billowing shadows.

His mind was a confusion of horrific impressions. He was content to let Lili tow him along behind her.

They ran along what seemed like miles of passages lined with rippling black silk. His head was spinning. At times it seemed to him they were running along the sides of a black-swathed tunnel; at times they seemed to be charging along the *ceiling*, while billows of sticky black silk, like sails of spiderwebs, clutched and clung to them.

He was aware of infinities yet to cross, and of raging, *hungry* things following them. He felt his energy had been drained out of him. He only wanted to stop, make peace with whatever was following, sleep, and dream.

"We can't make it," he said, weary to the bone, ready to sink into the soft billows and sleep forever.

"Don't *say* that, Uncle Tony!" yelled Leslie, tugging frantically on his hand.

"All right, pumpkin," he said stupidly. But he continued running, while Leslie pulled him along by the right hand, and Lili by the left.

Then the black-silk corridors turned into red-lit hallways. They were back in the dream of the hotel.

"Too far," he murmured, thinking of the nearly endless interlocking corridors that led back to the world he once had known.

But neither Lili nor Leslie were listening to him. They were relentlessly pulling him along corridors where partially aroused sleepers were pounding on doors, fumbling at locks, calling out to the runners to halt. Dimly Tony sensed that what had happened in the heart of the nightmare had sent a shock wave through all the dreamers whose individual dreams fed the collective nightmare Tony and Lili and Leslie had struck down. Tony suspected that the crawling horrors that had geysered out of the creature were the separate nightmares of all the dreamers in all the rooms along all the corridors— real *and* dreamed—that made up the nightmare hotel whose hallways spiraled through near infinities.

Doors on both sides of them were yanked open; screeching, fumbling beings, neither awake nor asleep, grabbed for them.

Tony sensed these were merely extensions of the dream, trying desperately to pull them back inside it. Their dreams had fed it; now he doubted they could exist outside of it. The dream was dying; its death throes could be seen in the clutching, scrabbling hands that caught at them as they ran down corridor after corridor. Several times Tony used the blocking abilities that had served him so well in football to clear a way for them through halls where waking dreamers—male and female—barred their way.

Then there was smoke in the passageway. He knew they were nearing the outside world.

There was a bellow from behind. Shocked by the sound, Tony tried to look behind him and stumbled. His fingers, locked with Lili's and Leslie's, stopped them in mid-flight also. All three tumbled into a heap in a smoky corridor. Two doors were opening; pale hands were fumbling through after them.

But what had distracted Tony was the black goblin, which had followed them from the core of the nightmare. It was loping down the hall in pursuit, clawed hands ready to rip them from throat to groin.

Tony scrambled to put himself in a defensive position, as did Lili. Leslie shrieked and rolled herself into a ball against the nearest wall.

With a screeching bound, the black monster was on them—
—and just as quickly was slammed back, heels over head, down the corridor. Vic, brandishing what looked like a length of heavy metal curtain rod with ornamental fleur-de-lis finials at both ends, stood watch over them, panting like some demonic guardian of the way.

"Vic—" Tony began.

"Haul ass, soldier," Vic commanded, "and take your company with you."

Tony struggled to his feet. Lili had already helped Leslie up and was watching Vic uncertainly.

The black goblin had also regained its feet. With a roar it cannonaded down the hall at Vic. Vic gave the momentary impression of a man unaware that fate is charging down on him, like a locomotive out of control. He seemed more interested in examining the metal fleur-de-lis on the curtain rod than in the ebony engine of destruction racing toward him.

Then, at the last possible moment, while all three—Tony and Lili and Leslie—were shouting warnings at him, Vic suddenly spun around, with the curtain rod held like a pike, and slammed it into the goblin's throat. The creature gave a strangulated "*Auuughk!*" as the fleur-de-lis, like a spear point, rammed through his throat and out the base of his skull. His momentum lifted him off the ground as Vic let the opposite end of the makeshift spear drop to the floor behind him. The impaled monster and the skewer tumbled into a heap against one wall of the corridor.

"Nice going," said Tony weakly.

"Tell me about it later!" yelled Vic. "We're not out of this yet."

The exertion had opened the wound in his arm. Tony could see fresh blood pumping out over the dried blood. But there was nothing they could do now. He grabbed Leslie in his arms and sprinted for all he was worth.

Somehow they managed to avoid the toils of the waking dreamers. Then they plunged back into the dream-smoke, where the nightmare figures still wandered through an inferno fifty years extinguished. Tony was able to keep Leslie from seeing the worst of the horrors endlessly blundering through the smoke and fear.

By the time they reached the huge hole burned through the floor, their eyes were watering and they were all coughing from the increased real smoke in the air. Tony insisted that Vic cross first, then Lili and Leslie. While he was crossing, dark tentacles whipped up from the darkness below, wrapping themselves around his legs, yanking him off the narrow ledge of flooring. Only quick action by Lili and Vic, grabbing his arms as he was yanked off his footing, saved him from being dragged into the black pit yawning below.

While Leslie and Lili anchored him, Vic produced a pocketknife and managed to saw through the two black, fleshy tendrils that held him prisoner. These spilled thick, red-black ichor over his legs before he was cut free.

Then they were running/stumbling down the hall toward the last juncture. But the end of the hallway suddenly exploded into flame, forcing them back toward the pit mouth. A nest of whole and truncated tentacles erupted out of the dark hole, on the border of nightmare, effectively blocking any retreat back the way they had come.

"Down here," yelled Tony, waving his companions toward an alcove terminating in a boarded-up window. RE ESCAP was faintly visible above the window frame. They were all hacking and half blinded from the thickening smoke. Fire was roaring hungrily down the corridor after them. All four attacked the boards sealing the window with vigor arising from desperation. The barrier remained obdurate for a moment, then Vic punched a board loose, and more followed rapidly.

"I can see the fire," Leslie screamed.

Tony lifted his foot and kicked out the last obstructing slats. Fire had framed the end of the alcove as Tony handed Leslie through the opening and set her down on the rusty balcony outside. Lili climbed through next, then Vic, with Tony following, the fire so close behind him that he found the soles of his shoes smoldering when he dived through into the cool night air.

Vic was jumping up and down on the antique fire ladder, which creaked and groaned but only dropped a short way to the ground. "We'll have to drop the rest of the way!" he shouted.

Fire jetted through the punched-out boards. "So, jump already!" yelled Tony, scrambling down after the others. Way down along Cabot Street, he could hear the sirens of fire engines and ambulances rushing toward the Hotel Bethel. Fire was erupting in gouts through window after window of the second and third stories. Tongues of flame were spouting into the eaves, sending fire east and west along the roofline.

One by one they dropped into the thick weeds below, none of them sustaining more than minor abrasions.

The roof of the hotel over the west wing suddenly went up in a fireball of flame and debris. A terrible howling from inside the explosion threatened to burst their heads in two. All of them dropped to their knees, their hands pressed to their ears, screaming in answer to the death-scream from deep inside the burning ruin.

Then the sound was gone, as though consumed by the fire. Smaller fireballs burst through the roof.

The four climbed to their feet. Holding hands, they staggered toward the Paxton Street gate, coughing and pausing frequently to wipe their stinging eyes.

The fire engines were converging on Cabot Street. They could hear more sirens in the distance. It would only take a matter of minutes for the police and fire departments to force the main gates to the hotel. For the first time in fifty years, Tony realized, the hotel grounds would be crawling with people. He looked at the blazing structure and realized that the fire department would be able to do little to control the fire. The building was finished; so, he hoped, was the nightmare it had contained.

"I want to go home, Uncle Tony," Leslie whimpered.

"So do I, honey. We all do."

"There's a key to the gate in that flowerpot," said Lili, indicating one survivor of a pair of ornamental urns flanking the entranceway. Vic fished the rusty metal key out and jiggled it in the lock. After a moment's stubbornness the key turned. Vic dragged the protesting iron gate open.

"Ladies and gentlemen," he said, smiling through his soot-streaked features. "Shall we . . .?" He bowed from the waist, waving them through the opening with exaggerated politeness.

But Lili held back.

"What is it, Lili?" Tony asked, while Vic and Leslie watched with concern.

"I can't leave here, Tony," she said, shivering. "I'll die outside. I belong to another time."

"You belong here, Lili," he said. "You belong with me."

"Oh, Tony, I wish I could believe that." She sobbed, turning away from him. "But I was part of that." She gestured back towards the blazing hotel. "I can't exist now that it's gone."

"Lili," said Tony softly, embracing her. "Don't do this to yourself . . . to *us*."

"I'm afraid, Tony. I've never been so afraid in my life."

"Take my hand," he said. "You'll see I'm right."

Her fingers were like ice intertwined with his own.

Together they took a step toward the open gate.

Suddenly Lili began to age before his eyes. She was turning to an old woman in front of all of them.

"Oh, Tony," she croaked, "it's true." She pressed her wrinkling hands to her face.

"No," whispered Tony, "I won't believe it. It's a lie. It's some last piece of the nightmare. It's only as true as you'll let it be."

"Oh, Tony," she said with a sob, her face still buried in her hands. "If only I could believe . . ."

"*I believe,*" said Leslie, "and I want to go home and sleep. So you come on *now!*" She grabbed one of Lili's hands and tugged her toward the gate, ignoring the young woman's protests.

"And I'm not about to leave you here," said Tony, taking her other hand. "This is only the nightmare: *Give it up, Lili.*"

"All right," she said, letting them pull her through the gate.

The instant she stepped through, the illusion of her aging vanished. Lili was as young as she had been earlier.

"See," said Leslie. "I *told* you."

"Yes," said Lili, laughing and crying at the same time. "You sure did."

"Home," said Vic wearily, "home, home, home."

"Uncle Tony," asked Leslie suddenly, "this isn't still a dream, is it?"

"No, pumpkin," he answered, feeling Lili's hand squeeze his. "It's no dream; it's the best thing we have going."

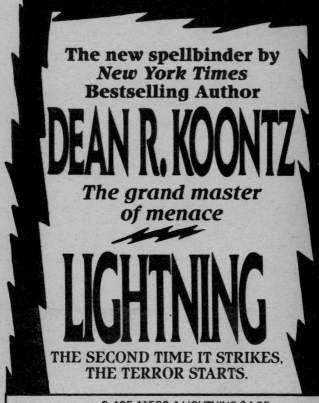